# THE
# LAIR

## A.B. MICHAELS

THE LAIR
Copyright 2015 by A.B. Michaels

ISBN 978-0-9915089-4-5

Red Trumpet Press
P. O. Box 171162
Boise, ID 83716
www.redtrumpetpress.com

Design by Tara Mayberry
www.TeaberryCreative.com

*For Anna*
*Thank you for sharing your*
*wonderful home town with me.*

OTHER BOOKS
BY A.B. MICHAELS

*Sinner's Grove*
*The Art of Love*

# ACKNOWLEDGMENTS

Many thanks to my early draft critique group: Donna, Dynisha and Nicole, you were collectively kind and honest with your feedback—a stellar combination!

Rachel, what can I say? You are the better angel of my nature—showing me where I can make a good story so much better. I appreciate your wisdom.

As always, Tara somehow turns my vague cover ideas into works of art that truly communicate the story within. Ah, to have that kind of talent!

Cheryl, thanks for keeping me on task and for getting the word out, a job that entails an endless stream of details. Thank goodness for spread sheets!

And Mike, you're one in a million. What would I do without you? I'm the luckiest girl in the world—and it's a pretty big world.

# CONTENTS

—✦✦✦—

# PROLOGUE

**W**hy *can't I see?* Mirela Pavlenco woke up in utter darkness, her eyelids heavy, as if they'd been pressed down by a leaden weight. Struggling, she lifted them enough to make out her surroundings, but even then her vision blurred. She was lying on a bed in a room, but not the room in her residence hotel. It was painted a different color, and there was no window. The air reeked of something old and musty, and there was no lavender candle, like the one she lit each day to remind her of Mama's garden.

She turned her head and saw a small nightstand with a drawer, and on it a spindly lamp shed a weak light throughout the room. She tried to reach over to make it brighter, but her left arm wouldn't move. Neither would her right. Her brain, still groggy, finally registered that her arms couldn't move because they were tied to the bed.

Mirela raised her head slightly and realized with a growing sense of alarm that her legs were spread and both feet were tied to the bed as well. She was held completely in bondage. Terror began to coil itself around her. Panic, a feral creature, stalked her.

She tried to stay calm, but couldn't catch her breath and draw air past the knot in her throat. Tears began to trickle down her face. She called out in her native Romanian, "Someone—anyone! Help me, please!" There was no response, only the occasional rumble of what sounded like a train in the distance. She tried again, in the language she had only recently begun to learn. "*Aiuto! Per favore!*"

She tried to think of how to escape, but perversely, her thoughts kept returning to her childhood village of Bârsana. She could see her mother in their cottage garden, carefully tending her onions and her cucumbers, coddling her tomatoes, cutting sprigs of lavender to set in a little pot in the kitchen.

"Why do you want to go so far away, *puiu*?" her mother asked. "You are so young."

"I've got to go," Mirela told her with firm resolve. "There has to be something more out there for me, and I am going to find it!"

Now a hysterical laugh almost escaped her as she realized how gullible she had been. She'd assumed her clear skin, thick blond hair, and womanly figure would open doors for her.

"You are so beautiful, Mila," the carpenter Simu Fidatof had told her on too many occasions to count. On last St. George's Day, he had even worn the mask of *Sangiorz* and burst into her cottage, carrying a small bouquet of alpine pinks and fire lilies, laughing as he fondled her and stole a kiss. Her mother had laughed as well, crying out, "Who is this?" and offering him the traditional eggs and wine to leave them alone. But Mirela had known it was Simu by his big and clumsy hands. Though he was an honorable young man and smitten with her, she did not want to spend the rest of her life being groped by him.

It seemed like fate was smiling on her when, just after her seventeenth birthday, she'd heard about job openings in the city of Baia Mare. She had traveled there and listened to the man as he made his speech: "We are looking for strong girls who want a better life...girls to work in the hospitality industry...do you want to see what life is really like in Western Europe? We can make it happen." She was old enough to make her own decisions, despite her mother's concerns ("You are leaving me alone, little one."). It wasn't Mirela's fault their father had left them so many years ago; why should she sacrifice her happiness just to keep her mother company? She made her decision and left three weeks later.

Now, lying here, she was filled with regret; how could she have been so stupid? At the time, it all seemed so safe. The company man had been clear and straightforward, with no funny business. He'd even given her a choice of country and she'd chosen Italy—known for its beautiful churches, just like those of Maramureş. Only Italy's churches were of stone, not wood, and they were overwhelming. The company had paid for her train ticket, assuring her the hotel she worked for would cover her fees and living expenses until she earned enough to pay her own way. Strong, bright girls are in high demand, the company man had said; you will be promoted in no time at all.

The only thing that had seemed strange to her was the tattoo he'd insisted she have put on her hairline, just behind her right ear. He told her it was to help identify her until she learned to speak Italian. It seemed a small enough request. The design was of a very small golden tree, visited by a tiny blue butterfly. Even though she'd been scared of the needle, it turned out not to hurt very much, and it was a pretty little mark. In fact, she came to think of it as her own little secret, like wearing red silk panties beneath her maid's uniform.

The door opened and in the dim light of the hallway beyond she saw an older woman with dark hair talking with a tall, white-haired man in a suit. He looked vaguely familiar, but Mirela couldn't recall where she had seen him. The two of them glanced in at her and the woman nodded before entering the room and shutting the door. Mirela recognized her from the hotel. "*Signora,* please, you must help me!" The woman could speak some Romanian; they'd even talked a little on Mirela's first day. She remembered the woman's perfume. It smelled like roses.

"Do not worry, *puiu,*" the woman said soothingly. "No harm will come to you."

Mirela winced at the endearment—"little chick." It was the same one her mother used. How could this woman pretend to care about her when it was obvious she did not? "Why am I tied down like this? What happened to me?" Mirela tried but failed to keep the fear out of her voice.

The woman, brisk in her movements, brought a pan out from underneath the bed. She carefully cut off Mirela's panties. "Come, you will use this now," she said.

Mirela was mortified, but desperate to empty her bladder, she complied with the woman's directions. Afterward the woman did not replace Mirela's underwear. She merely tossed the cut garment into a nearby waste can as if she were straightening up a room.

"It won't be long now," the woman said, and left.

"Until what?" Mirela cried after her. "Until what?!"

Her mind finally beginning to clear, she began to piece together the events of the night before. She had gotten off work and felt good about the tips the hotel guests had left in their rooms that day. The entire floor had been taken over by a group of salesmen and throughout their stay they had flirted with her as she rolled her cart down the hallway. Many of them had left her five and ten euro bills—one had even left her a twenty euro bill and put a business card on top of it. On it he had written in Italian, "Call me."

The tips had brightened Mirela's day because she missed her friends in Milan, where she had worked until a week before. *A transfer to Verona means you are being promoted*, the letter read. *You will work there for two weeks and then you will receive a new position*. Mirela was proud to think she was being promoted after just four months. She imagined the extra money she would send to her mother, as if to say, "You had little faith in me, but look at me now."

To celebrate the end of the work week, Mirela and her new friend Dobra had gone out for a drink and some dancing. Dobra was from Croatia; she was a big, buxom girl who loved to dance to the hip hop music that was so popular now. Mirela had agreed to accompany Dobra to banish her own loneliness, if only for an evening.

She remembered the dim smokiness of the bar...the loud, pounding rhythm of the music...and two young men who had come up to them as they sat with their drinks. The men looked respectable enough and the taller of the two asked Dobra to dance. The other one sat with Mirela and talked to her—or tried to, since he was Italian and couldn't speak her native Romanian. They laughed as he tried to teach her the word "lovely" in Italian and she taught him "handsome" in her language. She remembered excusing herself to go to the restroom, and coming back to find him waiting for her. But after that there was nothing—no memories until she woke up in this place.

What had he done to her?

The door opened again. This time the white-haired man entered and closed the door behind him, locking it with a distinct *click*. As he approached the bed and was bathed by the light of the lamp, Mirela realized who he was.

"*Signor Direttore*," she pleaded, "*per favore*. I have done nothing wrong."

The man didn't reply. He only looked at her and reached for the neckline of her dress. She instinctively tried to raise a hand to stop him, but could do nothing.

"How old are you?" he asked in Italian.

"Only seventeen," she whispered. "Please."

He nodded, as if she had given him the correct answer. "*Perfetto.*" He carefully peeled the neckline of her dress down to reveal her breasts, which were heaving now with anxiety and threatening to spill out of her bra. He calmly took a pocketknife from his trouser pocket and cut the bra apart.

"*Signor, per favore,*" she repeated, tears running down her cheeks. "*Io sono vergine.*"

"*Che fortunato,*" he murmured, before unzipping his perfectly tailored pants.

Sometime later, after the man had finally climbed off her, Mirela lay silently, too numb to react. The labored breathing, the grunting and moaning—all was quiet now. A memory floated by: Simu, pressing his large calloused hands against the front of her dress. She thought, now, that those hands would feel good and strong and safe. She thought of her mother and the garden and the lovely little sprigs of lavender. She thought of the wooden churches of her village and wondered where God had gone to. She barely noticed when the man pulled on his pants, leaned over and squeezed her breasts. She thought, how can someone so old be so strong? He did something strange before he left. He put his hands together as in prayer, bowed very slightly and said to her, "*Sawasdee.* Learn that and you will please them." She didn't know what he meant, but it did not matter now. Tired beyond measure, she closed her eyes and slept.

# CHAPTER ONE

—‧✦‧—

"You are absolutely getting off in Frankfurt. You are *not* going to follow me all the way to Milan!" Daniela Dunn stood in the aisle of the rapidly filling 747, an oversized carry-on bag slung over her shoulder. She leaned over and hissed the words at the tall, raven-haired detective sitting in the aisle seat of row twenty-nine.

Gabriele de la Torre—Gabe to his friends—didn't say a word. He simply smiled and stretched out his long, muscular legs, obviously settling in for the transoceanic flight.

"What, you're going to ignore me now?" she said. "After I told you and told you—"

"Is there a problem, ma'am?" A very attractive blond flight attendant paused while checking the overhead bins, glanced at Dani, and smiled at Gabe as if he'd just made *People Magazine's* "Sexiest Man Alive." Dani glared at him before mumbling, "No, I...uh..."

The attendant glanced at Dani's boarding pass. "You're back in row thirty-seven, seat B. That's—"

"I know which seat I'm in," Dani interrupted.

The attendant turned crisp as a Granny Smith apple. "If there's no problem, I'll have to ask you to please take your seat. You're holding up other passengers who are trying to get settled. We have a very full flight."

Gabe sent Dani a patronizing look before addressing the attendant. "I hope we don't wear you out," he said with a melt-in-your-mouth smile—the kind of smile Dani wanted to wipe right off his face.

The attendant matched him wattage for wattage. "We're here to please," she chirped before stepping into the next row to allow Dani to pass.

"I'll talk to you later," Dani muttered as she made her way back to seat thirty-seven B, bumping her bag into several seated passengers along the way. "Excuse me," she said. "Sorry...Pardon me." She found her row and wriggled between a gawky teenage boy wearing enormous headphones and a middle-aged man with perfectly cut hair, sporting a Bulgari wristwatch. She learned shortly after takeoff that he was an Italian banker who traveled a lot and was more than eager to "practice my Eeenglish" over pasta and a fine chianti. In fact, since Dani was *una bella donna di mondo*, would she be available the next time he was in San Francisco on business? He could text her when he arrived.

*It will be a cold day in hell before this "woman of the world" hooks up with you, creep.* "I'm sorry, I don't text," she lied. As she politely rebuffed him, Dani glanced down at the man's hands. She could see the slightly pale circle where his wedding ring normally fit his tanned finger; no doubt he'd slip the ring back on just before he returned home to his wife. *Yecch*.

Weary of making chit chat with Don Juan, Dani pulled out her iPod and tried to distract herself. No such luck. She leaned over to peek down the aisle. Several rows ahead, her nemesis wore his own headphones, looking totally relaxed. His seat was tilted back and she could see that his thick black hair was showing no signs of thinning, damn him. His strong bronzed hand was drumming on the armrest. What was he listening to? She thought of his hands, and how the backs of his fingers were sprinkled with tiny black hairs. His nails were blunt and clean, she knew, because she had served him so often at the restaurant. She wondered idly what those hands were capable of...

What? What did his hands have to do with the fact that he had no business being on this plane?

The nerve of Gabriele. For the past fourteen months, ever since he'd joined the Marin County Investigation Division, Detective de la Torre had made it his life's work to get under Dani's skin. Well, perhaps that was a slight exaggeration, but still. First he'd tried to come on to her, using their shared heritage as a line. They were both from northern Italy; surely they could get together some evening and talk about their cultural roots? Fortunately she'd put a stop to that pretty quickly. In no uncertain terms she'd told Mr. Dolce & Gabbana that although he seemed like a nice enough man, he held no physical attraction for her whatsoever. It was a lie, of course, but she wasn't about to share why they couldn't make a go of it.

Her brush-off was a gamble. Gabe was single and didn't like eating by himself, so he was a regular at her restaurant, part of the inn she owned in Little Eden. She didn't want to lose his business, so she had tried to be firm but not rude. It appeared to be working. He still ate at her place without seeming to harbor any bad feelings.

Oh, who was she kidding? Gabe had dropped any romantic interest in Dani in a flash—so quickly that she wondered if she'd imagined his interest all along. He still flirted with her, but there was a slightly mocking tone to it, as if he dared her to take him seriously. Of course, she didn't. She couldn't. Now he was simply a friend who liked to tease her—a good friend most of the time, and a meddling friend at times like these.

Dani glanced at the businessman, who had asked the flight attendant if she had any Italian newspapers. She came back with a copy of *Corriere della Sera*. As Don Juan leafed through it, a photo on page three caught Dani's eye; it was a stock shot of her father, Armando Forcelli. The headline read, DRUG USE SUSPECTED IN FATAL JOYRIDE OF HOTEL HEIR. Immediately, tears began to well up and Dani quickly fumbled in her bag for some tissue, hoping neither of her seat-mates would notice.

Several days earlier she'd learned that her father, the son of one of Italy's most famous hoteliers, had died in a boating accident. As his sole beneficiary, she was in fact headed to the Forcelli family compound in Verona to attend her father's funeral and sign some papers pertaining to his estate. She told herself there was no logical reason to feel so emotionally vulnerable. She'd seen her father only a handful of times over the past dozen years, ever since…ever since she left Italy. Yet it was as if her feelings had climbed aboard a roller coaster and wouldn't get off the tracks. She'd be fine for a while and then a memory would flit by of her *babbo* carrying her on his shoulders down the long picture gallery…or taking her to a special place in the old city he said had the best gelato in all of Italy. She'd remember the scent of his cologne, just a hint of lemons and spice…and the feel of her small hand encased in his big warm one. Then the tears would start to flow and she'd wonder, panicked, if they would ever stop.

She allowed herself the luxury of imagining Gabe next to her, holding her tight and telling her to just let go. It would feel so very good. But he wasn't next to her and it was up to her to keep it together. So she would, no matter what.

Still, she couldn't help wishing her mother had come along on the trip. Paula Dunn had been a gorgeous, vibrant flight attendant when she'd fallen head over heels for Dani's father, a spoiled but charming playboy and Cigarette boat racer who never grew up, not even when he got Paula pregnant with Dani. It was Dani's grandmother who forced him to marry Paula. Nonna Stella wasn't going to let her youngest son get out of line.

Although she'd kept her maiden name, Paula Dunn had given up her career and tried to be a good wife. All that came crashing down when Dani turned fifteen, and since then she and her mother had lived a much more "normal" life in the States. Dani had even used her mother's last name to keep a safe distance from her wealthy and famous Italian family. Her father had reluctantly agreed; he knew the offspring of wealthy people were often targeted by kidnappers.

Although they'd never actually divorced—the Forcelli family didn't believe in it—Dani's mom had eventually found someone new: a nice man named Herb Roscoe. Herb was so good to her mom that Dani hadn't minded too much when Paula moved from Little Eden, on the northern California coast, to live with Herb in Phoenix. Dani *was* worried that she couldn't run the inn on her own, but her mom had set her straight.

"You've got everything you need right there," she'd said, tapping Dani's forehead. "I have the utmost confidence in you." And she'd been right.

That same vote of confidence had enabled Dani to take a very deep breath and decide to fly back to Italy by herself. Paula, nursing Herb and his recently broken hip, couldn't go with her. Surprisingly, Paula had been the one with reservations.

"If you don't feel like you can handle it, I'm totally okay with you begging off," she'd told Dani on the phone. "Then, when Herb's better able to get around without me, I'll fly back with you."

No, Dani had assured her, she could do it. She *would* do it, on her own.

Except it hadn't turned out quite that way. Dani couldn't help herself. She unbuckled her seat belt and stood up briefly to see what Gabe was doing now. It looked like he was watching a movie—it must be a comedy, because he was laughing. She could see the strong lines of his throat as he tilted his head back and guffawed. He didn't seem at all worried that others might think he was strange for laughing at something nobody else could hear. He was so comfortable in his skin; she envied him that.

"I'll do whatever I can to help you," Gabe had told her after finding out about her father's death. She never dreamed he'd go so far as to follow her to Italy!

Dani sat back down and closed her eyes. What an exhaustive summer it had been, and it was barely August.

It had started simply enough. Professor Ethan Wolff and his family were renovating the old artists' retreat near Little Eden, known by the locals as "Sinner's Grove." Dani had offered her computer skills to help research the many artists who had lived there during its heyday. One of those artists had in fact been her own great-grandfather Luzio Furlan.

So much had happened since the beginning of the project that Dani still couldn't process it all: vandalism, arson—even murder. And behind it all, the theft of several priceless pieces of artwork, two of which may have been stolen by her very own ancestor. She knew she'd seen the paintings somewhere in her childhood home, and she was determined to return them to The Grove Center for American Art, where they belonged. All that, plus the news of her father's death, had thrown Dani into an emotional tailspin. And where had Gabe, the local 'constable,' been throughout all of it?

Right there. For her.

She frowned.

She'd never asked him, but there he was all the same. She felt in her bones that she could trust Gabriele de la Torre. Given her background, that by itself was a miracle. The problem was, his idea of help and hers did not mesh *at all*. She couldn't believe her eyes when she'd seen him in the security line at the airport. It must be a coincidence, she'd thought. But no. He was headed for the same gate, the same flight, and no ranting and raving on her part had convinced him to pack it in and go home.

At one point she'd gotten so agitated that other passengers in the terminal were beginning to look at them with concern. While Dani silently counted to ten to keep her temper in check, Gabe had actually announced to those within earshot, "Don't worry, it's just a lovers' quarrel. She really is crazy about me." Dani had just about lost it over the smiles and knowing looks these *strangers* had sent her way. It was mortifying.

"You are despicable," she'd told him after dragging him off to the side of the departure gate. At that, he'd leaned over and whispered in her ear, "Maybe, *bella*. But if I leave now they'll think I've planted a bomb on board. Wouldn't want that, would we?" She felt the hairs on her neck respond to his warm, ginger-scented breath. She scooted back and glared at him; his expression was about as innocent as a snake's.

Then it dawned on her: perhaps her mother, along with her restaurant employees Paolo and Nina, had put him up to it. "Okay, what did they offer you to babysit me?" she'd demanded. "A year's worth of Risotto del Veneto?"

"You wound me, Daniela," he'd replied with a grin. "As much as I love your risotto, you know I'd hold out for nothing less than Ravioli della Toscana and Venetian Meatloaf."

"I'm serious," she insisted. "What did they tell you?"

For the briefest moment, Gabe had turned serious as well. "Jenna told me about your father, and I asked Nina for your flight information. That's it. I took some comp time and here I am." He shrugged. "End of story."

Dani had searched his dark-brown eyes for any hint of dissemblance and found none. She stared at him a bit longer than she should have, and finally, to break the spell, she'd turned abruptly around and stalked over to a vacant seat. They hadn't spoken another word until they'd boarded and she'd hoped against hope he'd have a change of heart and ask for his luggage back.

He didn't.

So here they were, heading to Italy, toward who knew what...

Flying was one of Gabriele de la Torre's least favorite activities. He had to work hard to take his mind off the fact that a four hundred and fifty ton machine was actually carrying several hundred people, including him, more than six miles above the earth. He'd gone through all the standard distractions: reading Brad Thor's latest thriller, listening to Zeppelin on his iPod, watching "Ghostbusters." The original movie, which he'd seen four or five times over the years, was still the best. For the past hour he'd been chatting with a nice little old lady from Palo Alto who was on her way to visit a family friend in Bergamo. About twenty minutes into the conversation she had offered to give him the name and phone number of her grandniece, who was a student at the University of San Francisco.

"Rina's cute as a button," she'd told him with a wink. "And she's going to be a nurse. Always good to have a nurse in the family."

"Ma'am, as delightful as Rina sounds, you really shouldn't go around giving out her name and number," he'd gently chided her. "I could be an ax murderer. I'm not, of course, but I could be. I think Rina's probably better off handling her own social life."

The lady had poked Gabe playfully on the shoulder. "Oh come on," she said. "I can tell a Prince Charming when I see one."

Sometime later Gabe excused himself to use the lavatory. On his way to the rear of the plane he noticed a sharp-looking guy in his forties sitting next to Dani; the jerk was obviously making a play for her. Gabe instinctively bristled, and before he thought better of it, he leaned across the man and said to Dani, "How's it going, darling? Do you have the airsick bag handy?" He ignored her look of outrage, and turning to the man in mock confidence, he added, "I can never get her to sit with me on these long trips. She gets nauseous on almost every flight and she's afraid she'll… you know…so she insists on sitting separately." He patted the man on the back. "Good luck."

As Gabe continued making his way down the aisle, he could hear Dani apologizing to the jerk. The plane hit some turbulence and he reached out to steady himself on the back of another passenger's seat. God, he hated flying. Yet despite his nervousness, he had to smile. It didn't take eyes in the back of his head to imagine the dawning horror on the face of the predator sitting next to Dani. Was she really gonna reach for the bag? Was she going to lose it? Dani was no doubt furious, too. Those exquisite eyes of hers would be shooting fire right about now.

Back in his seat, thankful the old lady next to him had dozed off, Gabe considered what do to about Ms. Dunn. The thing is, she had a right to be ticked off with him, for a whole host of reasons. Who wouldn't be annoyed as hell if someone claiming to be your friend insisted on bulldozing their way into your private life, especially at such an emotional time?

But where Dani was concerned, Gabe would bulldoze a city if he had to. The relationship he'd originally nurtured as a favor to one of her relatives had morphed into something different… something that reached far deeper than he'd ever intended. When he'd heard she was making the trek back to Verona to deal with her estranged family, he just couldn't let her do it alone, even if it meant betraying a confidence he'd held for such a long time. So he'd called in favors, taken the time off and booked the same flights.

Gabe wasn't sure where he stood on the issue of fate versus free will. Do you make your life happen or does it happen a certain way whether you want it to or not? More than once, in both his career and his personal life, he'd felt that events had taken place for specific reasons; he just wasn't always sure what those reasons were. Or maybe subconsciously he'd pushed for those same events to happen. Either way, it felt right to be on this plane, to be watching over Dani. Being able to settle an old family debt while he was there was icing on the cake. He just hoped Dani could find a way to forgive him when she heard the rest of the story—a story he'd neglected to tell her ever since he'd met her.

He spent the rest of the flight figuring out how to accomplish that goal without getting his head bit off.

—◆◇◆—

"Let me get this straight. You lost my reservation, you have no more cars, and no one else is available to help me. It's almost midnight, and all you've got to say is '*Mi dispiace*'? 'I'm *sorry*'?"

What Dani's voice lacked in energy, it certainly made up for in sarcasm, Gabe thought. The poor girl was exhausted, but she was still a fighter. The thin-faced clerk behind the counter looked beyond her to Gabe for support, but Gabe simply shrugged. *It's out of my hands, buddy.*

"*Sì signorina*," the clerk said. "It appears you cancelled your reservation…" He typed in a few more key strokes. "…yesterday." He stretched his neck while he waited for her reply. Gabe imagined the guy's collar was feeling pretty tight right about now. It wasn't easy getting reamed by a beautiful woman, especially at the end of a long, tiring day.

Dani scanned the other car rental desks. At such a late hour nearly all of them were deserted. Her eyes settled on Gabe, who was standing casually at the end of the counter. He raised his eyebrows in inquiry.

"Don't play the innocent with me," she said. "Nina no doubt cancelled it, thinking you'd come to my rescue. You two probably planned this."

Smiling, Gabe pantomimed a courtier's sweeping bow with the hand that held his own car rental contract. He then held out his other arm to beckon her.

"Sir Galahad you're not," she said. She sighed and extended the handle of her rolling suitcase while trying to maneuver that humongous bag of hers onto her other shoulder. Gabe waited patiently, knowing that if he went to help her, she'd probably bash him over the head with it.

"Look, the only reason I'm taking you up on your offer is that I'm ready to fall asleep where I stand. Besides—" she smiled sweetly, "—if I can do anything to make your life more difficult, like make you drive out of your way, then, hey, why not?" She handed him the directions to her childhood home.

"*La Tana della Pantera*," he read. "The Panther's Lair.'"

"Pretentious, I know," she replied, stifling a yawn. "It is what it is."

Negotiating the streets of Milan, even in the dead of night, took a while, and it was well past one by the time they headed out on the A4 East Expressway toward Brescia and Verona. Now that it was just the two of them, with no distractions, Gabe figured he had his best shot at explaining to Dani who he really was. After a year, she probably assumed she knew him, but she was about to discover he'd left quite a few parts of his story untold.

"Uh, Daniela," he began, "I've got something to tell you before we reach La Tana." He dared not look at her as he continued. "You remember how I told you we were from the same part of Italy. Well—" He glanced at Dani. "Oh shit."

She was sound asleep. Not just lightly dozing, but seriously deep in dreamland. Her short dark curls had fallen across her eyes, and her mouth was slightly open. She was breathing softly, steadily, the sleep of one who has finally, after a long while, relaxed. It was the sleep of one who feels safe. Gabe gently brushed her curls aside and willed his hand away. His heart thumped in his chest. He wanted this woman. Wanted to care for her. Protect her. And yeah, be honest with her. For once.

Only it wasn't going to happen tonight.

Gabe continued the drive in silence. By three in the morning they had reached the western suburbs of the city of Verona. Even after so many years, he knew the turnoff to the Forcelli estate by heart and was glad Dani wasn't awake enough to wonder how he knew it without first checking the directions. They pulled up the long, dark road that led to the mansion known by everyone in the district simply as La Tana. Gabe pressed the intercom at the security gate and heard a faint, tinny voice call out, "*Chi e?*"

"Daniela Dunn," he replied. "She's expected. *La aspettano.*"

The massive gate swung open and Gabe continued up the drive. Dani hadn't stirred. Good. Maybe he could drop her off and beat feet before she even became fully aware of what had transpired. He parked the rented Fiat and unloaded Dani's bags before nudging her gently awake. "We're here," he murmured in her ear. "Time to go."

Still groggy from her much-needed nap, Dani blinked a few times and looked around. "You found it...?"

"Not a problem," he said quietly, and helped her out of the car. The front door was massive, better suited to a cathedral than a private home. Gabe's shoulders tensed up. Of course the Forcelli's would try to match the Church in opulence, if not piety. Taking a deep breath, he rapped the large bronze door knocker— a panther's head, what else—and hoped that at this obscenely early hour he'd catch a break and the one person he dreaded above all others wouldn't respond.

Didn't happen.

"Gabriele!" the woman said as she opened the door. "What are you doing here?"

"Good morning, Aunt Fausta," he said. "I've brought Daniela home."

# CHAPTER TWO

*If looks could kill, I'd be a dead man.* Gabe watched Dani's reaction turn from shock to confusion to awareness and finally to sheer outrage, all manifest in the movement of her magnificent eyebrows. She seemed to have no desire to make a scene in front of his aunt, but he'd probably hear plenty from her once they were alone.

"Welcome home, signorina." Fausta Lombardi's voice held no trace of warmth. She was wearing a dark crimson robe, her hands clasped primly in front of her. "The family has been expecting your arrival for some time. We didn't realize my nephew would be escorting you." She looked at Gabe pointedly, her expression stern. "Indeed, we had no idea the two of you were even in touch with one another."

Dani shot Gabe a look of true venom. "We wanted it to be a surprise." She practically spat out the words.

Fausta glanced at Gabe before saying, "You may leave your luggage here. Follow me, please." She escorted them into the entry hall of the *palazzo*—an imposing, but ultimately empty space. The floors were highly polished mahogany and the rough-textured, cream-colored walls displayed stark religious artwork: a madonna and child on one wall, a large crucifix on another. Dani seemed to have forgotten both Gabe and his aunt as she gazed at the austere furnishings. Her demeanor was guarded, her expression wary. He didn't like the sensation that she was far away.

"Does it seem as though you never left?" he asked.

"Yes," she said. "As if it were yesterday."

Fausta, who had been watching them, finally spoke. "You will come with me, please, Daniela. I will show you to your room. You will find it has not been changed significantly since you were last here."

Dani drew a sharp breath. "No! Ah, no. I prefer to be near... Gabriele." She placed her hand on Gabe's forearm. "You...understand, Fausta, no?"

*What? Where had that come from?* Gabe looked at Dani, expecting her to say "Just kidding," but although she had the decency to blush, her eyes told him emphatically not to say a word. He bit his tongue and smiled sheepishly at his aunt.

"If you'd rather we stay at a hotel..."

Fausta visually skewered the two of them and pursed her lips. "This is most irregular. I do not think Signor Forcelli would approve—"

"I am not looking for Uncle Santo's approval," Dani interrupted. "He's the one who asked me to come. If he wants me to stay, then he'll have to accept Gabriele as well."

"I was speaking of Signor Forcelli the Elder, your Uncle Aldo," Fausta said calmly. "As you know, he is quite religious in his outlook. But I suppose we can put you in a suite in the north wing, where your grandmother resides when she visits. It will perhaps afford you the…privacy you seek." She allowed the word to hit its mark before adding, "I must first have the rooms aired out, however." She pulled a small cell phone out of her pocket, dialed a number and spoke quietly into it before snapping it shut again. "Come this way, please. You may wait in the library."

Dani felt like she'd been thrust in the middle of a bad gothic novel. She'd expected a small hug, or at least a warm hand clasp from the long-time family housekeeper and estate manager. Dani remembered Fausta Lombardi as a starkly beautiful woman with a regal bearing who took care of the entire Forcelli household, as well as her own family, with quiet, graceful competence. She was the mother of Dani's closest childhood friend Agnese, and she'd often served as a parent, albeit a strict one, when Dani's own had been so often absent. She was still fully in charge, apparently, but her beauty had hardened into a stone-like countenance. Dani had been gone from La Tana for the last twelve years. What had happened to sour Fausta during that time?

More importantly, what was Dani to make of the bold-face *liar* standing next to her? Once Fausta left them in the upstairs room, she turned to Gabe. Although she barely reached his chin, she shoved him in the chest. "How dare you not tell me you were related to Fausta!" she said. "All this time, and you've known about my family from the beginning!"

Gabe didn't deny her charge, but tried to rationalize his behavior. "Look, I tried to tell you, honestly, but the timing was never right. You were always too busy telling me to get lost."

"Oh, that's bull pucky," Dani shot back. "Don't you dare try to make this somehow my fault. You had plenty of opportunities to come clean with me. The question is, why didn't you?"

"'Bull pucky'? Who says 'bull pucky'?" Gabe tried on one of his trademark lopsided grins.

Dani sharpened her glare. "Don't try to change the subject. You held valuable information back from me and I want to know why." She stopped as the full implication of his betrayal hit her between the eyes. "It's not a coincidence that you moved to Little Eden, is it?" She waited, hoping against hope there was some reasonable explanation. "Is it?" she repeated, her voice breaking.

He looked at her, opened his mouth, and then closed it without saying a word.

Oh god, there's more to this, Dani thought. There's more to *him*. Suddenly her eyes filled with tears. On top of everything else, finding out that Gabe was a fraud was just too much. She had never felt so completely alone.

Gabe lightly caressed her upper arm. "I'm not one of the bad guys. Really."

Dani looked up into his face, searching his eyes for some indication that he spoke the truth. He looked sincere, but how could he be if he'd kept his connection to her family a secret ever since they'd met? She retreated into the realm of facts. "Why don't I remember you?" she asked tartly.

"I moved to the U.S. when I was ten. You were, what? Six? Seven? By that time my mother had been ill for a while and I'd spent most of my free time with her. I never lived at La Tana, so it's no wonder you don't remember the times I visited."

"Why'd you leave Italy?"

A look of regret, and maybe shame, crossed his face. "My mom was getting worse, and my parents felt it best that I not be around her. So my dad took me away."

His tone was bitter; apparently he hadn't wanted to leave.

"So Agnese would be your cousin."

"Yes," he said, "although I haven't been in contact with her."

"I don't remember much about your mother, except that she was very sick."

Gabe turned away, seeming to look at the books on one of the many shelves in the room. "Yes she was. After I left I only saw her one more time...at her funeral."

Dani's impulse was to comfort him, but she refrained. He wouldn't want her pity; besides, she was still angry with him. He couldn't be trusted. "So you and your dad just took off and left Fausta to take care of your mother, is that it?"

Gabe winced and she regretted her words. He'd been just a kid, for heaven's sake; he wouldn't have had control over his life, just as she'd had no control over hers.

Gabe's voice was flat. "Yes, that's exactly what happened. Fausta took care of my mother just like she took care of Agnese and the members of your family. It's what she does."

He was right. The titles "housekeeper" or even "estate manager" fell way short of describing the role Fausta had played in all their lives. "Where is Agnese now, by the way? Did she marry? Does she have kids by now? We wrote for a while after I left, but then she stopped."

Gabe shook his head. "No. Agnese never married. In fact, I've heard she lives in a convent now and sells a skin care line for the Sisters. Does pretty well."

"A convent? Is it the same school she and I went to? That's the last thing I pictured her doing. She was so pretty and so nice, even when we were going through that awkward pre-teen stage. I assumed someone had snatched her up." As she said it, it occurred to Dani that neither she nor Gabe had been "snatched up" either. Dani had her own reasons for remaining single, but what about Gabe? Why had a hunk like him stayed a bachelor for so long?

There was an awkward silence, which Dani filled by plopping herself down on one of the leather couches in the large, cold room. "I couldn't care less about a stuffy room at this point," she groused. "I'm ready to drop."

Gabe sat down on the sturdy coffee table in front of Dani. He leaned forward, resting his elbows on his knees, and looked her in the eye. "Speaking of which, what was that 'I prefer to be near Gabriele' routine all about? I know you're pissed at me, but you're not planning on smothering me in my sleep, are you?"

The thought of Gabe and "sleep" and what those images conjured up caused Dani to momentarily lose focus. She reeled in her thoughts and reasoned that while she now knew she couldn't completely trust Gabe, he was the lesser of two evils—and there *were* evils in this house; she just didn't know exactly what they were. The fact was, she did feel safer around him, however misguided the feeling. She moistened her lips before speaking. "I don't know, temporary insanity, maybe. I just…I just want to keep an eye on you, that's all."

Gabe looked at her intently and she knew…she *knew* he didn't buy that excuse. He put his hand on her knee and squeezed it gently, saying nothing, for which she was extremely grateful. It was the first agreeable thing he'd done since they'd left San Francisco, and her eyes began to tear up again. She reached for her bag to see if she had any tissues left. Gabe reached into his back pocket and handed her a handkerchief.

"Do guys still carry these?" she asked.

"This guy does…and yeah, it's clean," he said.

Dani snickered, glad to break the tension. They'd reached a semblance of *detente* when Dani heard Fausta's voice.

"Your rooms are ready now. Please follow me."

No one said a word as Dani and Gabe followed Fausta up a wide marble staircase to the third floor and down two long hallways before reaching a set of ornately carved double doors. Fausta opened them to reveal a sophisticated yet inviting sitting room that brought back positive memories for Dani of the times she had spent there in the company of her grandmother, Nonna Stella. According to Dani's mother, shortly after Nonno Ciro had died that terrible night twelve years ago, Stella had declared her independence from the Forcelli family, which consisted of her three grown sons. She'd moved to an elaborate penthouse at the Stella d'Italia Verona hotel. Apparently she rarely returned to La

Tana, which was probably why Fausta had authorized the use of the matriarch's suite.

Dani noticed that her bags, as well as Gabe's, had been brought up and were sitting side by side near the door. A wistful sensation passed over her, which she quickly suppressed.

"The bedroom is through that doorway." Fausta gestured absently as she walked over to the large bay window across the room and pulled the drapes closed. "And there is a small alcove to the right which contains a daybed—" she paused and looked at Dani over her shoulder, "—should you require it."

Dani felt herself blush and avoided looking at Gabe as she busied herself with her luggage. "Thank you, Fausta. Can you tell me...what time is the funeral mass today?"

"It has been scheduled for three p.m. and of course the burial will occur in the family cemetery here at La Tana at six. There will be a buffet in the Great Hall for invited guests afterward. The chef's menu is quite impressive." She opened her cell phone and began tapping it, continuing to watch the screen as she spoke. "I do not know if you are aware, but we kept the vigil as private as possible, given the awkward circumstances. Nevertheless the outpouring of condolences and the involvement of the press have been substantial. Fortunately we have been able to control the message fairly well, and I believe we will be able to ensure that all is in place for an effective service."

Puzzled, Dani turned to Gabe, who returned her look of bewilderment. Fausta was talking about her father's funeral as if it were a hotel opening! Unbidden, her eyes welled up again and she noticed Gabe raise his eyebrows, willing her without words to keep it together in front of Fausta. She nodded slightly, and sighed.

"Then we'll—I'll…uh, we'll be able to sleep in."

"Yes, signorina. You'll note I have had a refreshment tray sent up to you, and breakfast will be served until eleven a.m. Now if you have no further need of me, I'll bid you goodnight."

"Of course. Thank you. Oh, Fausta? How is Agnese? Is she here?"

"No. Not at the moment. Goodnight."

Silence reigned in the wake of Fausta's departure. Dani didn't bother to fill the void, instead concentrating on finding her sleep shirt and toiletries bag.

Gabe watched her for a minute, saying nothing.

"*What*?" she finally asked, exasperation and fatigue coloring her tone.

"Nothing. Just…you look tired." He watched her steadily as he walked toward her. When he drew close she held her breath, only to let it out in a discreet whoosh as he leaned down to pick up his bag. "I'm gonna crash on the daybed, okay? We're both running on empty."

"Um, yes. Of course. Sure. I'll just…" She gestured toward the bathroom. "I'll just use the…"

"…bathroom. Got it." Gabe smiled slightly, then turned and checked out the fruit and cheese tray Fausta had provided. Selecting a ripe pear, he bit into it as he walked over to the alcove, kicking off his shoes along the way. As if she didn't exist, he unbuttoned his shirt and pulled it out from his pants. He emptied his pockets, reached for his belt and paused, finally noting that she hadn't moved from her spot. Their eyes locked.

"I'm going," she said.

He nodded. *"Buonanotte, bella."*

Gabe awoke from a restless sleep to the muffled sound of some-one pleading. He automatically checked the lighted face on his watch. It was four thirty in the morning; he'd been asleep for less than an hour. As the fog of sleep cleared and he remembered where he was and who he was with, he heard the sound again. It was coming from the bedroom. He shot up and knocked on the door.

"Dani?"

She didn't respond, but the plaintive sounds continued. He tried the doorknob and gave a small prayer of thanks that at least Dani hadn't mistrusted him so much as to lock him out. He opened the door slowly and in the near darkness he saw her shift-ing restlessly in the large four poster that dominated the room.

"Dani," he called in a slightly louder voice.

Again, she didn't respond. Dressed in an oversized pink T-shirt and nothing else, she had kicked the covers off the bed. Gabe tamped down the desire to join her; now was not the time to be imagining her sweet legs wrapped around him.

He approached the bed and leaned over. Dani's cap of curls was slightly damp. He repeated in a slightly more forceful tone, "Bella, wake up. It's just a—"

"What are you…No! No! Don't…hurts…No…please!"

Gabe froze. Dani wasn't talking to him. Tears running down her cheeks, she was rigid, straining against unseen bonds, talking to someone else. Pleading with someone else. Someone only she could see.

Someone who had hurt her.

Terribly.

Gabe sat on the edge of the bed next to her and began to gently stroke her face.

"Daniela," he murmured. "You're okay now. It's Gabriele. I'm here, sweetheart. It's okay." He kept up the soothing mantra, hoping to get through to her without jarring her awake and scaring her to death.

She didn't awaken fully, but after several moments she did respond to his calming words and touch. She heaved a sigh and rolled to her other side, curling into a more relaxed sleeping pose. Gabe pulled the covers over her, brushed her curls back and kissed her on the forehead. He left the room quietly, poured himself two fingers of Chivas from the sideboard and sat down to wait for dawn.

# CHAPTER THREE

—◆❖◆—

At six in the morning, the air surrounding La Tana was still cool enough to bite, but Gabe knew that wouldn't last long. He relied on memory to take him along the narrow paths behind the estate, up the terraced hillside planted with grapevines and olive trees that overlooked the city.

Running the hills of Marin back in California kept him in good shape; it took several minutes for his lungs to bellow. Today he needed the workout—needed to purge himself of his toxic thoughts.

Despite the darker influences of his childhood, Gabe had always been, at heart, one who played by the rules. It was one of the reasons he'd gone into law enforcement. But hearing Dani in the throes of an anguished dream that his gut told him was based on fact, Gabe had reverted to a primitive state. It was all he could do not to wake Dani and demand to know what had happened so that he could avenge her. But doing that would have scared the hell out of her, which was the last thing she needed. So he'd spent the remainder of the night brooding over who could have violated her. How recently had she been harmed? Could someone from Little Eden be responsible? *I'll find out who did this to you*, he vowed silently. *And when I do…*

An hour into his run, damp with sweat and figuring he was too tired to tear anybody's head off, Gabe re-entered the servants' gate leading back to the grounds of the estate. As a boy he had entered La Tana many times this way, to see his mother, to see his aunt and his cousin. He had always felt privileged, like he was entering the castle of a king. But today, in the cold morning light, the building looked shabby and tired. He noticed some fissures in the limestone that the groundskeeper had packed with plaster. *It's crumbling*, he thought as he ran his hand along the scars.

Fausta, a cell phone to her ear, held the door open for him while talking to someone on the other end of the line. The cadence of her rapid Italian brought back a flood of memories.

"No, I want *all* the flowers delivered to the cathedral…yes I know it will be crowded. Deal with it." She snapped the phone shut and turned to Gabe. "Where have you been?"

"Keeping the ladies salivating," he joked, patting his sweaty T-shirt. "You know I'm irresistible, Aunt."

The pretty lady he remembered would have played along, chastising him while holding back at least a ghost of a smile. The Fausta of his memory was nowhere to be seen, replaced with a still striking but grim-faced chatelaine.

"Apparently Signorina Dunn thinks so," she said, her eyes signaling her disapproval.

Gabe wasn't as tired as he thought; he felt his adrenaline surge. "What is your problem, Fausta? Any colder and you'd freeze me on the spot. You did the same thing to Daniela last night. She didn't deserve it and I don't either. What gives?"

He watched, fascinated, as his aunt's visage transformed subtly yet unmistakably into the face and character of the woman he remembered. *You don't even need a Halloween costume,* he thought. *You're that good.*

"I'm sure it's the strain of the circumstances," she said smoothly. "Armando Forcelli was much beloved. He will be sorely missed. Come sit down, have some breakfast."

Gabe refrained from snorting as he sat down at the large prep table in the kitchen. Dani's father had been by all accounts a spoiled, immature playboy who probably ran one drunken speedboat race too many. The only people who might have considered him beloved were those who sucked at his financial tit; apparently he was known among the Eurotrash set as one hell of a tipper.

Fausta ordered one of the kitchen helpers to bring Gabe a cappuccino and some *cornetti,* which he inhaled. She sat watching him for a few moments before asking, "Why are you here, Gabriele? Did Santo ask you to come?"

Gabe didn't bother to obfuscate. It didn't matter how much his aunt knew at this point; he intended to clear it all up anyway. Still, he couldn't help feeling defensive about what he'd done.

"No," he said. "The last time I spoke with Santo was maybe four months ago. When I moved to Marin he called and asked me to keep an eye on Dani, and let him know if anything out of the ordinary happened to her. Our conversations, if you could call them that, lasted maybe ten minutes, at the most. Given what he's done for our family, I could hardly refuse him, now could I?"

"Looks like you took your job seriously."

Gabe paused to rein in his anger; he probably deserved all the scorn she was heaping on him, but Dani didn't. "It's not like that," he said. "Dani and I are…friends. Good friends. She needed some support to get through this and her mother wasn't able to join her. So I volunteered. Besides, it was time."

Fausta raised her eyebrows. "Time for what?"

"Time to balance the ledger. Time to pay back the debt."

Once again Fausta's face changed, this time to one of tight-lipped righteousness. She stood up and gestured to the kitchen help. "Iolanda, Natalia, leave us, please."

Once they were alone she sat back down and took both of Gabe's hands in hers. Her gaze was direct, piercing. "To what debt are you referring?"

"Come on, Aunt Fausta. You know which one. The one for Mama. I've made some good real estate investments over the years. I can transfer two hundred grand today. That should cover it…and then we'll be even."

Fausta's tone was clipped. "That debt has been wiped clean."

Gabe rose out of frustration and began to pace. "What the hell are you talking about? My old man died before he could do anything about it, and there's no way you could have paid for Mama's care all those years. Ciro came through for us, and when he died, Santo continued the support. I owe them."

"No," Fausta said. "Santo and his father struck a bargain and it was fulfilled."

"Fulfilled how? What'd you do, take on a second job?"

"You could say that. But regardless, the debt was paid. You owe the Forcelli family nothing. *Nothing.*"

"I'll believe that when I talk to Santo directly," Gabe said. "In the meantime, I'd appreciate it if you'd soften your attitude toward Dani. Jesus, she just lost her father."

"A father she hadn't seen in years, and who'd rarely bothered to visit her," Fausta pointed out.

"Don't talk to me about the way fathers ought to treat their children. Mine was no saint, and I don't recall seeing Uncle Rico around Agnese much either. Of course it didn't help that both of them got themselves killed."

Fausta shrugged. "Men are often a disappointment."

"Is that why you put Agnese in the convent?"

Fausta pinned Gabe's eyes. "How did you know that?"

"The Forcelli household's a favorite topic of conversation around Verona, even among the local police."

"You are in contact with Marco, then?"

"Ah, so you know he had a thing for Agnese a while back. Which means you also know she told him to get lost. Come to think of it, maybe *you* ran him off."

"Bah! Agnese was much too good for the likes of him. His family—"

"—was no different than ours: servants and tradesmen. When did you become such a snob?"

Fausta sniffed. "My family line was meant for better things, that is all. And besides, I had nothing to do with her decision.

Agnese moved there herself straight from graduate school. She... finds it comforting there."

"Is she going to take the veil?"

"No. She works in the convent garden, sells herbal products for the Sisters. She is happy enough for now."

Gabe took a stab at humor. "What—no arranged marriage in the offing?"

"You never know." At that moment her cell phone rang and Fausta took the call. "Yes?"

Gabe headed for the door. It was time to grab a hot shower and check on Dani. Hopefully she'd been able to sleep a few more hours and would forget all about the nightmare once she woke up. This afternoon's service and burial was going to be tough enough without that hanging over her head. Maybe he could distract her; maybe she'd lean on him just a little. He could hope.

"I'm sure Dani would like to see Agnese," he said on the way out. "Maybe we'll see her at the church." He thought he heard Fausta say "I doubt it," but when he turned, she was thoroughly engrossed in her telephone conversation, completely oblivious to him.

—◆⟨⟩◆—

Dante Trevisan stood transfixed at the window in Mother Maria Annunciata's office, gazing down at the convent garden below. Agnese Lombardi walked deliberately around the beds of primroses and daffodils, expertly pinching back dead blossoms and thinning the plants. She moved with fluid grace, her ebony hair pulled gently back with a plain blue ribbon, her figure only hinted at through her workman-like cargo pants and denim shirt. *She has no vanity whatsoever,* he thought. *She has no idea that she is perfect.*

"She is a beautiful woman, is she not?"

Dante turned to see Mother Maria standing in the doorway, smiling at him. He smiled back. The abbess of the Convent of Our Holy Sisters of Rectitude was nearly as tall as he, with a gentle face and shrewd eyes. He wondered what color her hair was. They had known each other all of Dante's life, but he couldn't remember ever seeing her without her habit.

"I brought you the quarterly reports," he said. "Your herbal soaps and creams are taking off. Online sales have increased twenty-five percent."

"We have Little Agnese to thank for that. Her skill in the garden is infused with the Holy Spirit, and her knowledge of such cosmetic processes is otherworldly." She grinned. "Of course it helps that she has a master's degree in holistic health."

Dante nodded and turned back to the window. "She is otherworldly," he murmured.

The nun walked up and put her hand on Dante's arm. "She will never take the veil," she said. "She is troubled by something. And she is lonely...as you are."

"You left out that she could have her pick of any eligible bachelor in Verona—or the world, for that matter. I have nothing to offer her."

The Mother's hand tightened on Dante's arm. "Never say that," she admonished. "You have more character in your little finger than—"

A knock at the office door interrupted them. "Enter," she called.

A young nun opened the door wide to let Aldo Forcelli into the office. A man of medium height with thinning hair and a husky build that belied his placid demeanor, Aldo looked relieved to see Dante speaking with the nun.

"Hello, Papa," Dante said.

Aldo glanced at Mother Maria before turning back to his son. "I'm glad you're still here. Your uncle would like to speak to you at the reception this evening. He mentioned something about a human resource matter."

Dante couldn't hide his annoyance. "Doesn't Santo ever take a day off? Not even for his brother's funeral?"

"One might ask the same of you," the abbess said, squeezing his arm gently before letting him go. "Why don't you take a stroll in the garden before you leave? The flowers are...lovely right now. I have business with your father that I must discuss."

"As you wish. Let me know if you have any questions about the report."

Dante nodded to his father before leaving. "I will see you at the cathedral."

—⊹✦⊹—

Dante paused to bolster his courage before approaching Agnese in the garden. She had turned on a hose to water the plants and didn't hear him come up behind her. He reached out to tap her shoulder and she jolted, shouted "Hey!" and sprayed the hose high, almost drenching the two of them.

"I'm sorry!" Dante called out. "I didn't know how else to get your attention." He couldn't quite hide his grin; neither could she.

"You're lucky I didn't drench your Armani suit," she admonished, turning off the nozzle. "You wouldn't want to attend mass looking like a drowned rat."

"It would be a problem," he agreed. "Are you not attending?"

"Me? No. I'm more interested in the living," she said. "Your Uncle Mando is in a better place now. He won't notice I'm not there."

"I'll...we'll—miss you." Dante could feel his awkwardness returning. He didn't understand it: women generally desired him, and he'd had many of them. He was experienced and confident in the ways of the flesh. But this small female, whom he'd known all his life, had somehow worked her way far past his libido and into his heart until he was consumed by the flame of wanting her. Only her.

Yet she had parried every one of his attempts to get closer. She seemed content to keep her distance and he didn't understand why. "Well, are you sure I can't tempt you into coming to the memorial at La Tana afterward?" he asked. "It's your childhood home, after all."

He watched, perplexed, as her sparkling eyes faded into dullness.

"Not any longer," she said, and turned away from him, busying herself with the hose. "You'd better go now. You don't want to be late."

Dante paused, not knowing what to say or do. He finally turned and walked back the way he came.

# CHAPTER FOUR

—◆✦◆—

The requiem mass for Armando Pietro Rodolfo Forcelli took place that afternoon at the Basilica of San Zeno Maggiore. The twelfth century Romanesque church wasn't the largest in Verona but was certainly one of the most beloved. Even Shakespeare admired it: he'd set the marriage scene between Romeo and Juliet in its celebrated crypt.

Dressed in a simple black dress and veil, Dani sat stoically in the section of the transept that had been set aside for family and close friends of her father. She couldn't see the nave of the church, but Fausta had boasted that a steady stream of limos and luxury cars had been flooding into the city, headed toward the basilica, all day. Following custom, the estate manager had seen to it that posters announcing Mando's death and funeral mass were plastered all over Verona. The result was a church jammed to overflowing. Filled with a sad disgust, Dani could only imagine the funeral of one of Europe's most flamboyant playboys was the place to see and be seen.

"Your father was an important man with many friends," Fausta had commented earlier in the day. "It's a pity you didn't stay more in touch with him once you left."

Dani had ignored the veiled insult. Frankly she was too tired to fight back. The desolation she felt at the loss of her father merged with the stress of the long flight and the stab of betrayal she still felt at Gabe's duplicity. He hadn't moved to the same California town she lived in by accident and she wanted to know why. Worst of all, the old nightmare she thought she'd banished years ago had come back with an intensity she'd hoped never to experience again. Somehow she'd come out of it, but deep sleep had eluded her for the rest of the brief night. Early in the morning she'd heard the shower running, but afterward Gabe had gone back to sleep in the alcove. After lunch they'd kept a polite distance, only conferring about the service they were about to attend.

Dressed in a dark-gray suit with a crisp white shirt and navy tie, Gabe looked like a cover model for *Gentleman's Quarterly*. Normally she'd be salivating, but today all she really cared about was storing up enough physical, mental, and emotional strength to get through the service and what would follow. Gabe sat next to her now, offering by his simple presence a pillar to lean on. *Or maybe I just can't bear to think of myself as totally alone.* Once again her mother came to mind—the only person she knew without a doubt that she could trust. She missed her mother fiercely.

Because of the bloated condition in which the Italian Coast Guard had found her father's body, everyone agreed that an open casket was out of the question. As she stared at the ornate, flower-bedecked coffin on display, Dani tried to keep her tears in check, but after a few futile swipes she gave up, letting them roll silently down her cheeks. So much time had gone by, so many missed opportunities. And now there would be no more chances to patch things up; she would never see her father again. How had it come to this?

In the beginning, her parents had seemed happy enough, at least according to her mother.

"Your babbo really adored you," she'd told Dani many times. "He loved being your daddy." Mando really was a doting papa when he was home; the problem was keeping him there. His powerboat racing provided a convenient excuse for traipsing all over the world, yet for a while he seemed to have curbed his appetite for other women.

Eventually, however, Dani's mom must have realized the only way to truly keep her husband satisfied was to be there for him—wherever *there* happened to be. Thus began Paula's ill-fated plan to travel with Mando while leaving Dani within the safety of La Tana. A year before Dani was born, Fausta had given birth to her own daughter, Agnese, and the two little girls became inseparable. With beautiful, popular parents and a secure home life complete with a built-in playmate, it all seemed so perfect... until it wasn't.

Dani pushed the memories aside and tried to focus on the monsignor's homily, which seemed to go on forever. After several minutes the priest concluded his assertion that Mando was on his way to eternal bliss, and sat down. A man rose to speak whom Dani hadn't seen for the past twelve years. He was tall, impeccably dressed, and still powerful-looking, with a full head of thick white hair that swept straight back from his high, tanned forehead. He had the air about him of a Machiavellian prince, one so powerful that no one—not even the Church—dare cross. He filled the podium and it was clear to all in the vast sanctuary that he was in control. Dani glanced at Gabe and noticed he had straightened in his chair.

"Monsignor, distinguished clergy, members of the Forcelli family, and dear friends, it is with great sadness that I stand before you today to say farewell to my beloved brother Armando…"

Uncle Santo. The man who had been the patriarch of the family for as long as she could remember, even though he was the second son behind her Uncle Aldo. The man who had wrested de facto power from her grandfather Ciro before he had even passed away. The man who demanded fealty from everyone in his domain.

Dani let his polished words recede as she assessed her reaction to him. Anxiety? Yes. Fear? Not *exactly*. Santo had ruled the family so thoroughly that never once had she ever heard his authority or judgment questioned. As the saying goes, it was always his way or the highway. Yes, he had been a father figure of sorts, and yes, he had been there for her when the monster had tried to hurt her so long ago.

But now, through the prism of distance and time, Dani chafed at the notion of re-entering that stilted orbit. She could feel the knot in her stomach. As assertive as she'd been over the past several years—she ran her own business for heaven's sake!—Uncle

Santo was still the last person she'd ever want to cross. Those kinds of insecurities ran deep.

But what was there to be stressed about, really? He had no power over her now. She would sign whatever papers needed to be signed, ask him about the strange artwork she remembered, and return home.

She glanced again at Gabe and this time he looked back, smiling crookedly and handing her one of his ever-present handkerchiefs. She took it with a silent thank you and breathed deeply. Gabriele de la Torre could be overbearing at times, no question. But she knew, instinctively, that he had her best interests at heart. For some reason, she just wasn't sure she could say the same about the members of her own family—beginning with Uncle Santo himself.

*What a circus*, Dani thought later. Mando's burial was supposed to be a family affair held at the family cemetery at La Tana, but privacy was impossible. Perhaps because of that, Fausta had hired professional mourners to ensure the appearance of overwhelming grief. The three women wore traditional, flowing black dresses as if they'd just come from a matinee performance of *Macbeth*. When directed to begin, they sent up a plaintive wail that rendered the brief ritual even more surreal than it already was.

Superstition held that the souls of the deceased really didn't want to leave the earth, so it was necessary to put cherished items in the casket to give them comfort on their way to the hereafter.

According to Fausta, Mando was going to his reward with a scale model of his beloved forty-two-foot Ducati Cigarette boat and a bottle of Chivas Regal. Even though she was her father's heir, no one had thought to ask Dani what she thought about any of it, and she had to admit, after being gone for so long, there was no reason for anyone at La Tana to care about her feelings. One more layer of sadness settled about her shoulders.

Once the pallbearers had lowered the casket into the ground and the priest had blessed it, Fausta had one of her assistants hand out small pouches of dirt to everyone. One by one they filed by Mando's open grave and dumped the contents in. Santo led the procession, stoic and silent. Nonna Stella followed, crying softly for her youngest son. In spite of her fashionable charcoal-colored suit, Dani's grandmother looked much smaller and frailer than Dani remembered. Cousin Dante, tall, light-haired and movie-star handsome, offered his arm to his grandmother for support. Behind them walked Aldo, who murmured a prayer and made the sign of the cross as he passed his youngest brother for the last time. Fausta followed, then Gabriele. But when it was Dani's turn to walk by, she couldn't bring herself to empty the pouch onto her father's casket. It was all too final. Too real. Instead she clutched the little bag tightly, as if she were a little girl again, holding tightly to her babbo's hand.

After the family, a few close friends filed by whom Dani vaguely remembered, and they were followed by strangers whom Dani figured were probably just hoping to be considered part of the inner circle. Each one took the leather pouch, now empty, and put it in their pocket or purse. The pouches were embroidered with her father's name and the words *Vai con Dio*—"Walk with God."

Dani felt a spurt of panic as she took in the theatrics of it all. She glanced at Gabe to see if his reaction was the same as hers: *Is this really happening? It's unfolding like some bizarre wedding reception of the dead, complete with singers and party favors!* Gabe's somber expression gave none of his feelings away; he was a study in proper funeral etiquette. The only sign he gave was the supportive arm he slipped around her waist, and Dani felt tears prickling yet again. She closed her eyes and stubbornly fought them back, buoyed by the feel of Gabe encompassing her. *It's okay. I am not alone*, she reminded herself. When she once again took in the scene, Santo was staring at her.

The reception that followed at La Tana continued what Dani was coming to think of as "the farce." Fausta had opened up the Great Hall and transformed it into a lush garden with miniature cypress and fruit trees, and enormous coils of ivy interwoven with periwinkle, narcissus, and violets. All the mourning bouquets had quickly been transported from the church and now competed for space along with artistic displays of roses and lilies. The scent of flowers was cloyingly sweet, almost too much to bear. The atmosphere reminded Dani of the last extravagant event she had attended here. Memories of that earlier time threatened to derail her and she concentrated on banishing them from her mind. *That was then, this is now* became her silent refrain.

Had this been the wake of an average *Veronese*, friends and neighbors might have brought bowls of pasta, crisp garden vegetables, fresh-baked panini or perhaps some *torta di cioccolata*—classic, Italian style comfort food. But this was the death of a Forcelli, and that called for something else entirely. Fausta hadn't exaggerated about the menu. The executive chef of the Stella d'Italia Verona had been called in to oversee the preparation of a spectacular buffet, one that touched only briefly on local favorites before branching out into an international feast. Succulent bites of chateaubriand shared the spotlight with pigeon breast *en croute* and *foie gras* with truffles; yubari melon balls complemented morel mushrooms and rack of lamb. Fausta had even ordered a larger-than-life ice sculpture of a dove whose base was surrounded by Beluga caviar and Oysters Rockefeller. It was over the top.

As guests made and devoured their selections, waiters passed around flutes of Campari and champagne while discreetly taking orders for more fortifying cocktails. While they ate and drank, those who wanted to climb another level in the social strata made sure to connect with those who already had. And watching over everything were dark-suited centurions with ear buds—Santo's hired guns, no doubt. They kept discreet eyes on the crowd, lending an even greater sense of consequence to the proceedings.

But peel away the veneer and the scene could have been a sales incentive gathering, or a Vegas retreat for CEOs; it had nothing to do with the loss of a father, or a brother, or a son.

Gabe had stayed near Dani throughout the ordeal, never imposing, just letting her use him however she needed to, as an attentive date, a sounding board, or simply a solid presence. Only once had he left her side, to go and speak to one of the security guards. From her vantage point she could see them shaking hands, and then embracing. Obviously Gabe knew the goon.

"What, are you in need of some cop bonding already?" she asked when he returned. Even she didn't like the sarcasm in her voice, but her escort ignored it.

"Oh, that was Marco Clemente," Gabe said, sipping his champagne. "He's a detective with the state police force, but he's moonlighting tonight. We were *amici* way back when." He leaned closer and whispered, his breath tickling her ear. "Believe it or not, we were occasional pen pals. But don't tell anyone. It's bad for our tough guy image." He straightened and smiled at her. "We've stayed in touch through the years. He visited me in L.A. once, and I went to his wedding. His wife's a sweetheart. " He drained his glass. "You know, he had a thing for Agnese, but she shined him on. Now he's happily married with a *bambino*. Too bad for my cousin. Marco's a good guy."

The family had eschewed a formal receiving line, which relieved Dani because participating in that would probably have sent her over the edge. Nevertheless, a few individuals who somehow recognized her as a member of the family stopped by to give her air kisses and murmur platitudes.

"We're sorry about your loss."

"*Poveretto.*"

"We will miss him."

And Dani dutifully responded with similar banalities: "*Seite molto gentili*, you are very kind."

Dani took time to visit with her grandmother, who looked worn out and stayed only briefly before returning to her penthouse at the Stella d'Italia Verona. They made plans to visit in the next few days. Dante sought Dani out to give her a hug and shake Gabe's hand, then apologized for having to rush off because Santo wanted to meet with him over a business matter.

"Right now?" she asked, incredulous.

Dante shrugged. "It's ludicrous, I agree. But you know Santo. When he says jump…"

"Yes, I know." Dani watched her cousin stride across the room and counted herself lucky she hadn't had to interact with their uncle for the past twelve years.

An hour later her luck ran out. Uncle Santo headed straight toward them, leaving no avenue of escape. As he drew near, Dani found herself moving closer to Gabe.

"I am sorry we have not had a chance to speak until now, dear niece," Santo said, capturing her eyes with his. "I trust you are being well taken care of?"

Dani couldn't help but shiver at the glitter in his eyes and the way he had said "dear niece." It sounded almost…intimate. She glanced at Gabe before responding. "I…we…that is, yes, we are, Uncle. Um, you of course know Gabriele de la Torre, Fausta's nephew?"

Santo shifted his gaze to Gabe and the light in his eyes dimmed. "Yes, we are acquainted."

"More than acquainted, Signore." Gabe said, extending his hand. "I am sorry for your loss, but I am glad to see you after so much time. In fact, I would like to make an appointment to see you in the next day or two, if your schedule permits."

"You would like to see me." Santo continued to assess Gabe, his tone slightly condescending. Gabe didn't seem to notice.

"*Sissignore*, about a financial matter."

Dani watched the two of them. Something was definitely going on here, and it didn't seem to be connected to her or the funeral. Had helping her only been an excuse for Gabe to come to Verona on business? She chalked another mark under the "What I don't know about Gabe" column. The man had a lot of explaining to do.

"Very well, then. I believe I will have some time tomorrow morning. You may contact my secretary at your convenience." Santo verbally dismissed Gabe and turned again to Dani. "And you, dear, you must come to me as well...separately, of course. We too have financial matters to discuss." His eyes didn't leave hers and Dani felt a frisson of unease. Unconsciously she slid her arm around Gabe, but didn't dare look at him for fear he'd give their charade away.

"Yes," she said to Santo, her chin lifting slightly. "I suspect we do."

After a gaze that lasted too long for Dani's comfort, Santo nodded to the two of them and walked away. He was soon surrounded by a trio of older Middle Eastern men who seemed to be introducing themselves to him.

Dani immediately turned to Gabe. "What do you mean, you have something financial to talk to Uncle Santo about?"

"What do you mean by pretending we're a couple?" Gabe countered.

Dani immediately made to drop her arm, but Gabe quickly turned her to face him and locked his arms around her waist. He smiled slowly, in a way that, were she any other woman, would have clinched the deal right then and there. As it was, she couldn't suppress the warmth that had begun to spread all through her at the feel of his body so close to hers. The "rightness" of it shocked her; she stilled to soak in the feeling and barely noticed that he had gone still as well, the teasing look in his eye replaced with something much more intense. Something that made her uneasy but in a totally different, totally wicked way. She blinked to rid herself of the feeling and took a deep breath to will herself back to sensibility.

"I…I'm sorry," she said, pushing against him slightly. "It must be the emotion, I guess. I shouldn't use you like that."

Gabe released his hold, but kept one hand resting lightly on her hip as he bent down to her. "I'm not complaining," he whispered. "You may use me however you want, whenever you want, bella. I am yours. Completely."

Dani snorted then. *That* was the Gabe she knew: lighthearted and teasing. She felt on safer ground. "You're not getting out of it that easily. Come on, you still haven't told me. What business do you have with him?"

Gabe looked across the room for a moment before looking back down to Dani. "It's a long story—one that's about to reach a conclusion."

"What do you mean by that?" Dread settled over Dani like a shroud and she barely got the next words out. "Does it have anything to do with why you moved to Little Eden? Is your work ending there, too?"

Gabe smiled. "No. Dani, I—"

"*Scusi,* Signorina Dunn?"

Gabe and Dani turned to see a slender woman dressed in black with a veiled hat. It was difficult to see her face, but it was obvious she was distraught.

"*Sì,* signora?" Dani said.

"I...I knew your papa. He was a lovely man." The woman's voice broke on the last words, and she reached under her veil to wipe her eyes.

Dani looked at Gabe, puzzled.

"I...am sorry," the woman continued. "This is difficult." She reached out to Dani to give her a hug, which Dani awkwardly returned. "He would have been very proud of you."

The woman looked around as if checking to see who was near. She then took Gabe's two hands in her own and kissed him on each cheek before turning and walking quickly away. Within moments she was lost in the crowd.

"That was strange," Dani said. "I've never seen that woman before in my life. Do you know her?"

"No, but I think she wants to know me," Gabe joked. He held up a small piece of paper the woman had surreptitiously pressed into his hand.

"What? Let me see that." She made to snatch the paper, but Gabe held it out of her reach.

"Uh uh uh," he said, grinning. "This is my backup plan for when you've had your fill of me." He stuck the paper in the front pocket of his slacks and held up his hands. "Okay, now you can come and get it."

Dani wasn't about to go sticking her hands anywhere near his "pocket." "*Tu sei pazzo*," she grumbled. "*Completamento pazzo.*"

"I'm crazy all right—crazy about you." He wiggled his eyebrows at her. "Now may I interest you in some fish eggs on crackers? The grub here certainly doesn't compare to your cooking, but it'll do in a pinch."

"No, I mean it, certifiable," she said, amused at how this exasperating man had somehow managed to get her through the day's events intact and even smiling. "Well? Lead on," she added, and took the hand he offered.

—◆◇◆—

It was midnight by the time the two of them returned to their suite. Dani was exhausted. The funeral and reception had obviously taken its toll on her. Gabe didn't comment on the dark smudges under her eyes, and voiced no objection when she said she was turning in. He only hoped she would sleep until morning without the terrors of the night before.

He was still wired, however. Knowing he would finally settle accounts with Santo kept his mental engine running. So many years in the making, and now he'd finally be able to close the chapter. And maybe open a new one with Dani if he were lucky.

He looked to see if the small refrigerator under the wet bar had been stocked with liquid sleeping aids and was gratified to find a couple of Birra Moretti. "You're not a Heineken, but you'll do," he muttered, and flopped down on the couch with one of the lagers.

Out of habit he pulled his shirt out from his slacks and emptied his pockets on the coffee table, dislodging the forgotten scrap of paper in the process. *That was one strange lady,* he thought, and it struck him that she didn't seem like she was in the frame of mind to be hitting on anybody. He opened the paper and read it, straightening up as he did so. "Holy shit," he said.

The paper read:

*Nando Forcelli was murdered. Tell no one.*

*Meet me tomorrow 1 p.m. Giulio's in Mizzole. Please help.*

# CHAPTER FIVE

—✦✦✦—

Santo Forcelli, the president of Stella d'Italia hotels, sipped the last of his cappuccino as he read the morning papers in his private office. He found the write-up on the funeral mass and reception to be adequate and made a note to have his secretary send the editor of *L'Arena* some flowers. All in all, the unfortunate situation with Mando had turned out to be quite positive. Everybody loved a scandal, which brought free publicity, and if the Forcelli clan was seen as grieving the sudden loss of their wayward son, so much the better.

The sound of his secretary over the intercom was unexpected. "Excuse me, signore, but there is a Signor Gabriele de la Torre to see you. He says he made an appointment with you last evening."

*Christ, it's only nine in the morning*, he thought. *Anxious little bastard.* "All right. Send him in."

"Yes, sir."

As de la Torre entered his office, Santo made a point not to get up, which any idiot would take as the insult it was meant to be. Unfortunately the man didn't indicate by either expression or mannerism that he knew or even cared that he was being disrespected. Either de la Torre really was stupid or he'd been in America too long. Santo thought it must be the latter. Americans, in his experience, put very little stock in class distinction; in fact, they generally had no sense of class whatsoever. Daniela's mother was a perfect example of that.

Santo observed the man's muscles, which were considerable beneath his shirt and jacket. He was a strong-looking buck; no wonder Daniela had attached herself to him. He grew hard at the image of the two of them having sex and that irritated him. He was glad to be sitting down.

"You did not waste any time," he said, indicating with a nod that de la Torre should take a seat.

"I have a full schedule today…as I'm sure you do as well," de la Torre replied, dwarfing the chair he chose to sit in.

Santo eyed the interloper for a long minute before speaking. "Why did you come with Daniela?" he asked. "Are you fucking her?" He watched the man wince at his words. *So he has feelings for her.* "Does she know you've been spying on her for the past year?"

De la Torre stared at him. Santo noticed the man was clenching his jaw. "I don't know why you're insulting your niece, and I don't particularly care. Our business has nothing to do with her."

"Doesn't it?" Santo leaned back in his chair and calmly took a cigar out of the custom, engraved humidor that the sultan of Brunei had given him for "services rendered" a few years back. He took his time clipping the end of the cigar, lighting and inhaling it before he spoke again. "'De la Torre.' That was a noble name... once upon a time. Perhaps you are trying to resurrect it after what your family obviously did to ruin it."

Before the buck could react to the insult, Santo continued. "You feel you owe me for your mother's care, which is why, at my request, you've been willing to keep me informed as to my niece's activities without her knowledge. Now you've come to tell me you will no longer do my bidding, clearly because if you don't already have the woman, you want her, and if she learns you've been spying on her, she will no doubt kick you out of her bed. So you aim to alter the terms of our agreement by offering me a financial settlement. Do I have the facts right?"

Santo continued to gaze at de la Torre and was pleased to see that he'd scored a direct hit. The younger man was working hard no doubt to keep himself from reaching over the desk and grabbing Santo by the throat. *A pity he doesn't try it. The stiletto in my top drawer would look stylish jutting out of the bull's neck.*

"I have done nothing since I have known Daniela to cause her any harm. I simply answered the occasional questions of a concerned but far-off relative as to her safety and social status."

"Bravo," Santo said, clapping his hands slowly. "I'm sure you have rehearsed that many times. But the fact remains, she doesn't know, does she?" De la Torre's silence told Santo what he needed to know. He smiled. "So what may I do for you?"

"I have calculated what it must have cost your family to care for my mother for the years she suffered from her disease," de la Torre said. "I believe it is roughly two hundred thousand dollars.

I can wire that amount to your bank at any time and from that point forward I would like to call it even between our families."

"Two hundred thousand dollars? Where, may I ask, did a mere policeman get that kind of money? You haven't gone to the dark side, have you?"

"It's none of your damn business where the money came from, just that it's legal."

"So you've scrimped and saved and now you're going to restore honor to your family's name by repaying a decades-old debt. It's admirable. But once you turn over your nest egg to me, what will you have to offer your lady love?" Santo made a show of pondering the ceiling. "Ah, wait. I see. Now that's she's an heiress, it won't matter, will it? You'll live off her."

De la Torre stood up and Santo felt a moment of true fear. The man wouldn't go berserk, would he? He might be so quick that Santo couldn't get to the knife in time. De la Torre leaned his hands on Santo's desk in a gesture designed to intimidate.

"I've told you before," he said carefully, as if he too feared losing control. "This has nothing to do with Daniela. Simply tell me where to send the money and I will send it. Then we will never have to speak again."

Santo rose slowly, in part to show he wasn't cowed by the younger man, and in part to move closer to the door in case de la Torre was stupid enough to attack him. "Much as I would love to take your money, my own honor dictates that I cannot," he said. "I made an agreement with your aunt many years ago and she has taken care of the debt. If you feel the need to compensate anyone, compensate her."

"I don't understand," de la Torre said, straightening to his full height. "How could she have paid you so much money on a manager's salary?"

"Money isn't…everything," Santo replied as he walked around his desk toward his office door. "I thank you for your, shall we say, "reporting" services, but now that Daniela is back with the family I will have no more need of them…and she will have no more need of you. Your debt having been discharged, I'll expect you to leave La Tana as soon as possible."

The brute looked him in the eye. "With all due respect, the decision as to when I leave is up to Dani, not to you."

"We will see about that," Santo murmured. He held the door open. "Now if you'll excuse me, I have much more pressing matters to attend to." He met de la Torre's glare with a bored expression of his own. The young man brushed past him, and as he passed Cristina's desk, Santo called out, "Signor de la Torre?" When he turned, Santo said, "What were you, ten or so when you left your mother? It's a pity you never saw her alive again. But rest assured, the only real suffering she endured was the loss of her little boy."

*Sometimes one doesn't need an actual knife to inflict a mortal wound.* A grim smile on his face, Santo returned to his desk, agitation still simmering throughout his body. De la Torre was nothing. *Nothing.* He drew on his cigar and exhaled, as if to rid himself of the nuisance.

He'd been truthful about having more important issues to deal with. His very silent "partners," owners of the Azure Consortium, were beginning to pressure him, but not for anything that hadn't already been discussed within the family. For years his parents had argued about extending the Stella d'Italia hotel brand. His father was all for it, but his mother refused to leverage the company. Santo realized early on that he'd have to marginalize her to run the operation his way. Fortunately his own marriage to Ornella Orfeo, pathetic though it was, had provided enough capital to expand and upgrade their properties, elevating the Stella d'Italia brand to the elite cadre of European hoteliers.

But now, he agreed, it was time to take their operation to the next level. The consortium had purchased the ailing hotel chain Alberghi Paradisi specifically to resell it to Stella d'Italia. The acquisition would mean holding debt, to be sure, but the profit potential was considerable, and all it took was fifty-one percent of the family vote to approve the sale. His mother's forty-nine percent couldn't be counted on, damn her, but that had never mattered before, because in his will, Santo's father had given each of his sons seventeen percent. With Mando and Aldo each voting their shares with him, their combined votes had always carried the day...

...until Mando balked. The question was, why? Their last conversation had been cryptic. Mando implied he knew something wasn't right with the company, but gave no details. Sources told Santo that his brother was screwing the human resources director of their Milano property; maybe she had his ear. No matter, he'd already put Dante on her trail. He would ferret her out and see what, if anything, she knew.

Santo stubbed out his cigar. He had few regrets in life. He had not only taken care of his extended family, but seen to it that they all prospered. For years, his brothers had understood he put the family's interests first and they had willingly gone along with his wishes. But telling his shadow partners about Mando's newfound obstinacy had been a mistake. Without his knowledge they'd taken action, thinking they would solve his problem. But they had only changed the nature of it. Now that Mando was gone, Daniela was the linchpin. For that reason, only one path stood out in stark relief: Daniela had come home and once more it was time for her to follow the course he would lay out for her. But she was no longer a shy, respectful teenager, which meant his strategy would have to change. He pushed his intercom button once again.

"Cristina, I would like you to send a message to my niece Daniela Dunn and tell her I would like to take her to lunch today. Tell her I will have my driver pick her up at La Tana at twelve thirty. And tell Signora Petrovic that our lunch meeting will have to wait. When you have finished with that, please come into my office. I have need of you before my conference call at ten."

"Yes, Signor Forcelli."

While he waited for his secretary, Santo continued to drum his fingers on his desktop. The image of the muscle-bound policeman who seemed to have forgotten his place came to mind again. Images of Daniela and the stud in bed once again intruded, and lust cohabited with fury. At that moment the cell phone in his desk vibrated. He reached into the drawer, pulled it out and answered it.

"You saved me a call," he said.

—◆❖◆—

*I could kill him with my bare hands*, Gabe thought on his way out of the executive suite. The tension he felt from having to keep from decking Santo had caused his shoulders to knot considerably and he needed to punch something to loosen them up; too bad the prick's face wasn't available. Until today he'd had only a passing acquaintance with the Forcelli patriarch. As a young boy, he'd always considered Santo the amorphous "boss man." In more recent times, during the few telephone calls regarding Dani, he'd sensed the older man's condescension. But in person Forcelli had shown utter contempt toward Gabe and what was obviously a painful subject, the death of Gabe's mother. But more than anything, the man had seemed proprietary toward Dani, as if she were way too good for Gabe. Maybe she was, but that was for her to decide, not her uncle. God, what an asshole.

After checking his watch, he hailed a taxi outside the corporate headquarters adjacent to the company's downtown hotel. He had enough time for a run at La Tana before heading to Giulio's in the nearby village of Mizzole to meet the mystery lady. He debated whether or not to tell Dani where he was going. The note had said "Tell no one." Did that mean not even Dani? That seemed ridiculous, but then, why hadn't she given the note to Dani to begin with? He decided to take this first step solo, just in case it didn't smell right. He could always bring her up to speed later.

She was still in their suite when he returned. Dressed in a pretty, peachy colored summer sweater and cream-colored slacks, she looked like a two-toned Popsicle and he wanted to lick her from top to bottom. It helped that she had slept peacefully the night before; her natural energy seemed to be back.

"I missed you this morning," she said. "Did you go for a run?"

"Uh, no, I'm going now. What's on your agenda today?"

"Well, that's what I wanted to speak to you about. I got a call from Uncle Santo's secretary telling me he wants to take me to lunch today. I...I was wondering if you would like to come with me."

Gabe hesitated. The last thing in the world he wanted to do was deal with Santo again, but any other time he'd gladly suck it up to support Dani. She obviously didn't like the man. Still, he couldn't stand up the mystery woman—what she had to say was too important. "Uh, well, I'd like to, but...but I'm going to see Marco for lunch."

Dani stared at him for several moments, as if evaluating him. "Really?" she asked.

"Um, yeah. I just spoke with him a few minutes ago."

"I see. Well, then the man calling himself Marco who just called saying he'd like to invite us to dinner tomorrow night because he's busy with work today must be a different Marco." She cocked her head, waiting.

He sighed, running his hand through his hair. *Busted.* "I... uh...you remember that note last night..."

The expression that crossed Dani's face showed surprise, then hurt, and finally a strange vindication, as if he'd proven her right about his lack of character all along. "Ah." She nodded and turned to head back to her bedroom. "Well, enjoy yourself."

"Wait," Gabe said, starting toward her. "I don't think you—"

Dani waved him away. "Really, I mean it. You're on vacation, you shouldn't be babysitting me."

Gabe stared at the door that had effectively been shut in his face. He considered his options. He could tell her the truth and really freak her out, or he could mislead her for a little while longer until he found out more information. He decided on the latter course, although he felt like a shithead about it. No matter what, he was going to have to engage in some serious damage repair when he got back.

—◆·◆—

By mid-afternoon Gabe had just finished his second glass of *birra*—sadly, not nearly cold enough to combat the sticky heat that caused him to regret not wearing running shorts. After more than an hour, the mystery lady still hadn't shown up. He checked the piece of paper she'd given him yet again. Yes, he was at the right place, and yes he'd been there since one p.m. He looked around. This time of day the trattoria was nearly deserted; in fact, the only other customer at an outdoor table was a beefy man wearing sunglasses and a baseball cap with foreign lettering on it, playing some sort of game on his cell phone. Either that or he was writing a novel at breakneck speed. At any rate, the guy had been tapping away since shortly after Gabe sat down.

Maybe I've been pranked, Gabe thought. Or maybe Santo set this up to make sure I wouldn't show up with Dani for lunch. No, that didn't make sense. The mystery woman had come up to them just as Santo left them at the reception. Besides, Dani had only learned about the lunch invitation this morning; how would Santo know if she was going to show or not?

He called the waiter to get his tab and reached into his back pocket for his wallet. After pulling out some euros he looked up to see a woman approaching him. She was wearing a large floppy hat and sun glasses, but he could tell it was the same woman from the memorial reception.

"Signor Gabriele de la Torre?" she asked softly.

Gabe put the money on the table and spoke just as softly. "How do you know my name?"

"You were mentioned as Signorina Dunn's escort for the funeral. It was in *L'Arena,* the newspaper." The woman looked around furtively and lowered her voice even further. "You read my note."

"Obviously. Listen, signora, I don't know what you—"

"*Scusi,* will you come with me? *Per favore?* I do not have very much time."

Glancing over, he saw the guy with the cell phone stand up as well. Gabe accompanied the mystery lady down the alley, back toward the main street of the neighborhood. The phone guy followed them.

Gabe's sixth sense kicked in. At the corner, the woman turned right and continued walking briskly. Halfway down the block Gabe gently took her by the arm to stop her in front of a book shop. She looked up at him and started to tug, so he tightened his grip.

"Bear with me," he said quietly. And more loudly, in Italian, "You're always in a hurry, darling. I need to get a book for Rafael." He paused and appeared to be perusing the books displayed in the window. Phone guy walked by, but stopped two storefronts down. Gabe glanced at him; he looked innocuous enough, once more checking his cellphone and tapping. Gabe waited a minute, then took the lady's arm and turned her in the opposite direction. "Dammit, I forgot something at the café," he said in a loud voice.

"What's—"

Gabe leaned down as if to kiss her on the neck. "Shhh. Play along," he whispered. They continued walking back the way they came.

Phone guy followed.

Shit.

Out of habit Gabe felt for his shoulder holster, which of course he'd left back in California. He picked up the pace, and when the woman began to turn around he squeezed her arm again to keep her facing forward. "How well do you know Mizzole?" he asked.

"I grew up here." Her voice was strained.

"Then get us lost," he said.

The woman's eyebrows shot up and panic swept over her face, but self-preservation must have quickly taken over because she nodded, took Gabe's hand and immediately crossed the street, heading toward a small passage between two larger buildings off the village square. Gabe glanced back to see phone guy crossing the street, heading their way, still on his cell phone. *Probably calling in reinforcements,* Gabe thought, once more lamenting his lack of weapon. *This woman better know what she's doing.*

They were jogging now; thank God she was wearing sensible shoes. She took them through the alley and onto another street before ducking into a *panetteria*. The yeasty smell of the bread reminded Gabe of Dani's freshly baked focaccia back home. It crossed his mind how cruel it was to take this particular escape route when he couldn't stop to appreciate it or buy a loaf. He had no idea what the woman was up to.

"Look, I know a local cop," he said. "Where's the nearest precinct office?"

"No!" the woman cried. "My way is better." She waved hello to the woman behind the counter and headed to the back of the shop. With his free hand Gabe put his finger to his lips and the clerk smiled indulgently. They entered the kitchen where a middle-aged man was cleaning off a giant dough hook. "*Ciao* Rudi," the mystery lady said. *"Non ci ha mai visto."* Rudi grinned and waved his hand. "Sì. Sì."

They headed out the back door and kept running, down backstreets, through private gardens, along a park path, under a stone archway. The woman showed no signs of slowing down; she seemed to be running on adrenaline. Gabe glanced behind and to either side. No sign of phone guy. They'd probably lost him several blocks back. He tugged on the woman's arm to stop her.

"Good job," he said. "Now will you please tell me what the hell is going on?"

"I will, but follow me, *per favore*. It's not far now."

It seemed she really did know where she was going. They headed down several more streets until they came to a nondescript door. She knocked, looking both ways as she did so.

Ironically, Gabe felt much less comfortable leaving the street. "Look, lady, if this is some kind of scam—"

The woman stopped and peered up at him, taking off her sunglasses to look at him directly. Her eyes were dark and alert.

"No scam, signore, I assure you. Trust me, please." Her tone was impatient, as if she were a teacher and he an unruly little boy who had pushed her buttons one too many times. Gabe frowned at the all-too familiar memory.

After a moment the door opened and an older, white-haired woman beckoned them in. He followed the younger woman through a small, sparsely furnished house that was centered, like many Italian homes, around an interior courtyard. She led the way outside, motioning to a rickety iron table set with two chairs.

"Please. Sit. *Mamma, due espresso, per favore*?" She sat down and took off her hat. Without the disguise she was an attractive brunette who looked to be in her early to mid-forties.

"You may speak in Italian, signora," Gabe said. "Look, I have no clue who we were running from just now. But you seem to. What's this all about?"

"My name is Carla Rinaldi," she said. "Until very recently I was the human resources director at the Stella d'Italia Milano." She reached into her purse and pulled out a cigarette. "Do you mind? I am a little nervous these days." She chuckled weakly. Gabe shook his head and she proceeded to light up, her hands shaking slightly in the process.

"Why aren't you working there anymore? Were you let go?"

Carla started to speak, but her mother interrupted, bringing a tray with the two espressos and a plate of biscotti. "Thank you, Mama." She took a sip of the rich coffee. It seemed to calm her down. After several moments she began to speak.

"Signor de la Torre, as soon as I found out Mando had been killed, I left my job and my apartment. Everything. In fact, I am scheduled to take a train to Rome in two hours. From there I plan to take a flight…well, away."

"What do you mean, Mando was killed? From everything I've been told, he took his powerboat joyriding in the middle of the night, fell out, and drowned."

Carla nodded. "Yes, I know that's the report, but it isn't the truth. You see…I was with Mando that night. In Siracusa."

"Were you and he seeing each other?"

The woman bestowed a ghost of a smile. "You mean, was I his mistress?"

Gabe shrugged. "Your word, not mine."

"I suppose the world would see it that way," she admitted. "Legally he was still married to Daniela's mother. But our relationship was so much more than that. I loved him very much."

Gabe felt sorry for the woman; she obviously cared for the guy, but she couldn't openly express her grief as a lover would. Still, the relationship wasn't really the point.

"If you were with him, why did he take off in his boat? Did you have a fight?"

"No, nothing like that. In fact, Mando was ill that night. He suffered from migraines, and he could tell when one was coming on. Something about the light—he became very sensitive to it, so he knew what to expect. He was scheduled to race in a qualifying heat the next day, and he didn't want to be incapacitated, so he left after we had dinner and returned to his room to take the prescription medication he had brought with him. The medication made him drowsy, which he liked, because he knew the only way to improve his condition was to sleep. There is no way he would have taken the medication and then gone out on his boat."

"You weren't staying in the same room?"

Carla blushed at that. "No. Mando and I…We began as casual business colleagues. He would occasionally attend hotel promotional events and over time our friendship grew into something very strong. He was a public figure, and we—I—did not want the world to intrude on our privacy. Our relationship was…beautiful. And we took precautions to make sure it was not destroyed by the *paparazzi*. Do you understand?"

"I do. So you made an early night of it. Had you been drinking? Maybe he—"

"No. Absolutely not. Mando always said that alcohol inflamed his head even more and he never drank when he knew he was going to take the medication."

Gabe reached for his ever-present notepad and pencil. Carla watched him, her hands repeatedly flicking the cigarette. "Back in the States I'm a police detective," he said. "Did you know that?"

Carla shook her head. "The paper said you were in law enforcement, but it did not say in which capacity. I have heard that police in America are not as susceptible to corruption as they are in Italy."

"That's debatable," Gabe said drily. "But don't worry, I'm only taking notes to keep track of the timeline. So you parted company when?"

"I would say around ten fifteen or ten thirty p.m. We said our good nights. His room was four doors down from mine. I watched him enter his room. He...he blew me a kiss." Carla's voice broke; Gabe reached for his usual handkerchief and offered it to her.

"Thank you. You are very kind."

"So he enters his room around ten thirty. Did you hear any noises after that?'

Carla shook her head. "Not until, I don't know, around eleven or eleven-fifteen, I heard some men talking while they walked down the hall. They were not speaking Italian, although one of them spoke whatever language it was with an Italian-sounding accent. It was...it sounded Eastern European, but I'm not sure which country. One of them sounded as if he were breathing hard. I wonder—if I had opened the door, would I have seen that man carrying Mando? Could I have done something to save him?"

"Signora Rinaldi, you should thank your lucky stars you didn't open that door. If you had, and if what you surmise is true, you might not be talking to me today."

"I believe you are right. But as you can see, I am still in danger...for the same reason that Mando was killed."

"Okay, let's cut to the chase. You think Mando was murdered. Why?"

Carla took a moment before answering. Gabe could tell she was afraid to share what she knew.

"I'm on your side, remember," he said softly.

Carla paused, then nodded. "Stella d'Italia hotels cater to a very exclusive clientele, primarily businessmen. Each property is required to employ as many guest-exposure workers as possible, including housekeeping attendants, from eastern or northern

Europe." She smiled ruefully. "Gentlemen really do prefer blonds, Signor de la Torre."

"I must be the exception that proves the rule," Gabe said. "Please go on."

"Many of the maids who come to us are from rural areas of Eastern European countries, such as Slovenia, Romania, and the Ukraine. These young women, most of whom are very attractive, are quite innocent and unused to city life and its many dangers. I was alerted by our director of housekeeping that her staffing levels had been erratic the last several months and she was irritated because it was beginning to require more training hours than usual and was affecting employee morale."

"What was going on?"

"She had been sent a number of temporary housekeeping personnel from other Stella d'Italia properties to help with a large booking, but within a few weeks, two of them had left the company. Apparently this had happened several times before, whenever temporary staff were brought in. She assumed one of our competitors was offering a better employment package, so she finally brought the situation to my attention. I mentioned it in passing to our general manager and said I would be looking into it. He got back to me a few days later and told me, quite emphatically, not to pursue the matter. He said the corporate office had assured him it was part of the normal ebb and flow for that department."

"Something tells me that didn't sit right with you."

Carla smiled for the first time since he'd met her. "You are right. I did not bring it up again with either my director of housekeeping or my general manager, but in my spare moments I quietly created a spreadsheet showing turnover trends over time."

"So, was the competition stealing your best workers?"

"I honestly wish it were the case, but no. I selected a handful of names and talked with my counterparts at other Milano properties. The women had not joined any other hotel staff. I then traced the lost employees back to the Stella d'Italia property they had come from and talked discreetly with their home supervisors. Most of the temporary employees had indeed returned to their original positions, but none of the employees I was trying to locate had done so. Some of the supervisors, just like my own director of housekeeping, were annoyed because they too thought they had lost good workers to a better employment situation."

"Did you talk to anyone else about what might have happened to them?"

"No, I kept it to myself. I did not know what the answer was, only that those above me did not want me to find it."

Gabe nodded. "But you kept digging."

Carla shrugged. "Yes, certainly. I tried to track some of them down from their last known residence in Milan, but each one had left her living situation without giving a forwarding address. Yet there were no complaints to the local authorities, which is odd, except that they hadn't been in Milan for very long, so I suppose they wouldn't know too many people who would miss them. I find the situation quite perplexing."

"Maybe they decided to leave the hotel business altogether. Isn't there a lot of turnover at that level, anyway? Maybe as women got to know Milan, they decided they preferred it to the last place they worked, and found not only new positions, but better living situations."

"Yes, that does happen frequently, but in those cases there is almost always a forwarding address because many of these young women receive packages and letters from home. And do you know what I found most disturbing of all?"

"Tell me."

"The pattern repeated itself at different hotels. For example, the director of housekeeping at the Stella d'Italia Firenze would receive a request to provide specific staff members to work temporarily at another Stella d'Italia property. A few weeks later some of those workers would return, but some would not. At other times, the director would receive extra temporary employees from various properties, usually in advance of a large booking—a conference, for instance—and a few of those temporary workers would leave their jobs."

"Who was making these requests?"

"Sometimes they were made from one hotel director to another, but sometimes they came down the chain of command from the corporate office. It did not happen that often to any one hotel, so no one thought to report it." Carla smiled briefly. "It so happens that my director of housekeeping is a particularly vocal woman."

Gabe leaned back in the wrought iron chair and took a sip of coffee. "You're saying you think women are somehow being kidnapped from the Stella d'Italia Milano?

Carla stubbed out her cigarette and reached into her purse. She took out a stack of spreadsheets which she placed on the table in front of Gabe. "I'm saying, Signor de la Torre, that I think it is happening at virtually *all* the Stella d'Italia hotels. I told Mando what I had discovered, and I believe he was murdered because he was about to expose the operation. Let me show you what I mean."

# CHAPTER SIX

—·✦·✦·—

"I'm sorry you wish to speak English," Santo said. "Have you forgotten your native Italian, then?"

"I am a bit rusty," Dani admitted. She was sitting across from her uncle in a secluded booth in the back of the Tesoro di Mare restaurant, a five-star establishment located on the seventeenth floor of the Stella d'Italia Verona. She was perusing a menu, which her uncle hadn't bothered to look at, when the waiter arrived to take their orders.

"Well, you must try the *Aragosta Fra Diavolo*," Santo said, leaning forward on his elbows and looking at Dani intently. He wore a heavy gold ring on his right hand which showcased what looked like a bluish-black sapphire. "The seasoning is superb."

Dani loved lobster, but hated it when someone was so arrogant as to tell her what to order. "Um, no thanks, I'm allergic to shellfish," she lied.

Santo gazed at her, his eyes signaling his disbelief. But all he said was, "How sad. I do not remember that about you. Then try the *Pesce Spada alla Siciliana*. It is quite exquisite as well."

"I'll have the mushroom risotto, thanks." She handed the menu back to the waiter, holding her hand over her wine glass when he began to pour from the bottle that Santo had selected. "Just iced tea, please."

*Score two points for me.* Dani had been deflecting her uncle's overbearing behavior ever since she'd turned down his offer of a driver earlier that morning. After Gabe showed his true colors, she'd given herself a pep talk worthy of a halftime locker room speech at the Super Bowl. No more feeling so tense and, well, *anxious.* She was a grown woman now. She couldn't rely on anyone but herself, so she'd better buck up. No one was going to push her to do anything she didn't want to do—not even her dictatorial Uncle Santo.

"You are quite…grown up," Santo commented. "You are not the shy young sprite who grew to womanhood at La Tana." He paused, as if appraising her. "I find I like the change. Very much." He took a sip of his wine and made the gesture of a toast to her.

Dani felt the hair at the back of her neck stand up. Overbearing she could handle; it was this…this *courtliness* of his that felt so odd. She'd sensed it last night at the funeral reception, and now he was at it again. Santo must have noticed her uneasiness.

"I'm sorry if I have embarrassed you," he said. "You have turned out to be an exquisitely beautiful woman, and I believe such beauty should be acknowledged, if not celebrated."

*Point Santo.* It dawned on her that he was doing it on purpose; he *wanted* to make her uncomfortable. But why? She was screwing up her courage to ask him when the waiter brought their entrees. As they ate, Santo shifted the tenor of the conversation, retreating to safer topics such as Dani's degree in hospitality management and her current position as owner and manager of the Havenwood Inn.

"You see, hospitality is in your blood," Santo said. "You were born to this calling."

*Calling?* A funny way to put it. She might have said "career" or "line of work." But running hotels was obviously much more important to Santo. "I enjoy innkeeping," she said carefully. "It's an honorable way to make a living."

Santo smiled. "Of course it is. Which is why I would like you to rejoin the family business, now that you are a part owner. I have in mind a position you may find irresistible."

Dani took a sip of iced tea to hide her shock. Work for him? When Santo had mentioned "financial matters" the night before, she assumed he'd meant signing documents related to her father's estate. But a job offer? He had to be kidding. Finally she found her voice.

"Are you talking about me joining Stella d'Italia here in Italy?"

"In Italy, yes, but not with our original brand. We feel that ten properties bearing the Stella d'Italia name are sufficient to maintain its elite status. However, we are in the process of signing a contract to purchase the Alberghi Paradisi hotel chain. They operate thirty-five three-star properties throughout the country—the perfect 'inns' for an 'innkeeper' such as yourself. I would put you in charge of the entire operation, *cara*. What would you say to that?"

"I would say that my father hasn't even settled into his grave and you are moving *way* too fast for me. You don't even know if I am qualified for the job."

Santo's face showed a hint of irritation before he smoothed it over. He probably wasn't used to pushback. "But I know all about you, Daniela," he said. "Did you think I wouldn't keep track of a close member of the family? I know from a reliable source that you are more than capable of doing what I ask." He looked at her intently; she didn't have to ask who his source was.

Her anger at Gabe resurfaced, but something about the way her uncle said those words, and the way he had let the endearment *cara* slip, put Dani even more on edge. "How long have you been considering this?" she asked.

"For some time. If my poor brother hadn't died so suddenly, I would have contacted you eventually, after the acquisition was made, of course."

"Is this what you meant last night by 'financial matters'?"

"In part. After signing documents related to your inheritance, you will be able to vote your father's shares, and that will give us the majority we need to finalize the purchase of Alberghi Paradisi."

"Why do you need my vote if everyone else wants to do the deal?"

Uncle Santo took a sip of the Amaretto the waiter had brought for dessert.

"Everyone else wants to purchase the company, don't they?" Dani prodded.

Santo shook his leonine head. "Not everyone, no. Dear *Mama* enjoys putting the brakes on ideas large and small. But her forty-nine percent is moot once you give your approval."

Something didn't feel right. If this was such a great investment, why wasn't her grandmother on board? "I take it this deal has been in the works for a while. Did my father vote for it but die before you could get it in writing?"

"Not precisely," he said, his voice clipped. "The vote has yet to take place."

Dani frowned. "I'm not sure I understand. Why not?"

Santo's gaze bore into Dani. She could feel the anger radiating off him in waves. "My little brother didn't quite understand the situation. He seemed to be sorting through some misinformation at the time of his accident."

Now she *knew* something was off. "So my father, who never cared a fig about the hotel business, basically gave his votes to you, and you assumed he always would," she mused. "But this time he didn't. Why, Uncle Santo? Why didn't he rubber stamp his vote this time around?"

She watched, both unnerved and fascinated, as her uncle's face turned to stone.

"I have no idea," Santo said coldly. "You are right that Mando cared nothing for the business, only the lifestyle it afforded him." He paused to flick a piece of imaginary lint off the arm of his jacket. "He was very shallow that way. You, on the other hand, are the natural heir apparent to the Forcelli hotel dynasty. You would be the perfect champion to carry our family name to greater heights." He took another sip of the liqueur, slowly savoring it as if he had all the time in the world. But his free hand gave him away: he began to lightly tap his fingers on the table.

*He needs my shares desperately*, she thought. *He's even willing to bribe me with a dream job*. She began to gather her purse and jacket. "Uncle Santo, I'm flattered. Really. You've given me a lot to think about. But I will have to read the pro forma for the company and talk to Nonna Stella to hear her objections before I vote my shares."

"Where are you going?" he asked tightly.

"I...uh, I'm supposed to meet Gabriele in a little while."

"Then allow me to drive you where you need to go."

"No. No, that's quite all right, *grazie*. I'll just take a taxi. Thank you for lunch, Uncle. You've been most generous."

—◆—

Leaving the restaurant with a purposeful stride, Dani felt a curious mixture of elation and disappointment. Elation because even though Uncle Santo had tried his best to intimidate her, she had stood her ground. Disappointment because the person she most wanted to share her triumph with was now more interested in connecting with some stranger than spending time with her. *But that's good*, she rationalized. *That's the way it has to be*. But was it wrong to want to be near Gabe, just as a friend?

Determined not to wallow, she refocused on her victory, mouthing a fervent "Yes!" as she rode the elevator down to the lobby. She was no longer the biddable young girl Santo could order about. She had a mind of her own, and a good head for business, too. So she'd hear both sides of the merger issue and make up her own mind. If her decision didn't go Uncle Santo's way, he'd just have to deal with it.

She was about to exit the building when she realized just where she was. "Duh," she muttered as she changed course and went to a nearby bank of courtesy telephones. "Signora Furlan, *per favore.*"

To keep the public from intruding, Nonna Stella lived at the hotel under her maiden name. Josefa, her grandmother's assistant, answered the phone and, after conferring with her employer, gave Dani the code for the special elevator that led directly to the penthouse floor.

Dani traveled up eighteen stories, one level above the restaurant she had just dined in. Josefa greeted her warmly in English.

"Signora Forcelli will be so happy to see you," she said. She gestured down a hallway. "She is still despondent over your father's death. Perhaps you can cheer her up a bit."

Dani found her grandmother seated in a chair by the window, a full cup of espresso and several uneaten biscotti languishing on the table next to her. She wore a simple black dress and Dani noticed that her beautiful white hair, which Dani always remembered being perfectly coiffed, was in slight disarray. The old woman held a crumpled handkerchief in her hand and as Dani approached, she quickly dabbed her reddened eyes.

"Oh, Nonna," Dani cried, bending down to clasp her grandmother, her own eyes brimming. "I am so sorry." The two women hugged for several moments, one a mother, the other a daughter, both of whom had lost someone dear to them. After a bit Dani could sense her grandmother gathering strength.

"There, there, *cara*. No more of that," her grandmother said, patting Dani's back.

Dani smiled through her own tears as she sat on a nearby chair. "You're a fine one to talk."

"Yes, we are a couple of crybabies, aren't we?"

"I think we're entitled to be, at least for a little while. But truly, how are you, Nonna?"

"My son was almost sixty. He was the father of a grown woman, for goodness' sake. But to me he was always a little boy." She shook her head. "Perhaps that was part of the problem. If I never thought of him as an adult, why should he have considered himself one?"

"He did like to play, my babbo."

Stella snorted. "Yes, only your daddy's toys got more and more expensive…and dangerous. I suppose we shouldn't be surprised at what happened."

"What exactly did happen? No one has told me anything, and I'm not sure I can trust the newspaper accounts."

"He was down in Siracusa for a race. They said he had too much to drink and took his boat out racing in the middle of the night. He lost control, fell out, and drowned. That is all I know." Her eyes began to well up and she resolutely dabbed at them again. "I suppose we should be happy he died doing what he loved." She reached for Dani's hand. "So, tell me, how did you and Gabriele come to know each other? There was a time I would not have approved of such a union, but I can see that he has turned out to be a fine young man. And he is very easy on the eyes, as they say."

Dani could feel herself blushing. "It's not like that at all. About a year ago Gabe moved to the same town in California where I live and we...we struck up a friendship. That's all there is to it."

Stella looked at Dani intently before she spoke. "*Davvero*?"

"Yes, *really*."

Nonna Stella gazed at Dani and smiled tenderly. "It seems quite unusual that you should end up in the same part of a country so far away from ours," she said. "And by the way he looks at you, it seems he has more than friendship on his mind."

"Do you think so?" Dani found herself asking before she could check herself. Then, to make matters worse, she added, "So...what do you remember about him?"

"I remember a very bright eyed, active little boy whose mother, Eliana, was an excellent cook and whose father was a lazy do-nothing. And I remember how the light in that little boy's eyes dimmed when his no-account father decided to leave poor Eliana to suffer from that debilitating disease all on her own."

"On her own?"

"Well, with no one but her sister, Fausta, to take care of her. I suppose they didn't want Gabriele to watch his mother slowly waste away, but still, how cruel to take away her only real reason for living. I am only glad we had the resources to help out."

"What do you mean?"

"Fausta was such an excellent caregiver for all the members of our family, especially your Nonno Ciro—" here she paused, crossed herself and muttered, *Grazie a Dio* "—that he agreed to take care of Eliana's medical expenses. When Ciro died, Santo stepped in and helped until Eliana passed away."

"How sad that must have been for Gabe."

"Indeed. But it looks like he has come through the worst of it with no lasting damage. He's a police office, is he not?"

"Yes, a detective."

"How nice to have *some* law abiding citizens in the family."

Dani conquered her embarrassment, replacing it with indignation. "First of all, he is not a member of the family. And second, what do you mean by saying such a thing, Nonna?"

Stella waved her hand. "Oh, merely the rantings of an old woman. How long will you and your young man—because whether you want to admit it or not, he *is* your young man—be staying?"

Dani gave up denying that she and Gabe were a couple, but it gave her the chance to bring up Santo's offer. "I'm not sure yet. I know I have to deal with paperwork regarding the estate. But Uncle Santo asked me today to vote my father's shares in favor of acquiring Alberghi Paradisi. He even offered me the job of running the division. He also said you were against it, that you were always trying to block him. Why do you want to stop this venture?"

Stella looked at Dani, her eyes no longer clouded. She took Dani's hand in her own. "Please understand, my reservations have nothing to do with you or your abilities. In fact—wait a moment." She went to an elegant writing desk in the corner of the room, picked up two large manila envelopes, and brought them over to the couch. The one marked "Alberghi Paradisi" she handed to Dani. "These are the financials, including pro forma projections for the new hotel company. I am not impressed, but you may feel differently once you've analyzed them."

"Thank you." Dani took the envelope, pleased and proud that her grandmother trusted her judgment.

Stella then pulled out the contents of the second envelope and spread them on her lap. "It's true that I have always been more conservative where our family company is concerned. Neither your grandfather nor Santo shared my reticence, but fortunately, I was able to prevail. As a result, we have weathered up and down markets because of our envious cash position.

"But over the past few years I have sensed that something is not right with Stella d'Italia. I asked my accountant to give me a summary comparison of revenues, occupancy rates, staffing levels, and so forth. The numbers, while they would pass scrutiny from a legal standpoint, seem off to me. The problem is not too little funds, but too much. I called the accountant to ask him to dig a little deeper but was told he had quit the company." She handed the material to Dani. "I know you understand this business, *cara,* and I would like you to look at these figures and see what you think. If you find nothing amiss, and if you check the Alberghi Paradisi numbers and believe the merger would be beneficial to Stella d'Italia, then I will vote my shares with you."

"I take it you haven't mentioned your concerns to Santo?"

Stella caught Dani's eyes and didn't look away as she slowly shook her head. Dani swallowed hard and felt a chill run through her. She had always been wary of Uncle Santo, but only as a child would avoid an overbearing patriarch. But Nonna Stella was talking about something entirely different. Something dangerous, happening within their own family. She was counting on Dani to get to the bottom of it. Who knew what she would find? Her thoughts ran, as they often did, to Gabe. She could trust him to help her if she needed it, couldn't she? Of course she could. She took a deep breath, let it out slowly.

"Daniela?"

Dani gazed directly at her grandmother, letting her know without words that she could be trusted, that she would do her best for the family. "Let's see what you have here, Nonna," she said, and began to spread out the papers.

# CHAPTER SEVEN

—•✢✢•—

One of the few things Gabe appreciated about his old man was the fact that Angelo de la Torre had insisted Gabe keep speaking Italian at home. It was easy enough to do. The neighborhood in Staten Island where they'd moved was filled with first generation immigrants who brightened their drab little row houses with window boxes full of geraniums, pots of mouthwatering Bolognese sauce, and welcoming, tolerant hearts. Gabe spent countless Sunday afternoons lounging on the front stoops with neighbors in their seventies and eighties who shared stories of the old country and fed him for taking the time to listen. Despite the trouble he managed to get into before he left high school, Gabe figured those Sundays kept him from sliding any further down the slippery slope of delinquency. In the bargain he held on to his native tongue.

He was grateful for that skill now as he waited at the front desk of the precinct where his childhood friend Marco Clemente worked. Marco was Gabe's counterpart in Verona's state police.

As in any police station, barely controlled chaos prevailed. Gabe watched as suspects—many no doubt drunks picked up the night before—were finally reunited with scolding family members who had come to bail them out. Victims of non-violent crimes waited to give their statements: some officers were sympathetic, but others seemed too jaded to hide their annoyance at having to fill out yet another form. *Some things are universal*, Gabe thought.

"Hey, buddy," Marco said as he came from his office down the hall. He was a stocky, barrel-chested man with powerful arms and legs, reddish blond hair, and a ruddy complexion that had earned him the very un-PC nickname of *Pellerossa*, which meant "red man." Gabe and his buddies had shortened it further to *Indio*. Marco greeted Gabe with the traditional two-sided air kiss. "Did you get my message about dinner tomorrow night? Gina's going all out."

"Uh, yeah, I did. Looking forward to it," Gabe said. "But there's something important I wanted to talk to you about. Is there someplace we can speak privately?"

Without hesitation, Marco grabbed his jacket from a nearby hook. "I'll be back shortly," he told the officer on duty. "Come on," he said to Gabe, "let's take a walk."

Verona was returning to its normal buzz after the midday respite. Gabe followed as Marco set off for a specific destination. Two crossed streets and three alleyways later they came to a small trattoria. An older man came out from the shadow of the interior.

"Good afternoon," he said formally. "Please come in." Marco and Gabe entered the small restaurant, which had yet to pick up any afternoon customers.

"Two espressos, please," Marco ordered. After the waiter left he asked, "What is troubling you, my friend?"

Gabe decided to get right down to it. "What do you know about Armando Forcelli's death?"

"A fair amount," Marco admitted. "I'm handling the paperwork locally, although it appears to be just a shitload of bad luck for the guy. Accidents happen."

"What if I told you I had reason to believe it wasn't an accident?"

Marco, who had been leaning back in his chair, tipped forward. "I'd say 'tell me what you've got.'"

"I'm not sure I've got anything at this point. What I'd like to know are the particulars of what went down that night."

Marco took out his iPhone and called up a file. He scrolled through the data to find what he was looking for. "The body was found at five a.m. approximately three hundred yards off the coast of Siracusa, in the gulf there. You know where that is, right?"

Gabe nodded. "East coast of Sicily."

"Yeah. They host part of the Ocean Grand Prix down there—the place to be if you're into that shit. Anyway, the tide was coming in, or he would have been long gone. The boat was a thirty-nine-foot Cigarette pleasure craft belonging to one of his racing syndicate partners. They found it a half kilometer north of the body. Apparently it just kept going until it ran out of gas."

"How did they know he was in that boat—did they dust for prints?"

Marco searched the document. "Uh, no, they didn't take prints, but apparently he was seen in the boat with the partner and some others that afternoon. They probably figured his prints would be all over it." He continued to scan the report. "Ah, it says his shirt was found stuffed under one of the seats. He'd been seen wearing the same color shirt earlier in the evening."

"Okay, so it's established that he was in the boat at some point, you just don't have hard evidence he was in it that night."

A note of defensiveness crept into Marco's response. "Well, how do you say it in the States? 'If it looks like a duck and it walks like a duck…'"

"Yeah, yeah, okay, so probably it's a duck. So, what about the body? Any marks? Signs of trauma?"

Marco checked again. "Surprisingly few. A bruise to the forehead and a contusion at the back of the head, probably caused when he hit the water."

"Do they know which side of him hit the water first?"

"Doesn't say. Why?"

"Nothing, just…" Gabe paused to consider the information. "It's strange he'd have bruises both front and back."

"So he bounced around when he fell out."

"Yeah, but if he fell out of the boat at a high rate of speed, wouldn't there have been much greater impact? I mean, you slam into anything at eighty miles an hour and you're going to do some serious damage, even if you're only falling three or four feet."

Marco shrugged. "I don't know, maybe he wasn't going fast when he took the plunge. He could have been so blitzed that when he hit a wave and went over, he couldn't get back in and that was that."

Gabe took a sip of his espresso. Maybe he wasn't used to the extra jolt of caffeine, but he felt wired, his brain moving in several directions at once. "But there was no alcohol in his system, was there?"

Marco looked at Gabe sharply. "How did you know that?"

Gabe stared back at him. "If you already knew that, why did you imply alcohol might have been a factor?"

Marco tried to glare, but quickly gave it up, shaking his head. "I'm sorry. I've been told not to waste too much time on this, but I confess I've been uneasy about it ever since the toxicology report came back. They didn't find anything in his system except a drug for migraine headaches, known to cause fatigue but not erratic behavior. And why, on a cool evening, would he have taken off his shirt?"

"I take it he wasn't wearing a life preserver."

"No, which doesn't make sense if he was sober and intended to drive fast, especially at night."

"Any witnesses nearby?"

Marco scrolled down through the notes. "Apparently nobody heard or saw anything out of the ordinary. Just the usual low throttle noise of boats maneuvering within the marina."

"How did he get access to the boat, by the way?"

"The slips are private, accessed only by key. The boat's owner had given Forcelli a set of keys earlier that day and told him he could take the boat out whenever he liked, but—and this is another strange aspect—"

"Let me guess. The lock on the gate was tampered with."

Marco nodded. "And a set of keys was found in his hotel room, in the pocket of his jacket. So we're left with the theory that he forgot he had the keys, but so badly wanted to take the boat out alone, in the middle of a cold night, after taking a medication that made him drowsy, he figured out how to jimmy the lock on both the slip and the boat. Then he headed slowly out across the water, stripped off his shirt, fell quietly into the water and drowned. Oh yes, and there's one more thing."

Gabe said nothing, simply looked at Marco with raised eyebrows.

"There was no water in the lungs."

"Implying he didn't drown," Gabe finished.

"The coroner says that in about ten percent of cases, drowning victims do not inhale water. Still, that is one more question we have no answer for."

Gabe and Marco sat pondering the evidence in silence; Gabe could sense that Marco was as frustrated by the conflicting details as he was.

"Look," Marco said at last. "If this is something other than a freak accident involving an aging bad boy, I would like to know about it. But I seem to be the only one who cares. Hell, I even wondered at one point if someone had it in for him—didn't want him to compete in the race for some reason. But neither the family nor my superiors, nor the boat owner nor the racing authorities want this to go any farther. They certainly don't want to make this out to be some kind of foul play."

Gabe wasn't ready to tell Marco about Carla Rinaldi and whoever was following her just yet, so he took another tack. "I don't know that I have anything right now except a few more questions. Such as, did anyone take into consideration the speed of the boat? If Forcelli was out joyriding, why wasn't the throttle at full speed? If it was at full speed, why was the boat found so close to the body? If it wasn't, why was Forcelli moving so slowly? And what could cause someone to not breathe in any water once they fell overboard? Could it be they weren't breathing *before* they hit the water? And who was the last person to see Forcelli alive? Maybe they can shed some light on the circumstances."

Marco sat up straighter. "We know that Forcelli dined with a woman earlier that evening. Several eyewitnesses have said they saw the two of them together. We have identified the woman as a Signora Carla Rinaldi, an employee of the Stella d'Italia Milano. Unfortunately we haven't been able to locate her."

"Doesn't anyone think that by itself is strange?"

Marco shrugged. "Like I said, nobody wants to dig any deeper. Bad for the public image."

Throughout the conversation, Gabe had been jotting down details and ideas in his notebook. He tapped his pencil on the table, trying to make sense of the disconnected facts. Still, even more important questions remained; he decided to lob one at his friend. "So, Indio, what can you tell me about human trafficking in your neck of the woods?"

Marco went still. "What does that have to do with any of this?"

Gabe leaned forward in his chair. "What if Forcelli's death wasn't an accident? What if he knew something and someone wanted to shut him up?"

"All right. You know something, Gabriele. I can feel it. You must tell me what kind of fantastical connection you are making here."

"Okay. Look, I've heard something. I'll not say who it is, but I will say the source is credible. And the source says there might be something unsavory happening within the Stella d'Italia hotel company related to their back-of-the-house employees. That's all I know. I swear."

Gabe felt Marco's piercing look. *It's a good thing I play poker well.* He was not going to take this farther until he did some digging on his own.

"Stella d'Italia is a relatively small hotel company run by the iron hand of Santo Forcelli with the help of his nephew Dante Trevisan." Marco shook his head. "There is no way such an illicit operation could exist without at least one of them knowing about it. Are you absolutely certain about what you've heard?"

Gabe nodded, and as he did so, Marco's words sunk in. Dante. Santo. If what Carla said was true, one of those two men had to be involved. Dani had seen her uncle just a few hours ago, and maybe he or even Dante had ordered someone to follow Gabe. Suddenly he felt the need to make sure she was all right.

"I've got to go," he said abruptly. "If I hear anything more, I'll let you know. In the meantime, I'd try to keep the Forcelli drowning case open as long as I could. Where's the boat, by the way?"

"Still in police custody, but they're going to release it tomorrow."

"If it were me, I'd dust for prints. Something may turn up. If it's a hit job, chances are they wore gloves, but you might try the cleats. Sometimes you need finger dexterity to untie a tight rope." Gabe tapped his pencil again. "It's probably way too late, but I'd dust the security gate, too. Picking locks is also hard to do with gloves."

"Damn it, you're right." Marco scrolled his notes again. "Looks like we could also follow up on who else booked the hotel that night. Maybe there's a connection that's not related to the boat race."

Gabe got up and beckoned the waiter before turning to his friend. "Let me know if you find anything, okay? If Forcelli's death turns out to be a homicide, it could be just the tip of the iceberg."

The waiter waved Gabe off. "Arturo likes to have a cop come by once in a while," Marco said. "Hey, what's your motto? 'To protect and to serve'?"

"Yeah, but mainly to get at the truth. Thanks for the information, Marco. I owe you. I'll see you tomorrow."

Marco nodded. "Until then."

—⋅✦⋅✦⋅—

Gabe jogged back to the main street and tried to flag down a taxi. Inwardly he cursed the fact that he hadn't lined up a local phone card so that he and Dani could stay in touch. He put that at the top of his to-do list, along with sitting her down and explaining everything that was going on. Well, almost everything. Did he really need to get into his arrangement with Santo over the past year or so? He'd only talked to the guy a few times, and each call had lasted ten minutes, if that. Gabe hadn't told Santo anything the old man couldn't have found out by other means. Still, as they say, the "optics" weren't good. Santo had asked Gabe not to mention the calls, and Gabe, feeling beholden, had agreed. It looked sneaky, and it was. What if Santo told her before Gabe could explain himself? Hell, what did that matter at this point? That was nothing compared to the sewage Carla Rinaldi was digging up.

"Come on. Come *on*," he muttered, checking up and down the street. "Where's a cab when you need it?" Frustration warred with a niggling sense of fear, and he couldn't shake the thought that Dani might be in some kind of danger. But Santo wouldn't do anything to her, would he? She was his niece, after all. Yeah, but Mando had been his *brother*. He shook his head. *Okay, wait. Just because Carla Rinaldi suspects foul play doesn't mean Santo's at the heart of it.* Yet after his confrontation that morning, Gabe knew it wasn't a stretch to think that Santo could pull something like that off. "Asshole" didn't begin to describe the man.

Just then he spotted a taxi and whistled for it, waving for good measure. "La Tana della Pantera," he told the driver, and jumped in the back.

Marco kept his distance as he watched his old friend enter a taxi. Once it sped off he dialed his cell phone.

"*Direttore*," he said. "I have some interesting information to share."

As he had each week for the past several months, Dante Trevisan stood outside the door to classroom two seventeen in the health sciences building at the University of Verona. He was waiting for Holistic Health Practices 110 to finish for the evening. After so many classes, the students were used to seeing him in the hallway. The students emptied out and he returned with half smiles the coy flirtations of several cute coeds as they passed by. With a well-placed look, he could have had any one of them, but the one he truly wanted was always the last to leave. Dante had taken it upon himself to escort her home.

"I think you're right to advocate for botanicals, Giuseppi," Agnese Lombardi said to an earnest young sycophant as she locked the classroom door. "But much of the problem I feel lies with the public's impatience. Holistic healing processes typically need more time to work than modern pharmaceuticals. *Andrographis paniculata*, for example, is quite adept at breaking up bacterial aggregations, and has been used for thousands of years for the treatment of upper respiratory infections. Yet what is overwhelmingly prescribed?"

"Modern antibiotics!" The boy squeaked like a seal barking for a sardine.

"Precisely, which of course has led to their decreased potency through overuse. It's a growing problem." She looked over and saw Dante. He smiled and was gifted one in return. "At any rate, I think it will make an excellent term paper. I'll see you next week."

The young man gave Dante a sullen look and headed reluctantly down the hall.

"You need me," Dante said. "Desperately." He took her laptop case as they walked toward the exit.

Agnese barely contained a grin. "Oh is that right, Signor Trevisan? How so?"

"To protect you from the likes of lovesick puppies like Giuseppi there. Last week it was Giorgio what's-his-name, and the week before that—"

"Oh, stop. It's not that bad."

"Yes it is, but I don't mind pulling bodyguard duty. It saved me from a far worse fate."

"Really? What?" Agnese sounded genuinely concerned.

"Why, having to sit through a semester's worth of herbal remedies and admonitions to cut sugar, wheat, milk, and meat out of my diet." Dante patted his stomach, which he was pleased to admit was in still in pretty good shape. "I do love my pasta and cannoli."

Agnese responded with mock seriousness. "I am glad to have saved you from such a dire circumstance. Taking one of my classes could indeed be a fate worse than death." They left the building and began walking toward the convent.

"By the way, I'll have you know I make delicious homemade pasta," she added, a touch of defensiveness in her tone. "And my Bolognese sauce is pretty good, too."

It came out before he could stop it. "I'd love to try it sometime."

Agnese said nothing, leaving them in awkward silence.

*When am I going to learn?* Dante wracked his brain for a safer topic and remembered seeing Dani. "I'm sorry you missed the memorial service," he said. "My cousin was there with your cousin, and Gabriele looked quite happy to be with her." He smiled and turned to her. "If they got together, I hope that wouldn't make us too closely related."

Agnese stopped, the radiance gone from her face. "It wouldn't matter." After a moment she added, "You don't really have to walk me home each week. I can fend for myself."

"I know." The truth was painful, but he said it anyway. "We both know it's more for me than for you." The look of sweet agony she gave him nearly broke his heart. He kept his hands in his pockets to keep from reaching for her and felt the weight of the gift he'd brought. "Oh, I almost forgot." He pulled out a small wrapped package and handed it to her.

"What's this?"

"Open it."

"You are always bringing me things. It's not necessary."

"And that's the best time to give a gift, wouldn't you agree?"

Agnese nodded. "I suppose." She opened the package to find three six-inch long test tubes that had been wrapped with decorative copper wire, one end of which formed a hook.

"I found them near the Piazza Duomo," he said. "I thought you could hang them up in the lab. You know, put herbs in them or something. They're little vases. I know how much you love flowers, and…"

Agnese looked up at him. "Thank you. They'll come in very handy."

"Good. Good." They were almost at the convent. The walk was always too short, but he'd learned long ago not to ask her to linger for even a coffee. "Well, you're back, safe and sound once again. No drooling little teenage boys to fight off this time, but you never know."

Agnese had pulled her key out to open the gate but paused a moment before inserting it. She didn't face him as she said, "It's hopeless, you know."

Dante reached out to turn her gently toward him. "Don't say that. Don't ever say that. Just tell me how I can change and I'll change. I'll do whatever it takes."

She looked up at him with tears pooling in her eyes. "There's nothing to change," she said. "It's simply who we are." She took her laptop case from him, opened the gate, and went inside.

"I'll be there next week," Dante called to her retreating figure. "And the week after that. And one day you'll let me in."

She faced away from him but waved her hand behind her. "Thank you again for the vases. I will treasure them." He could hear a hitch in her voice.

"And I will treasure you. Always," he murmured as he turned and walked back up the street.

—◆◇◆—

"Okay, so where is she?" Gabe asked his aunt after searching all over La Tana. "It's after six o'clock. She ought to be back by now!"

"It is not necessary to take that tone with me, Gabriele." Fausta's tone was as frigid as her demeanor. "She refused to go with the driver that Signor Forcelli had sent for her. She took a cab instead. I assume she met him for lunch. Perhaps they had much to discuss."

"So Santo isn't home either? Can you call and ask him when they're due back?"

"Signor Forcelli doesn't clear his schedule with me," she said. "His time is his own."

As if to prove that point, Santo himself walked through the door. Gabe had to force himself not to pounce on the man, but couldn't help demanding, "Where is Dani?"

Santo looked at Gabe as if he were a servant who had mistakenly called at the front entrance instead of the back door of the estate. He calmly handed his jacket and briefcase to Fausta, taking time to check his appearance in the foyer's elegantly carved mirror before answering. "I thought she was with you," he replied. He smiled cynically at Gabe. "Have you lost your lover, Signor de la Torre?"

*Don't take the bait,* Gabe cautioned himself. "Just—are you saying you haven't seen her this afternoon?"

"I'm saying that after lunch she said that she was meeting you. Now if you will excuse me."

Gabe watched as the man turned and walked down the hallway. Fausta looked at Gabe, eyes blazing, as she followed her employer.

*Okay, she's probably out seeing the sights. Nothing to worry about. She'll be fine.* Gabe kept up the mental pep talk as he stalked to the suite, determined not to lose it as his blood began to boil.

—✦✧✦—

Four hours of pouring through the accounting summaries for Stella d'Italia had led Dani to one conclusion: whoever was doctoring the books, *if* they were doctoring the books, was doing an excellent job of it. She'd uncovered some irregularities, not in the account reconciliation, but in the unusually predictable fluctuation of certain expenses within the human resources budgets, as well as accounts receivable. She would have to check prior years to be sure, but it seemed that housekeeping employees in particular were flowing in and out of the hotel system at an oddly regular rate. It also seemed as though large payments from different companies showed up routinely on the books of every hotel, albeit a different location every month, and the amounts were surprisingly uniform. Few people would notice unless they compared the numbers of every profit center over time.

Dani could feel a building tension in her neck, so she put the spreadsheets away and rooted in her purse for her usual headache medicine. Stella had excused herself an hour earlier to take a nap and now that it was time to leave, Dani decided not to wake her. She wrote a quick note saying she'd be in touch and left the penthouse, hoping some fresh air would help clear her head.

The Stella d'Italia Verona was a glorious hotel perfectly situated in the heart of the city. Dating from the Renaissance, the building catered to businessmen with unlimited expense accounts as well as well-heeled tourists who didn't mind staying in ancient landmarks as long as their accommodations were the latest in comfort and style. Dani smiled as she pictured the Havenwood Inn back home. It too was considered an architectural treasure, but in northern California, age was measured in decades, not centuries. Still, the idea of hospitality was pretty much the same the world over and throughout time. It was a worthwhile profession to provide food and shelter for weary travelers.

Dani thought about returning to La Tana, but the estate was so stark and cold; no wonder her grandmother had fled to town. Besides, the idea of being there, waiting, when Gabe returned from his tryst—and that's what it was in her mind, a *tryst*—was beyond unappealing. She decided to explore the city a bit instead. *After all, it is my hometown.*

Most Americans, if they'd even heard of Verona, pegged it to *Romeo and Juliet*, since Shakespeare's most famous play was standard fare for high school English classes. But for Dani, Verona was much more complex than that. It had been a major crossroads city during Roman times and its amphitheater was one of the most well-known of the Roman ruins anywhere in the world. Dani remembered the city walks she took with her father as he told her of the many warlords who had ruled the city and its people over time.

"But the spirit of its people remained unchanged, no matter who was in power," he told her once. "You must never lose your spirit, *topolina*." Dani remembered pouting and telling her father that she wasn't a "little mouse," and him laughing and tousling her curls and asking her why, if she wasn't a mouse, did she like so much cheese on her spaghetti? But she had to wonder now. Had she lost her spirit?

From what she remembered, her childhood had been good. She had been happy. What attention she lacked from her traveling parents was made up by the rest of her family: her grandparents, her uncles—even Fausta and her daughter Agnese. Dani had no cause for complaint. But whatever happened to her at the age of fifteen had taken something from her. Something that no therapist or hypnotist or well-meaning mom or school counselor had ever been able to give back. Heck, they hadn't even been able to tell her what she was missing. Over the last twelve years that hole, that void, had kept her from becoming a woman in the truest sense.

But ever since she'd met Gabe de la Torre, the desire to fill that hole had warred with her fear of it, and the need to know what kept her broken grew along with the feeling that maybe, like all the professionals kept telling her, her brokenness was only in her head...and that was the scariest thought of all.

She rounded the corner and found herself on Via Capello, at the site of the *Casa di Giulietta*. Juliet's House. *Oh great,* she thought, *that's all I need, to be inundated with love.*

She walked into the courtyard with the other tourists and gazed up at the balcony which was supposedly the inspiration for the famous scene in the play. Amidst the group of visitors, a teenage couple stood next to her, dressed in matching torn jeans, arm tattoos, and lip rings. They must have been inspired by the sight because they began "sucking face" as she and Agnese used to say. Dani smirked. What if their rings got tangled? Would they have to call in the fire department? The teenagers were oblivious to passersby, and Dani realized the joke was on her. They certainly hadn't lost *their* spirit. For however long it lasted, they were in love and weren't afraid to show it. *Good for you,* she thought, and walked on.

After stopping for a small plate of pasta, Dani decided she really should head back to La Tana. Her headache had faded, replaced by a fatigue that seemed to reach down into her very bones. She began her usual litany: So what if Gabe wasn't there? So what if he spent the night elsewhere? They were just friends, right? She had no claim on him, nor he on her.

*Oh shut up*, she scolded herself. *You're full of it.* And it dawned on her what her father meant so long ago. If you can't be honest with yourself, if you can't be true to who you really are, no matter what anybody thinks you ought to be, then you really have lost your spirit. The truth was, she was crazy about Gabe, but she had driven him away out of fear, and she didn't even know why.

It was approaching nine o'clock when the taxi dropped her off at the mansion. Fausta let her in with a reproving look.

"You are late," the housekeeper said. "You should have alerted someone as to your schedule."

"You're right," Dani said wearily. "I apologize."

"I am not the one you should apologize to. Your uncle—"

"I'm here now," Dani interrupted, her ire returning in a flash. "Good night."

She made her way up the stairs to the suite, more tired than she'd been since arriving in Italy. A warm bath, her Kindle, and she'd be one happy—

Just then the door swung open and Gabe stood there, towering over her, eyes blazing, looking every inch the irate father. He reached out, grabbed her arm, pulled her in the room and shut the door. In rough, harsh tones, he took her to task. "Just where the hell have you been?!"

# CHAPTER EIGHT

—◆✦◆—

D ani looked shocked at his outburst. She obviously didn't
have a clue how important she was to him. He should have
throttled back, lightened up, but he couldn't; his heart was racing
too fast to calm down even if he'd wanted to.

She tried to pull away. "Why are you grilling me? I'm not the
one who announced I was going to hook up with some stranger!"

Hook up? Did she really think…? "Now, wait a minute—"

Dani continued to struggle. By the looks of things she seemed
more pissed than he was!

"What's the matter?" she said. "Are you ticked off because
your new friend has a 'no sleepover' rule?"

"Oh, for God's sake, you little *idiota*—" With that he brought
her up against his body and kissed her. No, *devoured* her. All the
fear, all the worry, all the desire he felt for this difficult woman
poured out of him and into her—there was nothing he could do
to stop it.

She resisted at first, but within seconds melted against him and opened fully to his assault. He reveled at the feeling of her softness against him. He had wondered about it, fantasized about it, so many times, and it registered in the back of his mind that reality was far, far better than anything his paltry brain could have imagined. He softened the kiss but took it deeper. He felt as if he had truly come home.

After a few moments of pure bliss, Dani seemed to regain her senses and began pushing gently against his arms. Reluctantly he broke the kiss and relaxed his grip.

"I'm not sorry I did that," he said defiantly, his chest heaving. He was gratified to see that Dani was breathing heavily too. "Are you going to bite my head off?"

Dani shook her head, apparently still in shock. He could tell by her eyes that she was confused about what had just happened between them. That, or she'd decided to humor him. The adrenaline that had coursed so violently through Gabe's body began to recede, replaced by the overwhelming sense of relief that she had returned to him unharmed. He took her in his arms again, not to devour or possess, but to cherish. Just for a moment. As he wrapped his arms around her, he lowered his head and inhaled the familiar scent of the woman he couldn't help loving.

"I was starting to lose it," he admitted. "I have been waiting for hours. I had no way to contact you. And I thought…I thought something might have happened to you."

Dani gradually pulled away. "As you can see, I'm all right," she said. "I'm sorry I scared you. I…I didn't think it mattered."

"Never think that," he said huskily. "You matter…believe it."

After a moment Dani stepped back, shaking her head slightly. Gabe felt she was slipping away, so he took her hand. "I don't know about you, but I need to sit down."

Despite her half-hearted protestations, he drew her down onto the couch and put his arm around her in a non-threatening, comforting way. She sighed and put her head on his shoulder. They stayed that way for a few minutes.

"So what happened to your date?" Dani finally asked in a neutral voice.

It bothered Gabe that Dani would think so little of him. He was the one to pull away this time. "It's not what you think," he said. "Carla isn't—"

"Carla," Dani repeated, as if testing the name. She nodded then and smiled slightly. "I am really sorry," she said.

"About what?"

She waved her arm around the room. "About all of it. About you feeling the need to follow me here, to protect me somehow…" She laughed bitterly. "I can just imagine how Nina and Paolo back at Havenwood made it sound: "Our poor little Daniela has to deal with her family all alone…"

"I told you, they didn't say anything of the sort," he said, trying to keep the irritation out of his own voice. "I came because…" He rubbed the back of his neck. "Because I care for you, for Chrissake."

"Hence the rendezvous with Carla," she said, nodding. "I get it—"

"No, you don't get it!" he shot back. "Carla has nothing to do with this—with us!"

"Oh, I see. I'm supposed to trust you, is that it?" Her voice was calm, but her flashing eyes telegraphed her skepticism. "I may not be a rocket scientist, but even I can see there's a little problem in that department. Of course Uncle Santo was kind enough to let me know just how he'd been keeping tabs on me."

Gabe winced at her words. "I've been meaning to explain," he said.

Dani moved away from Gabe and sat on one of the chairs facing the sofa, her hands resting primly in her lap. "Please do."

Gabe held back a smile; it seemed she preferred being indignant to being vulnerable. "It's a long story."

"I'm all ears."

"On the contrary, your ears are the perfect size for your beautiful head."

"I'm waiting."

It was Gabe's turn to sigh. "You know I grew up near La Tana. My mom was actually a cook for a few years here, and my father was a gardener, until they fired him for being drunk on the job. My mom came down with Lou Gehrig's Disease and eventually, well, she got worse. They'd always planned to move to America, and my mom didn't want to stand in my dad's way, so she insisted we go. That part you already know. But what you may not know is that your grandfather paid the bills for my mother's care for years before she died. Toward the end she needed someone twenty-four seven." He paused, the memories intruding. He remembered the last time he saw his mother, how she tried to reach out to him, her eyes so big and luminous. And how his father held him back, pushing him out of the room despite—or perhaps because of—his tears.

"Go on," Dani said gently.

He shook off the emotion; it was old news, and Dani deserved the straight story. "I was just a kid, but even then I got it that we were piling up a big debt that had to be repaid. My old man died a few years after we moved, so I knew it was up to me. I owed your grandfather. I owed your Uncle Santo. Do you understand?"

"Yes, I think I do."

"Do you? Because the thing is, when you owe somebody like that, it's pretty difficult to say no to them when they ask you to do something, especially something that isn't going to cause anybody any harm."

"And you figured spying on me fell into that category."

Gabe shrugged. "Santo found out through Fausta that I was tired of L.A. and wanted to make a move. I was deciding between a couple of police departments and he strongly encouraged me to move to West Marin. That had been my first choice anyway, so I said, what the hell. It was only after I moved that he told me you were living in Little Eden."

"Oh—I'm amazed he didn't get you the job."

"Ouch," Gabe said, pulling an imaginary arrow from his chest.

"Sorry, but I wouldn't put anything past Uncle Santo when he wants something. So tell me, what did he want?"

"Only to hear the basics about you from time to time," Gabe recounted. "Cross my heart. I talked to the guy maybe three or four times, tops. All he wanted to know was if you were married, and if not, were you tied to anyone. He also wanted to know the status of your business and whether you were making a go of it."

He chuckled. "I told him that you had missed your calling, that you should have been an executive chef, you were that good. I told him that I alone gave you enough business to stay afloat." He noticed Dani was chewing her lip. "What?" he asked.

"Oh…nothing. It's just…I don't understand why you didn't tell me from the beginning who you were."

"Santo asked that I keep my connection to your family to myself. I think he felt you'd be more open with someone who had no connection to your past. At first I didn't care, so I was willing to oblige him. Later, when I did care, I figured I was in too deep. I didn't want you to hate me and never talk to me again." He paused. "I didn't want to lose what little I had of you. I was a coward, plain and simple."

Dani remained silent. He couldn't blame her; he'd screwed things up big time. The only question was, would she ever forgive him? "Never would I intentionally hurt you, Daniela. *Never.*"

"I know that," she finally said. "But I think maybe you want more than I can…than I'm willing to give."

"What do you think I want from you?"

Dani gave a nervous laugh. "I don't know. Friends with benefits?"

Gabe shook his head slowly, looking her directly in the eye. "At the very beginning, maybe. But…" He watched as her eyes began to fill. "Hey," he said, reaching for her. "Don't—"

She waved him away, wiping her tears briskly with one of her knuckles. "Gabe, I just can't be what you want," she breathed. "Which is why I have no right to even ask you about Carla. What you do is your own business."

"Dani, I'm going to tell you about Carla, but first I want us to get something clear between us. I care for you…a lot. Are you saying you have no feelings along those lines for me?"

Dani looked at her hands and didn't respond. He finally reached over and tipped her chin up. "Dani?"

The look she gave him squeezed his heart. The light had left her face. "I don't want to lead you on," she whispered. "I'm just no good at this."

"You're very good at sitting here and being near me," he whispered back. "And you're extremely good at kissing." He smiled gently. "What is it you think you're lousy at?"

"So many things." She smiled sadly. "My baggage has baggage."

Gabe smiled back. He would do anything to avoid hearing they were toast. "Tell you what. I'm good at shouldering a load or two, but not until you're ready to let go of it. Okay?"

She looked at him and shook her head. "I don't understand you. But to be honest, I could use a friend right now." She pointed a finger at him. "Just a friend, mind you. No benefits. No expectations, no—" she glanced at the bedroom "—you know. Just a friend. Someone I can trust…really *trust*. And I will be the same for you. And that's all I can be for now. Maybe that doesn't make sense, but—"

"I'll take it," Gabe interrupted. "I'll be that friend to you. But *bella*?"

"Yes?"

"I have one request."

"Which is?"

"I'm a very affectionate man by nature, and my every instinct is to be...affectionate...with you. So if I cross the line occasionally, cut me some slack, okay?"

Dani grinned for the first time that night. "I suppose I could cut you some slack, Constable...sometimes."

*That* was the Dani he knew and loved. Gabe could tell she was feeling better because she'd used the old nickname she'd called him back in Little Eden. He knew their relationship had a long way to go, but somehow, tonight, he felt they'd turned a corner—and he wasn't completely discouraged by the path that lay ahead. Now wasn't the time to bring up his talk with Carla Rinaldi or the corroboration he'd gotten from Marco. Tomorrow was soon enough to dampen her spirits once again.

"I'd be much obliged," he said with mock formality. "Now, much as I'd love to spend the night with you...talking, of course... I'm beat. Here, I'll give you a lift home." He stood up and abruptly swept her off her feet.

"Oh!" Dani cried, grabbing his neck for balance. "What are you doing?"

"Showing you how well I carry baggage," he said with a grin. He carried her to her bedroom, gently laid her down and put his arms on either side of her face. He kissed her gently on the forehead. "*Buonanotte...amica.*"

—◆—

Dani thought after clearing the air with Gabe and setting the parameters of their relationship that she would sleep like a proverbial baby. But, perhaps more like the few real babies she'd known, she found it hard to fall asleep, and when she did, she had fitful dreams. Only these dreams weren't about what she imagined had happened to her at a disastrous party when she was fifteen. They were what she found herself longing for *now*...with Gabe.

In the dream she was back at the Havenwood Inn, working in the office behind the front desk. It was late at night and the bell had rung, alerting her that someone wanted to check in.

There, standing before her, was Gabe, looking impossibly handsome in a crisp white shirt and sports coat.

"May I help you?" she asked.

"Yes. I'd like a bed for the night. With you in it."

It being a dream, she said, "Of course, come right this way," and took him to her bedroom on the third floor, where he proceeded to undress her and explore every inch of her body with his hands and mouth. She welcomed him and there was no fear or pain or disgust—only an incredible sense of passion and belonging, rightness...and *love*. Dani woke with a start, feeling agitated and somewhat embarrassed. Was she annoyed because her dream hadn't followed the platonic protocol she'd set with Gabe earlier in the evening? Or was she frustrated because she woke up before she could complete the most erotic scene she'd ever imagined? She suspected the latter. And she realized the sexuality of the dream was only part of it. The other part—the love—scared her more than anything else.

# CHAPTER NINE

—◆✦◆—

*Sleep is overrated*, Dani thought as she willed herself to get up the next morning. A peek out the window of her sumptuous bedroom told her it was going to be another crystal clear day, unlike her brain after tossing and turning all night.

She pulled on a tank top, sweatpants, and hoodie, hoping a run would help clear her head. She felt a combination of excitement, trepidation, and, strange as it seemed, joy. "Today is the first day of the rest of your life," she murmured, tying her shoes. And, she decided, she was going to make it productive. First, refrain from waking up Gabe so as to avoid any "post heavy talk" awkwardness. *Do not check him out as he sleeps.*

After her run she'd be in better shape to talk to him, which, like it or not, she had to do. Last night, she'd all but forgotten to tell him about her uncle's off-the-wall job offer, her grandmother's concerns, and the strange accounting issues she'd uncovered after pouring over the books. That's why she'd been so late returning to La Tana. Well, sort of. Not wanting to return to an empty suite and wait for Gabe had certainly figured into it.

Whatever his "date" with the mystery woman had started out to be, it hadn't ended well, or he wouldn't have been back—for hours, he'd said—worrying about her.

He said he'd be her friend, someone she could count on. But maybe, over time, he could be…more than that. The idea set her pulse quickening. Maybe…maybe he could help her get over this weird fear—the panicky sensation she got when a man approached her in a physical, sexual way. Gabe said he'd do anything for her. He admitted he was "affectionate," which even she knew was code for being attracted to her.

What was that term she'd learned in Psychology 101? "Successive approximation." That was it. Like if you were afraid of snakes, the way to get over that fear was to start with, say, a picture of the snake, then maybe watch a TV show about them, and then go to a zoo and finally hold one of the creepy reptiles. She smiled. She had an idea that letting Gabe loose as far as sex was concerned would be like joining the cast of *Snakes on a Plane* on her first day. There had to be some way they could ease into it. When he'd grabbed her the night before, she'd felt the familiar panic only for a second; after that, her body had taken over and she'd felt this incredible…desire. What a feeling! Like all the endorphins she'd ever felt from a great run had all converged into one giant, overwhelming rush. If anyone could get her over her phobia, Gabe probably could.

But was that fair to him? Didn't he deserve someone without all the problems she knew she had? Maybe if she could get him to approach it like he was doing her a favor, as a friend, it wouldn't be such a big deal. They could even agree that anything they did here in Verona would stay here—like Vegas. He could help her out and she wouldn't hold him to anything once they got back to Little Eden. It could work. It could.

Buoyed by the thought, she took a fortifying breath and opened the door, thinking she'd just tip toe by the alcove. As she passed it, she couldn't help but peek around the corner.

It was empty.

By the look of the sparsely populated fruit bowl and ransacked pastry tray, Gabe had already fortified himself and taken off. He'd left a note, however. It read:

I want to tell you about Carla. Meet me at the upper garden pavilion

Like air escaping a balloon, Dani's spirits deflated. Who was this Carla, anyway? If Gabe professed to care for Dani, why was this woman important? Gabe had talked about being a support for her, but she had to grudgingly admit, it worked both ways. Maybe he was attracted to the woman and didn't know what to do about it. Maybe he was seeking Dani's advice. Well, she would be happy to give it; he was her friend and that's what friends are for, right?

Then why did she suddenly feel so…*sad*?

No, that would never do. She shook off the thought, took a biscotti, and headed down the hall, passing a woman in a nurse's uniform coming from the opposite direction. "*Buon giorno,*" she murmured.

"*Buon giorno.*"

As the woman passed, it dawned on Dani that there must be someone in need of medical attention. "*Scusi, signora,*" she called after the woman. "C'è *una persona malata?*"

"La *Signora Forcelli, signorina. Soffre di enfisema.*"

"Ah, *sì, grazie.*" Of course, Dani thought, feeling guilty. How could she have forgotten? Her Aunt Ornella lived in a suite of rooms down the hall on this very floor. She'd had emphysema for years and was attended by nurses around the clock. Uncle Santo never mentioned her, and neither did anyone else in the family. It was almost as if she didn't exist. Suppressing a shudder, Dani made her way down the back stairs and out the back, vowing to stop in and see her aunt later in the day.

The gardens behind La Tana weren't totally overgrown, but they did look forlorn, as if they longed for better days. Dani started to climb the stone steps that wound their way up one side of the vineyard and ended at a folly at the top of the hill. She and Agnese had spent many afternoons in the gazebo, pouring over fan magazines and gossiping about the goings-on at the convent school, knowing they were safe from judgmental ears. Even though Fausta was an employee, Dani had always deferred to her, even feared her a little. It seemed as if the housekeeper controlled virtually everything at La Tana, especially her daughter Agnese, almost as if Agnese were a princess in a tower. In fact, whenever they were out on the grounds of the estate and heard Fausta calling sternly for Agnese, Dani would tease her friend by saying,

"Time to go, Rapunzel." Agnese possessed such a good nature that she never took offense—but she always obeyed her mama. No doubt Fausta would have wanted her to attend the funeral and Dani wondered why her friend hadn't shown up. She resolved to see Agnese as soon as possible, too.

"Up here, bella," she heard Gabe call from above. Shielding her eyes, she could just make him out at the top of the staircase. She continued her climb and took Gabe's hand when he offered to help her up the last incline to the plateau above. She noticed he didn't let go as they walked to the small but ornate pavilion set in a clearing surrounded on two sides by evergreens, which marked the beginning of the alpine ascent beyond. Memories assailed her as she took in the circular benches, situated to take advantage of the view down the valley on the opposite side of the gazebo. She remembered the vista well: slightly below was La Tana, standing watch over an ancient but still beautiful town, which itself was nestled along the banks of the swiftly flowing Adige River.

"Why are we here?" she asked. "Couldn't you have told me about Carla back in our suite?"

Gabe motioned for her to sit. "I wanted to talk to you away from the house," he said.

Dani frowned. Maybe this thing with Carla was more serious than she thought. She steeled herself for the worst. "All right. I'm here. What do you want to tell me?" The next words to come out of his mouth nearly floored her.

"Carla Rinaldi was your father's...girlfriend. And she believes he was murdered."

"What?!"

"You heard me." Gabe took her hand again and waited.

Dani shook her head. "That can't be. He…he…It was an accident." She searched Gabe's eyes for some sign that he was kidding, or just speculating. But he gazed directly back at her with something akin to pity. Or maybe he was just feeling bad as the bearer of bad news.

"I've done some checking and I think she's telling the truth," he said quietly.

Dani began to pace the gazebo, her thoughts warring with her emotions. Why would someone kill her babbo? Why would they take him from her? Her eyes welled up and Gabe reached for her.

"Let me tell you what I know," he said.

Dani sat and immediately felt the solid presence of Gabe's arm around her. She concentrated on her breathing while he spoke.

"Carla slipped me that note at the reception saying to meet her yesterday at one, that she knew your father had been killed, and to tell no one. When I met her she was on her way out of the city. She knew if and when they connected your father to her, she might be next."

"But how—"

"She dined with your father that evening. Apparently they often traveled together, but stayed in different rooms to avoid the paparazzi. He suffered from migraines and had turned in early after taking medication. She said he would never drink in that condition, and that the meds made him sleepy. Her room was several doors away and a short time after they said good night she heard a commotion in the hallway. Two men were talking and it sounded to her as if one of them were carrying a heavy load. She feels terribly guilty, thinking that if she had only opened her door, none of it would have happened."

"Or maybe she would have gotten hurt too," Dani said.

"Exactly what I told her. Anyway, I met Marco at his precinct afterward and verified what I could without giving her away."

"Why didn't she go directly to the police?"

"She's scared shitless, worried about corruption. And Dani, her story checks out. There was no alcohol in your father's system, only the migraine meds. Marco's following up on some other evidence, but it's starting to look like someone killed your dad and made it look like an accident."

"But who? Why?"

"We're working on that. Carla was the human resources director at the Stella d'Italia Milano. She'd gotten wind of some strange business related to disappearing housekeeping staff members, not only in her hotel but throughout the company. She makes a compelling case for the possibility that there's been some human trafficking running through the system. She told your father about it, and her theory is he died on account of it."

Dani shook her head. "But Stella d'Italia is relatively small, and my uncle runs it with an iron fist. How on earth could someone pull that off without him finding out about it?"

Gabe's silence spoke volumes and Dani turned to him, her eyes wide.

"Wait a minute. You don't think *he*...?"

Gabe shrugged. "All I know is what Marco told me. He basically agreed with you. He said there's no way something like that could be going on in that company without either Santo or Dante—or both—knowing about it."

The cool of the morning had nothing to do with the shiver that traveled down Dani's spine. "Human trafficking" was a polite label for the sex slave trade. Could her uncle or cousin really have anything to do with such a disgusting crime? It was unthinkable, and her hackles rose. "Who is this Carla person, anyway, Gabe? Do we really know if she's telling the truth? Maybe she was a plant by some competitor or something. Maybe—"

Gabe held up his hand. "You're right. We don't know a lot about her. But Marco confirmed she was your father's companion and was employed by the Milan hotel. Apparently when her director of housekeeping first brought some odd staffing issues to her attention, she began to look into it, but was called off by higher ups. She did some research anyway and found out things weren't adding up." He paused and looked intently at Dani. "Maybe the most important thing is, my gut tells me she loved your father very much. And she is afraid she's going to get killed for it. If she had anything to do with his death, why would she take a chance just to keep a case open that even Marco admits nobody wants to pursue?"

*Not adding up.* The words struck a chord with Dani. There *was* something odd going on, at least with the numbers she'd looked at. Her grandmother had sensed it, and Dani had seen it. Could there be any connection? "I, um, I learned something yesterday. I don't know if it means anything, but…"

Gabe looked alarmed. "What? Did Santo say something?"

Dani shook her head. "No. It was after I left him at the restaurant. I stopped by Nonna Stella's apartment and she asked me to look over some figures. It sounds odd, but she was concerned because there's too much money flowing into the books—and she's right."

"What do you mean?"

"Every month there's a twenty to thirty thousand dollar entry from a different company, flowing into a different hotel. It's not always on the same day, but it falls once within each month. They're apparently paying for "miscellaneous services rendered," which is line-itemed as an accounts receivable from the executive office."

"So, what—they book a lot of meetings?"

"That's just it. I checked against both guest and conference room bookings but the companies aren't paying to use hotel facilities, at least not under the name they're billing under. Occasionally hotel execs will consult with companies regarding large events, but even for Stella d'Italia those fees seem excessive."

Gabe reached into his pocket for his notebook and began writing in it. "Can you get me a list of the companies?"

"I can do better than that. I'll run a search to see if they're linked in any way."

"That's right." Gabe smiled warmly at her. "I forgot you're the resident computer geek back home at The Grove."

Dani straightened her shoulders. "Nothing wrong with us geeks. So, once I get that information, what are we going to do about it?"

"*You* aren't going to do anything," Gabe replied, still jotting down notes. "I'll take the information back to Marco and we'll see if we can construct some sort of theory based on the facts."

Dani put her hand on his forearm; it was well-muscled and covered with soft, dark hair—a man's arm, strong and capable. But entirely too chauvinistic for her taste.

"Excuse me, but this is my family we're talking about. If there's something sinister going on, I need to know about it. I need to know who's involved and I need to protect those who need protecting. So we're going to work together—" her chin jutted mutinously "—or...or we're going to work apart."

Gabe methodically put his notebook away and slowly put his hand behind her head, his gaze boring into her. "This is not just a family squabble. This is not a game. This is something that could be very, very dangerous for those involved, which is why I don't want you anywhere near it."

"I hate to tell you this, but you're out of your jurisdiction, Constable. And if you think I'm just going to sit back and let you slay whatever dragons you think might be out there, you are sadly mistaken. Besides, I can help you."

Gabe looked skeptical. "How?"

"For starters, I can visit my cousin Dante and ask him about the accounts. That would be a natural thing for me to do for my nonna. And he might be able to clear the whole thing up...or not."

"It's the 'or not' I'm worried about."

"Well, we won't know unless I talk to him, so that's what I'm going to do."

Gabe sighed. "Look, how about we go see him together? At the very least, promise me you won't do anything until I get both of us local cell phones. I can't go through another night like we had last night. I have too many gray hairs as it is."

Dani looked at his slightly wavy hair and sure enough, there were a few telltale strands in it. She couldn't help herself; she reached up and ran her fingers through the thick, soft mane. Embarrassed at her own lack of control, she turned it into a joke. "They give you character, but I can pluck them out if you want."

"I'll pass," he said, and pulled her up from the bench. "Just promise me you'll let me know where you are at all times."

Dani frowned. "Well—"

Gabe tilted his head so he could look directly into her eyes. "Dani?"

"*Va bene, va bene. Sissignore.*" She signaled her frustration with a wave of her hands, and started to jog back down the hill.

"Dani?" he called after her.

She stopped and turned, hands on hips, letting him know she wasn't happy with him. "What?" she called back.

"I can help with this…I want to help."

"I know," she said, resignation in her voice. "I know."

The corridor was quiet as Dani made her way down the wing of La Tana that housed Santo's wife. She'd always been a sickly woman, and she became even more so after Dani's cousin Ciro, Ornella and Santo's son, passed away. Little Ciro was five years older than Dani and lived at the same estate, but only rarely had he deigned to play with Dani and Agnese. At first she'd thought he was a stuck-up creep, but time had revealed a sadder truth. His juvenile onset diabetes was severe and he'd died of complications from it when he was sixteen. Dani vaguely recalled a funeral— much more intimate than her father's had been. She remembered Ornella with her distinctive, unnaturally red hair, looking painfully thin and dressed completely in black. A dark veil covered her face. There was no need for professional mourners because her aunt had loudly and painfully expressed the loss of her only child. One of Dani's sharper memories of her Uncle Santo was his cold, unyielding demeanor that day. He hadn't wept or carried on; in fact, he'd seemed to find his wife's vociferous grieving distasteful. Dani could still remember thinking he looked mad at his wife and wondering why her aunt should shoulder the blame for Ciro's death. Shortly after the boy was buried in the family cemetery, Ornella took to her rooms and was rarely seen out of them again. In the spirit of self-absorbed pre-teens everywhere, Dani remembered giggling with Agnese that La Tana had its very own Mrs. Rochester, although they'd argued as to which of them would have to play Jane Eyre to her Uncle Santo, who was way too old to be a romantic hero.

As she reached the door to her aunt's suite, Dani could hear quiet voices and an intermittent mechanical hissing sound. It reminded her of a science fiction movie, as if her aunt were somehow being kept alive in a pod. She shivered at the thought and knocked quietly on the door. She was startled when a man in a suit opened it.

"Sì?"

"Uh. *Buon giorno*. I'm here to see my aunt. If you could tell her that Dani is here to see her."

"*La faccia entrare, Guglielmo, per favore,*" she heard a woman call weakly from within. The man opened the door and Dani walked into what was for all intents and purposes a hospital room. It smelled strongly of antiseptics. A set of built-in shelves along one wall contained a plethora of medications and supplies. Nearby, a heart monitor beeped quietly. Aunt Ornella was propped up in a large hospital bed with side rails and a rolling tray upon which her breakfast sat. She had a cannula in her nose that was connected to the hissing machine, which supplied her with oxygen. A clamp on one of her fingers was connected to the monitor, and her forearm had a needle stuck into it from which a tube led to an IV stand. A severe-looking nurse who appeared to be in her fifties was fixing the pillows behind her patient's back. Ornella looked incredibly frail; she probably weighed less than one hundred pounds. Her hair was very thin, but held the same vivid red color that Dani remembered from so long ago.

"How are you, Aunt Ornella?" Dani asked. She stood by the bed and took Ornella's unencumbered hand in her own.

"I'm glad you're speaking English," she said. "I get so little opportunity to practice it." The older woman gestured to herself in the bed. "As you can see, I am but a shell, Dani. A shell. I am waiting for this disease-ridden body of mine to give it up and I suspect it won't be that long."

"Oh, don't say that," Dani said. "You are...you are..."

"I know what I am, and pretty words won't change the truth of it. But I'm glad you are here. I wanted to tell you that I am sorry for the loss of your father. I liked Armando very much. Did you know I always called him 'little brother'? Because I was an only child, you see, and he was just the kind of fun-loving little brother I would have liked to have." Ornella stopped long enough to take a bite of the pastry sitting on her tray. She washed it down with what looked and smelled like Doctor Pepper. "It was a crime for him to die so young," she said pointedly. "A crime."

Dani sensed her aunt wasn't talking in metaphors. She looked around to see if anyone was listening. "What do you mean, a *crime*?"

Ornella smiled then and spoke to her staff. "Guglielmo, Zuleta, you may leave us for a few minutes. I am fine here with my niece for the time being."

The man and the nurse left and Ornella gestured for Dani to lean over. "I am always careful what I say around them," she confided in a near whisper. "They seem loyal, but you never know what money will buy, do you?"

Dani frowned. "I'm not sure what you mean, Aunt."

"So young. So trusting," Ornella said, squeezing Dani's hand. "Tell me, what do you know about my husband's latest business venture?"

The question took Dani by surprise, although she tried not to show it. "Do you mean the Alberghi Paradisi acquisition? Not very much. Only that because of my father's death, Uncle Santo needs my votes to make the purchase. Why? Is there something I should know?"

"One hears things," Ornella said. "Even in this prison cell. Santo visited me last month. He needs funds, so he tried to sell me on the merger, said that it would strengthen the company. 'To what end?' I asked him. He doesn't like it when I say things like that." She paused and took another sip of the giant soft drink. "So he went to my solicitor looking for a side deal, but Mauricio told me the numbers simply didn't match Santo's enthusiasm. Something is wrong there. Very wrong."

"But—wouldn't Santo know a good business proposition when he saw one?"

Ornella inclined her head. "Perhaps. But there is something else going on. There is danger. I can feel it." She sighed and leaned back against her pillow.

Her aunt's cryptic comments were starting to give Dani a headache. She hated it when the answer to a research question eluded her and this felt the same way. She silently counted to ten before speaking. "Well, Aunt, knowing Uncle Santo as you do, what do you think could be behind it?"

Ornella looked at Dani for several moments as if deciding how much to confide in her. "Santo is a filthy human being," she finally said. "He is evil."

"Oh come now, *Zia*. I know yours wasn't the happiest marriage—"

Ornella barked with laughter that held no joy. "You have no idea what my husband is capable of—and with whom." She gestured for Dani to come closer with the arm that held the I.V. "Do you want to know something funny?"

"I...I suppose so."

"You probably don't remember, but years ago I was, shall we say, curvaceous." She placed a hand under her sagging left breast and lifted it. "These were bountiful and I thought Santo would be pleased. But he was not. It turns out he preferred a more *prepubescent* look." She raised her eyebrows as if to silently add *you know what I mean*. "I tried to diet and could not bear it so I started to take pills and I started to smoke, and I lost weight. So in order to lose more weight, I took more pills and smoked even more. Now you see where that has led. And now I can eat whatever I want and still I lose weight. Funny, no?"

Dani shook her head. "But surely Uncle Santo…"

"Once he had my dowry and I had given him Ciro, Santo had no use for me. And after our little boy died, well, then he cared even less. I could have had a perfect body and it wouldn't have mattered because by then I was way too old to interest his cock. I'm only sorry it took so long for me to figure that out." Ornella looked deeply into Dani's eyes. "Ask him where he goes on vacation every year and ask him why. And when he lies to you, determine the facts for yourself. You will see what I am talking about… and then you will finally know the truth." At that point Ornella starting coughing violently. Dani didn't know what her aunt was trying to say, but it was obviously making her upset.

"Should I get the nurse?" she asked, faintly alarmed. She turned for the door, but Ornella shook her head, reaching for the soft drink again. Dani held the straw for her as her aunt drank the soothing liquid.

"No, this is the way it is," she managed to get out. Dani reached over to rub her aunt's back and Ornella began to calm down. The woman lay back on the bed and closed her eyes. It smelled as if the bed linens or Ornella herself needed to be changed. "Soon I am going to see my little Ciro, but because of Guglielmo and his colleagues I will leave on my terms, not Santo's."

*What was she talking about?* "I'm sorry, but I don't follow you," Dani said.

Her eyes still closed, Ornella spoke wearily. "Who do you think Guglielmo is?"

"I don't know. I confess I was puzzled when I first saw him. I assumed he was some sort of aide, but he doesn't look the part."

Ornella turned her head on the pillow and opened her eyes. "Not an aide, my dear—an armed guard."

Dani couldn't hide the look of shock on her face. "Why, Aunt? Why does Santo have someone guarding you?"

Ornella shook her head slightly; her wisps of bottle-red hair lay dank upon her scalp. "Santo doesn't employ the guard, I do."

"What? Why? Who are you afraid of?"

The old woman spoke in a whisper, as if she had run out of her allotment of energy for the day. "Your Uncle Santo, of course."

# CHAPTER TEN

—◆◆◆—

Back in her own suite, Dani sat on the sofa with her laptop open, the spreadsheets her grandmother had given her laid out on the coffee table. She breathed deeply for several minutes, trying to get herself back on an emotionally even keel. It wasn't easy. She was still trying to wrap her mind around what Gabe had told her, coupled with her grandmother's warning and her Aunt Ornella's admission. *Murder*, for heaven's sake. *Armed guards*? Dani knew her uncle was a forbidding, controlling man, and it was no surprise his marriage had failed, but still, this went way beyond a typical family feud. Dani worked to channel her brain into thinking rationally and logically. "Focus," she muttered. "Connect the dots."

Earlier she'd called her nonna to say hello and recount her visit with Ornella. She'd decided against filling her grandmother in on the more disturbing news she'd learned. That could wait until there was proof.

She'd also made a quick phone call to her cousin Dante, who sounded happy to meet Dani and Gabe for drinks at a café in the Piazza Bra around four. Gabe had left a note saying he would meet her in the main lobby of the Stella d'Italia Verona at two p.m. She tried to feel irritated that he was ordering her about, but deep inside it felt too good to have someone care enough to want to keep track of her.

Dani began to look for connections between the companies listed on the monthly accounts receivable reports. Based on their names, the companies that had paid the high sums to each Stella d'Italia hotel over the past year seemed to have nothing in common. One month it was Skyline Property Management; another month it was Cloud Imports. Still another entry was Sicurezza Mondiale and a fourth, Casa Italia. Strangely, none of them had dedicated or social media websites, and none showed up in industry blogs. Finally she hit pay dirt through a sweep of the country's Register of Enterprises filings. Any legitimate Italian company had to have tax identification and VAT numbers. Although none of the companies seemed to be subsidiaries of another, the same names kept cropping up on virtually every company's registration application. Those names pointed to what seemed to be a holding company called Azure Consortium. "The plot thickens," she mused aloud. "What does Stella d'Italia do for Azure?"

The door to their suite clicked open, jolting Dani out of her reverie. She looked up to see Fausta enter the room, a stack of towels in hand. The two women stared at each other for an awkward moment before Fausta broke the silence.

"*Scusa,*" she said coolly. "I did not realize you were here."

"Well I am," Dani said, feigning cheerfulness. "Is there something you needed?"

"No, I…was simply checking to make sure your accommodations were as they should be." She paused slightly before walking across the room, glancing at Dani on her way to the bathroom. Dani stood up quickly.

"I'll take those," she said, reaching for the towels. "Fausta, really, we are family. You don't need to treat us as if we're hotel guests."

Fausta firmly held on to the linens. "Please, allow me." She walked around Dani and into the bathroom. When she came out again, Dani tried again to break the ice.

"Here, will you join me for some—" she looked around, noticed that Gabe had left only a few small pastries and an orange "—um, coffee?"

Fausta glanced at the papers on the coffee table. "Yes, that would be nice. Thank you."

Dani reverted to her own innkeeper's sensibilities and poured a cup for Fausta as the woman sat primly on a Queen Anne chair to the side of the sofa. "It's been such a long time since I've seen you, Fausta," she said gently. "I remember when you taught Agnese and me the correct way to serve, just like this."

A brief smile crossed Fausta's lips. "That was indeed a long time ago," she replied. "You have traveled far since then."

"Yes, I have," Dani said. "Even though it was a painful journey, for me at least." She met Fausta's knowing eyes. *Of course she understands why I left.*

"Agnese missed you," Fausta offered with a trace of sadness. "She...she had to grow up quickly after that. I suppose you could say you took her childhood with you, but it was all for the best."

What? Fausta seemed to be talking in riddles. How had Dani taken Agnese's childhood away? "I hear Agnese traveled some as well," she said to lighten the mood. "University, then graduate school. And now she lives with the Holy Sisters?" Dani smiled. "That's certainly not the way I pictured Agnese. She was always much too pretty to live in a convent."

The empathy that Fausta had appeared to share with Dani seemed to vanish, replaced by a look of painful pride. "Yes, Agnese was and is a beautiful girl. And I don't think she'll remain there indefinitely. She will come around, but for now she prefers her privacy." Fausta's implied warning piqued Dani's curiosity. She decided she had time for one more visit before meeting Gabe for lunch. She was about to cut the conversation short when Fausta looked again at the papers on the table.

"You have brought work from home?" she asked.

The came easily to Dani's lips. "That? No, it's uh, just some financials related to a project Uncle Santo is working on. He asked my opinion, and—"

"Ah, the Alberghi Paradisi?"

"Yes. You know of it?"

"Bits and pieces," Fausta said. "I believe it was coming to fruition just before your father's untimely death."

*This woman knows more than she lets on, but how much more?* "You're right," Dani said. "Uncle Santo must be confident that it will go through because he offered me the job of running the company."

"What?" Fausta was clearly shocked by Dani's statement. "Do you...do you mean to take it?"

"One never knows," Dani answered with a small shrug. "As you can see, I'm studying the situation."

Dani was taken aback by the outrage Fausta was trying so hard to conceal. Why should it matter if Dani joined Stella d'Italia? Or was Fausta simply angry that she wasn't in the loop?

Fausta carefully put down the coffee, which she hadn't touched, and rose, smoothing out her skirt as she did so. "I'm sorry but I must get back to my duties," she said.

"Of course." Fausta had reached the door to the suite when Dani called out to her. "I saw Aunt Ornella earlier this morning and she said the strangest thing."

Fausta paused without turning. "Oh? What was that?"

"She said she feared Santo might kill her, which is why she employs an armed guard. Why on earth would Santo want to kill his own wife?"

Fausta slowly turned to look at Dani. "Signora Forcelli should have left La Tana, like your grandmother did, long ago."

"Why, Fausta?"

"Secrets, signorina. It isn't healthy to know too many of them."

The look on Fausta's face sent shivers down Dani's arms. Was she sending a warning? A threat? Dani tried to make light of it. "What about you?" she asked. "You must know where *all* the bodies are buried."

Again, Fausta's smile was fleeting. "You are a quick study, signorina." The estate manager then quietly left the suite.

It took Dani barely a minute to realize she'd forgotten to ask the woman about the two paintings Dani's great-grandfather had brought back from The Grove in the 1920s. Surely Fausta would know about them. She ran to the door and opened it. Fausta was at the other end of the hall and Dani ran after her.

"I'm sorry, I forgot to ask you. I seem to remember a couple of paintings from when I lived here. They were a matched set. I don't recall exactly what—"

Fausta's eyes bore into hers. "Secrets," she whispered, and continued on her way.

—◆·◆—

While Dani visited her aunt, Gabe spent the morning dealing with the items on his mental checklist. First he rented two cell phones for them to use during their stay. No way was he going to repeat the agony of not being able to reach Dani when he needed to.

Next he called his buddy Sam Barker to check on the status of the Sinner's Grove investigation back in Marin. A fellow detective, Sam had taken up the slack when Gabe explained his impromptu trip to Italy. Sam paid attention to details, so Gabe figured everything was probably in order. As soon as his friend picked up, however, Gabe realized why he should have waited. Sam was not thrilled to get the call.

"It's two a.m., dude."

"Shit, I'm sorry, man. Did I wake you?" Gabe could hear a feminine voice in the background asking Sam who it was.

Sam chuckled. "Lucky for you I wasn't exactly sleeping."

Gabe grinned at his cell phone. "So, how's it going?"

"What, you mean right now? You want a play by play?"

"Ha ha. I'm talking about The Grove."

"Shaping up real nice," Sam said. "All but a couple of paintings are accounted for and the perp is looking at second degree murder for making the old man stroke out."

"Fifteen to life—not bad," Gabe said.

"Couldn't happen to a nastier individual."

"Amen," Gabe said. "What about the kid? He turn up yet??"

"No, not yet. How are things with you?"

"All right, I guess. Dani's family is a piece of work—she's got some complicated shit to work through. But she's okay. I'm hangin' in."

Gabe heard the woman's voice again in the background. It sounded like she was using her feminine wiles to coax Sam back to whatever they'd been doing before the call. Sam murmured something to her that Gabe couldn't hear, then got back on the line. He sounded distracted. "Uh, when you coming home? Word is, The Grove is going to have a multi-million dollar jewel collection as part of the Grand Reopening. Little Eden's town council is freaking out about it and asking the sheriff to come up with some foolproof plan for increased security. The lieutenant wants you in on it and asked when you were due back. I told him 'soon.'"

"As soon as I can," Gabe agreed. "Hey, thanks again for filling in, buddy. I owe you big time."

"Oh, I'm keepin' score," Sam said. "Gotta run." Gabe could hear the grin in his voice.

"Right, man. See you soon."

*Never a dull moment at The Grove*, Gabe thought. The new Grove Center for American Art wasn't due to open until early October, but already they'd dealt with a massive art theft that nobody realized had been happening for *decades*. And now they were adding priceless jewels to the mix? That oughta be fun.

The last item on Gabe's to do list was the most important of all—borrowing a firearm from Marco. It had taken some arguing, cajoling, and even some guilt-tripping, but finally his friend had agreed to let him use his wife's Colt Cobra. She dropped it off at the station and Gabe stopped by Marco's office to pick it up.

"Nice little antique," Gabe said, hefting it in his palm. "Lightweight, too. Gina know how to use it?"

Marco snorted. "Hell, yes. Our first date I thought I'd play Marco the Macho Guy. Took her to a gun range and she smoked me. That's how I knew she was the one."

Gabe smiled and adjusted the shoulder holster so it would fit his much larger body. He had to admit, he'd felt naked without a sidearm; the snub-nosed pistol wasn't much, but it would do in a pinch. "Thanks for this. I don't intend to use it, but it's a load off knowing I can protect her if I need to."

He noticed Marco didn't even bother to ask whom Gabe meant by "her."

—◆◆◆—

"Are you actually questioning my judgment in this matter, Fausta?" Santo addressed his estate manager, who uncharacteristically had shown up at his office a few minutes earlier and asked for an audience with him, ostensibly to "go over the menu for an upcoming dinner party." What rubbish. There was no need to see him in his office for that. But he'd complied, only because he wouldn't put it past her to slip some stool softener into his food if he didn't. She was wily, and right now, livid.

"I do not understand why you have to have your niece underfoot when she was perfectly happy...with my *nephew*...running that inn. You don't even know her, and yet you have gone so far as to offer her a job with Stella d'Italia?"

"Obviously Daniela's been talking to you. Of course I offered her a position. She is capable, but more importantly, she is family. As for your nephew, he is of no consequence to my niece—especially now that she has come home. He knows I expect him to be leaving La Tana at the earliest opportunity."

Fausta leaned over Santo's desk. He leaned back reflexively. Where had this presumption come from?

"Are you that blind? Can you not see the way they look at each other?" She straightened up and pierced him with a look. Her voice was strident; it was getting on his nerves. "You and I have an...understanding...that goes back many years," she said. "I am waiting for you to honor your end of the bargain."

Santo glanced at his watch. Yesterday it was that prick Gabriele and today it was Fausta. Who'll show up next—the gardener asking for a raise? "You are overstepping your bounds, Fausta. I pay you to run my estate, not the people in it." He picked up a memo from his desk and scanned it, dismissing her. "Leave such matters to me."

Fausta didn't move and he looked up. She was glaring at him and for a moment he thought of a gypsy flashing him the Evil Eye. "You know what I want…what I have been waiting for, patiently, all these years. I intend to have it, and I will not let anyone stand in the way of it—no matter how important she is to you."

Her words stopped him cold. "Are you threatening me?"

"I am informing you." She opened the door. "I'll take your menu suggestions under advisement, but I can't promise you anything…*Signore*." Fausta's voice was now devoid of all inflection. She turned and left his office.

Santo sat back in his chair and contemplated Fausta's little diatribe. His estate manager was a strange one, always had been. He'd never truly understood what his father saw in her. But she was loyal, he'd give her that. Loyal to the Forcelli name, which he appreciated. What she really wanted was out of the question, but it wouldn't hurt to placate her if and when he could. He examined his manicured nails and noticed a few had been chewed. He'd only been half joking about the stool softener. Fausta was capable of so much more.

Not an hour later, Santo heard his secretary, Cristina, talking outside his office to the man he called "the pig." His blood began to boil. This scum was far worse than any gardener.

"Ah, lovely lady," the pig said. "I'm sure your boss will see me, even though it is such short notice. He and I have business to conduct. Very important matters."

Santo anticipated the buzz on his intercom; it came within seconds. "Signor Forcelli, there's a—"

"Send him in." Santo tried to maintain a calm voice, but it was difficult to keep his fury in check. How dare the pig show up here, of all places! At the warehouse, yes; even at one of the outlying hotels. But not here; not in his domain. He barely had time to straighten his suit jacket before the swine lumbered into the room. Fredo Moroni was a fat man with swarthy, mottled skin and thinning, gelatinous hair. He wore a dull brown suit whose middle button strained across his protruding midsection. The remains of a stain of some sort could be seen on his grayish shirt. He was repulsive.

"Santo, buddy, how goes it?" Moroni began circling Santo's spacious and elegant office, pausing to admire several objects that had been carefully chosen by the company's interior designer for their masculine appeal. A bronze nude graced a pedestal; along one wall several prints extolled the virtues of Roman Verona. "Nice tits," he said, referring to the sculpture.

"Did you come here to compliment my artwork or do you have a purpose?" Santo asked with irritation.

"You wound me, Santo. I come bearing gifts." Moroni handed Santo a package addressed to the President and CEO of Stella d'Italia; it was clearly marked *confidential by courier*. "You might want to lock the door."

Santo tossed Moroni a disgusted look, closed the door to his office, and opened the small padded envelope, which contained a single DVD. *I don't have time for this*, he thought. "I assume you want me to view this now."

Moroni inclined his head. "If you would be so kind."

The program opened on a man, sitting at a desk, cast in shadows.

"Good day, Signor Forcelli," the man said. "We would like to say we are saddened by your loss, but are ever mindful that events often happen for a reason. Some time ago we explained to you through our intermediary that we wished your company to purchase Alberghi Paradisi, which our holding company acquired two months ago. As you know, we are not in the hotel business per se—that is your line of work—but we feel that market conditions are ripe to expand our trade. That hotel chain provides a broader base of distribution than Stella d'Italia, which, as you know, is limited." The shadowed man spoke in deep, measured tones, with a cultured Eastern European accent.

"We understand your constraints, which is why we helped you overcome one of your obstacles. But your continued reticence in this matter is becoming problematic. We wish to see some progress—a letter of intent or understanding, perhaps. To give you an incentive, we offer you a glimpse of the following."

At that point, the scene dissolved into a grainy overhead shot of a man and a teenage girl having rough sex. The girl was pleading with the man to stop. When he finished, he climbed off the woman and the camera revealed the man to be Santo himself.

The tape cut back to the Eastern European man. "We expect you to move the process along," he said. "You have until the end of the month. We will be in touch." At that, the DVD faded to black.

"You fucking bastards," Santo muttered as he realized what had been captured on the video.

"It would be a terrible shame for the CEO of the great hotel company Stella d'Italia to be caught in such a scandal," Moroni said. "Here, I'll take that." Santo gave him the DVD and the slug calmly broke it into small pieces before throwing it in the trash. He had strong hands for a man so obviously out of shape. "Of course, there are other copies," he remarked.

"Of course there are." Santo's sarcasm was obvious. "Will that be all?"

Ignoring his rudeness, Moroni sat heavily in one of the large leather chairs facing Santo's desk and reached into the humidor in front of him. "I'd love one, *grazie*." He calmly rolled the cigar between his stubby fingers, sniffed it, clipped the end, and lit it, all without saying a word.

Mentally eviscerating the pig, Santo said nothing and sat back down behind his desk. "I'll ask one more time," he said deliberately. "What else do you want?"

Moroni leaned back in the chair, inhaling deeply, holding it, and exhaling with satisfaction. "Cuban," he said with a sigh. "Delicious."

Santo was about to explode. He rose from his chair, but Moroni waved him back down.

"Sit. Sit. I'm here on a mission. My superiors asked that I deliver that message to you, as well as get a progress report. So here I am." Moroni continued to smoke the cigar as he looked intently at Santo. "I'm waiting," he added.

"I don't know why your *superiors* are so impatient. I told Stolar some time ago that I am negotiating."

"Negotiating for what? Do you not control your own family? Our two companies have worked hand in hand for quite a while now. And my bosses feel it is time to take our alliance to the next step. You have something we want. We now have something you want. Quite simple, really."

Santo gripped the edge of the desk. "No, it's not. I cannot simply purchase Alberghi Paradisi without a majority vote of the shareholders. We are talking millions of euros here."

"What's holding up the vote? Yours is a privately held company. You told us it would happen quickly."

"It seems the deciding family member needs more information before making her decision. I have decided not to pressure her, but it is difficult. *She* is difficult."

Moroni continued to gaze at Santo through the haze of tobacco smoke. "The only difficulty I see is that once we release the video of your, shall we say, relationship with the busty little Romanian, your life, or the reputation of your company, isn't going to be worth shit."

Santo bristled. How *dare* this cretin lecture him? He was the head of Italy's premier hotel company. He could buy and sell this swine a hundred times over. "If I go down, Azure goes down with me," he countered. "Not only will you lose your conduit through Stella d'Italia, but your expansion plans through Alberghi Paradisi as well. So don't threaten me."

Moroni shrugged. "It sounds as if your little niece from America isn't the pushover you thought she'd be. So, how can we help you resolve your little family squabble?" He puffed again. "You know the services we provide."

"You didn't provide much service the other day."

"That was unfortunate," Moroni said. "The little birds flew away before we could clip their feathers. But your niece, now, that is another story."

Santo rose from his chair, walked over, and used his imposing height to tower over the seated thug. "Don't even think about *persuading* her—in any way, shape or form. She is mine to deal with. *Mine.*"

"Yours?" Moroni smiled. "It sounds as though she means more to you than just a voting bloc, Signor Forcelli. *Tsk tsk.* You are still married, are you not?"

Santo stared at Moroni for several moments until the germ of an idea began to sprout. He thought about what Fausta had said and rapidly turned the possibilities over in his mind before calmly sitting back down. "I will not need your help with my niece, but perhaps you can provide assistance in another matter, and do it right this time. I will contact you through the usual channels later today. It should help us in all aspects of our...endeavor."

Moroni rose and bowed lightly. A subconscious acceptance of his inferior status, Santo thought with satisfaction.

"As always, Azure lives to serve both its customers and its suppliers," the pig said formally. "We will not let you down." He paused before adding, "Just make sure *you* may say the same."

Santo inclined his head slightly in acknowledgment. "As always."

Before he turned to go, Moroni glanced at the humidor. "May I?"

Santo reached into the humidor, pulled out two cigars and handed them to the brute. "With pleasure," he said grimly.

After Moroni left, Santo contemplated the changes that had occurred—and would occur—within the Forcelli family. The name...the reputation...the dynasty must be preserved at all costs. Family was everything. It had always been everything. He would not be the one to break the tradition. His thoughts strayed and he grew hard.

After several minutes he called Cristina into his office and told her to lock the door. "You know what to do," he said. She dutifully leaned over his desk and spread her legs. Without saying a word, he hiked her skirt to her waist. She was not wearing panties, per his standing instructions. He fondled her pale buttocks and fingered her, noting that she must like what he routinely did to her because she was already wet. He unzipped his trousers and quickly donned a condom before impaling her from behind. As usual her cries were subdued as he held her hips and pumped methodically into her, bringing himself to orgasm in quick, hard thrusts. By now she was finely tuned to his needs. She knew not to look back at him or make eye contact. Perhaps, as he pushed into her, she thought about what she would buy with the hundred-euro note he gave her after each session. She had no cause for complaint. There was only one problem.

"I'd like you to do something for me," he said after finishing.

"Yes, Signor Forcelli?" The girl really was very pretty. With short, bouncy golden curls, soft breasts and a heart-shaped ass, she looked much younger than her twenty-six years. She was a fairly decent secretary as well.

"Dye your hair black for me," he said. "I want a change."

"*Sissignore*," she managed faintly, before smoothing down her skirt and returning to her desk.

# CHAPTER ELEVEN

—⊹⊹⊹—

A small sign on the frosted glass door read *Lozioni dal Cielo*. Dani grinned because the nerve center for Lotions from Heaven, the all-natural, online skin care company, was actually an old high school science lab. She knew this because she had spent a year dissecting worms and frogs there as part of her coursework at the Convent of Our Holy Sisters of Rectitude, one of Verona's more prestigious convent schools.

Dani knocked on the glass. Hearing no answer, she tried the door and it opened. She walked in to see Agnese, dressed in a lab coat, standing at a counter in front of several petri dishes backed by stoppered bottles, an eye dropper in her latex-gloved hand. Her dark hair was tied back with a ribbon and she was wearing glasses.

"Yes, what is it?" she asked, so focused on her work that she didn't bother to look up.

"Just a voice from the past," Dani said.

Agnese turned and paused for a second before hurriedly peeling off her gloves. "Dani? *Dio mio*, is it you?"

"One and the same." Dani's eyes immediately welled up; not until that moment did she realize how much she had missed her childhood friend. Agnese ran up and encased her in a heartfelt hug. She was teary-eyed, too.

"Now this reunion was way too long in coming," Dani said, chuckling as she looked for a Kleenex to dab her eyes. "You stayed in touch for a while, but then you stopped writing. I missed you terribly."

"And I missed you. I…suppose life got in the way. And such a sad reason for your visit. I'm so sorry to hear about your father. God bless him."

"Thank you. I looked for you at the memorial service."

Agnese squeezed her friend's arm and stepped back. "I am sorry about that also. I…I was not able to make it."

"Listen, I talked to your mother earlier today. She said you prefer 'the quiet life,' as she put it, and that you didn't like to be disturbed. She seemed to be warning me to steer clear of you. What's that all about?"

"My mother…well, you know Fausta. She wants to control everything and everybody. But she no longer controls me, and it rankles. I think she's hoping I'll be too lonely here and come running back to La Tana."

"Is there a chance of that happening?"

Agnese shook her head. "Not a chance in hell I'll ever go back there."

Something was going on between Agnese and her mother, but Dani felt it was not her place to ask about it, at least not until they were able to rekindle their once-close relationship.

Instead she looked around the lab. It was obvious the room was no longer used for teaching. Except where Agnese stood, the long countertops were now bare of microscopes and Bunsen burners. Gone were the cases of mounted butterflies and spiders that had always given Dani the willies. But the huge periodic table of the elements was still hanging on one wall, and the desk that had once been the domain of Sister Mary Catarina, the science teacher, remained. Now it obviously belonged to Agnese. She kept it orderly, without a stray paper or pencil out of place. The shelves above the counters were equally tidy: sections filled with bottles were labeled alphabetically with what must have been ingredients for the skin care products. One row read *Basil, Bay,* and *Bergamot.* Another listed *Camphor, Cardamom, Carrot seed,* and *Cassia bark.* And so it went around the room.

"You always were organized," Dani finally said. "I envied that, you know."

Agnese laughed. "Come on. You hated that about me—I was always too regimented for you, remember?"

Dani wandered over to the counter where Agnese had been working. On the partition in front of her hung three cute little vases that looked like test tubes. They contained fragrant sprigs of herbs. She smelled lavender and mint.

"Maybe back then, but now, oh I could use a little tidiness in my life." *What an understatement.* Dani thought about all the complications that had cropped up in just the past few weeks and

wished for the kind of serenity she sensed Agnese was searching for as well. "You know, your mother put your products in our
suite, and—"

"Then it's true. I heard you are with my cousin. Are you
two...that is—"

"No, no. Definitely *not*." Dani waved her hand dismissively
to make the point. "We're just friends. That's all. He's a detective
near where I live in northern California."

"Really? What a coincidence."

"Not such a coincidence. Uncle Santo hinted that it would be
a good idea for Gabe to relocate there and he agreed." She took a
deep breath and let it out. "It's a long, irritating story, believe me."

Rather than ask her to elaborate, Agnese seemed to turn in
on herself. She moved to stand next to Dani and busied herself by
lining up the already straight petri dishes. She began to put on the
latex gloves she'd worn earlier. "Now that you've had a chance to
try our products, what do you think?"

Apparently Agnese was glad to change the subject, too. "I
love them," Dani said. "Especially that lavender-lemon body butter. It feels so sinfully good."

Agnese smiled. "Yes. It's one of our most popular items. But
we're expanding our line. I'm testing a new fragrance now." She
tipped her glasses down to mimic an erudite professor. "It's all
very scientific, you know. One drop of this, two drops of that.
Once we've determined the new scent, we take the formula to a
small manufacturer here in Verona who creates the product line
to our specifications. We're hoping to launch it in the fall."

Dani nodded absently. Agnese was obviously committed to her career, but why was she living here at the convent? She was too beautiful and loving not to have a special someone in her life. Then again, maybe she did. Dani had noticed a picture of Dante on the corkboard behind Agnese's desk. Actually it was a newspaper clipping from a recent society function. Everyone in Verona society knew that Dante Trevisan was illegitimate, but as the top gun for Stella d'Italia and a gorgeous man to boot, he was probably invited to many parties of the upper echelon just to glam up the event. Maybe he and Agnese were an item. Only one way to find out. "So how's my cousin doing?"

"Your cousin?"

Dani grinned. "Yes. My cousin. Dante. You know. The gorgeous hunk you have a picture of hanging behind your desk? I saw him briefly at the funeral. That wavy blond hair and those hazel eyes? Wow. In fact, Gabe and I are going to see him this afternoon. Would you like to join us?"

Dani couldn't have orchestrated a more awkward reaction if she had emptied a bottle of fire ants down Agnese's blouse. Her friend's face turned a bright pink and she actually stammered a series of excuses as to why she couldn't go. It was painful to watch, and it was obvious that seeing him was the last thing she wanted to do.

"So, uh, you see, it wouldn't be…that is, I couldn't…I wouldn't—"

Dani laid her hand on Agnese's arm. "That's all right. I didn't realize there was or had been something between you."

"Oh, there isn't. There isn't," Agnese said forcefully. "And there never can be. He is…he is not someone I could ever be with."

Dani tipped her head. "Are you saying that because his parents weren't legally—"

"Married? No, of course not. He is one of the most honorable men I've ever known."

"Then what's the problem?"

"It's me, Dani. I'm not good enough."

Dani shook her head. "That's not true. You're a beautiful person."

"No. It *is* true. And there isn't anything to be done about it."

Dani looked at her dear friend and saw the pain emanating from within. Something kept Agnese apart from a person she obviously cared a lot about. Dani recognized it all too well because she felt a similar pain regarding Gabe. She put her arms around Agnese. "We are a sorry pair, aren't we?" she whispered.

"We are," Agnese agreed. They smiled at one another, bridging a gap that had been too long in the making, rediscovering a friendship that thankfully had never truly died.

"I've got to go," Dani finally said. "Promise me we'll talk more before I leave? I can't bear for us to part again like we did so long ago."

"You can count on it," Agnese said, giving her a final squeeze.

—◆⋅⋆⋅◆—

"I think Agnese has a *tendre* for Dante," Dani said later as she and Gabe walked to the Piazza della Erbe. As instructed, she'd met him in the Stella d'Italia lobby. He'd picked up a couple of local cell phones and given one to her, programmed with his number and that of his friend Marco. Then, instead of having a late lunch in the hotel, he'd suggested they amble over to the popular marketplace held in the nearby square and grab a bite to eat while playing tourist. It sounded like a perfect break from all the unsettling news she'd been given over the past week.

"First of all, who uses the word 'tendre'?" Gabe asked. "Isn't that some sort of Jane Austeny kind of term?"

Dani playfully thumped him on his arm. "Gee, I'm shocked you even know who Jane Austen is. I'll have you know it's the perfect description for the kind of wistful attraction she seems to have for him. But for some reason, she doesn't think she's good enough."

"Why? Has she gotten fat or grown a beard? Because I remember she was a very pretty little girl…and I was only nine at the time."

"Well, she's grown into a gorgeous woman, so that's not the problem. I wonder if they had a relationship at some point, but had a falling out?"

"We can always take the direct approach and ask him," Gabe said. "Now, speaking of gorgeous women, before I start to gnaw on your beautiful bones, let's get something to eat."

Dani nodded, unwilling to read too much into his flirtatious comments…or feel elated when he took her hand. He had warned her of his affectionate personality and she vowed to keep reminding herself that his actions didn't, and couldn't, go beyond that.

But still, his hand felt so warm in hers. So solid. She couldn't deny she felt proud to be walking next to him and letting the world think they were a couple.

"What do you feel like?" he asked. "Antipasto? Pasta? Salad? Given what you whip up for Havenwood, you must have a pretty sophisticated palate."

"Um, not really. I could go for just about anything." She felt the tiniest twinge of conscience related to her cooking ability, but quickly set it aside.

"Okay then," he said, pointing to a stall with a bright green awning. "This place looks respectable. It's got a line and the customers look like locals. I think we're good to go here." Gabe proceeded to order a meat lasagna, salad, bread, and *vino da tavola* for himself; Dani stuck with a salad and a bottled water. "You're eatin' like a bird, bella," he admonished as they found a bench to sit on. "Don't be trying to steal my zagny, now."

"Okay, here's a factoid," she pointed out. "Most birds eat around half their weight every day. So in my case, I'm good for... well, for..."

Gabe made a production of looking her over from top to bottom. "I'd say fifty-five pounds, give or take," he said with a grin.

"Something like that," she muttered. They ate their lunch in companionable silence, with Gabe, despite his earlier teasing, actually feeding Dani a large bite of lasagna from his own fork.

"What's your expert opinion?" he asked, his eyes glued to her lips as she took the morsel off the fork. "Granted, it's not as rich and satisfying as yours." Distracted by him, Dani paused with her lips still around the fork and Gabe playfully tugged it away. "You must like it," he said.

"It's...it's fine," Dani stammered, completely undone by Gabe's dark-as-sin eyes. "Really. I like it very much."

"I'm glad," Gabe murmured, and she didn't think he was talking about the food. He did break off a hunk of bread, however, and offered it to her. Once again they ate in silence and she savored both the bread and the moment. Once they'd finished, Gabe gathered the remains of the meal, tossed it in a nearby trash can, and pulled Dani up from the bench. "And now for the best part," he said. "As of right now we are officially in search of Italy's most delicious gelato."

"Oh," Dani said, her eyes wistful. Gabe immediately saw the change in her expression. "What's the matter, bella? What's wrong?"

"Nothing. Sorry." She attempted a smile. "It's just that my babbo would take me to get gelato when I was a little girl...and he always said it was the best gelato in all of Italy."

"Well, in honor of your babbo, then," Gabe said, wrapping his arm around her shoulder, "let's find the place your dad called the best of the best."

It was ridiculous, he realized, but strolling down the ancient streets of Verona with his arm around Daniela reminded Gabe of a sappy song from *The Sound of Music*, which he'd been forced to watch with a girlfriend—whose name he couldn't even remember—one Friday night when he was still in high school. It was the scene where the Captain von Trapp dude finally makes his move on Maria and they sing a duet, something about "I must have done something good." Because right then Gabe felt like he was the luckiest guy in the world. Dani, who'd gone through something so horrible she couldn't even talk about it, hadn't rejected him outright, even though he'd given her no good reason to trust him. She must know how much he wanted to touch her, and when he couldn't stand it anymore, she'd put up with it. And those kisses last night—they had blown him away. So yeah, he must have done something good, at least once.

Finding the gelateria that Dani thought she'd gone to as a kid, they'd both gotten cones and wandered back toward the Arena, Verona's most important monument. It was a Roman amphitheater that at one time had held thirty thousand spectators for God knew what kinds of horrific events. It had incredible acoustics and these days it was used for concerts and a world-famous summer opera festival. They walked by one of the side entrances, which was open. Men were bringing in what looked like portable sound equipment.

"Shall we go in?" he asked.

"Why not?" Dani said. "Lead the way."

They scooted by the technicians and made their way to the back of the Arena, opposite the stage. Gabe began to climb the stone steps, stopping about halfway up and taking a seat. "I remember coming here once with my mother when I was about seven or eight," he said. "My mother loved opera and my father hated it, so she brought me instead. We couldn't afford those padded seats down there, so we sat up here. I remember when everyone began to light the candles at twilight. It was pretty awesome as I recall."

"I came here once or twice myself," Dani said. "We were stuck in those seats you were talking about. I would much rather have sat up here. And yes, when the candles began to flicker, it was magical." They sat there, soaking up the atmosphere for several moments. Dani broke the silence. "Tell me, what was it like to have to leave your mother like that?"

Gabe took his time before answering. He gently took Dani's hand and intertwined their fingers. He was willing to talk about it, but he wanted something to hold on to.

"I didn't believe it was happening at first. My mom had always seemed healthy, but then she began to have problems with balance, and little things like tripping and problems getting dressed. Her speech began to slur and I remember my father, asshole that he was, actually screaming at her, accusing her of drinking. She went to the doctor but it took a while to diagnose her with ALS because she was so young."

"I vaguely recall when your mother came to live at La Tana. She was in the room next to Fausta and Agnese. I think Fausta's husband had died by then. Sometimes Agnese would take me to visit her. I remember she was beautiful. She had long black hair that Fausta made sure was always shiny and clean. And she had enormous eyes that smiled when we came into the room. She was happy to have us play near her bed. I didn't think then how lonely she must have been. I'm so sorry, Gabriele."

Gabe rubbed his thumb gently across the back of her hand. "What's a young kid supposed to know about that sort of thing? I'm just glad you were able to bring her a little bit of happiness now and then." He paused to look out across the Arena, a sharp pain slicing through his heart. "I wish I could have."

"You said your dad and mom decided *together* that you and your dad should go to America. So that's important to keep in mind. You mom wanted that to happen."

"Yeah, well, that didn't make it any less painful, for me at least. My old man and I had never gotten along. I think he figured I was a bit of a mama's boy, because I wasn't into contact sports—and I don't mean soccer. He liked to fight, and looked for any excuse to do it." Gabe laughed bitterly. "He would have been real proud of me later on, though. If only he hadn't gotten himself snuffed."

"How awful! What happened?"

"I never found out exactly, and the police never cracked the case either, although let's face it, it wasn't a high priority for them. We lived in a rough part of Staten Island and I'm pretty sure he decided he could make more money on the wrong side of the law. I didn't see him much. My uncle—my dad's brother—had sponsored us, so I spent a lot of time with him and my cousins. I was thirteen when my dad died."

Dani's eyes welled up and Gabe gently brushed her tears away. "You're a regular crybaby, you know that?"

"*Mi dispiace*, signore," she said. "So...thirteen's got to be a tough age to lose your dad, much less be stuck in a foreign country."

Gabe shrugged. "It wasn't so bad. I'd picked up English quickly and by then I'd grown a bit physically. Soon I became the spittin' image of my old man, at least when it came to fighting. So it didn't take long for kids to stop calling me 'Little Orphan Gabie.'"

"Oh my, your uncle must have wondered what he'd gotten himself into."

Gabe grinned. "Nah, my Uncle Tony and Aunt Linda were used to hardscrabble kids like me. The neighborhood was also tight—lots of folks from the proverbial 'old country.' I used to hang out with them on the weekends to make sure I kept up with my Italian. But what really saved me, I think, was my uncle's buddy Ronny Splain. He was a local police sergeant who sort of took me under his wing."

Now it was Dani's turn to grin. "Something tells me this was a case of 'keep your friends close and your enemies closer.'"

"You've got that right. Sergeant Splain used to let me help out at the precinct. It was probably against the rules or something, but he did it anyway. And it took. After I got out of the service I went back to school in law enforcement, and you know the rest of the story."

Dani covered their clasped hands with her own. "And you never saw your mom again. Why?" she asked softly.

"I meant to," he said. "I had picked up the odd job here and there after high school and saved just about enough to fly back here, but then my cousin Rico ran into some trouble with his car and needed a loan, so I told myself I'd put it off a year or so. Then

I joined the Army and figured I'd take my first leave and visit her. But it didn't happen."

"She passed away?"

The feelings rushed over him in a wave: regret, longing, sadness, relief knowing his mom no longer suffered…so many feelings. He could only nod.

"Well, she adored you and knew you loved her. I can tell you that."

Gabe looked at her. "How so?"

"There were photos of a little boy with dark hair on the walls. And hand-drawn pictures, too. I think one of them was a horse, and I remember one of those turkeys you make by tracing your handprint. And there was a stack of letters by her bed."

"I hated writing letters," Gabe said, "but I did like to draw. I wondered why my Aunt Linda kept all of them."

"Now you know."

"I guess I owe her a thank-you."

Dani nodded. "A big bouquet of roses wouldn't be bad, either." She glanced at her watch." I think we'd better get going if we're going to meet Dante at the Piazza Bra at four."

"Yes, ma'am," Gabe said.

They made their way back down the Arena steps and headed in the direction of the piazza. Suddenly Dani stopped and reached into her purse. "Shoot, I almost forgot to tell you. I found a connection between all those companies listed in the accounts receivable spreadsheets."

"Yeah? What's the story?"

She shrugged. "They're all part of some holding company, I think. The Azure Consortium. Some places it's listed as Consorzio Azurro. Should we mention it to Dante?"

"No, let's feel him out a bit first. See how he reacts to the idea of the merger and the HR problems. Okay?"

"You're the expert," she said.

"I could say the same about you," he said, stuffing the list in his pocket. "And Daniela?"

She stopped at the tone of his voice. "Yes?"

He raised her hand—the one he'd been holding off and on during their lunch—and kissed it, looking directly at her, hoping to let her know what was happening in his heart. "Thank you for a most enjoyable time."

She swallowed, caught by his penetrating gaze. "Um, thank you too."

He leaned in to kiss her, but she looked over his shoulder and stepped back. Gabe turned and saw that Dante had spotted them. He was standing up and waving them over.

"*Alla prossima,*" he murmured. "Next time."

# CHAPTER TWELVE

—◆❀◆—

D ante kept a full schedule. Taking time off in the afternoon for socializing wasn't his usual style, but other than the funeral, it had been forever since he'd seen his cousin Daniela. He remembered the occasion well, for all the wrong reasons. He'd graduated from hotel management school in Switzerland, gotten an MBA from Yale, and returned to Verona to enter the family business. Stella d'Italia was hosting a large reception at La Tana for suppliers and major clients, and Santo had insisted he attend. Early in the evening he'd seen Dani, an adorable sprite at fifteen, trying to act like a diva. He recalled grinning at her because she looked like a little girl playing dress up. Unfortunately she'd grown up that night in a way no young girl should. The "incident," as Santo called it, would have been bad enough, but their grandfather Ciro had died that same night of a massive stroke.

But, the most memorable part of that evening had to do with someone else entirely. As if it were yesterday, Dante remembered seeing Agnese for the first time as a man sees a woman. She'd barely registered when he was younger—just another little girl running around the estate. But that night, even though she was only a year older than Dani, she was light years ahead of her in elegance and, in his humble opinion, beauty. They spoke briefly, but she was painfully shy and left way too soon. At sixteen she was far too young for his twenty-four years, but he recalled thinking, wistfully, *someday*. Now, twelve years later, he feared the someday of his dreams would never come.

He looked up from his musings at the cafe and saw Dani from halfway across the piazza walking with Gabriele, Agnese's cousin. Dani had grown into a lovely young woman, and it was obvious Gabriele wanted her. He didn't remember the guy from his childhood—of course he was a few years older, which is a lifetime when you're young. How had the two of them ended up together so far from Verona? He stood up to wave them over, quirking his lips when he saw he'd foiled an attempted kiss. *Welcome to the club, friend.*

"*Ciao*, Dani," Dante said, bussing her cheeks. He briefly shook Gabriele's hand. "*Buona sera*, Gabriele."

"Call me Gabe, please."

"*Va bene*." Dante signaled for a waiter and looked at the couple. "*Caffè?*"

"*Sì, per favore*," they both said.

While waiting for their drinks, they made small talk, speaking in English for Dani's sake. Yes, Dani loved living in the town of Little Eden and running a small inn. Yes, Gabe loved the area as well—it was a big change from his years as an LAPD cop. How had they gotten together? "Coincidence," Gabe said at the same time Dani blurted, "We're not together." Dante left that one alone. After that, Dani had quickly changed the topic and asked about Agnese, of all people.

Taken aback, Dante countered with, "What about her?"

"Well, I saw her earlier today and noticed she had a newspaper clipping of you on her bulletin board, and I thought—"

"She did?"

"Yes, she did. But when I asked her about it she got all flustered. It seemed like maybe you two had been an item at one time..."

"I wish," Dante muttered.

"Oh, then you're not?" Dani asked.

"Why not?" Gabe pressed. "Dani says my cousin's a knock-out, and she's available, so what's the hang-up?"

Dante could tell Gabe was trying to lighten things up, so he didn't give in to his impulse, which was to throttle the guy with all the pent-up frustration he'd been carrying around. Instead he said with a calmness he didn't feel, "Look, let's just say we're friends and leave it at that."

Gabe shrugged. "Whatever you say, man. Seems like a waste, that's all."

There was an awkward silence among the three of them. "Daniela, I'm sorry your father's gone," Dante finally offered. "I didn't see him all that often, but he was always kind and respectful to me. He was a good man, and a thoughtful one, despite the way he was often depicted in the press."

"I'm glad you think so. I don't think my father was the shallow playboy they made him out to be, either. I mean—" she paused to glance at Gabe, "—I learned recently that he had a close relationship with a woman who...whom he cared for very much. Perhaps you know her—she works at the Stella d'Italia Milano. Carla Rinaldi?"

"Carla Rinaldi? That's odd. Santo—at the reception, in fact—asked me to get in touch with her. He said he needed to discuss some personnel matters. She's the human resources director at that hotel. Or I should say, *was* the director. She quit without giving notice and we can't seem to locate her. I wonder...*mio Dio*, I hope she's all right. If they were really a couple, she must be shattered."

"Are you still looking for her?"

"No, I assumed it was moot, since she'd left the company. But in light of what you've told me, perhaps I should. I hope she has a support system, family nearby or something."

"Ah, well, maybe she's taking the time to mend a broken heart." Dani glanced again at Gabe, whose eyebrows raised slightly as he gave her an almost imperceptible nod.

*What's going on here?* Dante thought. *Why do I suddenly feel like I'm being tested?*

—·◆·◆·—

Dani felt something shift inside as she took Dante's hand across the table. She knew instinctively that she could trust this man. "Cousin, I'm glad we were able to meet someplace away from La Tana and the company headquarters." She took a deep breath before continuing. "You probably know my father left his estate to me, which means I am now in charge of voting his share of stock."

"That makes sense," Dante said. "But that shouldn't be of immediate concern, should it? I mean, Stella d'Italia has actually increased market share during this downturn, we have no impending capital expenditures—"

"Well, not according to Uncle Santo," she said.

Dante looked at Dani and Gabe, but Gabe sat expressionless. "What do you mean?"

"I mean our uncle didn't wait twenty-four hours after the funeral before putting pressure on me to vote my shares in favor of acquiring Alberghi Paradisi. He even offered me the plum job of running the new subsidiary."

Dante's jaw dropped. "Are you serious?"

"What the hell?" Gabe exclaimed simultaneously.

Dani gave her partner an apologetic look. "You heard me. He said he needs my votes because Nonna Stella won't budge, and he needs to know soon."

"What about my father's vote?" Dante clenched his hands. "Never mind. I already know. He'll vote with Santo no matter what. And after I told him…"

"Told him what?" Gabe asked.

"Told him the hotel deal wasn't worth the asking price, that it wasn't a good business model and wouldn't do anything except bring the Stella d'Italia brand down. I've been through the numbers. Nonna Stella is right."

"So just to be clear, you don't think it's a good idea," Dani said.

"That's right. In fact, it's a terrible idea. It's a bad investment, pure and simple. But my father…he's…oh, never mind. Look, you know the business. You should look at the numbers and see for yourself."

"That's exactly what I told Uncle Santo—that I needed time to check out the financials. But he seems to be in a bit of a hurry."

"Yeah, so much so that he'd bribe you with a dream job." Gabe's voice dripped with sarcasm. "Sorry, Dante, but your boss is a first class prick."

"He's been called worse, I can assure you."

The waiter brought their drinks and Dani paused to think of how her cousin must feel about all of this. "How long have you worked for the company, Dante? Ten years?"

"Try over a dozen."

"And it looks like you've risen pretty high up," Gabe said. "You must be good at what you do."

"Oh yes, I made it to chief lackey, all right." Dante's bitterness was unmistakable. "But despite both my training and experience, neither my uncle nor even my father trusts my judgment. I'm thinking it might be time for me to make a change, family business or not."

"Ah, there's one other thing," Dani said.

Dante looked at her skeptically. "I'm afraid to ask."

"Well, it's just that…we think there might be some, shall we say, 'irregularities' happening in the company."

"Jesus. Who is 'we'?"

"Well, Nonna Stella, for one, and—"

"The hell with it. I think we need to bring Dante into the loop," Gabe broke in.

Dante looked at the two of them. "This wasn't just a friendly little 'Hey, let's catch up with Cousin Dante over coffee' session, was it?"

Dani and Gabe slowly shook their heads. "We think there's some major shit going down in your company, and we needed to make sure you weren't part of it," Gabe said.

"Gabe's right. This goes way beyond an ill-advised acquisition. There could be extensive criminal activity involved. My father—"

Dani's voice broke and Gabe put his arm around her.

"How do you know this? You've been here—what? Three days?"

"I know it sounds crazy," Gabe said, "but we were approached, both of us, with information…credible information. I've talked with a good friend of mine—maybe you know him, Marco Clemente? He's with the state police and he's been helping me piece the story together, discreetly, of course."

"What makes you think you can trust me?" Dante asked.

Dani shored up her emotions and regarded him. "From your reactions, you're either a fantastic actor or you've been kept in the dark about all this stuff. Besides, call it woman's intuition, but I refuse to believe that Agnese could feel the way she does about a criminal."

Dante was about to refute her assumption about Agnese when Gabe interrupted.

"Let me sum it up, Dante. I read people pretty well. Back in the States I'm a detective, so it's part of my job. But just in case we got it wrong and you're dirty, remember this: if I find out you've ever done anything to hurt Daniela in any conceivable way, either directly or indirectly, I'll come after you and I'll see that you pay."

Dante and Gabe appeared to take each other's measure, and Dani liked what she saw. Dante was a decent man who wanted to do the right thing. He was the perfect man for Agnese if she could only see it. *Just like Gabe's the perfect man for me—if only I weren't so screwed up.*

"Tell me what you can," Dante said at last. "Let me see how I can help."

—·❖·—

An hour later Dante parted company with his cousin and her protector. They'd filled him in on the puzzle pieces they had so far gathered. His Uncle Mando murdered? Carla Rinaldi in hiding? It seemed unbelievable. Even more incredible was the idea that Stella d'Italia was somehow being used as a human trafficking conduit.

Yet something in the back of Dante's mind kept niggling at him. A thought. A feeling. A sense that something wasn't quite right had been percolating within him for more than a year. He'd never mentioned it to anybody because he'd never had anything of substance to point to. And was Santo in the middle of it all?

They all agreed it would be a bad idea for Dante to blow the whistle or instigate an obvious investigation, even within the confines of the company. Whoever was involved in this might panic, or worse yet, be so good at covering their tracks that they'd never get to the bottom of it. He could take some surreptitious steps, however. He'd at least drill down into the suspect income sources and see how many could be justified; see if he could establish a timeline of some kind. Maybe he'd find something they could use as evidence. And during his scheduled meeting with Santo to talk about Carla Rinaldi, he could probe a bit to see where his uncle was coming from. Perhaps it was all a big misunderstanding…or perhaps the man had something he was desperately trying to hide.

Dani and Gabe had gone back across the piazza to buy flowers; apparently they were headed over to Marco's for dinner… the same Marco who had lusted after Agnese and been rebuffed. *Grazie a Dio*. Dante pulled out his cell phone.

"Papa? I'd like to take you to dinner. Are you free? Good. I'll pick you up after mass." The one thing Dante could address openly was his father's complacency and weakness. It was time to lay his cards on the table once and for all.

—•✦✦•—

Dante waited impatiently by the steps for his father, whom he knew to be a creature of habit and admittedly not much imagination. Aldo Forcelli went to the six p.m. mass every day at Santa Maria Antica, which was an easy commute because he worked at the church as a lay minister. He had taken on several positions over the years, including sexton, lector, and altar server. These days he was performing the duties of Extraordinary Minister of Holy Communion, in which he served the Lord's Supper to housebound members of the parish. Dante knew it was the closest to ordained priesthood his father was ever going to get, and, not for the first time, he felt a twinge of guilt that his birth had kept his father from the calling he'd felt all his life.

By now the parishioners would be receiving the benediction; soon they'd exit the church, his father among them. Like clockwork, Aldo appeared.

"Dante," Aldo greeted him, his arms widening for a hug.

Dante, who towered over his father, kissed him dutifully on both cheeks. "Come, I told Mauricio to hold a table for us."

The two walked along the Corso Sant'Anastasia for several blocks in silence before turning onto a side street and entering the trattoria. They had had relaxing dinners there many times over the years, but tonight Dante had no stomach for idle talk. Over a plate of pasta and a glass of wine, he got down to business.

"Earlier today I met Dani and her friend in the piazza. She tells me that Santo is already pressuring her to vote her shares in favor of acquiring Alberghi Paradisi. Grandmother must have said no, which means that you have said yes, and he needs Dani's assent to bring him over the top. Why are you going along with him, Papa? We had this conversation weeks ago. It's not a good business decision."

Aldo began to scratch the back of his neck; the action caused Dante to twitch slightly in commiseration. His father had suffered from psoriasis for years and Dante had read that stress can cause the skin condition to flare up. Maybe the hotel deal was the cause of his father's latest discomfort.

"I know we spoke about it, but you must understand, Santo is the head of Stella d'Italia. He's been making decisions for the family business for the past twenty-five years, even before our papa passed away. Both Mando and I trust him to know what is right."

"But Mando is dead, and in his place is a woman who knows a lot more about the hotel business than her father ever did. And excuse me, but you have a son who was trained at Les Roches, of all places. And at Yale. I know this business, and I know a good opportunity from a bad one. I've poured my heart and soul into this company for over a decade, and still you people don't trust me."

Dante saw his father wince.

"'You people'?" Aldo asked quietly. "You're part of this family, too, Dante."

"Am I? My name isn't Forcelli, it's Trevisan. And because of that, I'll never be a true member of the family, at least not in Santo's eyes." Anger began to build. "Did you ever notice that I never refer to Santo as 'uncle'? It's because he asked me not to refer to him as such…ever."

"Perhaps to keep it more professional at work," Aldo offered.

Dante looked at him. "No, Papa. I was fourteen at the time."

He watched as his father began to scratch more forcefully. Aldo dipped a corner of his napkin in a glass of water and pressed it to his skin. He breathed deeply, as if to calm himself. "I would have married your mother," he began, "but she…she had to move overseas. She left you in my care and there was nothing I could do."

Dante slapped his hand on the table. "*Enough.* I will not take that any more from you."

"What do you mean? Take what from me?"

"That farce about my mother giving birth and then leaving me with you. You must truly think I'm an idiot if you think I don't know who my actual mother is."

Aldo froze, his eyebrows lifted. He began to scratch even harder and Dante reached over to stop his father's manic behavior. "It's all right," Dante said.

His father wasn't ready to give up the charade. "Who..." he stopped. Swallowed. "Who do you think your mother is?"

"Every good Catholic boy knows that the faithful Sisters of the Church had maiden names before they married Christ. The venerable abbess of the Convent of Our Holy Sisters of Rectitude wasn't always Maria Annunciata, was she?"

Aldo looked down at the table, as if ashamed. He shook his head.

"No," Dante said. "Once she was the young and innocent, and as I understand it, very pretty and very religious Luisa Trevisan. That is, until she made the mistake of spreading her legs for—"

Dante was cut short by a powerful slap across his face. "Don't you *ever* talk about Mother Maria that way again," Aldo hissed. "She is a veritable saint compared to us."

Dante stared at Aldo as he rubbed his jaw. "I believe that's the most gutsy thing I've ever seen you do, Father. I applaud you. But you're wrong. The abbess—my mother—is as human as the rest of us. She's intelligent, shrewd, and loving. And she can be bossy and even short-tempered at times. I've worked with her for years. I know her. And I know she made a mistake and slept with a young man before she was married, and that mistake turned out to be me."

"No, you are wrong," Aldo said fiercely. "You may have been unintended, but you were never a mistake. Never. You have been the joy of our lives. You have given us a reason to stay within each other's sphere. Our devotion to you is second only to our devotion to Christ. And Christ granted us the miracle of never having to choose between you and Him. If you believe nothing else, you must believe that."

"The fact remains," Dante continued, "that my illegitimacy has stifled my career with Stella d'Italia, and I'm tired of it." He ran his hands through his hair. "Hell, it's ruined my personal life, too."

"What do you mean?" his father asked. "Your parents' marital status has nothing to do with who you are. And you are good enough for anybody."

Dante let out a long breath. "Apparently not good enough for Agnese," he said.

His father looked at him sharply. "What about you and Agnese?"

Dante waved his hand. "She likes me, I believe, but she is unwilling to take our acquaintance any further." He frowned. It was embarrassing even to be talking about this, as if he were a heartsick teenager handling his first crush. He expected his father to respond in his usual gentle manner, but instead he saw signs of hidden anguish on the older man's face.

"Agnese is a beautiful young woman and a sensible one, now that she is away from her mother," his father said. "You must be patient. I...I think she will come around."

"You sound as if you know something special about her, Papa. Fill me in. Please."

His father shook his head. "It is not for me to say."

"But—"

"I said no!"

Dante stared at his father, who looked on the verge of coming unhinged. What was he hiding?

Aldo, still visibly upset, took a drink of his wine. "As for the proposed merger," he said, "I want you to know I do believe you when you say it shouldn't happen. I find it...difficult...to confront Santo, but I will talk to him. I promise you that."

Much was left unsaid, but at least in the matter of the vote, Dante felt something uncoil inside. "Thank you, Papa."

Aldo raised his glass. "To family," he said.

"Right," Dante said, his expression tight. "To family."

Later, while drinking grappa on his balcony overlooking the Adige River, Dante began to brood about what his father had said concerning Agnese—or rather what he hadn't said. He'd also drunk just enough of the brandy to give him the courage to do what he'd been contemplating ever since dinner. He took a cab to the Convent of Our Holy Sisters of Rectitude and sat down on the wrought iron bench situated just outside the convent's gate. Knowing that when she wasn't teaching, Agnese worked most evenings in her lab, he took a chance and texted her:

I'm sitting on the bench outside the convent and need to see you.

I won't leave until you come out and talk to me.

Then he waited.

And waited.

It grew dark and still he waited. After a while the adrenaline that had carried him to the bench began to drain away, and he fell into a light sleep. When he awoke, Agnese was sitting calmly next to him. Even though it wasn't a particularly cold evening, she had brought a blanket and it covered both their laps. She wore a deep-red cap over her hair and she smelled of lemon and lavender.

"You showed up," he said, his heart beginning to thump joyfully in his chest.

"You said you needed to talk to me, so here I am."

He heaved a sigh. Why was she the only one he felt comfortable talking with? Because she just *was*. "Tonight I told my father I knew who my mother was."

Agnese said nothing.

He waited for her to speak, until it dawned on him what her silence meant. "You know, don't you?"

She looked at him for a long moment before nodding. "You are the luckiest man in the world. She is everything a mother should be, and more. I love the abbess with all my heart."

He paused to collect himself, afraid he would lose it and start whimpering. His heart was so close to the surface and ready to burst. Could she hear it pounding? It felt thunderous in his chest. His whole life long he'd feared the revelation of his birth, and the one person he cared about knowing more than any other had just told him it was all right, that he was *lucky*.

But he had more to confess. "I have tried not to let my...lack of legitimacy...get in the way, but it has. At Stella d'Italia and... and elsewhere."

"Those who would hold your parentage against you are fools, and they aren't worth your time, not in the slightest." She said it without hesitation.

"Do you really believe that?"

Her lips softened in a gentle curve. "I really do. I always have."

He took a moment to steel himself for the worst. "Agnese, you care for me. I know you do. I can feel it in every pore of my being. Yet you tell me we can't be together because of who we are. If my pedigree isn't an issue, what is holding you back? Is it something about the person you are? Because if it is, I can assure you that..."

He paused, stunned, as the beacon that lit her from within slowly flickered away, leaving a cold, empty shell. She began to reel her loveliness in, as if she had showed him her treasures and now it was time to wrap them up and put them away. She would not look at him, but when he turned her face to his, she wore a guarded expression that masked the intense emotion beneath. He decided to meet it head on.

"There is something about you my father refuses to talk about. I think it causes you great pain. What is it?"

"It's none of your business," she said, her tone flat and businesslike. She stood up, brushing off her sweater. "Listen. I know you handle the accounting for the convent and that you visit the abbess frequently. It's inevitable that as long as I am here, our paths will occasionally cross. But I think that from now on it would be best if those meetings were kept to the confines of the convent."

The problem with finally speaking the truth was that you could go too far and cross the line. Dante couldn't help the frustration that seeped out. "You talk about the confines of the convent. Is that where you intend to spend the rest of your life? Trapped in there, mixing potions for others to enjoy while you sit and grow old in your little laboratory? My God, Agnese, you were no more meant to be a nun than the man in the moon."

Agnese laughed bitterly. "A nun? You're right. I am certainly no nun." She unlocked the gate as she had the other night after class. "Please don't seek me out again, Dante. Ever."

Dante watched her go and belatedly noticed that she'd left the blanket for him. He leaned back on the bench and wrapped the soft covering around himself, letting the tears spill over his eyelids at last.

# CHAPTER THIRTEEN

—⋅✦⋅✦⋅—

It was nine p.m. and Santo was just settling in to his "massage therapy" appointment. His favorite masseuse, Brigitta, worked at the Stella d'Italia Verona but came to his office regularly to "work out the kinks." Brigitta was in her twenties but looked about seventeen. Deep tissue massage was just the beginning of her skills.

Few people remained in the company offices at such a late hour. He'd kept Cristina late, as usual, but even she was about to head home for the night. Which is why it surprised him to hear her through the intercom.

"Signore, your brother is here to see you."

For a moment Santo wondered which brother it was—until he realized he had only one brother left. A pity. "Tell him I am occupied."

There was a moment of silence, then, "He says it's very important. He—"

The intercom cut off and the door to Santo's office swung open. Aldo stood in the doorway while Cristina sent Santo a beseeching look. "I tried to tell him, signore."

Barging in was simply not Aldo's style; it must be important. "Wait outside," Santo said to the two women.

The masseuse gathered her clothing and squeezed past Aldo with a soft, "Excuse me." Santo calmly sat up, hopped off the portable table and wrapped a towel around his waist.

Aldo pointed to the door. "Did your secretary do something to her hair? She looks quite different. Reminds me of someone."

"I'm going to assume you didn't interrupt me at this hour just to ask me that," Santo said. "What is so important that it couldn't wait until I returned to La Tana?" He walked over to his desk and reached into his humidor for a Cuban, clipping it nonchalantly. He offered one to his brother, knowing Aldo would decline because he'd never smoked a day in his life, and knowing it irked his brother that Santo invariably offered anyway.

"I'm happy to wait for you to get dressed," Aldo said.

"I wouldn't dream of wasting your time," Santo rejoined. "Have a seat."

Aldo sat ramrod straight in the chair, his hands clasped in apparent supplication. He was mild-mannered and gutless, always willing to go along with whatever Santo decreed, even though at two years older than Santo, *he* was the titular head of the family. Ciro, their father, had picked up on Aldo's weakness immediately and exploited it whenever he got a chance.

"Here's the little altar boy," he'd say, or, "You came out two years too early. Santo should be your big brother, not the other way around."

Looking at him now, Santo wondered which came first, his brother's infatuation with Christ or his humiliation at allowing himself to be bullied by his own flesh and blood. Once, their father had blistered both of them verbally for some minor transgression. Santo had given it right back to the old man and gotten slapped for his efforts. Aldo had left the room and disappeared. Santo later found him in La Tana's private chapel, mumbling a prayer: *But the Lord has become my stronghold and my God the rock of my refuge. He will repay them for the iniquity and wipe them out for their wickedness.*

Wickedness. Santo had always loved the sound of that word.

"I want to talk to you about the Alberghi Paradisi acquisition," Aldo began, his voice surprisingly firm. "I have talked to Dante at length about it and he feels it is a bad investment for Stella d'Italia."

Santo said nothing. He puffed thoughtfully on his cigar and gazed at Aldo. "This is what you pulled me off the table to say?"

"Therefore I choose not to vote for the purchase," Aldo continued. He paused, apparently waiting for Santo to react. "Well?" he finally asked. "Have you nothing to say?"

Santo tapped his cigar and sat back in his chair. It was leather, beautifully upholstered, and made no sound as he rocked slightly back and forth. "You will vote your shares with mine," he said, "as you have always done, because that is the way we do things."

"Listen," Aldo said, "I don't think you understand—"

"No, my dear brother. It is you who doesn't understand. Your son merely works for Stella d'Italia. He does not own it. He does not run it."

"He will own it, at least part of it, when I give him my shares," Aldo said. "I don't want to resort to extreme measures, but if I have to, I will."

Santo puffed indolently on his cigar. His movements were fluid and he took his time before responding. But when he did, he looked directly at Aldo, his eyes blazing with carefully banked rage. "Shall we talk of extreme measures, Aldo? How about this headline for *L'Arena*: 'Bastard son of luxury hotel owner caught embezzling funds from company; admits mother was whore before becoming abbess of local convent school.'" He found pleasure in the stunned look on Aldo's face.

"You would do something as vile as that?" Aldo choked out.

"Without blinking an eye," Santo said. "Now listen carefully, for I am only going to say this once. I did not build Stella d'Italia into a five-star brand just to turn it over to a bastard nephew who just happens to be able to read a profit and loss statement." He rose. "Now, I really must get back to my massage. You know the way out."

Aldo rose, a look of pure hatred on his face—a look Santo had never seen on him before. "The only bastard in this company is the head of it," Aldo spat.

"As you wish," Santo said. "And brother, don't cross me on this. I have asked Daniela to head the new division, but she is perfectly capable of taking over Dante's position as well. And she is *family*."

After Aldo left, Santo found himself contemplating Aldo's prayer of so long ago. *He will repay them for the iniquity.* Payback came in all forms, didn't it? Perhaps God had meted out his own divine justice by blessing Aldo with a strapping, intelligent son while Santo's only issue had been a sick weakling with so many health problems he'd died before he even became a man. Suddenly his cigar tasted fetid and he stubbed it out angrily. *Soon I will remedy that,* he thought with cold determination, while thoughts of Dani swam in his head.

He pressed his intercom. "Cristina, tell Brigitta I am ready for her now."

"You will love this *Recioto*. It goes extremely well with Gina's *torta*," Marco said, uncorking yet another bottle. Dani smiled, shaking her head even as she held out her glass for the sweet wine. The evening with the Clementes had turned out to be a total delight. The young detective and his wife accepted Dani and Gabe into their modest home as if they'd been friends forever—which of course, Gabe and Marco had been. But Marco's wife had been equally warm and inviting, so much so that it took no time at all to feel completely at ease. Dani was surprised not only by how fluent Gabe was, but how her own Italian had finally started to kick in, even after a dozen years of speaking only English. From traditional antipasto through a *grigliata mista*—barbequed pork and chicken served with grilled vegetables and polenta—the wine and the laughter had flowed readily. After the first couple glasses, Dani hadn't even minded when her hosts started talking so fast that she couldn't always make out what they were saying.

Gina Clemente was blond, buxom, and beautiful. It was obvious by the way Marco found any opportunity to touch her that he adored her as well as the chubby eight-month-old, red-headed son they had created out of their love for each other. Earlier in the evening, Gabe had wasted no time in picking little Eduardo up, tossing him in the air, and then bussing him soundly on his belly when he caught him. Two or three times and little Eddie announced his approval with squeals of delight. Dani had wanted to call out "Be careful!" but was glad she didn't, because it was immediately apparent that Gabe knew exactly what he was doing.

"Ah, Gabriele, you are as bad as Marco," Gina admonished with a smile. "For that, you must calm him down when it is time for bed."

Gabe held the baby up and looked him directly in the eye. "We have been challenged, my little man. And we will meet that challenge, no?" Eddie gurgled and grabbed Gabe's nose in response. Gabe looked at Dani and grinned. "Uh oh," he said.

*Is there anything sexier than a gorgeous hunk of a man holding a baby?* Dani gazed at Gabe while sipping from the wine glass that had been continually filled all evening. She held his eyes for an instant and an overwhelming sense came over her, that he was thinking the same thing she was. *We can make one of those. We* should *make one of those.* She shook her head. That was ridiculous. Preposterous. Except that a little thought made its way to the forefront of her mind: *Is it? Is it really so impossible?* She dared not think like that…should she?

A little while later, Gabe was indeed dispatched to put Eddie down for the night. Marco volunteered to show him the ropes and give him moral support. While they were gone, Gina wasted no time before extolling Gabe's virtues.

"Marco has known Gabe all his life, and says he's the salt of the earth," she said. "Did you see how good he is with Eddie? It's obvious he likes kids…and it's obvious he's head over heels for you."

Out of habit, Dani attempted to set the record straight. "No, we're just friends. Really."

"Uh huh, right. So the way he stays close to you and is always seeing to your comfort and keeping your body close to his—that's all just friendship, you say?"

"Well, he's…affectionate," Dani said.

Gina laughed and tilted her glass toward Dani in a mock toast. "Well here's to friendship and *affection* then. May Marco always feel that way toward me! Come, I will get dessert, and you can tell me what you thought of tonight's meal. Gabe says you are a master chef. Maybe you can give me some pointers."

Once in the kitchen, Dani couldn't help but set Gina straight, and the young woman let out a sigh of relief. "I could tell from the beginning you were a lovely person," she said. "All I really worried about was whether or not you'd like my cooking. Thank you for clearing that up."

"Well, you can see you have nothing to worry about on that score. Only, don't tell Gabe, okay? I have never lied to him, but I've never exactly told him everything. And my chef and his wife seem to think it's funny, so I have let them run with it. Now I'm kind of worried about what he'll do when he finds out."

"Finds out what? That you can't boil water? Dani, the way that man looks at you, that is going to be the least of your problems." As Gina spoke she sliced pieces of delicate, mouthwatering apple cake and put them on a tray along with a pot of espresso and four tiny cups. Dani followed her back to the living room where Gabe and Marco were in the midst of what seemed to be an intense conversation. As the women approached, the men stopped talking. Gabe casually folded a piece of paper that Marco had given him and put it in his jacket pocket. He then leaned back and patted the seat next to him.

"So, Dani, I hope you jotted down the recipes from dinner tonight. I bet the mixed grill will be a real winner back home."

*Back home.* That sounded wonderful. Especially since the way Gabe said it implied he considered it his home, too. She was beginning to feel a flush throughout her body and she thought at first it was too much wine. But then she realized the truth: *she wanted him.* She almost laughed out loud at the sensation—one she never thought she'd experience in her lifetime. "Uh, yes, Gina was very helpful. She's, um…she's a good cook."

"Good?" Marco said, putting his arm around his wife's waist and giving her a smacking kiss. "She's not just good. She's incredible…in every way."

"Ah Marco, cut Dani some slack. Remember, she's in a league by herself when it comes to cooking." He put his own arm around her and squeezed. "Right, Daniela?"

Dani looked at Gina, who raised her eyebrows and smiled. "I suppose I am," she said.

The conversation turned to exclamations over the dessert, which turned out to be an old recipe handed down from Gina's grandmother. Dani, who tried to limit her sweets to the occasional gelato, found herself sighing with pleasure as she closed her eyes and let the buttery, sugary apple confection melt in her mouth. When she finally refocused, she caught Gabe looking at her lips. He looked up and their eyes held.

"Did you ever do this in the States?" Marco asked.

It took Dani a few seconds to shift her thoughts from "doing something" with Gabe. "I'm sorry. Do what?"

"Little rinsers." He had served espresso with sugar and was pouring a few drops of grappa into their nearly empty cups. "It's a tradition here in Veneto."

"Oh yeah, I used to indulge once in a while with my uncle and his friends," Gabe said. "Sometimes the old traditions are the best." He winked at Dani. "Bottoms up."

The four friends spent another hour in good-hearted conversation. They talked about Verona, the town they'd all grown up in, and how it had changed over the past several years. Dani enjoyed the banter but eventually felt herself coming down from the rush of the caffeine and feeling the effects of so much alcohol. Snuggling up to Gabe, it was so tempting to put her head on his shoulder, close her eyes, and listen to the singsong cadence of her native tongue. Gabe didn't seem to mind and it felt so wonderful…

"I think it's time to get this party girl back to La Tana," Gabe said, putting his hand lightly on her thigh to wake her up. "Come on, sweetheart. Let's let these good folks have their beauty sleep."

It was past midnight when they made their farewells. Gina hugged Dani and whispered "Your secret's safe with me," and Dani hugged her back, not sure whether Gina meant the fact that Dani couldn't cook, or her lust for Gabe. They made plans to get together again during Dani and Gabe's stay.

"I'll be in touch," Gabe said to Marco and the two exchanged looks that Dani couldn't decipher.

Dani didn't mind it a bit when Gabe put his arm around her as they waited outside to hail a taxi. It was dark, yet she felt safe. So safe. And yet excited, too. An idea kept running across the stage of her brain: "Why not tonight? Why not tonight?" Dani's mind wasn't sure what it meant, but her body certainly did.

— ✦✦✦ —

"Remind me to monitor your intake, sunshine," Gabe muttered an hour later. They'd gotten back to La Tana and Fausta had grudgingly let them in. Dani was practically asleep on her feet. "Hey, you can always give us a key," he'd joked, but his aunt hadn't said a word.

Once in their suite, Dani had perked up enough that Gabe could point her in the direction of her bedroom. He reluctantly bid her good night. *God she was beautiful.* Perfectly proportioned and so graceful, although she didn't put on airs *at all*. He'd spent the entire evening fighting the impulse to touch her everywhere, even in places that demanded privacy at the very least. He'd known instinctively she'd get along great with Marco and Gina, and she hadn't disappointed him.

Man, she was killing him. He rubbed the back of his neck to rid himself of the knot he felt starting to form. Both tired and wired, he couldn't tell which was more to blame, the booze or the stress of keeping his desire in check. He reached into the small refrigerator for a beer before realizing he was already half pickled, so he opted for water instead. Damn, he was thirsty. Drinking half the bottle before he'd even pulled his shirt out of his slacks, he sat down to focus on the investigation. Maybe *that* would keep his libido where it belonged. He pulled out the report that Marco had given him earlier that evening.

"I think we're on to something," Marco had told him quietly. "We found a match."

He was just beginning to scan the document when the bedroom door opened and Dani appeared. Her hair was tousled and she walked a bit uncertainly, like she was slogging through mud in high heels, even though she was barefoot. She wore a short, ivory-colored cover-up of some kind and she looked nervous.

"I'm ready," she said.

He looked at her quizzically. "Ready for what, bella?"

"For us...you know." He didn't have a chance to reply before she tottered up to him and threw her slender arms around his neck, locking her lips with his.

After his initial shock, Gabe took a moment to enjoy the feel of Dani's curves against him. Despite all the alcohol he'd consumed, his body still reacted immediately, hardening in response to her softness. She felt so damn decadent—like falling into the most luxurious bed when you've been sleeping on the floor all your life. And oh, did she smell good, like some small, sweet flower. He smiled inwardly at her earnest attempt at seduction, and cursed his inner cop—the prig who wouldn't let him take advantage of her while she was intoxicated.

Reluctantly he took her by the upper arms and peeled her away from his body. "Uh, sweetheart, I don't think this is a good thing to be doing…"

"What?" she asked, her voice soft and earnest. "Don't I measure up to your other women friends? Don't I? Just a little?" She stepped back and before he could stop her, she dropped the cover-up, revealing a perfect—and perfectly naked—female form encased in a five-foot-two-inch frame. Her breasts were full, high, cream-colored mounds with luscious pink nipples. Her waist was small and her hips slightly flared. She was biting her full lower lip, practically screaming for his approval.

An image flashed before him of Dani pregnant. She was ripe and luscious—the epitome of Woman. Instead of cooling him off, the thought of her big with child—*his* child—only made him hotter, and made what he had to do all the more difficult. He looked at her a long time, so long that he could see uncertainty, followed by embarrassment, overtake her. He reached down and picked up the wrap, putting it around her shoulders.

"I'm sorry," she mumbled. "I thought…" She turned to go, but Gabe took her shoulders and turned her back toward him.

"If you think for one second that I don't want to bury myself in you right now, you are sadly mistaken," he said roughly. He pulled her wrap off her shoulders once again, but only so that it imprisoned her arms, pressing her breasts together and lifting them. With his right hand he pushed the wrap beneath her breast, raising it even higher so that it spilled out of its cover and he could suckle it. Dani let out a gasp, automatically pressing herself against him. After a minute, Gabe realized he'd better stop before his body took over completely.

"When you and I make love, I am going to be all over you," he rasped. "You are going to feel me everywhere and know when I've taken you higher than you've ever been before." He tore himself away and covered her back up. "And the next morning, you're going to remember everything I did to you and want me to do it all over again. Count on it. Now go to bed."

"But—"

"Please," he said firmly, turning her around and practically pushing her back into the bedroom. It took several minutes after her door shut for Gabe's upper brain to start functioning again. "Keep your eye on the prize," he repeated like a mantra. "Keep your eye on the prize." The prize, in this case, was a Dani who felt no regrets about whatever physical gymnastics they might partake in together. He'd waited this long for the timing to be right; he could wait a little longer, even though it was damn near going to kill him.

A half hour later he'd sobered up enough to focus on transferring details from Marco's report to his own little notebook. Turns out a name from the hotel reservations list, Tino Abruzzo, had matched fingerprints uncovered at the scene, but interviews with the boat owner apparently showed no nexus between Abruzzo and the racing syndicate.

He was sitting on the sofa, working by the light of a small table lamp, when the light went out, pitching him into darkness. The small refrigerator stopped humming. The air from the suite's ventilations system stopped circulating.

There was no sound at all.

He opened the door to see if the sconces leading to their suite had been affected. All of them were out. It was completely black. "Must be a circuit," he murmured, wondering if the old house still used fuses. He made his way back to the daybed to stretch out and wait for a staff member—Fausta, no doubt—to deal with it. Worst case, he figured he could get back to his notes in the morning.

He must have nodded off because the light from the lamp woke him. Just as he remembered where he was, he heard a sound from somewhere down the hall.

Someone was screaming.

# CHAPTER FOURTEEN

---✦---

G abe's first thought was to make sure Dani was safe. He ran
into the bedroom and found her lying on her stomach, sleeping soundly, one arm stretched overhead and the other tucked
under her chin; neither the loss of power nor the muted screams
had disturbed her one bit. At that moment, nothing would have
suited him better than to crawl under those covers and wrap himself around her; instead he whispered *"Grazie a Dio"* and hurried
back into the hallway, donning his jacket and sticking the snub-nosed pistol into his pocket on the way.

He came to the next wing and had just turned the corner
when he saw Santo and a man dressed in a suit running up from
the opposite end of the corridor. The man stopped at a set of double doors, much like the ones to Gabe and Dani's suite, stumbling
by a chair that had been left in the corridor. He quickly opened
the door and headed inside.

"What is wrong?" Santo called out sharply to Gabe in Italian.
"What's happened?"

"Hell if I know. I heard a scream and came to check it out." Santo stalked into the suite and Gabe followed. The room was dimly lit and a young woman in a nurse's uniform was leaning over a hospital bed, desperately performing mouth to mouth resuscitation on a woman whom Gabe belatedly realized was Santo's chronically ill wife, Ornella. It was obvious by the way the gaunt woman stared unwaveringly at the ceiling that she was well and truly dead. The man in the suit came up to the nurse and whispered something in her ear, motioning for her to stop. She looked up to see Santo and began crying.

"Signor Forcelli. I am so sorry. I don't know what to say. All was well with Mrs. Forcelli and I was sleeping in the bed in the alcove. I didn't even notice that the electricity had gone out. I didn't realize that the ventilator was not working. I am so sorry, signore. So very sorry."

Gabe noticed the nurse seemed as distraught over displeasing Santo as she did over the fact that her patient had died. Santo's expression was rigid. He shot Gabe a look that said, distinctly, *What are you still doing here?* "Well, there is nothing more we can do tonight," Santo announced. "I will call the doctor and have him come and make the pronouncement." With that he turned and left the room.

"Man, that is one cold fish," the man in the suit remarked.

"Excuse me," Gabe said, "but what are you...who—"

"Antonio Bonafacio of Veneto Security Systems, at your service," the man said, and bowed slightly.

"Security? I don't understand."

The man glanced at the nurse, who was still distraught over Signora Forcelli's death. "It's all right, Claudia. You are not to blame." He motioned to Gabe to join him near the door. "You see, the patient, Signora Forcelli…she didn't feel safe," the guard explained. "She hired our firm to keep a vigil outside her door, twenty-four hours a day. My shift started four hours ago." He shrugged. "It is a living…although it's apparent this assignment is over."

Gabe was still confused. "So if you're security for his wife, why were you with Signor Forcelli?"

"The lights went out and he asked if I would come with him while he went to check the circuit breakers. He seemed agitated. Apparently he feels somewhat vulnerable too."

"Ah. So Signora Forcelli needed oxygen at all times, then?"

"Yeah, she had bad lungs."

"How long was the power off?"

The guard pulled a pack of cigarettes out of his pocket. "May as well turn that off," he said to the nurse, pointing to the oxygen machine. He lit his cigarette. "At least I can smoke now, eh?"

Gabe felt like busting the guy's chops just on principle. "I said, how long was the power off?"

The man took a drag before answering. "I'd say ten to fifteen minutes max. Signor Forcelli came running up right after they went out and asked me to help him."

"What, he doesn't know where his own circuit box is?"

"I don't know. As I said, he was a bit flipped out himself." The guard looked at Gabe and squinted. "Ah, may I ask why you're asking all these questions? I mean, who are you?"

Gabe explained that he was a guest of the family and happened to be a detective.

"Ah, like those CSI guys on TV, eh? I can never figure out how they solve all those cases, and so fast, too."

*What a putz.* Gabe turned to the nurse, who was still sniffling and fussing around the body of Signora Forcelli. "So, she couldn't have gone even fifteen minutes without oxygen? And there was no generator backup?"

Claudia's tears started flowing again. "That's just it. She should have been able to make it that long. We didn't think a generator was necessary. We have portable canisters, should the need arise. I have been with her almost every night for the past six months and I did not realize she had deteriorated so much." The nurse began to cry in earnest. "Excuse me," she said, and retreated to the other side of the room.

Gabe walked over to Ornella's body and leaned over to examine her face closely. The nurse had closed the older woman's eyes, but her mouth remained open, as if she'd been fighting for her last breath, which of course, she had been. He was about to turn back when he noticed something odd: one of her front teeth was chipped. It wasn't a large break, but still..."Nurse? Could you come over here for a moment?"

Claudia reluctantly stepped forward and stood next to him. "Yes?"

"Did Signora Forcelli have a chipped front tooth when she went to sleep this evening?"

The nurse peered into her patient's face and frowned. "No, signore. No! Her teeth were fine earlier. I brushed them for her before she went to sleep."

Gabe turned to the guard. "I think you have more than a power outage on your hands here. I suggest you call the police."

—◆◆◆—

Dani was still in a state of shock. When she'd fallen asleep, the only thing on her mind had been Gabe's rejection...and promise. The next thing she knew, Gabe was gently shaking her and explaining that her aunt had not only died, but possibly been murdered.

Despite Gabe's suspicions, the doctor summoned by Santo recorded Ornella Forcelli's cause of death as 'complications from emphysema.' By six a.m., everyone involved in the incident had been interviewed by local investigators, including Dani, who'd been oblivious to it all. Ornella's room had been cordoned off and her body transported to the local morgue for an autopsy.

"Just a precaution, you understand," the officer in charge had explained to the group. "Whenever a death occurs that is out of the ordinary, we must take this step. It is the law. Her remains should be available in the next day or two for burial."

Gabe had gone back to bed as soon as his interview was over and suggested Dani do the same, but she was too upset to sleep.

Fausta, she noticed, had quickly stepped into her role as chatelaine, making sure that everyone, including members of the investigative team, were properly fed and made comfortable. She spoke quietly with Santo, who had cooperated with the authorities but who was still fuming that any investigation was necessary at all. Dani saw him nod and say, "Yes, yes, handle it," before he stalked out of the room. Fausta then turned to Dani and Aldo (who had also slept through the ordeal) and announced that unlike Mando's public mass and reception, Ornella would be laid to rest after a very small and very private service. "If you will excuse me, I must tell Signora Forcelli's family what has transpired." She then left the room.

Aldo made his own exit soon after, citing the fact that he was needed at the church "and must begin my prayers for Ornella." Dani couldn't help but envy both of them—they each had something to do, an activity they felt could somehow help the situation. Dani, on the other hand, felt completely powerless, and she hated it. She spent the rest of the early morning hours mentally rehashing everything that had happened. When Gabe joined her later in the library, she vented her frustration on him.

"I just spoke with Ornella yesterday," she said, pacing the room. Her head was throbbing both from her hangover and the tension of the whole ordeal. "She told me straight out how rotten Santo was and how he'd been practically begging her for money to buy Alberghi Paradisi. She said he even approached her lawyer for a side deal, but the guy looked at the numbers and told her it didn't make financial sense." Dani stopped and looked directly at Gabe. "She just about came right out and said my father was murdered because he wouldn't vote to buy the hotels. She told me she knew she didn't have much time left, but that she wanted to go out on her own terms, which is why she hired the bodyguards."

"Well, those were damn sure not her terms," Gabe said. "That woman was suffocated."

"How you can be sure of that before they've even done the autopsy?"

"Look. She hadn't shown any signs of distress when she went to sleep. But when the power goes out for a few minutes, she keels over and her tooth breaks off? Uh uh. My money's on the exam showing her airway was cut off with enough force that her tooth chipped in the process. And if they do their job right they'll probably find pillow fibers on her face or down her throat. The question is, why? Mando had voting rights, but Santo's wife didn't. Logic tells me your grandmother should be in danger, not your aunt."

"Okay, now you are really making me nervous." Dani wrapped her arms protectively around her body. "Are we safe here?"

Gabe took her gently by the shoulders. "I don't see why you wouldn't be. Santo offered you a job, didn't he? Now me, on the other hand…" He gave her a light squeeze.

Dani reached out to touch his arm, searching his eyes to see if he was kidding. "What are you talking about?"

"Santo made it crystal clear at our meeting yesterday that I'm not good enough for you and he asked that I leave La Tana as soon as possible."

The adrenaline that had receded over the past few hours surged throughout her body again. "Are you…are you thinking about leaving?" She swallowed hard. "I guess I wouldn't blame you. I mean, it's not your fight, and—"

"Shush," he said quietly. "I'm not going anywhere until you tell me to get the hell out, and probably not even then. I don't like what's going on here, but I'll be damned if I'll let you face it on your own."

Dani let out a lungful of air she didn't know she'd been holding. "Okay then. Where do we go from here?"

Gabe hesitated before answering. "Um…"

"Oh no, you're not going to pull the 'you've got to stay home, little lady' routine again, are you? Because I—"

Gabe took Dani's hand and led her to the sofa. His voice pitched low, he leaned toward her. "Listen to me, Daniela. Very carefully. Marco and I have a lead on one of the thugs who was there the night your father died. This guy's not a choir boy, so we have to meet him at his level. If we can scare him into turning, it might be the break we've been looking for. I cannot have you there distracting me. You could make it even more dangerous for all of us."

Dani looked into Gabe's eyes and squeezed his hand, trying not to show the palpable fear that seemed to have taken up residence inside her. "You…you and Marco know what you're doing, right? I mean, you won't take any unnecessary chances? I know Gina would kill Marco if he got himself hurt…" They both smiled at the ridiculousness of her statement.

"I do this kind of thing for a living, bella," he said, reaching out to stroke an errant lock of hair behind her ear. "So does Marco. Don't forget that. And we have too much to live for to blow it by being sloppy. I promise to call and let you know everything's fine. So no worries, okay?"

"Well, you can't ask *that* of me, Constable. But I will stay put until you get back."

"Beautiful *and* wise—I like that in a woman," he teased. Then, in a more serious tone, he added, "If you don't mind, I'd like to get those company names you talked about. There may be a connection between our guy and one of them."

Dani followed him back to their suite, grateful for the change in topic. Amidst all the turmoil she'd almost forgotten her humiliating attempt at seduction the night before, and she hoped against hope that Gabe had forgotten it too. What in God's name had she been thinking? Well, she hadn't been thinking, that's what. She resolved never to drink again and to keep their friendship right where it belonged: strictly platonic. Now if she could only stop herself from worrying to death about his safety.

⸻ ✦⦙✦ ⸻

"You are early," Santo said, looking up from the papers on his desk, cigar in hand. "Our meeting wasn't scheduled for another ten minutes."

Dante stood in the doorway to Santo's office. "If you'd rather I come back…"

"No, no, come in. Tell me what you found out." Santo turned back to his papers, as if Dante were an office boy telling him the mail was in.

Dante sat in one of the oversized chairs. He knew that Santo liked his petitioners to feel small in his presence, but fortunately the chair was just the right size for someone of Dante's build. "It's not good news, I'm afraid."

Santo looked up. "Oh?"

*Santo isn't used to hearing bad news*, Dante thought. *Maybe I can use that.* "The employee you asked me to locate, Carla Rinaldi, is nowhere to be found. She left her position abruptly and has apparently moved out of Milan permanently, with no forwarding address. I've heard rumors, however."

"What rumors?" Santo asked, his eyes locked on Dante's.

*Oh, he's paying attention now.* "That she knew something about the Alberghi Paradisi hotel acquisition and had told Uncle Mando what she knew. He was going to put a stop to it…and that's why he was killed."

Santo viciously stubbed out his cigar. "That's preposterous. Ridiculous. Mando had reservations about the leveraging, that's all. He was coming around when the accident happened—"

"I heard they are reopening the investigation as we speak."

"Who told you that?"

"Somebody who knows somebody. You know how it goes."

"No, I don't know how it goes." Santo leaned back in his chair, his focus now entirely on Dante. "But you'd be happy if the purchase didn't go through, wouldn't you?"

Dante shrugged. "You didn't consult me, but you obviously know I don't think it's a wise move. I told my father as much."

"Yes, Aldo had the temerity to tell me he wasn't going to vote for it…until I convinced him otherwise. I told him it wouldn't be a good career move for you."

Santo's demeanor screamed *Take that, you punk*, and it dawned on Dante that Santo must be so desperate to acquire the hotels that he'd risk all-out family war. But why? "I thought it was more for Dani's career than my own," he countered.

"Ah, so she told you, did she? Well, she would be an excellent addition to the company, and to the family." He leaned forward again, all business. "But that means the purchase must take place, and soon."

"What's the hurry, uncle?"

"I told you not to call me that. As to the other, I don't want Dani to get cold feet. She is capable of taking over a lot of responsibility, which would be helpful to you as well."

"Me? How so?"

Santo was in full bullshit mode now. "You work too hard, for one thing. You should get out more. Find yourself a woman. Quit pining over that whore Agnese."

Santo's casual remark hit Dante like a sucker punch. What had he just called Agnese? Dante had to work hard to keep from reacting. "What are you talking about?"

Santo, back in control, started fussing with the papers on his desk. "Come now. It's common knowledge you hold a torch for her. But trust me, you don't want soiled goods…even though she gives good head, I'll grant you that."

"I said, what are you talking about?" Dante glared at his uncle.

Santo looked up. "I thought you knew. Your father certainly did. Several years ago, Agnese shared my bed. She's nothing but a tramp, and given your background, you can't afford to go slumming. If you like, I can set up some introductions, the daughters of some of my wealthy connections. Your birth is a hindrance, but you're enough of a stud that I'm sure some young heiress will overlook your tainted pedigree."

At that moment, Dante didn't trust himself to speak. He slowly got up. "That won't be necessary," he said tightly.

"Did I say we were finished?" Santo's tone was smug; he obviously knew he had scored a direct hit.

"Oh, we're finished," Dante said. "I have work to do." He kept his breathing normal until he reached the door. He turned back to his uncle. "And Santo?"

"Yes?" Santo was smiling now.

"My father may vote for the acquisition, but you still have to convince Dani. So I wouldn't be taking a victory lap quite yet... not unless you have the funds to buy Alberghi Paradisi yourself." Dante had the brief satisfaction of watching the smile drain from Santo's face. He continued down the hall until he was stopped by Santo's young secretary.

"Signor Trevisan?" she asked shyly.

He almost barked *Not now*, but stopped himself in time. The poor girl wasn't to blame that her boss was an asshole. "Yes?"

"How is he?"

"Who?"

"Director Forcelli. Is he doing okay?"

Dante gestured back to Santo's office. "You mean him? Why wouldn't he be okay?"

The secretary clapped her hand to her mouth. "Oh, you don't know?"

"Know what?"

"Signor Forcelli's wife died last night."

"What?" Dante paused and looked back through the inner office at Santo, who was at his desk looking no different than any other day of the week.

"Yes, after so many years of caring for her. Isn't that sad? I suppose he came in to work to take his mind off his sorrow."

"Yes, that must be it," Dante muttered, and continued walking down the hall. *Jesus. They don't make them colder than that.*

Instead of returning to his office, he headed straight out of the building and began walking down Via Scala to the Corso Porta Borsari. At mid-morning the streets were crowded with high-end shoppers looking to spend their money on the likes of Pollini, Furla, and Max Mara. He didn't notice the pink marble of the walkway, or the bright red geraniums hanging from wrought iron balconies above the storefronts. He didn't feel the sun on his face or smell the tantalizing aroma of roasted almonds from a sidewalk vendor. He blindly walked on, not even mourning his sickly Aunt Ornella's death.

All he could think about was the bombshell Santo had laid on him. Agnese had been Santo's mistress? *Several years ago,* he'd said. How many years? Had she been with him during college? Or, God forbid, during *high school*? She'd gone to a convent school, for Chrissakes! How did those two concepts go together? Maybe Santo was lying to get under Dante's skin. But why? Santo had taken him for granted for so many years that he doubted the man had even given Dante enough thought to come up with something so hurtful. More likely he'd been telling the truth and had blithely assumed Dante knew about his sexual dalliance. And what about the conversation he'd had with his father over dinner? Dante's admission that he wanted to be with Agnese had definitely shaken his father up. Was Santo right? Was it possible his father had known about the affair all this time?

Dante felt queasy for the first time in years. He took a moment to thoroughly digest what his uncle had said. What if Agnese *had* had sex with Santo—would he feel differently about her? The answer was...maybe. If she really did sleep with him, what did that say about her character? Did she think it was okay to sleep with a married man? Did that mean she'd sleep with just about anybody? Okay, maybe he was being a hypocrite. He'd certainly had his share of women. But none of them had been married, and he knew that once he settled down, he'd be a faithful husband.

But if Agnese wasn't choosy about who she slept with, why hadn't she come on to him? He knew he was considered a good bet in that department. Yet she'd gone out of her way to avoid him, even though he could tell she liked him. Maybe she just didn't feel attracted to him.

Or maybe she simply wasn't that type of woman.

He paused in the middle of the path, hardly noticing the stream of shoppers skirting around him. What if...what if Agnese didn't want to get involved with him because of *her* background and not his?

It could be she felt ashamed about the decision she'd made to sleep with Santo earlier in her life. That could explain her unwillingness to set foot in La Tana. She just didn't want to be reminded of her stupidity. That must be it. If it were, could he look past that?

The answer was a resounding *Yes*. We all make mistakes, he thought. We all deserve second chances. He knew he couldn't talk to Agnese directly about this without more facts, so he resolved to talk to her mother. Fausta was so controlling, the chances were good she'd know what her daughter had done in the past and how Agnese felt about it now. If he approached the topic with tact, perhaps he could learn something that would help him get through to the love of his life. With grim determination, Dante hailed a taxi to take him to the villa.

# CHAPTER FIFTEEN

According to Marco's background check, Tino Abruzzo was a punk from the back streets of Rome who had risen above the petty delinquencies of his boyhood slum. He'd apparently rejected the local Mafia for a more cosmopolitan life of crime, because he'd been picked up before on charges involving Eastern European perps. Assuming he was their guy, Gabe wondered where Tino had learned whatever language he and the other guy had been speaking in the hotel hallway. According to Carla Rinaldi it hadn't been Italian.

They'd tracked Tino to a bar called the Sexy Maiale located near the Verona airport. Gabe grinned at the image of a "sexy pig." Airline records showed the young thug had a round trip flight to Rome scheduled later that afternoon. He had a sister back in his old stomping grounds, so he could be visiting her. Either that, or he had another contract job waiting for him in the capital. Another hour and they would have missed him.

Tino was just downing the third of three shots of grappa lined up on the table. Next to him sat a tall, muscular blond man who looked like he was in his late twenties. They were smoking cigarettes and playing a dice game without much enthusiasm when Gabe and Marco walked up.

"*Scusi*," Marco said as he wedged between the taller man and Tino. He leaned in and discreetly showed Tino a badge.

"Augustino Abruzzo? We'd like to talk to you outside, please."

"What the fuck?" Tino said. "I got no quarrel with you guys."

"Yeah, but the state's got a quarrel with you," Marco said. "Let's go someplace quiet and talk about it."

"Shit." Tino grudgingly got up from his seat. He threw down some euros, glanced at the taller guy—who had conveniently turned away— and went with them. Once outside he grew more belligerent.

"Look, my boss said the paperwork's in the mill for that assault charge. You don't have any shit on me and I don't like guys like you blowin' smoke up my ass."

Marco and Gabe looked around before taking Tino around a corner. Before the punk could react, Gabe frisked him and removed both his switchblade and his revolver.

"You got a carry license for these?" Marco asked.

"Fuck you," Tino said. "What do you want?"

Gabe looked at Marco and shrugged. His nod said *Go for it.*

"We've got your prints at the scene of the death of Armando Forcelli," Marco said. "You're in a big pile of shit, Tino."

Tino looked surprised as hell. *He must pride himself on his work,* Gabe thought with a touch of irony. He almost felt sorry for the guy, who was trying his best *I dunno what you're talkin' about* routine.

"Hey, didn't you read the paper?" Tino asked. "The guy offed himself joyriding."

Gabe shook his head. It crossed his mind that it was always the same dance between the suspect and the law no matter what country you were chasing the bad guys in.

"Look, *paisà*," Marco said. "We've got you and you're in deep. But you don't have to be."

"You help us out, we help you out. Otherwise…" Gabe's accent sounded a little squirrely, even to him; he hoped Tino wouldn't notice that little detail in a future interview. Regardless, they must have gotten their point across because he could see beads of sweat starting to form on Tino's upper lip. The jerk made one last stab at denial.

"Swear to God, I don't know shit."

"Okay," Marco said. "You wanna clam up, no problem. We'll take a ride downtown. We can hold you on that old assault charge until we get the gears grinding on the Forcelli case."

*Time to go fishing.* "Yeah, we might even tie you to the death of Ornella Forcelli," Gabe added.

"What? No way, man, I had nothin' to do with that one. That was—" He stopped, shaking his finger at Marco and Gabe. "I see what you're tryin' to do."

Marco pressed on. "Hope you like prison life, Tino. You've skated 'til now, but that's about to change. Better stock up on Vaseline. Hey, maybe you'll make it to Gorgona. I hear those inmates make pretty good wine."

Gabe snickered for effect.

Tino had turned into a sweat factory. He looked at Marco, then at Gabe, tapping his foot nervously the whole time. The guy was probably thinking, *Do they really have something on me?* Gabe raised his eyebrows in silent question. *You gonna take the fall for these guys, Tino? Really?*

"So...you said I didn't have to be in deep. What do you mean?"

"It means we need some information," Marco said. "We need to know why you killed Forcelli and who told you to do it."

Tino feigned a hearty laugh. "Right. You want me to squeal, and you think I'm just gonna walk away like nothin's happened?" He paused, frowning. "Hey, either of you wired?"

Both Gabe and Marco shook their heads and opened their jackets to prove it.

"Listen, Tino," Gabe said. "You make good money, right? You got some stashed away, no doubt. So take it and get lost for a while. We won't go looking for you as long as we have somebody else to go after. Understand?"

Tino looked at Gabe and cocked his head. "You don't sound like you're from around here."

"He's a transfer," Marco cut in before Gabe could speak. "Now what's it gonna be, Tino? You gonna talk with us, or you gonna walk with us?"

"Hey, come on, guys. I'm just a working guy, okay? I get a job, I do the job. They don't tell me much about it. All I know is they wanna expand and that bum Forcelli wasn't cooperating. Somethin' about a vote. That's it."

The offhand way Tino described murdering Mando Forcelli took Gabe over the edge. "You never even met the guy before you whacked him, did you, punk?"

Tino shrugged. "Just a job, buddy."

"Who's your contact?" Marco asked.

"Man, I can't tell you that," Tino said with a smirk. "You think I'm crazy?"

Without thinking twice, Gabe pulled Tino's own switchblade out and held it open at the thug's throat. He pressed hard enough that the prick could feel the pressure of the blade against his skin. Tino swallowed carefully and looked at Gabe with fear in his eyes. *That's right, asshole. Time to wonder if my hand is going to slip.*

"I...I don't know the contact," Tino stammered. "I get a call from someone. Some lady. I don't know her—"

Gabe pressed the knife even closer; a trickle of blood started its way down Tino's neck. "A name, Tino."

"Okay okay. Tetka. I've heard her called Tetka. Tetka Somebody. She's local. That's all I know."

"You get it on your cell?

"Yeah, but it's an unknown number."

"Let's see it," Marco asked.

"I get a new cell every week. Just got this one today."

"Lemme see it anyway." Marco held out his hand.

"Listen," Tino said. "I can't let you have this phone. I give it up, they know I've been made, and I'm done. Cooked. Lemme... lemme meet you someplace later, when I can figure out what I'm doin'."

Gabe stepped back. He pocketed Tino's knife, then took the bullets out of the revolver and handed the gun back to him. Marco handed him a card on which nothing was printed except a number.

"You're gonna think about it, and you're gonna call that number with more information," Marco said. "And you're not going to be stupid enough to think you can outrun us. You got it?"

"I got it," Tino said.

—◈—

It took Gabe several minutes to calm down after they let Tino walk back into the bar. Marco took a minute to jot down license numbers in the parking lot while Gabe ruminated about what he'd just done. Even he was surprised at how close he'd come to gutting the thug. Maybe the guy deserved it, but still…how much of his fury had to do with the fact that he was dealing with Dani's father's killer? Plenty, he decided. In all his professional career, Gabe had never gotten so emotionally invested. "Feels like shit to have one of Forcelli's killers in our hands and then just let him go," he said once Marco got behind the wheel.

"Yeah, I know." Marco headed down the road and onto the *autostrada*. "What's more, that could have been his partner next to him at the bar." They'd taken Gabe's rental to keep a low profile, but Marco knew where he was going, so he drove. "Tino had it right—maybe we should have recorded him."

"Would it have mattered?" Gabe asked. "I don't know how you play this back at the station, but in the States, that guy would have been out on bail quicker than a fifteen-year-old Romeo did-dling Juliet. At least we know for sure it wasn't an accident and you can keep the investigation alive, despite the fact that every-body and their brother wants it shut down. And we got a name out of the deal."

Marco glanced at Gabe. "Yeah, only because you were ready to slice the guy a new smile. What was that all about?"

"That asshole killed Dani's father. Didn't think a thing of it. 'Just a job.' I detest that kind of scum. The only thing he's good for is leading us up the food chain."

"Well, I'm not sure how far up we'll get with the name Tetka. Sounds foreign."

"I'll Google it," Gabe said. He pulled out his rental phone and tapped in the letters. "It means 'aunt' in Croatian. Maybe you'll find an alias in your database, like 'Big Auntie' or something. So what's gonna happen with Tino?"

"We'll give him a day or two and see if he has anything else to spill. If not, we'll bring him in on the evidence, see if it'll stick."

Gabe reached into his back pocket and brought out a slip of paper. "In the meantime, here's a list of companies we should check out."

"Why those?"

"Dani's been going over the Stella d'Italia books because Santo offered her a fancy job and she knows the industry. She found some weird financial activity running through several of the hotels—money flowing into, not out of, the company." He nodded to the paper. "That's a list of the companies associ-ated with the influx of cash. It may or may not be related to the back-of-the-house scam I mentioned to you before, but it's worth looking into."

"Your Dani's one smart woman."

"Naturally. She's with me…sort of." Gabe smiled as he watched Marco maneuver through Verona's downtown traffic. He looked down at the list. "Here, see if any of these sound familiar. Skyline Property Management…Italian House…Worldwide Security—"

"Wait."

"That one ring a bell?"

"Yeah, I think so." He checked his rearview mirror. "I'll have to double check, but I think that's the name of the company Tino checked in under. What about the name Consorzio Azurro?"

Gabe scanned the list. "Yeah, it's on there. She says it seems to be a holding company these others are all connected to through their VAT applications. How'd you know that?"

Marco frowned, concentrating on traffic. "I've just seen that name, that's all."

*He knows something he's not telling*, Gabe thought. "Hey, Indio, does your captain know you're digging into this? Goes a ways beyond handling the paperwork for a boating accident down in Siracusa." He looked his friend in the eye. "You stepping over a line for me?"

Marco scoffed. "Don't flatter yourself. Something rotten's going down in my town and I want to get to the bottom of it, that's all."

"All right, then. I say we pay a visit to Worldwide Security." Gabe punched in the address and the coldly efficient GPS instructor told them to make a U-turn.

"You're missing out, man," Marco said. "My GPS is a woman and she's sexy as hell. Gina hates her." The two men grinned at each other as the disembodied voice sent them on their way.

—⋅✦⋅✦⋅—

Dante arrived at La Tana and found Fausta checking the work of the downstairs maid. He wasted no time asking her about Agnese, even though she tried to divert him.

"You don't seem to be particularly sad that your aunt just passed away," she said. By the tone of her voice, it was apparent Fausta wasn't too broken up about Ornella's death either.

"I have other things on my mind," Dante said. "And I'd like to get some insight from you, if possible."

Fausta gave him a look that seemed a mixture of disdain and condescension. It rankled. "You want me to tell you why Agnese isn't interested in you. Why don't you ask her yourself?"

"She won't talk about it, and I thought you could enlighten me," Dante said carefully.

"Well, I really don't know except that I believe she is saving herself for someone." Fausta busied herself by fluffing pillows on the library sofa that didn't need fluffing.

Dante almost laughed at her use of the pious phrase "saving herself." "And who would that someone be?"

Fausta stopped and looked at Dante, apparently deciding she should confide in him, perhaps simply to put his mind, and heart, at rest. "Come, sit down," she said.

Dante sat next to her on the sofa. "What are you trying to tell me, Fausta?"

The housekeeper sat with her hands folded in her lap. "Dante, this is confidential, but given your keen interest in my daughter, I feel you should know. For many years your Uncle Santo has had a…a special feeling for Agnese. He is quite taken with her and knows that she can provide him with the heir he needs. I realize it is a May-December match, but who can dictate the path of true love? Now that Ornella has finally left this mortal world, well then…"

"Wait. Are you saying that Santo is going to marry Agnese now that his wife is dead?"

"Well, that's putting it rather bluntly, but yes, that is the plan."

"Whose plan, Fausta?"

"Why, Santo's plan. And Agnese's, of course."

Dante had to tread lightly here. "Are you certain? Because that is not what I have heard."

Fausta looked at him sharply. "What have you heard?"

"Just that Santo has no intention of marrying Agnese. In fact, my uncle expressly warned me off her, saying she was…how shall I put it…not 'morally pure.'" Dante watched as Fausta's eyes narrowed.

"Are you sure he said that?" she asked.

"Quite sure, although the language he used was a bit more coarse. He suggested that despite my tainted pedigree, I could do much better. I don't agree, of course." He paused and decided to cut to the chase. "Did they have an affair, Fausta?"

Fausta looked at him with wide eyes, pausing enough to confirm with her body language that at least Santo had been telling Dante the truth on that score.

Dante felt his stomach roil. How could Agnese have been taken in by him? "Now that Santo is free to make Agnese his wife, why wouldn't he simply tell me his intentions—why talk about her so crudely?"

Fausta didn't seem to hear him. "Why that bastard," she murmured. "After he promised…"

"Promised what?"

"What? Oh. He, uh, he promised not to speak about Agnese until the time was right. However, I am sure you misunderstood him…or perhaps he was trying to throw you off the scent. Yes, that must be what happened."

He had learned what he needed to; it was time to leave. "Yes, perhaps you're right. I'm sorry to have bothered you with this, but I had to be sure, you understand."

"Yes, yes. No hard feelings then, eh? I know that Agnese holds you in high esteem and that you will continue to respect her after her marriage."

"Of course."

Dante left the villa and decided to walk a while before calling a taxi from his cell phone. Was Fausta right? Had Agnese spurned him because she was waiting for Santo to make her his wife? If that were the case, why would Santo have been so insulting when he talked about her? As Dante processed what he'd learned, he began to piece together a theory of what had happened. Perhaps Agnese had fallen in love with Santo and become his mistress, thinking he would fall in love with her as well. And maybe he never intended to make an honest woman out of her. Dante wasn't a violent man by nature, but right now he wanted to punch something. How could a man take advantage of a young woman's feelings like that?

He considered Fausta's explanation. What if everything she'd said was true and Agnese and Santo were merely waiting to make their relationship official? Wouldn't Agnese want to spend time with him in the meantime, by taking any opportunity to visit La Tana? For that matter, why wouldn't they have simply continued their affair? But Agnese seemed no more eager to go to La Tana than Santo seemed to want her around. None of it made sense.

The one other person who could help clear up the mystery was his father. Aldo seemed to know about Santo's relationship with Agnese, whatever it was.

If what happened to Agnese turned out to be as sordid as it seemed, Dante realized he might never be able to avenge her directly. But perhaps he could still pay Santo back for his utter callousness. Dante knew that somehow the purchase of Alberghi Paradisi was more than just a business deal. He'd work with Dani and Gabe to find out why it was so important to his uncle. And he'd find a way to use that knowledge to bring him down. Dante's mind began to organize facts, prioritize options, calculate outcomes. He was a businessman at heart. Some colleagues, particularly those who found themselves on the wrong end of a deal, had even accused him of being cold-blooded. When it came to serving up revenge, that description suited him just fine.

For the first time in his life, Dante was glad he didn't share the Forcelli name.

—‣✦✦‣—

"We really miss you, Dani. Da's been asking about you constantly. When are you coming home?"

Dani's throat tightened as she heard Jenna's voice on the other end of the line. Yesterday she'd checked with Nina at the Havenwood Inn, not even bothering to chastise her employee for getting Gabe to come to Italy. All was well at home, as she knew it would be.

For the past several hours she'd poured over the spreadsheets that Carla Rinaldi had given Gabe, all the while waiting anxiously for Gabe's call. It hadn't come yet and Dani was beginning to worry. She needed to hear a friendly voice, and Jenna was that voice.

"I miss you all too," Dani said. She did miss them—more than she thought she would. "I'm not sure when I'll get to return," she hedged. "There are lots of documents to sign, and unfortunately my Aunt Ornella, who had been very sick, just passed away this morning."

"Oh, how sad for your family! How are you doing with all the…the grief and all?"

"I'm holding my own. Gabe is here, and he's been really supportive."

"Of course he is."

Dani could hear the innuendo in her friend's voice. When they'd met for the first time early in the summer, Dani had been amazed by how quickly Jenna picked up on Dani's attraction to Gabe. She'd even noticed it was mutual. And she'd never understood why Dani didn't act on it. If only she knew.

"No, it's not like that," Dani tried to explain. "We're just—"

"Friends. I know. It's still great that he's there for you. And you never know what it might lead to."

"So how are you and Brit doing?"

There was a smile in Jenna's voice. "Fine, fine. Change the subject if you must. The truth is, we couldn't be better. It sounds so corny, but he's my soul mate, Dani. We're even talking next steps."

"What? Wedding bells?"

"It's a possibility, but there's so much else going on…"

"You mean with the opening?"

"Among other things."

"Oh, what a tease," Dani said. "Come on, out with it."

"Okay. You remember the jewels that Reggie Firestone talked about, the ones that are part of the Amanda Firestone Collection?"

"Sure. Her grandmother used some of them as props in her nude modeling days at The Grove."

"Yep. Well, Reggie's going to loan them to The Grove Center for its Grand Reopening. We're even thinking of having nude models re-enact some of the poses."

Dani laughed. "Really? Wow—that ought to get them in the door!"

"I know. But here's what's funny. Remember the photographer who developed Da's negatives? Turns out he's my cousin—"

"Now, why am I not surprised to learn that? Your grandfather seems to be in contact with every branch of your family tree."

"And every leaf, it seems like. But Walker—that's his name—has taken on the task of coordinating the jewel exhibit and photographing it, which is great, except that he and Reggie are about to strangle each other over it."

"Why? She seemed like the most easy-going person in the world."

"Yeah, and so is he. But for some reason the sparks started flying as soon as they got together—almost as though they had a past like Brit and I did, but they'd never met before. So it's a bit of a tangle and we're trying to sort it all out. See why I didn't want to burden you with it?"

"No, that's okay. It's just…sometimes it's good to know that other people's lives aren't picture perfect either. Does that sound bad?"

"You mean like, 'misery loves company?'"

Dani winced. "That does sound bad." She could hear Jenna chuckling on the line.

"No. It sounds human," Jenna said.

Dani swallowed around a lump in her throat. Her friend Jenna had been through so much in her twenty-nine years: her parents had died tragically and Jenna herself, along with her grandfather, had almost been killed by a teenage nutcase. Fortunately that nightmarish episode was behind her, and Jenna and family were on track to open the new Grove Center for American Art. "Hey, I haven't forgotten about the missing paintings, by the way. I just haven't had a chance to look for them yet."

"You listen to me, Daniela Dunn. You are not—repeat *not*—to worry about those paintings. The gallery and the museum are virtually finished. If we have them, fine. If not, fine. I have no doubt that your great-grandfather Luzio came by them honestly, and they deserve to stay in your family."

"You are kind," Dani said, "but I won't be satisfied until I know just how the paintings got here…and if I am going insane for even thinking I've seen them. I really need to sit down with my Uncle Santo and ask him where they came from. But it's been… difficult."

"No worries, no hurry," Jenna said. "Just do what you have to do and come back to us with your luscious constable as soon as you can."

"He's not—"

"Yours. Right. Go on kidding yourself if you want. I'm just looking forward to saying 'I told you so.'"

"Say hello to the dear professor for me, will you? Tell him I do miss him dreadfully. Is he doing okay?"

"Yes, Da is doing great. It's amazing how relaxed you can be if you aren't worried about being killed all the time."

"There is that," Dani agreed. "Give my love to all, especially that gorgeous hunk of yours. We'll be back just as soon as we can."

"Will do. You take care."

After signing off, Dani paused to reflect on the fact that she had used the pronoun *we* instead of *I*. When had she started to think in those terms? Despite all her internal warnings, deep down she had to admit that more than anything else, she wanted more from Gabe than simple friendship. She had no doubt he'd be fine taking it to the next level, but for how long? When he found out how truly messed up she was, would he bolt? But in the meantime, would he be able to help her? Even if he stayed just long enough to help get her over some of her hang-ups, it would be worth it, wouldn't it? Yes, it would, and that's how pathetic she was. Having Gabe for just a little while was better than having no Gabe at all. But honor dictated she let him know what he was getting into, so he could make his own decision.

Dani shook herself and began to sort the pages she'd been working on. Enough of thinking about Gabe. He was going to call any minute with news about this whole mess and they'd be one step closer to going home. And that was the *most* important thing, wasn't it?

As if she'd conjured it, her cell phone rang. Only it wasn't Gabe, but Dante, asking if they could meet someplace away from La Tana. He'd done some digging, he said, and wanted to compare notes. She could tell from his voice that he was determined to get to the bottom of the situation with Stella d'Italia. And why wouldn't he? His whole career was on the line. Besides, she wanted to reassure him that she had no intention of usurping him in any way. The phone call with Jenna had only confirmed what she already knew in her heart: Little Eden was the place she wanted to be, even if she had to pretend otherwise to help Dante ferret out her Uncle Santo's plans.

She thought briefly about Gabe's admonition that she stay put and stay safe. Well, it cut both ways: he could have set her mind at rest hours ago by calling, but he hadn't. So, she'd at least still be within cell phone range.

Dante suggested they meet at the Caffè Veneto in the Piazza delle Erbe. Did she know where it was? Yes, she told him. She remembered it well from her childhood.

Dani had just enough time to hop in the shower and wash her hair before heading into town to meet her cousin. The bathroom sported a walk-in shower, which was heaven. Gabe, she noticed, had chosen the darker bath towel—*typical guy*—and hung it up to dry on a nearby rack. She had to smile. *At least he picks up after himself.* She put the lighter-colored stack near the entrance to the shower and set her cell phone on the counter so she could answer it quickly. After turning on the water, she waited a moment for it warm up, then stepped inside, letting the hot spray sluice over her body and relax her tense and tired muscles. She took her time lathering up and rinsing. Long, hot showers were one of God's greatest gifts and she admitted, if only to herself, that the only thing better would be a hot shower *with Gabe*. Dammit, why hadn't he called?!

Five minutes turned into ten and she negotiated with herself to enjoy the heat for a little while longer before reluctantly shutting off the water. As she reached for one of the towels, she noticed a small, dark speck on the cream-colored terry.

It was moving.

Dani snatched her hand away and watched, horrified, as a second speck—a bug of some sort—joined the first. She took a breath and reached gingerly for the tip of the towel in order to shake the offending creatures off. She tugged to straighten out the towel.

"What the hell!" she cried, jumping back into the shower stall. The dislodged towel revealed not just one or two, but what looked like hundreds of baby spiders crawling around a birthing sac that was guarded by what Dani knew was a female tarantula. It was huge and it was agitated. Freed from the folds of the towel, the spiders were now starting to crawl *everywhere.*

"Okay, okay, okay," she chanted, trying to calm herself down. "They won't hurt you. They're just little babies and that large brown scary thing is just their mama." Forcing her heart back down her throat, she leaped over them, grabbed the phone and took Gabe's damp towel off the rack in one fell swoop. She ran out of the bathroom, slammed the door shut, and found a table runner from the front room to stuff under the door.

"You stay in there," she told the arachnids through the door, and immediately felt like an idiot. She towel-dried her hair—thankful it was cut to take advantage of her natural curls—quickly got dressed, and headed out the door to find Fausta. Fortunately the housekeeper was already walking down the hall toward her.

"I thought I heard something," Fausta said.

"That was probably me, screaming bloody murder. There's a whole family of tarantulas in our bathroom. They must have crawled up into the towels you brought me."

"I am sorry, signorina. It is a very old house. I will have them taken care of." She continued to look at Dani impassively as she dialed her ever-present cell phone. "You are going out?" she asked as she waited for the person she had dialed to answer.

"Yes. I'm…going sightseeing. Something to take my mind off the sadness. You know."

"Yes, I know. Since you've been here, sadness has permeated La Tana, much like the *tarantole*."

As Dani waited for a taxi in front of the mansion, Fausta's words reverberated in her head. *Since you've been here…* Did Fausta actually believe Dani was the cause of all the trouble they'd been having? Or that she was making things worse? Fausta had been cold to Dani since she arrived. She'd mentioned "secrets." Did the housekeeper not even want her there? A cold sensation swept over her. Fausta had free rein at La Tana. Fausta had brought those towels…

Okay, now she was being ridiculous. Dani willed herself to calm down by taking deep breaths and letting them out slowly. It was one of the tricks she'd learned from therapists over the years to counteract her anxiety. *Tell yourself you have nothing to worry about and the worry will go away*, one of them had instructed. She tried the same strategy now. *They're only spiders, for heaven's sake. Fausta would never stoop so low. Nothing to get wigged out about.*

On the way into town, Dani clutched her cell phone, hoping it would ring. It didn't. "Men," she grumbled. If something bad happened to Gabe and Marco, she was going to fight Gina for first rights to at least maim them. Fast on the heels of that thought was a prayer: *Please, God, keep them safe*. Her nerves fraying, Dani fought tears all the way to the cafe.

# CHAPTER SIXTEEN

—·✦·✦·—

"**S**he's going to kill me," Gabe muttered as he looked at his dead cell phone. Between Dani's sexy come-on and the sketchy death of her aunt the night before, he'd forgotten to charge it. "I can't believe you don't have a personal cell phone, Marco."

"Don't blame me. Blame Gina. She's the penny pincher, says I don't need one because of my work phone. She's got a point. Look, I know we said we'd keep my line clean, but if you gotta, you gotta." They'd agreed not to use Marco's government-issue phone to link him directly with the Forcelli family; with so much corruption in the Italian police system, Marco didn't need to be part of a situation that even *looked* questionable.

"No, just pull over so I can use a landline someplace. I promised I'd let Dani know I'm okay."

Marco grinned at his childhood friend. "Well and truly hooked," he teased.

Gabe and Marco had run into a dead end related to Worldwide Security. The street address had turned out to be an abandoned warehouse near the train station.

"I'll bet the others on the list turn out to be shells, too," Marco said. "That sucks."

"Yeah, big time. What about the holding company, Azure Consortium? Maybe we can get a bead on that."

"Maybe," Marco said without enthusiasm.

Gabe glanced at his friend. "Hey, man, don't get discouraged. We've got options. Like you said, we wait a day or two for Tino to get back to us, and see if Dani and her cousin can make any connections within the company."

"You sure Trevisan's clean?"

"My gut says yes. He'd already nixed the Alberghi Paradisi purchase, said it was a bad investment. Santo seems so hot to make the move that he's pulling out all the stops. Maybe he's under pressure by somebody else. Something's rotten when you'd off your own brother to make a deal happen."

"No shit. Hey, I'm going to park on Garibaldi and we can walk to Erbe. I know a cafe where you can use the phone. Then I'll just walk back to the station."

Marco parked and locked the car, tossing the keys back to Gabe. As they made their way across the bustling piazza, Gabe saw something that stopped him in his tracks: Dani was sitting at a sidewalk cafe drinking and huddling close to Dante Trevisan. Gabe's brain told him it was no big deal: they were no doubt comparing notes about the hotel company. However, his emotions were on another track entirely: she lied to him! She told him she'd stay put and here she was out in the open where anybody could take a pot shot at her.

Despite what he'd told her earlier that morning, Gabe was beginning to worry about her safety. The more he dug into this mess, the more he wondered whether Santo was in fact the head of the snake. Santo might want to keep her in the family, but what if someone else was calling the shots? Someone who thought Mando and Ornella were expendable. If that were the case, why would Dani be any different? The thought of something happening to her started his heart racing. Setting his jaw, he stalked toward the couple.

Marco, who had also spotted them, stopped Gabe with his arm. "I always say Verona's just a small town at heart," he said lightly. "Guess you don't need the phone, huh?"

"She promised to stay at the villa," he ground out. "She shouldn't be out in the open like that."

"Hey, chill. Nobody's gonna pop her out here in public. And Dante's a brute in a suit. He's watchin' out for her. You gotta relax."

Marco's words penetrated and Gabe slowed down. He took a deep breath and looked at his friend, who shrugged as if to say *I know you got it bad, but now's not the time or place to let it show.* Finally Gabe nodded. "You're right."

Marco clapped him on the back. "As I've been demonstrating since you were six years old."

The two men approached the outdoor cafe at a more leisurely pace. Still, Gabe couldn't help feeling tense as he neared the couple, who continued to talk with their heads down. Finally Dani looked up, and Gabe couldn't help it, he almost laughed at her expression. It changed from recognition to outrage in the space of two seconds. She looked exactly the way he felt. He decided then and there to take the high road.

"What a small world," he said affably. "You saved me a phone call."

"Oh, you mean it actually crossed your mind to call?" Dani's tone was sharp enough to etch glass.

"Funny you should mention it," Marco interjected. "Gabe's been beside himself for the last hour because his cell died and he knew you'd be waiting for him to get in touch with you."

Dani's eyes narrowed and Gabe gazed back with the most innocent expression he could muster.

"True story," he said. Then, because he couldn't resist, he added, "Of course, I expected to call you at the *villa*."

Dani read his tone perfectly and raised her chin in defiance. "Well, when one has been waiting by the phone *all afternoon*, and finally gets an invitation to go out, what's a body to do?"

Dante had been watching the exchange like a front row spectator at a world cup tennis match. "Uh, we're glad you're here." He glanced at Marco with a puzzled expression.

"Don't worry," Gabe said. "Marco's working with us on this." He introduced the two men.

Dante shook Marco's hand. "I remember you from the memorial service," he said. "And I understand you know a mutual friend or ours, Agnese Lombardi."

Marco glanced at Gabe. "Yes, well, that was a while ago." He pulled up a chair. "So you've got some information to share?"

"Yes, Dani and I think we've got something you'll be interested in," Dante began.

"Let's hear it." Gabe sat down next to Dani.

With one last glare, Dani got down to business. She gestured to the sheets spread on the table, then looked up again at Gabe. "I dove into the numbers Carla Rinaldi gave you, and Dante pulled his own figures. Between us, we think we have an idea of what's been going on."

Gabe figured he and Dani would hash out their differences later; this was far more important. "What have you got?"

Dani rifled through several sheets. "In Rome, Milan, Florence, and several other properties, including here in Verona, housekeeping was beefed up considerably over the past six months in advance of slightly higher occupancy rates. But within two weeks the staffing numbers had dropped, despite the continued higher occupancy. That level of fluctuation is not the norm, not even with a staff sharing program among hotels."

Gabe peered at the spreadsheets. "So who's making the chess moves? Carla told me it seemed to be coming from corporate."

"That could be the case for the Milan property, but it's not so clear elsewhere," Dani explained. "It looks like many requests were generated locally, along the lines of 'Hey, can we borrow Sonia for a few weeks? She got good reviews and we're having a big crowd in the week of the fourth.' But that kind of give and take probably has to be sanctioned at a higher level."

Gabe looked at Dante. "Did you know any of this was going on?"

"Complaints never made it up to my level. I suppose because no one determined it was a sustained or system-wide issue."

"I can see why," Dani said. "The numbers aren't dramatic enough in any one property to cause red flags. It's only when you see the regularity with which it's occurring every month, even though it's at a different property, that you see something's not quite right."

"What about those weird company payments you uncovered?" Gabe asked. "Do they track with the staffing dips?"

"Well, they're not tied to the same hotels." Dani traced her finger down a column, then made an arc over to another. "One month the problem shows up in Florence, but the money flows into Milan. So I'm not sure if there's a connection."

"There has to be," Dante said. "Look, it's not unheard of in the hospitality industry to charge for one's 'consulting,' especially within the luxury hotel tier. The money might be an honorarium for serving on a board, or a 'thank you' for exceptionally good service. Maybe a company wants to pave the way for an advantageous booking down the road. The reasons are endless, and the fees I've traced have very common descriptions attached to them. But the strange thing is, five years ago those payments were a fraction of what they are today."

"And Santo's the only one who could have generated them?" Gabe asked.

"The only one," Dante confirmed. "He's connected at the highest levels. I cross- referenced the uptick in consulting fees with the increase in housekeeping staff fluctuation across all properties and the correlation between the two events is unmistakable beginning around the same time."

Gabe leaned back in his chair. "So the two are related and something fishy started happening around four to five years ago. Anything happen to Santo back then that you know of?"

"Nothing I can put my finger on," Dante said. "He's always kept his own counsel...except, wait. He did hire a new person about that time. A special assistant. Surprised the hell out of me, because Santo usually goes for very young, very attractive women. This lady is old enough to be my mother and she's built like a tank. She's from Eastern Europe someplace."

Gabe shot Marco a look. "Could she be Croatian?" he asked Dante.

"Could be. I'm not sure. She's a nice lady, don't get me wrong, but not the usual hire for the executive suite."

"What's her name?" Marco asked.

"Flora Petrovic," Dante said. "She's very efficient. Santo seems to be pleased with her work. Who knows—she may be the one helping him arrange the consulting jobs."

Marco looked up. "Wouldn't he keep that income for himself?"

"Not necessarily. Since he's generating the income as a result of his position with the company, he'd have to show it on the books. However, if it were done on his own time, most companies would compensate him for it. Given who Santo is, however, there's no real daylight between him and Stella d'Italia. He lives and breathes it."

"I wonder," Dani mused. "When I talked to Aunt Ornella, she said something odd. Something like, 'Ask your uncle where he spends his vacations, and when he lies to you, find out the truth.'

I was surprised he even took vacations. Where's he been traveling for the past few years?"

Dante looked sheepish. "You know, I never asked. It was such a nice change having him gone, I guess I focused on that. I'll look into it."

"So where do we go from here?" Dani asked.

"I think it's two-fold," Marco said. "If you can get a tighter sense of how the staffing changes match the occupancy spikes, as well as who moved from where to where, maybe we can model it and try to predict what's going to happen next. You said it doesn't seem to happen at the same hotel twice in a row, but maybe there's actually a rotation you can identify. If we know what workers are coming in—"

"Or who may already be in place," Gabe added.

"You're right," Marco said. "If we can identify who might be next, maybe then we can tail them and see what's going on."

"Great minds think alike." Dante reached into his briefcase and pulled out a small card-size box. "Look, we said we wanted to keep a low profile, so this isn't something I can do. But you can, Dani." He handed her the box, which she opened to reveal a small stack of business cards. They featured the Stella d'Italia company logo, embossed in gold, and the name "Daniela Dunn" in elegant script. Below her name was the title "Corporate Human Resource Analyst" and a phone number—Dani's cell.

"What's this?" she asked. Gabe leaned over her shoulder to look and nodded, understanding Dante's strategy immediately.

Dante shrugged. "Uncle Santo wants you in the company, you're now in the company. He just doesn't know it yet. You can go out and interview our housekeeping employees, and with the card, they'll talk to you."

"Makes sense," Dani said. "I'll start looking into the Verona employees who disappeared, like Carla did in Milan. One of them was named Mirela, I think. Maybe one of her co-workers knows something that can help me out."

"You mean, help 'us' out," Gabe said. "We're a team, remember?"

"Uh huh. A team. Right." Dani rolled her eyes. "Who are *you* going to be, my bodyguard?"

"If I have to be," he said, smiling.

"Ah, maybe you could be a trainee, or an intern," Marco suggested. "I know the perks you interns get back in the States."

"Very funny," Gabe said. "I'll be whoever you want me to be, as long as I'm there," he said.

"So we'll all touch base whenever we've got something, right?" Marco asked the group. Just then his phone beeped. He answered it and got up from the table. "Homicide. Gotta run."

The three watched Marco walk briskly across the piazza. "I've got to go also," Dante said, rising from his chair. I've got a dinner meeting and I want to follow up on some of the material we talked about today."

"Um, Dante?" Dani reached for her cousin's arm. "I hope you know I don't take these cards seriously. I have no intention of coming to work for Uncle Santo."

The look Dante gave her was serious. "Not him, certainly. But you might want to work for Stella d'Italia one day. Despite what we may uncover, it is a great and noble company."

Dani gestured to the cards. "Well, I won't shame you, even if it is just for show," she assured him.

"I know you won't, but we *must* clean house, and the sooner the better."

Gabe watched Dante stride off in the opposite direction as Marco. Dante seemed about as committed to bringing down Santo as a man could be. What had Santo done to him?

Dani rose from the table as well, but before she could leave, Gabe reached out and caught her hand. "I'm parked a few blocks away," he said. "I'll give you a ride back."

"No need. I'll take a cab," she said, her earlier aggravation back on the front burner.

"Dani, look. I—"

She held up her hand. "Really, no need to explain. Your cell phone died. You couldn't call. I get it."

"No, I don't think you do," he said, rising smoothly. He looked at her for a moment, took her face in his hands, leaned down and kissed her gently, yet completely. He could feel her stiffen slightly and then relax, becoming soft and pliable against him. He brought her closer, tilting his head and taking the kiss even deeper. He could feel her arms slide hesitantly around him for a few moments before she stepped away.

"What...what was that for?" she asked, touching her fingers to her lips.

He made a point of looking at his watch. "Because it's now almost seven o'clock in the evening and I didn't think I could go another minute without touching you," he said. "May I buy you dinner?"

Dani slowly shook her head. "No, I don't think so. I'll take that ride home, though. I'm exhausted."

Gabe nodded, not wanting to push things. At least she hadn't slapped him. But then, maybe she just hadn't wanted to make a scene in public. As he walked with Dani back to the car, Gabe couldn't help but wonder how he was going to keep himself from sliding irrevocably in love with her. It was a slippery damn slope and he had no idea what lay at the bottom of it.

Dante once again sought out his father, this time in the sacristy of Santa Maria Antica, where the older man spent every third evening after the six o'clock mass organizing the vestments of the clergy, as well as prepping the elements of the Eucharist that he would take to homebound parishioners the following day. The surroundings were as familiar to Dante as his own home. All his life he'd visited his father at this church, and the place had always evoked an odd combination of comfort and disappointment. Comfort because it never changed; disappointment because it was a constant reminder that Dante's father had wanted, above all else, for his son to become a priest.

Dante had entertained the idea briefly as a child, but as soon as puberty kicked in he knew he would never go down that saintly road. Being with a woman was just too vital for Dante's happiness to give it up, even for God. So it was particularly unnerving for him to see the unrequited love of his life walking up to the door at the same time.

Her dark, lustrous hair flowed halfway down her back; it had been years since he'd seen it untethered and it took incredible fortitude to keep from running his hands along its smooth path. She was dressed in a simple, modest blue dress that nevertheless couldn't hide her beautiful curves. She looked extremely distressed to see him. Given the way they'd parted the evening before, he could see why.

"Your father asked me to meet him here. Did he ask you as well?"

Dante shook his head. "No, he said nothing to me. Just a lucky coincidence, I guess." He tried to smile as mentally he began to regroup. He was here to ask—no *demand*—that his father tell him with certainty what had gone on between Agnese and Santo. Dante could feel, in his bones, that Aldo knew the truth. And it was time the truth came out.

But how could he even attempt to bring up the topic if she were present? It was an impossible situation. He would have to come back another time. "I'll just say hello to my father and leave you to it."

He was about to open the door when Aldo opened it from the other side, putting on his coat and turning off the light. He looked shocked to see Dante, but his expression quickly shuttered.

"Dante, I'm surprised to see you," he said.

"I didn't know you were meeting Agnese. I can come back another time."

"No," he said, taking a breath. "It could be a sign." He crossed himself and gave Agnese a strange look of sympathy. "I'm glad you came, my dear. Both of you, come with me."

Dante and Agnese exchanged looks; it was obvious she was as perplexed by his father's behavior as he was. They walked down the hall and through a side door into the sanctuary.

Santa Maria Antica was a small, Romanesque-style church. The structure dated back to the twelfth century, and some believed even before that. It was austere, with round arches, plain columns, and simple wooden benches. Dante had always felt it matched his father's modest, self-effacing personality.

Agnese seemed to read his mind. "You are at home here, Signor Forcelli, and I can see why," she said in a soft tone. "This place suits you."

"It does," his father agreed. He walked down the nave until he reached a tiny chapel off to the side. Inside was an altar that displayed a marble statue of the Virgin Mary. A rack of candles in front of the altar held a few votives, most of which had burned down and out for the day. Aldo quietly took a match and lit a new candle. "Sit," he said, pointing to a small bench.

"Father," Dante began.

Aldo held his hand up. "No, please. This will be difficult enough." He closed his eyes briefly, then looked directly at Agnese.

"One would think that when I light a candle here I am praying to the Virgin Mother," he said. "But it's to another Mary I pray. Do you know which one, Agnese?"

Looking puzzled, she shook her head. "No, Signore."

"I pray to Santa Maria Goretti. Do you know her?"

The horrified look on Agnese's face told Dante she knew very well who it was. For once, he cursed the fact that he hadn't paid attention in religion class when it came to memorizing the saints.

"Who is it, Father?"

Aldo continued to gaze at Agnese. "She is the Patroness of Youth and looks after the victims of rape," he said. "But more important, she is the patron saint of forgiveness." He looked at Dante. "I asked Agnese to meet me here so that I could ask her forgiveness—not for what I did so many years ago, but for what I didn't do. I am so very sorry, my dear. So very, very sorry."

Wait a minute. Rape? Agnese was raped?? Dante couldn't hide the look of shock on his face.

At his father's words, Agnese's face drained of all its color. She looked as if he'd struck her. Dante reached over to touch her but she flinched and stood up abruptly. She wouldn't look at Dante at all.

"I...I don't know what you're talking about. You have done nothing wrong. This is a...a mistake, I'm sure. Excuse me, I have to...I have to go now." She turned and hurried out of the chapel.

"Agnese, wait!" Dante called out, but she ignored him and continued walking rapidly down the nave until she was practically running. He turned back to his father. "Why on earth did you do that?!"

His father stood gazing at the statue, his broad shoulders curling inward as if he were in pain. "I needed to reopen a wound," he said simply. "I could see no other way to let the poison out."

"Are you telling me Santo took Agnese without her consent? When did this happen?"

Aldo looked at his son, his face awash in guilt and shame.

"When?" Dante thundered.

"I'm not sure exactly, but I think it started shortly after... after Daniela left the country with her mother."

There was a malignant pause between them as Dante made the mental calculations. "That would have made Agnese sixteen years old," he said with deadly calm. "You're saying it 'started' then. That implies he did it more than once. And you did nothing about it?"

His father had the look of a condemned man resigned to his fate. "I had my suspicions and I asked Santo about it, but he dismissed it, dismissed me for even asking about it. I convinced myself it couldn't really be happening, that Fausta wouldn't let it happen."

"But Fausta did let it happen," Dante said coldly. "And so did you. That's...that's despicable."

His father nodded, making no attempt to defend himself. "What is that saying? 'All that is necessary for evil to triumph is that good men do nothing.' But I am not even a good man, am I? I have lived with that fact for more than a decade. If it were not a mortal sin, and if I had more courage, I would relieve the world of my presence. But that young woman did nothing wrong and she deserves something better than living a life of shame and guilt for something she had no control over."

Dante ran his hands through his hair and felt like pulling it out by the roots. "But why bring it up with me here? Did you see her reaction? She couldn't even look at me."

"God put you here, at this place and this time, for a reason, Dante. Stop and think. Agnese cannot hide from you any longer. You know the ugly truth. Now that the wound is open, it's up to you to wash it clean…with love."

"Are you kidding? She'd already told me she didn't want to see me again, and now this?" Dread took up residence in his gut.

"Talk to God," his father murmured, turning back to the altar. "He will help you find a way."

"Like God helped you?" Disgusted, he got up to leave.

"Dante, wait. What did you want to talk to me about?"

"Nothing, it turns out. Nothing at all." He left his father praying to Mary, no doubt looking for more forgiveness than he could possibly find on earth.

# CHAPTER SEVENTEEN

—‧✦✦‧—

G abe was thinking he'd dodged a bullet as he and Dani began the drive back to La Tana, but after a few minutes she took a deep breath and said, "Wait. Do you know the way up to the castle?"

"What, you mean San Pietro?"

"Yes. I'd like to drive up there if you don't mind."

"Right now?"

Dani nodded. "I have something to tell you and I think I'd like to do it on neutral ground."

Gabe felt his stomach lurch. Shit, he shouldn't have given in to his impulse to kiss her. "Listen, Dani. I'm sorry about that kiss back there. I know you just want to be friends, and I got carried away, that's all."

"This isn't about what I want, it's about what *you* want. I've told you that I can't…be what you need. And I think it's time to tell you why."

Gabe swallowed, tried to keep his mouth shut. Dani was finally ready to talk, and that was a good thing, right? You get bitten by a snake, you've got to get the poison out in order to heal. He respected that. Hell, he *needed* that if they were ever going to get beyond where they were now. If only it didn't sound so ominous. "Fair enough," he said.

They wound their way up the Via Fontanelle and Gabe turned onto Via Castello, parking in the lot along the esplanade overlooking the city. It would be another hour before the locals and savvy tourists would walk or drive up the ancient hill to watch the sunset from one of Verona's prettiest vistas.

Dani got out of the car and walked over to the stone wall surrounding the imposing structure. The "castle"—actually a nineteenth century army barracks—stood on one of the oldest sites of the city. For two thousand years, every tribe, army, or government that claimed this region of Italy had held this plot of land because from its vantage point one could see for miles in every direction. Ironically, the violent, defensive requirements of the past now invited a veritable feast for the eyes. The icy blue of the Adige River set off the rich terracotta of the medieval rooftops; here and there intensely green cypress trees added to the vibrant palette. Throughout Verona, soaring church spires served as reminders that mankind's highest priority perhaps shouldn't *always* be to act in its own self-interest.

Dani hopped up onto the wall and sat with her legs dangling off the edge, a move that made Gabe smile. How many times had he and his friends walked these ramparts as acrobats in the circus? *One misstep, ladies and gentlemen, and the Flying Orsinis will tumble into the abyss!* He tried lightening Dani's mood. "Didn't your mother tell you not to get too close to the edge, young lady?" He levered himself up to sit next to her.

Dani smiled, a perfunctory twitch of the lips. "I don't think my mother ever came up here," she said. "My babbo took me here once and let me sit just like this. He held me to make sure I wouldn't fall. I felt like I was on top of the world."

Gabe looked out over the expanse of the city. "You were lucky to have him."

Dani glanced at Gabe and nodded. "Yes, I was. But he wasn't there when I needed him."

Gabe said nothing. He waited.

"Something happened to me when I was fifteen," she said after a pause. "At a big party at La Tana. You know, for clients and suppliers, people like that. It was like a big thank-you to them. I was trying so hard to act grown up. Agnese and I stole some alcohol and then we got separated. I had way too much to drink and… and I was almost raped by some man there. Uncle Santo caught the guy in time, but I guess in my mind he'd already done the deed. The experience freaked me out. In my mind it's real, you see. As if it actually happened. But it didn't. Not really."

She paused again and took in the view, but Gabe wasn't sure she saw anything except memories. He could see tears pooling in her eyes. He leaned toward her so he could take his handkerchief out of his back pocket. She took it and chuckled. "You and your handkerchiefs." She dabbed her eyes before continuing. "So you see, I have a hang-up about men that everyone has told me for the past twelve years is strictly in my head. Now that's pretty screwed up, don't you think?"

Gabe thought back to the nightmare she'd had their first night at La Tana. Her dream had seemed very real—not a fantasy at all. "How did your uncle find you?" he asked.

"I was in one of the rooms upstairs and I think the man—I don't even remember what he looked like—must have put something in my drink. But I guess Uncle Santo found us before the man could do anything because he sent the guy away and brought me to his office to calm me down. Then my Nonno Ciro had a stroke and Santo had to leave me. I think I must have fallen asleep or something, but the doctor who had come for my grandfather came and checked me out and they tell me nothing happened. I was fine. But I've never been able to get it out of my mind. I can't tell you how many therapists and counselors I've been to." She laughed bitterly this time. "One psychologist even said he thought I secretly wanted to be raped, and that's why I couldn't stop obsessing about it. He called it 'an adolescent case of wishful thinking.' Needless to say I refused to see him again."

"What an asshole," Gabe said. He chose his next words carefully. "So who was there to help you that night besides Santo, your mom?"

"No, my mom and dad were off at a race. But Santo and Uncle Aldo and Fausta were there, and Nonna Stella, after she dealt with my grandfather. Nonna was the one who had the doctor examine me, even though Santo assured her nothing had happened."

"What happened to the man who tried to rape you?"

"Uncle Santo said he didn't recognize him and that it would be a big scandal to check everyone who had come to the party. That's what he told Nonna, at any rate, and she told my mom, who later explained it to me. They figured 'no harm, no foul,' I guess. I barely remember any of it…"

"…except in your dreams," Gabe finished.

Dani turned sharply to look at him. "You…you heard me?"

He nodded. "The first night we were here."

"That's funny. I thought someone was with me at one point. In a good way, I mean. It felt…strange. Strange but comforting."

"Guilty as charged," Gabe said. "Have you had nightmares like that often?"

"Off and on for years," she admitted. "But then, gradually they went away. I was worried they might start up again once I returned to this place, and sure enough…"

Gabe put his arm around her and gave her a light caress. "I can't imagine reliving something so frightening over and over like that. You must be made of steel to have survived it."

"That's just it," she said irritably. "Why am I reliving something that never even happened?"

An idea began to form that was so unbelievable he couldn't bring himself to voice it. He wouldn't test his theory with Dani; she might think him as crazy as she thought herself. But he resolved to dig a little deeper. Who knew what he might find if he turned over some rocks? The important thing right now was just to be there for her. "I don't know why you have those feelings, but I'm beginning to think—as weird as it sounds—that it was a good thing you came back. Maybe you'll find the answers you're looking for."

"Maybe." Dani turned to face him, causing him to remove his arm from her shoulder. "But now do you see how impossible it... we...are? I mean, how stable can I be if I'm remembering things, feeling things that aren't even there? I wouldn't saddle anyone I care about with the likes of me."

Gabe gently tilted her chin so that she was forced to look directly at him. "Ah, so you admit you care about me...at least a little?"

Dani pursed her lips. "I must. Why else would I have done such a stupid thing last night?"

"What, coming on to me?"

Dani winced. "If you could call it that."

"Yeah, I'd call it that. I'm just sorry you were three sheets to the wind. Like I told you, when you and I take this to the next level—and trust me, we *will* take this to the next level—you're going to be firing on all cylinders." He waggled his eyebrows to make the point.

Dani threw her hands up. "Have you heard anything I've been telling you?" Her voice rose in frustration. "Because you don't seem to be taking any of it seriously."

"Not true," Gabe said. He pushed himself up onto the ledge and dropped gracefully back onto the esplanade before turning back to her. She turned around to face him and he leaned his hands on the wall, capturing Dani between them. "I'm absolutely serious when I tell you that no matter what actually happened that night, nobody...and I mean *nobody* deserves to go through what you've been through. But it doesn't make you damaged goods and it's damn well not going to keep defining who you are.

I won't let it. Now all I've got to do is convince you that I'm right."
He smiled to soften his high-handed rhetoric. "Come on, let's go
find dinner. He reached for her waist to swing her down onto the
pavement. "You really can trust me, bella. I won't let you fall." In
that moment, the tentative smile she bestowed on him as she put
her hands on his shoulders made everything right with the world.

They shared a bottle of Bardolino, a plate of spinach ravioli, and
two coconut gelatos, and for once, Dani gave herself permission
to spend time with Gabriele de la Torre without questioning why
he could possibly want to be with her as well. They walked along
the Corso Porta Borsari, exploring the side streets and grinning
at the pretentious window displays. Dani told Gabe about her
awkward introduction to America at the age of fifteen, and Gabe
related funny, self-deprecating stories about his teenage years in
New York. Each left unspoken the realities that had made both of
their younger lives so much more complex. Gabe described his
stint in the army and how he appreciated the structure, but not
for a lifetime. He fell in love with the weather in California, he
said, which was why he'd moved first to Los Angeles and later,
Marin. He craved the hills and the ocean and the Redwoods. And
Dani could tell by the way he looked at her that he craved her too.

Late in the evening they returned to their suite at La Tana.
Fausta had left a note informing them that Ornella's private
funeral service would be held in three days' time. She also mentioned that the *tarantole* had been taken care of.

"Tarantulas?" Gabe asked. "What's that all about?"

"It's a long story. Suffice to say I don't think Fausta's happy to have me here."

They commiserated about the change in Fausta's demeanor; they wondered aloud why she had stayed at La Tana long enough to turn sour. "Like a wine past its prime," Dani said.

They grew silent, both retreating to the mundane rituals of settling in for the night. Gabe hung his jacket on the back of a chair and emptied his pockets on the side table; Dani kicked off her shoes and rummaged through her purse for a comb. Finally, the elephant in the room could no longer be denied and Dani, with a deep breath, stepped into its path.

"You...you talked earlier about taking this...taking *us*...to the next level," she said, forcing herself to look directly at Gabe. He had stretched out on the couch, but at her words he almost snapped to attention.

"I did," he said slowly.

"Well..." The rest of her words came out in a rush. "Look, I'm not drunk, so no excuses this time. I'm pretty sure you're very good at this sort of thing. Can you just...can you just do whatever it is you do so that I can get over this fear of men and sex and everything?" She laughed nervously. "I'd like a sex life too, you know. Couldn't you just sort of...I don't know...loosen me up?" *Oh God. That didn't sound right at all.* She stopped on a whoosh of air.

Gabe looked at her as if she'd killed a dog. "No," he said.

—◆—

Gabe watched Dani as she registered his refusal. It didn't take long for her eyebrows to rise and her lips to tremble. He frowned, surprised at the disappointment he felt. He'd been primed, ready for…something. The evening had been damn near perfect, but how she proposed to end it just *wasn't*. He got up, reached for his jacket and turned to leave the suite.

"If all you want is for me to help you 'loosen up' so that you can have a sex life, I don't think I'm your man." He'd take a walk around the grounds so he could cool down and hope that Santo wouldn't use the excuse to have him shot as an intruder. Christ, this was turning out to be a lot more painful that he thought. Make love to Dani just so she can feel better about getting it on with somebody else? No. Way. In. Hell.

Dani reached out to touch him. "No, I didn't mean it like that. It's just that for so long I've been…closed up, you know? And there's no one I trust more than you to help me. You're more than just a friend. You understand me. Oh, I'm sorry. This is embarrassing." She let go and clasped her hands together.

Gabe looked into her eyes and saw the vulnerability there shining right back at him. Big mistake. He had told her repeatedly to trust him and she did. More than anyone else, she'd said. Could he do this for her and not lose his heart in the process? He didn't think so, but there it was. He loved the girl, plain and simple. And when you love someone, you'd do just about anything for them. Even take the chance they might not need you anymore. He sharpened his gaze. "Do you really trust me to do this, Dani?"

"Yes," she whispered.

"And you trust me enough to do as I say?"

She swallowed.

*She has to think about that one.* After a brief hesitation she nodded. He smiled at her courage. "All right then, my first question is, which language do you prefer, English or Italian?"

Dani cleared her throat. "Do we, um, even have to say anything? Can't you just…you know…"

Gabe shook his head slowly as he met her worried eyes. "Have you forgotten to trust me already, bella? Which will it be?"

"English, I guess. My memories of Italy and this particular subject aren't the greatest." She looked around their suite. "Should we…should we go to the bedroom? I mean—"

"Not yet, sweetheart. We have plenty of time. Right now I'm going to pour you a glass of wine, sit you down on this couch next to me, and tell you a story." Dani gave him a puzzled look but seemed to relax a bit at his instruction. If he didn't play this right, her nerves could get away from her and spoil the experience. Instinctively he knew he should go slow, so slow that she'd be begging for him when the time came. Well, he hoped, anyway. "One minute," he said, jogging into the alcove where he had stashed his luggage. He stuck a couple of foil packets in his pants pocket and returned, heading over to the small wine refrigerator in the living room. He opened a bottle of Soave, poured them each a glass and sat down, pulling her close to him. "Salute," he said, tapping their glasses gently.

"What is this story you want to tell me?" she asked.

"It's the story of a young man—well, maybe not so young anymore, let's just call him a man—who had lived in America for a long time. He loved his adopted country, he had made it his home, and he was generally happy. But every once in a while, he got homesick. So he'd look for something that would remind him of the happier times of his childhood. Usually he accomplished this by having Italian food…" At Dani's eye roll, he shrugged. "What can I say? He loved his pasta."

"Go on," she said.

Gabe took one of her hands in his. "So one day he walked into the charming restaurant of a nearby inn. He'd been told that someone from his hometown ran the place and he was curious to see the person he remembered only slightly as a skinny little girl—ouch!" He rubbed his arm where Dani had punched him. "As I said, he was looking for a skinny young woman…"

"What, like one of those age progression photos?'

"Hey now, you're interrupting my story," he said, squeezing her hand gently. "Take a sip of your wine, relax, and listen. So he was looking for a slightly older version of that little girl, but he didn't find her. Instead he met the most delicious, the most incredibly sexy woman he had ever seen."

Dani snorted. "I guess this guy had been living in a monastery, huh?"

"Not at all," Gabe said. "In fact, the man had had, shall we say, a fair amount of experience with women. For some reason they liked him—" he raised his eyebrows "—and he liked them back. But this was different." Gabe turned so that Dani could see and feel the truth of what he was about to say. "This woman just did it for him, and he knew it almost immediately." He reached over to thread his fingers through Dani's hair, changing into the present tense because he couldn't help himself. "She's exotic-looking, with shining dark curls that look so soft, he just wants to run his hands through them. Her skin is so velvety and pretty, too, and her eyes—whoa, they blow him away they are so big and bright. He watches her smiling as she talks to people in the restaurant and he can tell the people really like her. She has a warmth about her that makes the man want to wrap himself up in it...in her."

Gabe could tell he'd finally caught Dani's attention; she wasn't scoffing, wasn't rolling her eyes. She was listening. Intently. And maybe breathing a little bit harder. Good. He paused.

"Is that the end?" Dani whispered.

"Oh no, Just the beginning. The man immediately falls in love with her lips, you see. They're red and luscious and look like they're made for kissing...and other things. And in his imagination he takes the back of her head in his palm, brings her to him and kisses her. Like this." Gabe paused to look into Dani's eyes, assuring himself of her acquiescence before claiming her mouth completely. He turned his head slightly to take it deeper, compelling her to open her lips for him as he explored her with his tongue. He felt her hand glide up to hug the back of his head, and felt her tongue begin to dance with his. Somehow through the haze of lust, he heard his mind say *So far, so good*. Reluctantly he ended the kiss, pausing to rub his thumb across her generous, moist lower lip.

"So...what happened next?" she asked shakily.

*Yep. So far, so good.* "Well, you see the man's not content just to see the woman as others see her. He wants to see, and feel, and taste *all* of her. The parts that others don't see." Gabe took his hand and ran it lovingly down the side of Dani's face. "Being a red-blooded Italian-American male, he wants to see her body, to see if it matches the beauty of her face and her demeanor. For example, he wants to reach under the top she's wearing—" Gabe insinuated his hand underneath the front of Dani's blousy top, causing her to gasp "—and see if her breasts are as plump and as soft as he imagines them to be." He reached around and unhooked her bra, then cupped a breast, which he was thrilled to feel spilling out of his palm. He rolled it and pressed it against Dani's body, using his thumb to tweak her nipple, which had already pebbled. He did the same to her other breast, then ran his hand down to her waist. He could feel his erection beginning to strain against his pants. *Slow. Take it slow.* "And they are."

"Are...are what?" she stammered.

"Plump and soft." God, what was he thinking? How was he going to drag this out? He wanted to be on top of her, inside of her *right now.* He started to pull her top over her head and she paused, uncertain, before taking a deep breath and letting him finish the job.

"Oh," she said.

"Oh yeah," he said roughly, looking at her breasts for a moment before laying her down on the couch. He bent over her and began to suckle one, drawing the peak strongly into his mouth while Dani moaned and clutched his head to her. He laved the other breast and soothed it with his tongue before sitting upright. "Shall I go on?" he asked.

"Yes," she said without a trace of hesitation.

# CHAPTER EIGHTEEN

—◆◆—

Gabe hesitated. As much as he'd enjoyed Dani's positive responses to this point, from now on it could get dicey. Once again instinct kicked in and he figured it was time to turn over the controls.

"So all this time, while the man is fantasizing about the woman, it turns out she's been fantasizing about him too. For example, she wants to know what his body's like under his shirt, so she…" Gabe stopped and looked at Dani expectantly. She frowned, not understanding what he was up to, so he opened his arms wide and repeated, "She wants to know what his body looks and feels like under his shirt." He watched as comprehension dawned in her gorgeous eyes. It was a beautiful thing.

Dani took up the narrative. "So in her own fantasy she takes off his shirt and…and touches him." Gabe sucked in a gasp as Dani slid her small hands under his polo shirt and felt his lightly furred chest. Then she found his nipples.

"Ah," he said involuntarily, slightly jerking his body.

His reaction emboldened her. She nibbled on her lower lip as she pulled the shirt over his head and looked her fill. Then she touched him again, this time rubbing her palms across his pecs and down the sides of his chest.

Gabe couldn't help it. He stopped her hands with his own and looked into her eyes again.

"This is where the story gets really good," he said. "Ready to hear more?"

Dani returned his gaze, wide-eyed, and nodded.

"So after months of dreaming about each other, fate steps in and brings them together in the…in the…in a place with a comfortable bed."

Dani giggled. "That's real imaginative."

"Oh, but it was. Not the place, but the two lovers in the place. The man tells her what he wants to do to her. He doesn't sugar coat it. He doesn't use fancy words. He simply says, 'I want to kiss you and touch you and lick you *everywhere*. I want to stick my cock deep inside you and ride you until you scream with pleasure. I want to take your body and claim you as mine.'"

Dani blushed at the sex talk and the rosiness extended down her chest. Gabe realized how close he was to making good on that claim, so he had to physically move backward a few inches to remind himself what he wanted to have happen next.

He forged on. "But the woman says, 'That's all well and good, and yes, I'll let you take me, but first I am going to take *you*. I am going to look at your entire body and do what I want with it and then I am going to be the rider.'" With that, Gabe stood up and reached for Dani's hand. "Now we go to the bedroom," he said.

Dani looked up at him and hesitated. Then she took the glass of wine he had poured for her and finished it in one long swallow. She took his hand and let him lead her to the bedroom, where they both stopped in front of the bed. "So...take off your clothes and...and get on the bed," she commanded in a small voice.

"Yes, ma'am." Gabe tore off his shoes and socks, putting them next to a pair of sandals that Dani had left on the floor. The image warmed him—not that he needed warming at that point. As he took off his belt, pants, and underwear, he tried to focus on something other than the fact that he had a raging hard on that was going to go to waste if he got off too soon. But damn if she wasn't the sexiest thing he had ever laid eyes on. Her breasts were absolutely perfect, and she was so focused on him and his anatomy that she'd left modesty back in the living room. He loved it.

"You seem...big," she said, and he could hear the trepidation in her voice.

"It's a good thing you're in control, then." He climbed on the bed and lay flat, his arms splayed out to the side.

"I am, aren't I?" Dani's voice grew stronger. "And I can do whatever I want."

Gabe swallowed. "Within reason. I'm only human, you know."

With a smile, Dani quickly took off her skirt and stood at the foot of the bed watching him, clad only in her bikini panties. His erection saluted her scrutiny. She climbed on top of him and straddled his legs. "I like this," she said.

"I figured you might." He concentrated on things like cabbage soup and departmental paperwork—anything to combat the rising need in him to plant his seed in her. The image brought him up short. "Wait, I need something out of my pocket."

Dani hopped down, grabbed his pants and handed them to him. He retrieved the packets and set them on the nightstand. Seeing them must have given her pause, because she wasn't as eager to jump back on the bed.

"You have all the control," he reminded her in a gentle voice. "All of it."

She nodded finally and climbed back on, straddling him once again.

"That's my girl," he murmured.

"It's just that you're so...ready. More than ready. Maybe too ready."

The pretense of the story was gone; they were in the here and now. Although Dani seemed apprehensive, Gabe didn't think it was because of old memories; she seemed more wary of the mechanics involved. "I guarantee you that I will fit nicely, if you will let me play with you a little first."

"Play with me?"

Gabe didn't answer with words; he simply reached up and began to fondle Dani's breasts, which as she leaned toward him dangled so enticingly that he couldn't help but take one into his mouth again. The sounds coming from her told him he was on the right track. He took his erection and began to rub it back and forth along the scrap of bikini that kept him from her. Then he took a finger, slipped it past the barrier and explored her channel. It was warm and wet and ready, so he slipped in two. But whether or not this was really Dani's first time, it was still her first in a long time, which meant she needed to have it be the best it could possibly be. With his other hand he brought her face down to his and captured her lips again, his tongue mimicking the action of his fingers. He began to rub her gently and rhythmically, and could tell by the way she pressed herself on him that she was heading in the direction he'd hoped for.

She was concentrating now, finding her own pace. The fact that Gabe was taking such liberties appeared to be just fine with her. He felt her tension build, and he thought about the courage it took for her to be so vulnerable, and in a flash he felt honored and thrilled and proud to be the one to help her become who she was meant to be. For once in his life his own needs disappeared completely as he worked with her to make it happen, to show her it could happen. And then he felt her melt all around his fingers and a voice inside of him said *Yes*.

—◈— 

"Oh. My. God," Dani panted. "Oh, Gabriele…Oh!"

Dani's climax rolled like a giant wave across the surf, building higher and higher until it broke with such sweet chaos over her body that she imagined she was drowning in the pleasure of it. She found herself draped over Gabe, breathing heavily, waiting for her pulse to return to some version of normal. In a matter of seconds she realized two things: one was that she had yet to experience the actual act of sex, and the other was that Gabe was ready, willing and—by the feel of his rock-hard erection—very much able to help complete that experience with her.

She sat up and looked into his eyes. His gaze was steady and his lips were pressed in a firm line. She knew in that instant that he was paying a high price for waiting. And he was waiting for her. She knew that if she said she wanted to stop, he would calmly say "Okay" and still care for her, still be there for her. Tears welled up as she absorbed the meaning of that, and her love for this aggravating man intensified exponentially—maybe, she thought on a note of panic, to the point of infinity.

She took a deep breath and let it out slowly. "The lady had said she wanted to ride him first, but then she changed her mind," she said softly. She then moved to lie down beside him. She said, "I want you on top of me and inside of me, because I know you won't hurt me." The lady had vanished; it was only Dani talking to Gabe.

Gabe turned to her, leaning on his elbow. His expression, which had briefly betrayed disappointment, now rapidly turned inquisitive. He frowned, murmured, "Are you sure?"

Dani nodded and Gabe said "All right, then." He placed himself on top of her, keeping his upper body weight on his elbows. He nudged her legs apart and motioned for her to bend her knees. *There's no turning back now.* She barely had a moment to register that thought before he began kissing her again, passionately, single-mindedly, his mouth claiming hers without reserve. He moved from her lips to her neck, whispering endearments in Italian, words like *bella mia* and *sono pazzo di te. I'm crazy about you.* He pressed his body against hers, his hard, muscled planes moving rhythmically against her softness, preparing her for what was to come. He leaned over to get a foil packet from the nightstand, tore it open with his teeth and expertly donned it. Then he reached down between their legs to fit himself to her and entered her slowly. She was grateful for that, because part of her remained skeptical that he would in fact "fit nicely" as he had promised.

"*Tesoro mio*," he said, groaning slightly as he pushed inexorably into her body. "*Ti adoro.*"

Dani felt the pressure of him, but no pain. A thought flashed across her consciousness: *If you are a virgin and have a hymen, isn't it supposed to hurt more?* But she didn't think a second beyond that because once he was seated fully inside her, he began to move, and all sanity fled. Slowly at first, then building momentum, he thrust powerfully in and out of her until her own body took up a rhythm in sync with his, meeting him on his terms regardless of anything she might think about it. Another climax began to build and she started to whimper in tandem with his measured groans. Then, as if striking a match to a pile of kindling, he placed his hand between their legs to touch her exactly where she needed him to. She erupted again, crying out, lost in the blazing intensity of her orgasm, only dimly registering that Gabe had thrust once more and then held her fast as he too reached his peak. "*Mio Dio*," she heard him say before he buried his face on the side of her neck. She heard his rapid breathing and felt his heart beating as fast as her own.

Slowly their bodies came down to earth. Gabe pulled out from Dani and disposed of the condom. He didn't ask if he could stay in her bed; in fact, neither of them spoke. He simply lay back down, brought her close to him and pulled the covers over them.

It was all too much for her to process at the moment, so she did the sensible thing and fell asleep in his arms.

—◆◇◆—

It was nine o'clock the next morning before Dani stirred. The heavy curtains had been pulled aside, leaving the shears to filter the morning light. She was alone in the bed, but it didn't bother her, because she could hear the shower running. She figured Gabe was back from the early morning run he'd taken shortly after their last bout at lovemaking—their third of the night.

After the second time, they'd slept nestled together like spoons. She'd awakened sometime later to feel his arm move from around her waist down to between her legs. After a few minutes of play she'd turned to her back and opened her legs in invitation. Their lovemaking had been sweet and slow, with a dreamlike quality to it. Afterward she had fallen back asleep as if it were the most natural thing in the world to have a man fondle her awake, climb on top of her and make her moan in ecstasy.

Fully alert now, she tried to make sense out of what had happened during the past several hours—or more importantly, what *hadn't* happened. She hadn't frozen at Gabe's touch, or been repelled, or felt scared, or panicked. She hadn't thought about being a victim or feeling helpless or being overpowered. Gabe could have made her feel all of those things; physically he was so powerful in every way that she was no match for him. He could easily have taken advantage of that disparity. Instead, he had given her the power over *him*. He had let her take every step forward when she was ready and not before.

Dani stretched, feeling the twinge of muscles not accustomed to being used the way she'd used them the night before. She wondered briefly if last night meant she had gotten over her "issues." Maybe she could truly put the past behind her, whatever it was, and move forward. Maybe even move forward with Gabe. *A happy thought.* But even if that were to come true, it still didn't solve the mystery of what had happened to her—if anything—when she was fifteen. More than ever, she wanted to know the truth.

Just then Gabe walked out of the bathroom, a towel wrapped around his waist while he bent forward and vigorously dried his hair with another. Dani worried briefly about spiders in his towel, but thrust the thought aside. Instead she gazed at him, enjoying the view as the morning light caught his sculpted arms and chest.

"Keep looking at me like that and I'm goin' in," he warned, looking over at Dani and smiling. "Fourth time's a charm."

"You had your head down!" She cried. "How did you know I was…"

"Lucky guess, bella. If you were standing where I am now and I was in the bed? You could bet your last nickel I'd be looking…and planning…and hoping that your towel would fall off… just like this." And with that, Gabe dropped the towel and lunged under the covers, reaching for Dani and more than ready to take her wherever she wanted to go.

"Oh my gosh you have cold feet!' she squealed, laughing as she tried to escape his embrace. They mock wrestled until he had her lying on her back with her hands over her head.

Suddenly he stopped.

"Does this bother you?" he asked gently. "The arms, I mean."

Dani shook her head and her tone was serious. "Not with you. Never with you."

A look of relief crossed Gabe's face and he leaned in to kiss her. It didn't take long for the kissing to lead to touching and then to suckling and then to loving—this time in daylight, as if to proclaim once and for all that it was right and good for them to be together.

Afterward Gabe lay with his head on Dani's breasts while she ran her fingers idly through his still-damp hair. "I noticed when you lost control last night you reverted to speaking Italian," she said.

"Hmm," he said, pausing in his quest to root out her nipple. "I guess you can take the boy out of Italy…"

"…but not the Italy out of the boy?"

"Something like that." He raised his head to catch her eyes. "But I beg to differ on one point: I never lost control."

Dani smirked. "Uh huh. Constable, when you were huffing and puffing over me, I don't think there was any way you could have changed course."

Gabe sat up against the headboard and tucked her beneath his arm. She was surprised at the solemnness with which he spoke. "Bella, in my line of work, I've seen countless situations where the perp says, 'I just lost control.' That doesn't cut it. Ever.

You need to know that with me, there will never be a time when we make love that you aren't in complete control of the situation. I never want you to feel helpless again. Do you understand?"

Dani's eyes immediately welled up. Gabe was telling her he believed she'd actually been violated. He didn't think, like so many others, that it was just in her head. That realization brought with it a flurry of jumbled emotions: relief at having someone finally take her seriously, and fear that the person who had done such damage so long ago might still be out there, inflicting pain on other helpless girls for the past dozen years.

"Hey, that was meant to make you feel better, not make you cry," Gabe admonished. He carefully wiped her tears away with his thumb. He was about to begin kissing her again when he heard the insistent buzz of his cell phone. He tried to ignore it, focusing instead on taking Dani's mind elsewhere, but Dani wouldn't let him.

"Could be Marco," she said.

Gabe sighed, rolled over, and sat on the edge of the bed. He picked up the phone and nodded to Dani, letting her know it was indeed Marco's number. He listened for a minute and stood up, his entire body on alert.

"You're shittin' me," he muttered in response to what he was hearing.

Dani reached out to him. "What's wrong?"

Gabe looked at Dani and held his finger up. "Yeah, I'll meet you there," he said to Marco, and hung up. He immediately headed for the bathroom.

Dani scooted off the bed, reaching for her robe. Gabe had left the door open and was pulling on his jeans and socks. She stood in the doorway, hands on hips. "Gabe, you're scaring me. What is it? Did Marco find something? Tell me!"

As if he'd just remembered her presence, Gabe stopped dressing long enough to gently grasp her face between his hands. "I'm sorry. No…uh…nothing's popped up yet related to your aunt's death. Still waitin' on the autopsy. Marco just got some new information he wants to share with me, that's all."

"What new information?"

"Something…something about a witness. He's gonna fill me in. I told him I'd meet him downtown. But I need you to stay here until I get back, *va bene*? I won't be long, and then we can head over to interview those employees." He kissed her hard on the mouth before reaching for his shirt; a moment later he was gone.

Gabe's departure left an icy void in the room that had nothing to do with temperature. Dani felt down to her bones that he wasn't telling her the truth, and the pain of knowing that stopped her in her tracks. Gabe hadn't been up front with her from the beginning, and he still wasn't coming clean. She took a deep breath. Maybe it's nothing, she chided herself. Maybe he just didn't think it was that important. She tried that thought on for size, but it just didn't fit.

*Maybe,* she thought at last, *it's me who's not important enough.*

—◆❖◆—

"Jesus, the guy was executed," Gabe said thirty minutes later at the Caffè Veneto. Marco had bought them cappuccinos and just filled Gabe in on the homicide of Augustino Abruzzo, the same thug they'd shaken down the day before.

"Bullet to the back of the head, nice and tidy," Marco remarked. "The question is, did he take that bullet on account of us?"

Gabe felt like crap. "We've got to assume he did, which means they're feeling some heat. That's not good."

"No, it's not." Marco paused and took a breath. "Listen, I could get in real hot water over what I'm about to tell you, but this is getting serious and you've gotta know what's going on."

Gabe looked sharply at his friend. "What are you talking about?"

"It's no coincidence that I've been able to spend a lot of time on this case. I haven't been sneaking around. I've got the blessing of the director of a special task force that I've been a member of for some time."

"What, on human trafficking?"

"Yes. We've known something wasn't quite right here in Verona, and we've had signs that it's related to the hotel industry, but we haven't been able to pinpoint what's going on or who's behind it, although a shadowy holding company called Consorzio Azurro has popped up more than once on our radar. Stella d'Italia is small and privately held, so it's been impossible to penetrate their books. You coming to me with the evidence from Carla Rinaldi was the first break we've had in a while."

"You been using me, Marco?"

His friend stiffened. "I wouldn't put it that way. I wanted to bring you up to speed from the beginning, but was told not to. I'm just doing my job, and if it leaks out that I brought you into the loop, I'll be fired. But it's getting dangerous for you and Dani, and you deserve to know every angle of this thing. So do what you want with it."

Gabe and Marco sat in silence for several minutes. It dawned on Gabe that fate, if it existed, had intervened here. And if he had no power over such a thing, why would he let it ruin his oldest friendship? "Well, I can't say I'm thrilled you took this long to level with me, but better late than never." He clapped his friend on the shoulder. "What you shared stays between us. I'm as committed as you are to nailing these dicks, whoever they are, to the wall."

Marco looked relieved. "Okay. So," he said, getting back to business, "assuming you're right about them offing Santo's wife—and from what Tino almost let slip, it sounds like you are—they kept the scene clean this time around, except for the damaged tooth. Maybe the autopsy will show something more definitive, but I'm not gonna hold my breath. Still no hits on the name 'Tetka,' either. We know there are Baltic criminal organizations involved in the trade, but the fact that 'tetka' means 'aunt' in Croatian doesn't give us much to go on. We've got another lead, but nothing as solid as Tino."

Gabe sat up in his chair. "What have you got?"

"You told me Carla Rinaldi said there were two guys, so we know Tino had a partner. Only Tino was linked to the fake company and to the prints at the marina, but a guy checked into the room next to Tino five minutes after Tino did, so I ran his name." He pulled a file up on his phone. "Goran Novak. Thirty-two years old. Self-employed 'security guard.' Last permanent address was Zagreb."

"Carla said they were speaking some Eastern European language. If he's a Croat, that fits. You got a picture of him?"

"No, his record's clean."

"Well, the guy sitting next to Tino in the bar looked Slavic. Maybe it was Novak. Which means we might have set Tino up for his own murder. *Shit.* Any way you can bring Novak in for a chat?"

"No. There's no link between the two at this point. We can't hold him and we sure as hell don't want him to end up like Tino."

"You're right. No sense alerting them any more than you have already. So...what's next?"

Marco took out his wallet. "I'm going to run those license plates I took down at the Sexy Pig. If something turns up in his name I'll have him tailed, see if he leads us anywhere. Maybe he's a nervous type. Maybe he makes a mistake. Who knows? In the meantime, we'll see what Dante finds out, see if anything pans out with those missing employees, keep putting the pieces together."

Gabe nodded and reached for his own wallet but Marco waived him off.

"Least I can do, since you're practically on the force," Marco groused.

Gabe mustered a half smile. "Then by all means, let's get to work." They both got up to leave, but Gabe stopped Marco with his hand. "Hey, you mind checking one more thing for me?"

"Sure, what do you need?"

"I'm looking for the name of the doc who treated Ciro Forcelli the night he stroked out."

Marco threw his hands up. "Damn, don't tell me you think *that* was suspect! That was, what, ten years ago?"

"Twelve years ago, and no, that's not it. I…I think it was the same guy who cared for my mom. I'd like to stop by and say thanks, that's all."

Marco shot Gabe a look of compassion. "No problem, I can look it up. But wouldn't your Aunt Fausta know the guy? She took care of your mom after you left, didn't she?"

"Yeah, well, Fausta's, shall we say, *prickly* these days. I try not to get too close if I can help it."

"Don't I know it." Marco's lips twitched. "I'll send you the name."

"Thanks."

"No problem. Later."

As Gabe headed back to his car he started a mental checklist. *One: Do not let Dani out of your sight. These thugs are getting nervous and they don't mess around. Two: The doc who treated Ciro also checked on Dani that night. He might know something he's not telling. Three: We need to see if we can flush anything out about these missing girls. Four: I need to get back to Dani…now.*

# CHAPTER NINETEEN

—✦✦✦—

After Gabe left, Dani decided to search the mansion to see if she could find the two elusive paintings her great-grandfather Luzio had brought back from The Grove nearly a hundred years before. Fausta had alluded to "secrets," so maybe she knew they'd been stolen and not given to her ancestor as a gift. Dani wouldn't know the truth until she found them. She frowned. *And maybe not even then.*

She couldn't remember where in the house she'd seen them as a child, but they should be easy to spot; both were dark and moody, like the house, but they weren't religious in nature, like most of La Tana's furnishings. Instead, each depicted a woman in the midst of an extremely emotional event. She shuddered at the thought, made worse by the childhood memories that were already beginning to engulf her.

Growing up in a *palazzo* the size of La Tana meant learning how to run, not when any responsible adult could see her (Fausta would never have countenanced running), but whenever possible, darting past the cold, dark, sinister spaces to get to the good, warm, happy places. Dani and her parents had lived on the top floor, the only members of the family to do so. Her father had told her once it was because they were special, but now Dani realized they must have drawn the short straw in terms of accommodations.

Living at the top of the mansion meant running (and sometimes sliding) down the stairs one flight and racing all the way to the end of the north wing to Nonna Stella's welcoming suite, where she slept when her parents were out of town.

Agnese's room required an even longer sprint: all the way down to the ground floor and across to the opposite side of the mansion beyond the kitchen.

From the time she'd learned the estate's name meant "The Panther's Lair," Dani had been afraid of the dark stretches between the light. Had she been a boy, maybe she would have relished stalking the "panthers" of the house. But for a little girl with a vivid imagination, it was all too believable that wild beasts lurked behind the doors of those gloomy, forbidding halls. And wasn't she vindicated when one of them—of the human variety—tried to snatch her when she was fifteen? The key word, so everyone said, was "tried." The rest, she'd been told, was merely in her head.

Now, at the age of twenty-seven, Dani set out to truly explore her childhood home for the first time. She hadn't conjured the paintings out of her imagination; she remembered them from *somewhere*. No one but staff was home at this hour, so now was as good a time as any. She decided to search from the bottom up, and fully expected common sense to prevail over her childish fears.

That expectation lasted exactly two floors.

The ground floor and what Europeans called the first floor (which was logically the second floor, because didn't the ground floor have a floor too?) posed no problem—and revealed no paintings. Those levels housed the "public" rooms the family never seemed to use. By and large they were filled with religious artwork and sculpture that somehow appeared lonely, as if the pieces had been assigned a shepherd's task where no sheep could be found. The large front reception area, filled with wooden furniture created for short visits, smelled of vinegar and flowers past their prime. The dark paneled library, where she and Gabe had waited that first night, still reeked of musty books whose spines had probably never been cracked. Dani peeked into the ballroom and waited for memories to intrude, but none did. So much of La Tana was what architects called "transition space;" the true living areas of the house were few and far between.

It was only when Dani reached the next level up—where she and Gabe were staying, and where Aunt Ornella had died—that her heart began knocking against her chest, warning her to beware.

*Why now?* she thought with a tiny spurt of panic. She'd been staying at La Tana for a week—on this very floor—and hadn't felt afraid. But she hadn't felt quite so alone, either. Gabe had been with her, or she'd been coming or going or working; never had it been just her and...the *lair*. She tried to slow down her breathing.

It was just a house, right? Too large and way too pretentious, maybe, but still, just a house.

At the top of the landing she paused. She heard nothing. The space felt desolate.

The mansion encompassed four wings, each of which had its own hallway, dimly lit with wall sconces. To the far right was Nonna Stella's wing and the suite that she and Gabe shared; no need to check there. The next closest hallway housed Aunt Ornella's rooms. One by one she poked her head in, saving her aunt's actual bedroom for last. She doubted Ornella would have wanted the darkly themed paintings anywhere near her, but Dani hadn't paid attention when she'd visited earlier, and she had to be sure.

The yellow tape that marked the room as a possible crime scene sagged low across the doorway. The police would not be coming back, but no one, not even Fausta, had cared enough to remove the garish sash. She gingerly opened the door, stepped over the tape and flipped on the light.

Death greeted her.

Ornella's body was gone, of course, but the aura of loss lingered along with the slightly sour smell of a sickroom. Nothing hummed, nothing stirred. All was quiet. The bed lay empty, the soiled sheets still crumpled on top. The shelves still held the accoutrements of a life that no longer needed them: pads and tubing and small metal pans...a jar of body cream, some hand sanitizer. A person had lived in this room for many years, and even though she was ill and immobile, she still had thoughts and feelings and memories. Now there was nothing. Aunt Ornella had experienced untold sadness during her life and now even that life was gone. Dani fought past a lump in her throat. *Maybe she's with little Ciro now.* She sincerely hoped that was true.

As Dani suspected, the room held no paintings. She took a moment to collect herself before moving on to the third wing, which served as her Uncle Aldo's living quarters. Her sense of unease began to grow, and her heart, which had let her grieve briefly for her aunt, resumed its frenzied pulse. *You should not be here*, it seemed to say.

Pushing on through sheer willpower, Dani told herself she was doing no harm, merely touring the house. Her Uncle Aldo's rooms were unlocked—a sure sign he wouldn't mind her presence. *Right.* She found more religious artifacts and truly Spartan furnishings. Maybe Uncle Aldo considered himself a modern-day monk. Whatever he was, he was no connoisseur of Amelia Starling originals. Lia's paintings were nowhere to be found.

That left one wing to search: Uncle Santo's. As she forced herself to walk down the hall, memories finally began to assail her. She was ten years old and her cousin Ciro was having a family birthday party, too sick to invite outsiders. Uncle Santo stood in the main hallway, asking her to turn around and show him her new blue dress. She twirled for him and he smiled, giving her a piece of chocolate for her trouble. "You are a very pretty little girl," he'd told her.

She walked down the hall and visions emerged of another night. She'd worn blue then, too, but her dress was daringly short and the makeup Agnese had applied to her face made her feel much older than fifteen. She'd drunk a mixture of wine, rum, and

Coke, and way too much of it. Her stomach had begun to churn, like it was right now. Dani fought to keep her mind in the present, but the sights and sounds and smells of that earlier time were too powerful. She could hear the melody of the string quartet from the floor below. They were playing Verdi and she wanted so much to hear Avril Lavigne. She wanted to *dance*! But she had put on too much of her mother's Chanel No.5 and the cloying scent of it was making her gag. She could hear the murmur of voices and laughter and the clink of glasses and knew she had to find her room and lie down before she threw up all over her pretty blue dress.

And she remembered the man's arms as they came around her from behind and touched her small breasts and whispered in her ear with hot, liquor-smelling breath: "Come on, little girl. Let me show you something."

And she was saying "No...get away...please..." and tried pushing him away but the man just gripped her tighter and forced her up against a wall and she shut her eyes as he began lifting her little skirt and rubbing himself against her...

...and a deep voice, her uncle's voice, saying "Basta!" and the sound of a hard slap.

And the man whimpering "*Mi dispiace, signore*," and nothing more...until she felt another pair of arms, around her shoulders this time, leading her to a room and a couch.

Engulfed in her memories, Dani opened the door to her uncle's suite of rooms. A small lamp on a table cast a soothing glow over what looked like an office of some sort. She saw the same couch she'd pictured in her mind from so long ago. It was long and soft and black and her hands began to shake. She had sat on that couch, shaking like she was now, and her uncle sat next to her, brushing her hair back from her face and whispering to her that it was all right, that she would be all right now that her Uncle Santo was here. And when he left her, even for a moment, she felt alone and scared, but he came back and sat down next to her and handed her a small glass of water. Or she thought it was water, but it tasted strange. And he said it would make her feel so much better, if she would just drink it all, and she tried to, but she had already drunk so much. And then he helped her up and said, "You can lie down in my room. You'll be safe here," and he took her into the other room, and—

"Daniela, what are you doing here?"

Dani whirled around to see her uncle standing in the doorway. "*Mio Dio!*" she cried, clapping her hand to her mouth. Her stomach roiled and she thought her lungs were going to burst. "You...you scared me."

Santo stepped into the room and closed the door. Dani's heart beat even faster. *Get control*, she told herself. *He can't do anything to you. He won't do anything to you.*

"I said, what are you doing here?" He spoke the words more sharply.

"I...I...I..."

Santo walked over to a sideboard and poured himself a glass of some type of liquor from a crystal decanter. He poured another glass and handed it to Dani. "Brandy," he said.

She took the drink with severely shaking hands and immediately set it down so she wouldn't spill it.

"You're obviously upset," he said calmly. "My guess is that you were reliving that night."

Dani swallowed hard. He'd cut right to the chase. "You…you remember what happened?"

"Of course I do." He took a sip of his drink. "Here, why don't you have a seat and I'll tell you what I can—assuming you want to hear it, of course." He gazed at her benignly.

"Yes…yes, I do want to know." She ran her hands through her hair. "I was…I was looking for some old artwork I remembered from a long time ago, and memories just started popping up." She looked around. No paintings. "I can't remember anything that happened, really, except when I came in here, images started to bombard me."

"Please sit," he said, gesturing to his couch. He did not join her, but stood over her, exuding power. "I'm not surprised you remember being in here, because in fact, you were in here. This is where I brought you after the man tried to…have his way with you the night of the party."

Dani nodded. That much she knew. "What did happen?"

"I had left some papers up here in my office, and when I reached this floor I saw the monster with his hands on you. I…dispatched him and brought you in here to calm you down. You were, needless to say, quite upset, not to mention extremely inebriated."

Dani felt her face redden as long-held shame washed over her. "I remember, I felt sick. You gave me something…"

"Yes. What is that expression? A little 'hair of the dog' to settle your nerves."

"And then what?"

Santo paused, his glass halfway to his lips. "What do you mean?"

"And then what happened? I don't remember after that."

"Ah. Well, you...you fell asleep. There was a commotion in the hall and someone knocked on the door to tell me that my father—your Nonno Ciro—had had a stroke. I had to leave you momentarily, but I sent someone to fetch you back to your room, where you spent the rest of the night."

"My mother said you had a doctor examine me."

Santo walked casually back to the sideboard and poured himself another shot. "Yes. My mother was a bit manic in her grief. The doctor who attended my father could do nothing more for him, so when she heard you'd been...approached...she insisted the doctor check to make sure you were all right. I tried to spare you the indignity since I had seen the incident unfold, but she would have her way." He drank the rest of the brandy in one swallow. "She always has her way."

"But there was nothing."

"That's correct. Because nothing happened."

Dani sat quietly, trying to absorb it all. The story seemed to match her memories, but something was missing...something was incomplete.

Santo interrupted her thoughts. "I'm sorry for what happened to you at the tender age of fifteen, but I must confess I'm glad you are here now." He pinned her with his eyes. "Have you given any thought to my proposal?"

Dani rose from the couch. As shaky as she was feeling, it was time to shift gears. She'd never be able to go "head to head" with her uncle, but she needed all the height she could get, even if it was just a few inches over five feet. "I don't think Alberghi Paradisi is a good investment," she began. "I—"

Her uncle's studied benevolence dissolved in an instant. "You've been listening to your cousin," he bit out. "Dante has not been running this company for the past thirty plus years—I have. I assure you I know what constitutes a good investment."

"I was going to say, I've been looking at the numbers," Dani countered. "I understand profit and loss, Uncle. I can spot trends. Dante happens to share my view, but neither he nor Nonna Stella influenced me, if that's what you're implying."

"I'm implying nothing," he said, taking her arm firmly. "I'm telling you that you must vote your shares with mine to make this happen. It's imperative."

Dani looked down at the arm he held captive. *Santo's losing it,* she thought. The situation must be worse than they all imagined. She looked directly at him and pulled her arm away. "I'm not ten years old anymore, Uncle," she said, forcing herself to remain calm. "You can't force me to do anything."

"Oh can't I?" he murmured. He stepped back.

Still quivering, she turned to leave. "Thank you...for helping me to remember."

Santo paused, then spoke in a tone that demanded her attention. "You should know something, Daniela."

She turned and looked at him. "What?"

"There are others, close to you, who could be adversely affected if the vote does not take place, and soon. Do you understand?" He held her gaze a moment longer than necessary before walking to the door and holding it open for her. "Oh, and those two paintings you mentioned? They are unavailable at the moment. I would appreciate it...very much...if you asked for permission the next time you come to my chambers. I would be more than delighted to invite you in."

Dani tore her gaze away and headed back down the hall, trying desperately not to run.

Thoughts jostled for the front seat of her mind: *He's desperate. Desperate people do desperate things. He needed her vote and implied that people would get hurt if she didn't comply.*

*But there was something else.*

*Something darker.*

*The paintings. How did he know which ones I was talking about? How did he know there were two of them? I never said how many.* And perhaps worst of all: *I didn't see the room beyond his office.*

She felt a sickness inside—the same combination of pain and horror she'd experienced in so many nightmares as a teen. Had she conjured the feelings from nothing...or were they based on a memory?

One thing she knew with certainty: the Lair would eventually give up its secrets. The truth, she feared, would be unbearable and perhaps even dangerous. One thought emerged to crowd out all the others: *I cannot bear to have Gabriele caught up in this. I cannot risk him getting hurt on account of me.* She swallowed a sob, and once she'd turned the corner, she ran all the way back to her suite.

# CHAPTER TWENTY

—‣✦✦‣—

Several housekeeping employees of the Stella d'Italia Verona lived in a high-rise apartment on Via Santa Lucia, just a stone's throw from Verona's main rail station. Gabe watched Dani cover her ears as the teeth-rattling screech of brakes announced the arrival of yet another train.

"I used to live near a station," he commented. "You get used to it."

"I suppose you would," Dani said neutrally. It was the first thing she'd said since they'd driven over from La Tana.

Something was wrong. He'd felt it the minute he'd returned from his meeting with Marco. The soft, delectable woman he'd left in bed not two hours previously was nowhere to be seen; instead a very agitated, distant Daniela had emerged. He'd come back to find her pacing their suite, but when he'd offered an apology, she'd waived it away, saying without heat, "No, don't worry about it, really. I…I just want to get this all behind us, that's all." She didn't seem mad at him, which bothered him more than anything. Anger he could deal with, but a Dani without emotion? He didn't know what to make of that.

Dante had given them the name of two relatively long-term employees who could perhaps shed some light on one of the women who had recently dropped out of sight.

The two staff workers were like cotton candy and rutabaga. Ines was tall, blond, pretty, and ditzy. She obviously knew the effect she had on men and she reveled in it. Dobra, on the other hand, was big-boned, overweight, and unfortunately, shrewd. Gabe figured in the long run, Ines would be more forthcoming.

They lived in a tiny third-floor walk-up that seemed to have captured the heat of the afternoon and stubbornly refused to give it up. Dobra insisted on taking their jackets and hanging them on a coat rack in the corner. The living room consisted of a faded green couch, which the girls sat on, and two rickety chairs from the kitchen dinette set that Gabe thought might actually bend under his weight. A cheap fan blew a meager breeze that ruffled a couple of outdated magazines on the small, battered coffee table. He could smell the remnants of Indian curry—probably take-out, by the looks of the Styrofoam boxes overflowing a trash can in the kitchen.

Dani had opened their inquiry by explaining that Stella d'Italia wanted to make sure it was doing all it could to retain workers like Dobra and Ines and avoid hiring those who weren't cut out for the job. She plastered on a smile and piled the bullshit on thick. Gabe was impressed by how well she'd gotten back into speaking Italian after just a few days.

"We want to have more high quality employees like you two," she'd said. "So tell us, what kind of person was this Mirela—" she looked down at her notepad "—Mirela Pavlenco." Gabe didn't bother to interrupt because Dani had it wired. She probed for anything the two women might know about the kind of person Mirela was, who she socialized with, whether she was happy in her job, what might have prompted her to leave.

"She might have found a better job being a waitress or a dancer or something. I mean, she was sexy, you know?" Ines looked pointedly at Gabe and smiled. Despite the credibility of Dani's business card, both young women had been reluctant to talk at first. Gabe, ostensibly Dani's new "assistant," had therefore shamelessly turned on the charm, and Ines had taken the bait. Of the two, she showed at least a modicum of cooperation. Not so with Dobra.

"So, um, she was attractive," Dani said. "Is there anything else you can tell us about her? For example, did she make any new friends who came to see her?"

Both women shook their heads. "No, she was kind of shy," Ines said. "She didn't know anybody. You went out dancing with her once, didn't you?" She turned to her roommate.

Dobra shook her head again. "No. Not really. I don't remember."

"Well, *you're* both attractive, so there must have been something different about her," Gabe suggested. He glanced at Dani, expecting at least an eye roll, but she gave nothing away.

"No, there was nothing," Dobra said flatly. She sat with arms crossed under her pillow-like breasts and tapped her wide left foot on the floor. She needed a shower.

"Oh, she had something I thought was kind of pretty," Ines countered. "I mean, I would never do it. My friends who've done it say it hurts, although not too much, but still…but a lot of people do it these days and it's pretty cool, so maybe one day I'll…"

"You'll do what?" Gabe interjected, gracing her with a slow smile.

"Get a tattoo," Ines said, caught by his gaze. "Would you like that? I mean, do you like those? On women, I mean?"

Gabe glanced at Dani. "Uh, well, I suppose that would depend on where it is," he said, injecting some subtext into his tone. "Where was Mirela's?"

Ines lifted her golden shoulder-length hair as if she were about to pin it up. "Back here," she said, pointing to the back of her right ear.

"No, that wasn't anything. That was a birthmark," Dobra said. "You don't know—"

"If that was a birthmark, then I'm the Holy Father's daughter," Ines shot back, dropping her hair. "It was a little blue butterfly landing on a tiny gold tree."

"Sounds pretty. Did she like to show it off?" Dani asked.

"No," Dobra said at the same time Ines shook her head.

"I don't speak Romanian," Ines said. "You can ask Dobra. It just sounds like marbles in the mouth to me. I just pointed to Mirela's tattoo one time and said it was pretty, and she smiled and nodded. That was it."

Dobra took that moment to stand up. Gabe decided he wouldn't want to meet her in a dark alley; the woman was *large*.

"I really have to go to work now," she announced.

"You working a double shift?" Ines asked. "I thought—"

The look Dobra gave her roommate would have kept a case of Budweiser perfectly chilled; Ines apparently got the hint because she shut up.

"Well, um, thank you for taking the time to talk to us," Dani said. "We're trying to find out why some of our employees are leaving the company. Perhaps we should conduct more interviews before they decide to leave."

"Ya, that's a good idea," Dobra said, ushering them out the door. Just as she was about to close it in their face, Ines grabbed her purse and scooted by.

"I've got to go check the mail. I'll walk you down," Ines said.

She smiled and made small talk as they walked down the three flights of stairs. At the bottom, while Dani continued walking purposefully toward the car, Ines picked up a discarded flyer, pulled a pencil from her purse, and hastily wrote her name and number down. She handed the flyer to Gabe. "I...um...I'm not doing anything tonight. Maybe...maybe you'd like to talk some more about, well, you know, the job and all."

Gabe glanced at Dani's retreating figure before pasting a smile on his face. *Who knows? Maybe the little twit will share more without Dobra the Dragon Lady breathing down her neck.* "Great idea," he said, looking directly at Ines and grinning suggestively. "Why don't we go dancing? Maybe that place you said Dobra and Mirela went to. Is it around here?"

"Near Piazza Bra," she said.

"Perfect. I could pick you up at Caffè Notte—you know it? Say, eight thirty? We could get a bite to eat and then head over. He leaned forward. "But don't tell Dobra, okay? She looks like the jealous type."

Ines giggled and reached over to touch his arm. "It'll be our little secret. Until tonight, then."

Gabe inclined his head, offering her a slight smile. "Until tonight."

Ines waved goodbye with her fingertips and headed back up the stairs. Gabe transferred the phone number to his cell phone as he hurried to catch up with Dani. Once he reached her, she didn't acknowledge him, but kept walking, her face a study in control.

Gabe started to explain, but she cut him off. Not with anger, not with jealousy, but with something much more deadly: indifference.

"It's not important," she said, looking at him with lifeless eyes. "Not at all."

Gabe held his tongue. She couldn't mean it. Not after last night. He strapped himself into the driver's seat and waited for her to blow her top. Yell at him. Slap him, even. Anything to open the door so that he could explain why he'd just made a date with that little twit Ines.

But instead she merely stated, "That woman Dobra was lying."

Okay. Back to business, then. The other could wait. "No question about it," he agreed. "She knows something. And she did *not* like us being there."

"Maybe she had a thing against Mirela. If the woman was that attractive, there could have been some jealousy."

Gabe shook his head. "Given Dobra's less than friendly attitude, that's a possibility, but I don't think so. If that were the case, she could have called her a bitch, dissed her job performance, said good riddance and all that. She didn't seem to care about the Romanian girl personally. She just didn't want us to know anything about her."

"I wonder if Dobra's Romanian."

"Maybe. Or maybe she's Croatian. Marco's working on a lead in that direction."

Gabe pulled out his phone and began texting. "Speaking of which, let's see if he can scare anything up on Dobra Moretti." He put the phone on the dash. "So, bella, may I take you to lunch?"

Dani glanced at him. "Uh, no thanks. If you don't mind just dropping me back off at La Tana, I think I'll just get a snack and a nap. I'm...kind of tired. Didn't sleep too well." The moment she said it, her face turned bright red.

"That's my kind of insomnia," Gabe murmured, reaching for her. She flinched. *Yes, something had definitely happened while he was meeting with Marco.* "What's wrong, sweetheart?"

Dani avoided his gaze, but after a moment resolutely turned to face him. "About last night..."

"And this morning," he said.

"And this morning. It was...it was great and all, and really helped me out a lot, but..."

She looked away again.

"But you're sorry it happened and it will never happen again. Do I have that right?" Gabe tried to keep the resentment out of his remark.

"Something like that." She gazed back at him, imploring him with those big velvet eyes. "I told you I have baggage…"

"And I told you I'd help you carry it." Gabe's hands tightened on the steering wheel to keep from touching her.

"I know, and I appreciate all you've done, in so many ways, really. But I think I just have to take it from here," she said. "My family situation here is pretty messed up." She laughed harshly. "*Mio Dio, I'm* pretty messed up. I'm…I just don't want you getting stuck in all this…*miseria*. Maybe it's time you cut your losses and headed back home."

Gabe didn't respond immediately to Dani's insane comment because he knew that whatever he said he'd probably regret later. He took a moment to watch the activity at the train station across the street. Dozens of people were continually entering and leaving the building, like hardworking bees maintaining their hive. They all seemed to have someplace to go. Gabe wanted to be one of them, heading far away from the shit connected to La Tana and his and Dani's families. Hell yes, he wanted to go home. But right now he didn't have that luxury. And he knew it was going to get a whole lot uglier before they could leave it all behind. But one thing he was sure of: when they did leave, they were going to leave together.

He finally turned and looked at her. "You want to shelve the discussion about you and me, that's fine. You want to blow off the fact that we made incredible love, that's up to you, too." He tensed. *Better tell her everything.* "But there's something you need to know. The witness we talked to yesterday about his involvement in your father's death was murdered. Executed. Whoever's behind what's going on isn't happy we're asking questions, and they don't mess around. So yeah, to say there's some misery connected to La Tana is an understatement. And Dani? There's no way in hell I'm leaving you here to deal with it alone." He started the car and headed for La Tana, not bothering to comment on the tears that were quietly streaming down Dani's face.

—⟡⟡⟡—

Despite his warning and her tears, Dani didn't soften toward Gabe the rest of the day and Gabe decided not to push her. When they returned to the estate, she politely excused herself, went into her room, and shut the door. "I really am tired," she'd said. "I'm going to take a nap." Damn, he was tired, too. He wanted nothing more than to curl up behind her sweet body and lose himself in dreams of her. But she was having none of it. It seemed she'd retreated behind the same aloof barrier he'd been trying to win over for the past year. He didn't understand it.

He stretched out on the daybed for a cat nap of his own and promptly fell asleep. When he awoke several hours later, he was covered with a blanket and Dani was gone. At least she'd left a note. She was spending the afternoon and evening with Agnese, she wrote, and they'd be out late because they were going out to dinner and then to see *Aida* at the Arena. She might even ask Dante to join them, she'd added.

"Better you than me," Gabe muttered, feeling a twinge of sympathy for Dante. The end of that opera depressed him. The two lovers end up sealed in a tomb with no chance of escape. They die in each other's arms, supposedly feeling at peace, which some people might find romantic. But personally, if he found himself in that predicament with Dani, he'd be looking for a way to save her until his very last breath. Of course, that brought up the question of fate again. Did it exist? And if it did, should he just accept the course of his destiny, whatever it happened to be, or should he—could he—try to change it? He didn't know the answer, but he *was* sure of one thing. Now that he knew how good they could be together, no way was he going to give up on Daniela without a fight.

Unfortunately the fight would have to wait until tomorrow because tonight he was stuck courting Ines. Hopefully she'd give up *something* in the way of useful information. Gabe went for a long run around the estate, demolished the rest of the daily fruit and pastry tray, then grabbed a clean change of clothes and headed into the bathroom to take a shower. He washed his hair and shaved his five o'clock shadow, wondering idly if Daniela liked the forty-eight-hour stubble look that seemed to be so popular. If she did, so much the better—it'd be great only having to shave every other day. But thinking about her made him frown. Maybe she was sensitive. He hadn't checked to see if he'd left any marks or abrasions. Those wouldn't be good. Not on her delicate skin. Though he had to admit, he did like the idea of other men seeing the evidence of his claim. *Shit, now you sound like a Neanderthal.* Daniela brought that out in him like no other woman ever had.

He went downstairs and raided the kitchen, then spent an hour and a half back in the suite going over his notes, looking for any connections he hadn't made before. To kill some time he considered taking another nap, but decided to watch a spaghetti western on TV instead. It was great not having to deal with sub titles. In the evening, on his way out, he scribbled his own note and left it where Dani would see it:

Trying to pry more information out of Ines tonight. I'll share what I've learned when I get back.

—◆⋅◆⋅◆—

"Isn't the Labyrinth incredible?" Ines gushed later that night. The nightclub off Piazza Bra was dark, loud, and pulsing with the libidos of several hundred young men and women determined to get high, get moving, and get laid. Gabe had lost his fascination for places like the Labyrinth about ten years earlier. It didn't help that as a beat cop in L.A. he'd often had to break up fights—some of them deadly—between partygoers who lost control.

Ines met him wearing a skintight, fire-engine-red mini dress and four-inch stilettos, which put her at eye level with him. He wondered why women put themselves through the torture of wearing those mini stilts. If they did it to get a guy's attention, it worked—for about ten seconds. Besides which, the place was so dark, who could really tell what the other person was wearing anyway?

He bought Ines a whisky and soda, which she drank through a straw, and settled for just a club soda himself. Over pasta earlier she'd told him she was a *Veronese,* having lived in the city all her life. She liked working as a housekeeper at the Stella d'Italia because the hours were good and she got to meet all sorts of rich people, especially men, who gave her great tips. She didn't sleep with many of them, of course. She was very selective. Someday she was going to open her own hairdresser shop, once she saved enough money to take the course.

Over the next couple hours, Gabe worked his magic to get Ines to spill her guts. Yes, she said, the Labyrinth was the last place anybody saw Mirela Pavlenco. Mirela and Dobra had gone dancing. Ines remembered, even if Dobra didn't, because at the last minute Dobra had asked Ines to cover for her and Ines had been pissed because, *mio Dio,* what's the big deal about having to go dancing on a particular night? And Dobra had told her she and Mirela were going out for a special celebration. And then, poof, Mirela up and quits and doesn't tell nobody where she's going. Way to make friends, Mirela.

Gabe nodded and listened and refilled her glass. Ines began to talk more about Dobra.

"She used to be married to Adriano Moretti, but they broke up on account of her traveling to other hotels and helping out all the time," Ines explained. "He musta got lonely 'cause he cheated on her and when she found out she almost pummeled him to death. That's when she moved in with me." Ines giggled and took a sip of her drink. "But hey, I don't mind that she travels a lot. You've seen how small our place is."

"Where's she from originally?" Gabe asked.

"Croatia," she said. "She told me that a long time ago it used to be part of a country called Yugoslavia or something, but now it's all broken up." She waived her arm erratically. "It's not that far from here. You just go over the water."

"What brought her to Verona?"

"Oh, probably Romeo and Juliet, just like everybody else." Ines giggled again and swayed a little on her bar stool. "No. Not really. Her mother works in the corporate office and got her a job. They're a real close family." As she talked, Ines sipped through her straw and constantly surveyed the crowd, apparently looking for people she knew. "Uh oh," she said suddenly.

Gabe looked around the crowded room. "What?"

"See that guy over there dancing with that red-headed girl? That's Goran Novak. Dobra's going to be pissed."

Gabe snapped to attention. *Novak.* He looked in the direction she pointed. Sure enough, it was the same guy with Tino in the bar. Good thing Novak was too far away to notice them. Gabe turned subtly away from the dance floor just in case.

"Uh, why is Dobra going to be mad? Is that guy her boyfriend?"

"No. Her cousin. But Dobra can't stand Angelena, the girl he's dancing with. She thinks she's just out to take his money. I don't know. I like her, though. She has nice hair."

Gabe let her prattling wash over him. *Cousin. Mother.* The pieces were starting to click into place. Now if he could only—

"Uh oh."

Gabe turned back toward the floor. "See somebody else?"

Ines nodded and sipped again nervously, her eyes focused behind Gabe this time. A kid in skintight pants and a modified Mohawk walked up to them.

"What are you doing with him?" the punk asked.

Gabe stuck out his hand. "Gabriele de la Torre. A pleasure to meet you."

Apparently not in the mood for niceties, the kid only had eyes for Ines, and right now those eyes were tearing up. Oh, sweet Jesus, talk about Romeo and Juliet! Inside, Gabe chuckled. Evidently it wasn't his charms so much as Ines's quest to make her current boyfriend jealous. Why not play it up? "Oh man, is this your girlfriend? I'm really sorry."

"Yeah, she's my girlfriend," he said in English, which meant either he wasn't Italian or Gabe's accent sounded far more Americanized than he thought it did.

"Well, I meant it," Gabe replied in English. "I'm very sorry." He turned to Ines, who was staring at the young man and smiling. She'd obviously accomplished her goal for the evening. "Ines, I can see you…uh…have a lot to talk about. Signor, can you escort Ines home? I have to be going, and…"

"It's okay," Ines said. "Caesar will give me a ride home. But hey, thanks for the drinks."

"No problem." Gabe slapped the punk heartily on the back. "You take good care of her, you hear? *Lei è una donna molto speciale.*" *A special woman is right,* Gabe thought as he made his way out of the nightclub. *She might have just helped us crack the case.*

# CHAPTER TWENTY-ONE

—✦✦✦—

Dante was losing his patience.

"I can't let you in to see her. It is after hours." Mother Maria Annunciata spoke to Dante through the front gate. It was eleven o'clock in the evening and the Convent of the Holy Sisters of Rectitude had long since closed for the night.

"I must see her," Dante insisted.

"Come back tomorrow," the abbess suggested. "I'm sure she'll see you then."

"No, she won't, Mother Maria…" He paused to catch her eye. "Mother. I've been trying all day. She won't ever see me willingly. But do you remember telling me she is troubled? Now I know why. And I believe I can help her."

The abbess stood momentarily stunned at Dante's use of the word *mother*. He knew they would have a conversation at some point about the liberty he had taken, but not tonight. Tonight he had to see Agnese, to make her understand, before it tore both of them apart forever.

His mother stared at him for a moment longer and then unlocked the gate. "She is working in her laboratory," she said quietly. "Do not make me come after you, and for heaven's sake, do not raise your voices."

—◆—

Dante found Agnese bent over her microscope, so focused on her work that she didn't hear him come in. He didn't want to scare her, so he called her name softly from the door. She looked up at him and froze.

"How…how did you get in here?" she stuttered.

"The Mother Superior let me in. I have to speak with you, Agnese, but you refused to take my calls or answer my notes."

"I told you, we have nothing to talk about," she said dismissively, bending over her instrument again.

"Oh yes we do, and I'm not leaving until you face it…and face me."

She looked at him then, a weary expression on her face, as if she'd been traveling a long while and had come to a dead end. "How much do you know?" she asked.

"I know enough to ask you to speak to me about…about everything. And to do so from the heart." His own heart was breaking for her as he envisioned the mental anguish she must be going through.

He watched as she pulled herself together and faced him. "You really want to know the truth, Dante? Are you sure? Even though it will change completely the way you feel about me?"

"That's not going to happen. But yes, I want to know. Everything."

"All right then." She took a deep breath before releasing the toxins inside her. "Santo took me as his mistress when I was sixteen." Her voice was flat, without inflection. "I serviced him for two years, almost daily, and during that time I became pregnant and had an abortion. When I was eighteen I was able to leave for university, and minimized my visits home. Still, he had me on occasion for another year until I finally gathered the courage to tell him no more. So you see, the woman you think is so virtuous is not real. She is a fraud."

Agnese stopped speaking and looked down at her hands. They were trembling. Dante was silent. She nodded her head slightly, as if to affirm the fact that she had destroyed something of great value. But in reality she had taken the first step toward what he hoped would be their future. Her bravery humbled him.

"Agnese, look at me."

She didn't respond.

"Agnese, please," he repeated softly.

She finally looked at him, with beautiful dark eyes that begged him not to judge her too harshly, that said *This is me. Try to look past my ugliness.* He took her hands in his. They felt cold and he rubbed them gently to warm them.

"I have only one question, and although I already know the answer to it, I want you to tell it to me in your own words, because you need to, for your sake, not mine."

"What is it?" she asked in a small voice.

"Did you seek my uncle out? Did you want to be his mistress?"

The question shocked her. "No!" she cried. "Of course not. He was…it was…" She couldn't go on.

"Arranged?"

She nodded, the tears beginning to roll down her cheeks. "My mother said…my mother said we needed to pay for my Aunt Eliana's care, even though she had passed away by then, and for my college education…that it was the only way. She said it was a good thing because one day Ornella would die and Santo would marry me and that would make it all right."

Dante stepped closer and held her face, taking care to gently wipe her tears with his thumbs. "And you were a good, obedient daughter," he said.

She closed her eyes. "I didn't like doing it," she whispered. "I was glad when I got strong enough to say no." She sighed, as if remembering the end of a long, tiring race. "So glad." She looked up at Dante again. "There has never been anybody else."

Dante enfolded her in his arms. "Do you know," he said after several moments, "you have had only one lover, but I have had many. And some of the choices I've made in that regard weren't smart. But at least I could make the choice. You weren't able to. So I hope you will forgive me my past stupidity and be able to love me in spite of my many imperfections. Please tell me you love me, Agnese. Because I am crazy about you—totally, madly crazy about you."

"After what I just told you? How is that possible?"

"I remember someone telling me once that we couldn't be together because of who we are. Well, something awful happened to you, but that's not who you are, Agnese. Not by a long shot.

The person you are is intelligent, creative, loving, kind, and beautiful inside and out."

Agnese searched his eyes, looking, he supposed, for proof of his declaration. She shook her head. "But how can you be *sure*?"

He smiled. "I just am, as sure as I am standing here holding you at last in my arms."

He felt a stillness and a sigh ripple through her, and imagined a blossom in her garden unfurling to the sun. Her voice trembled when she spoke. "I have loved you forever," she whispered.

"Then I have one more question for you." He paused, leaned back to look into her eyes. "Agnese Maria Josefina Lombardi, I love you with all my heart and mind and body and soul. Will you be my wife?"

"Oh!" she cried, the tears beginning to fall again in earnest. "Dante…"

"Wait," he interrupted, suddenly afraid of her answer. "I want you to know something first. I desire you as a man desires a woman. You are the loveliest creature I have ever seen. I want to see all of you and touch you in places that will bring you incredible pleasure. I want to be inside you. I want to make *bambinos* with you. But I can wait. If you have…issues…about making love, then we can take it slow. We can work through them. I will never force you, never hurt you—"

Agnese put two fingers against his lips to stop his nervous recitation. "I know you would never hurt me, and I…well, in truth I have never really made love before."

She gave him a quirky half smile and his heart broke a little more for her. But she had a point. "When you put it that way, I suppose I haven't either. You would be my first…and my last. If you say yes."

"Are you absolutely certain? Because…because if you are, I say yes." Agnese reached up and clasped her hands around his neck. "Oh Dante, I say yes!"

Dante, laughing with tears streaming down his face, gathered Agnese by the waist, and kissed her as Odysseus might have kissed Penelope upon his return: forcefully, powerfully staking his claim to his beloved. Agnese responded shyly at first, but quickly began to match his passion with her own. After several minutes they reluctantly broke apart. He could tell she was as dazed and thrilled by what had just happened as he was.

"Do you know," she said with wonder, "that was my very first kiss."

Dante held her by the shoulders. "Darling, I am honored to give you your first one. And I will give you many, many more, I promise." He kissed her again, exuberantly. "But I've got to go now. Mother Superior said she would kick me out if I didn't. Besides, there are things I have to do."

Agnese searched his face again. "Tell me you aren't going to confront Santo about all this. It is in the past, and that bastard is not worth the dirt beneath your shoes. He is powerful, Dante, and he could hurt you." Her voice hitched. "I could not bear that."

Dante ran his hand lovingly over her hair. "Already you fuss over me as a wife fusses over her husband. I like that. But please don't worry. I know who Santo is. I know his strengths, and I know his weaknesses. I'm going to make him pay for what he's done to you, but in a just way. Trust me. Now before I go, let's find Mother

Maria and tell her our news." He kissed her hard one more time, took her hand firmly in his, and headed toward a future that filled him with indescribable joy.

—◆◆◆—

Dani shook her head as she followed the crowds leaving the Arena after the performance. She should have known better than to pick *Aida*, for heaven's sake! Given her state of mind, the last thing she needed to think about was a pair of doomed lovers. It just hit too close to home.

She and Agnese had spent the afternoon visiting and caught an early dinner together, but she was glad her friend had begged off seeing the opera; apparently she'd had to finish some lab work before tomorrow. Dani had considered asking Dante, but decided not to bother him. It just didn't make sense for any of them to wallow in the sorry state of their love lives. She felt a twinge of guilt for not telling Gabe about the change in plans, but let it pass. It wasn't her fault Agnese couldn't make it, and besides, if he knew she'd decided to attend the opera alone, he would have worried too much about her safety. He was already caught up in her family's troubles; he didn't need one more thing to stress him out.

Gabe. Right now he was probably cozying up to Ines. Had he learned anything more from her? Dani could tell after their interview with the two employees that he'd made a date to connect with the blond. Dani knew he was worried she might be jealous. He was so sweet, he wanted to explain in the car why he was doing it. Dani had cut him off, not because of the green-eyed monster, but because she had to start weaning herself from him. How could she do that except to freeze him out? If what her Uncle Santo implied was true, the sooner she could show that Gabe meant nothing to her, the safer he was going to be.

If only Gabe would listen to her and stay away! But he couldn't help himself because he was too busy helping *her*. Trying to get more information out of Ines was a typical Gabe maneuver and she loved him for it. And that's what made cutting him off all the more heart-breaking.

She took her time walking along the outside of the stadium toward the taxi stand, trying to clear her mind. The street lamps were low and she watched, fascinated, as several stage doors stood open, casting a peculiar light from the actors' dressing rooms onto the street. Many of the performers were still in costume, their faces heavily made up. They looked otherworldly, as if they were truly Egyptian soldiers who had somehow found their way to modern Verona for the night. Although she was on the other side of the street, she could tell they were smoking and drinking from water bottles, which seemed out of place. But it was the singsong cadence of their Italian voices that really threw her off. Wouldn't Egyptian soldiers be speaking Arabic? She smiled at the extent to which she'd been willing to suspend her disbelief.

She reached the curved end of the stadium and looked around. Where was the taxi stand? She was sure it had been on this side of the Arena. She began to feel uneasy. There were fewer street lamps and the departing crowd had thinned considerably. A car rolled slowly by and she quickened her pace. *Always act like you know where you're going*, she remembered from a self-defense class she'd taken. Out of habit she reached into her purse for keys to use as a weapon, but quickly remembered she was out of luck— Fausta had never given her one.

Clutching her purse tightly to her body, she scanned her surroundings. No one was near her and it was nearly pitch black. *Not a good situation.* Maybe she should go back the way she came. She glanced back and saw another vehicle driving along the street, a van this time, moving even more slowly than the car. Fighting back panic, she started walking even faster, breaking into a jog and cursing the fact she'd worn boots that definitely weren't made for walking.

It wasn't enough.

In the next instant she was grabbed from behind by two assailants and shoved into the van.

# CHAPTER TWENTY-TWO

— ⟨✦✦⟩ —

Dani couldn't tell how much time had passed. An hour? Two or more? Once inside the van, which seemed more like a delivery truck, a sweet-smelling cloth had been placed over her nose and mouth, and after a brief struggle, that was all she remembered.

Until now. She was lying on a bed in what seemed to be a large, empty room. There was minimal sound. Once in a while the floor would vibrate and she could hear a muted train whistle; she was probably near a station. Her hands were tied behind her back and she was blindfolded, but somehow she could sense a hollowness to the place. It was cold and she shivered, despite wearing the coat she'd had on all day. Her head throbbed slightly, as if she were hung over from a too-strong sleeping pill. She thought about screaming, but decided against it. They would have gagged her if her cries made any difference; apparently they were in a protected location. No sense making anybody mad for no good reason until she knew what she was up against.

*You will not panic*, she told herself. Logic told her that if who-ever it was wanted to kill her, she'd be dead already. This had to have something to do with her uncle and the hotel deal. Maybe they were going to force her to sign something related to the vote and then kill her. She had to make sure that didn't happen.

She struggled to sit up and realized someone else was in the room. A woman's voice, speaking softly in an unfamiliar lan-guage, came nearer. Was she speaking to Dani or to someone else? Dani felt hands help her to a sitting position. The woman wore a floral perfume. Rosewater, maybe. She led Dani to a chair next to a table and compelled her to sit in it. Then she left the room. Dani assumed someone else was still present, so she did nothing. Who was she kidding? There was nothing she *could* do, except wait.

Sometime later, she heard a door open. Two male voices, this time. Both speaking the same Eastern European-sounding lan-guage. One had a deep, cultured accent, and the other, higher in pitch, sounded as if the person were Italian, speaking a language he wasn't used to. She heard a chair scraping across the floor and the deeper voice spoke to her in formal English from across the table.

"Signorina Forcelli," he said.

"It's Signorina Dunn," she corrected him, keeping her voice as neutral as possible.

"My apologies. Signorina Dunn, then. Do you know why you are here?"

"I assume it has something to do with my uncle and the pur-chase he wants to make."

"What purchase would that be?"

"Alberghi Paradisi. That's who you represent, isn't it?" *Be bold*, she told herself. *Show no fear.*

The man with the deep voice chuckled. "In a manner of speaking, yes. My partners and I are curious as to why you are so reticent about voting your shares. We'd like to see if we might convince you to change your mind."

"By kidnapping me?" she said derisively. "Haven't you ever heard about positive reinforcement? It's a much more effective way to change behavior."

She wasn't sure, but she thought she could sense the man grinning across from her. He paused and she could hear his measured breathing. "In my part of the world," he said, "I'm afraid we are inclined toward more primitive means of persuasion."

"What part of the world would that be?"

"Croatia. Have you ever been there?"

Dani shook her head.

"A pity. It is a beautiful country."

"I'm sure it is," she said testily. "Can you tell me, is my uncle part of this 'means of persuasion' you seem to prefer?"

"Does it matter?" the man asked.

"Yes. I'd like to know the extent to which my own flesh and blood would go to achieve his goals."

"I would simply say we have less patience than your uncle. He seems to want to go about this in a more…personal way. But you sound like a woman of business. So, let us open the negotiations."

The absurdity of the situation struck her. Here she was, kidnapped, bound, and blindfolded, completely at their mercy, and they wanted to negotiate? What would it hurt to play along? "Yes, let's," she said, trying to pretend she was in any other business meeting. "For starters, the financials of Alberghi Paradisi aren't impressive. As it stands, it's not a good investment from a hotel management point of view."

"Ah, but there are other points of view," the man said. "Let me just say that the acquisition of that hotel company will reap many benefits for Stella d'Italia that will eventually have a most positive impact on your company's bottom line."

"How so?"

"That's of no import now. The critical data point for you is my assurance that your fears of weak financial performance are misinformed. If that is not enough to change your mind, then I'm afraid I must change tactics and inform you of the consequences of a *no* vote on your part."

Dani swallowed hard. She could tell that the man across from her had ceased playing the civility game. "Go on," she said quietly.

"Blindfold, please." Apparently the man with the deep voice was issuing an order to the other man in the room. A few moments passed and Dani felt her blindfold being untied. When her eyes adjusted she saw that, as she suspected, she was sitting at a table in a dimly lit, virtually empty room. The only item on the table was a small notebook computer. The man sitting across from her wore a hood reminiscent of the Ku Klux Klan that she had read about, except that it was blue. The other man in the room was standing off to the side. Medium height and overweight, he was also disguised. Knowing how powerless she was sent a bolt of terror through her before she could stop it. Her head began to pound.

"Are you going to start burning crosses next?" she asked, trying desperately to maintain a calm façade. She could see the seated man's eyes through the covering. They were icy blue to match the hood. She told herself they must want her alive; why else would they bother to keep their identities hidden? The man didn't respond to her taunt. He merely gestured to the fat man, who walked over and turned on the computer.

What Dani saw during the next few minutes nearly brought her to her knees. The quality was grainy, but the act against the woman and the fact that it was Santo was clear as day. Images started to form in her head and she fought to push them away. She felt bile rising in her throat and swallowed her fear.

"Turn it off," she rasped.

The fat man looked to his superior, and at the seated man's nod, he shut down the computer and returned to the side of the room.

"You can see Signor Forcelli's…motivation…for wanting to please us by acquiring Alberghi Paradisi. A *no* vote would have devastating consequences for the company, I would say. Do you agree?"

She nodded. "It would, I suppose."

The man steepled his fingers. "You suppose. You see, that is what worries me, Signorina Dunn. You *suppose*. Despite the rather stark evidence, you do not strike me as being completely convinced that your uncle's, shall we say, *exposure*, is worth making what you are convinced is a bad business decision." He paused. "I think perhaps it's prudent to lay out what your own consequences might be, should you vote against the purchase."

Dani sat up straighter. "What are you talking about?"

"You have a mother, do you not? A Paula Dunn, who lives with a man named Herbert Roscoe in a suburb of Phoenix known as Glendale. Is that correct?"

Dani didn't answer. She couldn't with her heart stuck in her throat.

"I shall take that as a yes," the man said. "You also have a lover, a Signor Gabriele de la Torre, a detective with the Marin County Investigations Division, who accompanied you here to Verona. He seems more than willing to put himself in harm's way to help you, even to the extent of questioning one of our operatives, who, I'm sorry to say, we had to…'let go' because of—well, trade secrets that might have been compromised. There are many other members of your family and close circle of friends that I could mention as well. Do you see where I am going with this, Signorina Dunn?"

"Yes. I see," she whispered.

"Good," the man said. "Then we'll expect you at the corporate offices of Stella d'Italia on Friday morning to sign the documents with your uncle. He'll be quite pleased, I'm sure, as will you. I understand he has great plans for you…on a number of levels." He turned to the man in the corner. "The blindfold, if you will."

The fat man came around to the back of Dani and once again covered her eyes. Afterward she could tell that the seated man had taken off his hood. An idea came to her and she spoke up despite the fact that her teeth were now chattering.

"I…I wonder if I might take a copy of that scene," she improvised. "I may have to convince my Uncle Aldo, who has been thinking of siding with my grandmother on this issue. Once he sees it, he will understand what needs to be done."

"Ah. A woman of action," the man across from her said. "No wonder Santo has his eye on you."

The chair scraped back and the man with the deep voice spoke in low tones to the fat man. "*Fino a Venerdì,*" the deep-voiced man said. She heard the door open and shut.

Until Friday. They had a day and a half to figure something out. The fat man came up to her from behind and breathed in the crook of her neck. "They mean business, *gnocca*," he whispered in Italian, and licked her. "Don't fuck with them." She could smell cigar smoke in his clothing. She felt his hand come around to the front of her blouse. He dropped something in the pocket of her jacket, which she prayed was a copy of the file she'd just viewed. Then the man squeezed her breast. Before she could react, he put another sweet-smelling cloth over her mouth. Once again, she struggled only slightly before blacking out.

As soon as he left the nightclub, Gabe called Marco with the information he'd gleaned from Ines, including the bit about the tattoo she'd described earlier in the day. Marco was still awake, but like Gabe's friend Sam, he wasn't exactly happy. Apparently Gabe had interrupted some "alone time" between Marco and Gina. Gabe made a mental note to stop pissing off his friends with late-night phone calls unless, like right now, it was absolutely necessary.

"Sorry, man," Gabe said, "I couldn't wait. First, can you send a patrol car over to the Labyrinth nightclub and have them take down license numbers? You'll probably find a match against the numbers you took at the Sexy Pig. If you do, the car's going to belong to our man Novak—the woman I was with ID'd him in the club tonight. It's definitely the same guy we saw with Tino at the bar. Hopefully you can put a tail on him pronto. Also, can you get me the background check you did on the name I gave you this afternoon? For Dobra Moretti?"

Marco agreed and Gabe ended the call. By the time Gabe reached his car, Marco had called back.

"Dobra Moretti. Maiden name: Petrovic. Native country: Croatia. She's been here about five years," Marco read.

"Okay, well Dobra was definitely one of the last people to see one of the missing employees, Mirela Pavlenco, before she disappeared. Apparently they went dancing together. Turns out Dobra's mother works in the corporate office of Stella d'Italia," Gabe said. "Remember Dante mentioned that special assistant Santo hired? I checked my notes, and bingo. Flora Petrovic. But here's the kicker. Goran Novak is Dobra Petrovic's cousin, which means Flora Petrovic is his aunt....Yep, you got it. Tetka."

Thirty minutes later, Gabe's satisfaction with starting to put the puzzle together was completely forgotten in light of one glaring fact.

Dani was gone.

He'd gotten back to La Tana about midnight, fully expecting to find her in their suite. No such luck. In fact, he'd found his note exactly where he'd put it and no sign that she'd been back to the estate since she'd left him sleeping that afternoon. Okay, the three of them went over to Agnese's after the opera, he reasoned. They decided to yak some more. Maybe they drank too much and Dani decided to spend the night. Women did that sometimes, right?

But in his gut Gabe knew better. Dani would have called him or at least left a message at the house. She knew how much he worried. He swallowed his pride and called her, but got only voicemail. Then he tracked down Fausta to get Agnese's phone number. Rather than give him the number, Fausta called her in front of him.

"Agnese hasn't seen her since they had dinner together," Fausta said, arching her severe, dark eyebrows.

"Are you kidding me? Let me talk to her." Gabe practically tore the phone out of his aunt's grasp. His own hands were trembling. "Agnese? Please, are you being straight with me? Because Dani left a note saying she was attending *Aida* with you and Dante tonight."

"I'm sorry, Gabriele. I had to pass on the performance. I haven't seen her. Truly. And I can tell you, Dante isn't with her either. Perhaps she stayed over at her grandmother's."

Convinced that Agnese was telling the truth, Gabe handed the phone back to Fausta. Then he called Dante, just to be sure. Agnese was right—Dante hadn't seen Dani either. In fact, she hadn't even asked Dante to go to the opera in the first place.

"The little bird has flown from the nest," Fausta said, her tone devoid of any concern. It was too much.

"Why wouldn't she?" Gabe shot back. "This place is a living nightmare…and you're the star of the show." He left Fausta standing with her mouth open while he ran back up to his suite and dialed Marco again.

"Dani's disappeared," he said. "Do me a favor and ask to speak to a Signora Furlan at the Stella d'Italia Verona. That's Dani's grandmother. Wake her up if you have to, okay? She'll answer if the police are calling. See if Dani went there tonight and let me know right away, will you? Right away! I'm heading over to the station now. I'll meet you there."

Fighting down the anxiety that threatened to overwhelm him, Gabe grabbed his coat and headed back downstairs to his rental car. His mind buzzed with all the possibilities: Dani was tired of Gabe and had gone to stay with her grandmother. She'd decided to book a hotel room for the night…she—hell, there were only three logical explanations, and none of them were good. Either she was hurt and couldn't contact him, or she was being held against her will and couldn't contact him, or she…or she— No, he would not go there. That was not a possibility for his Dani. She was okay, he told himself. She was okay.

Dear God, let her be okay.

Just as he was pulling into a parking space near the station, his cell phone rang. "*Sì*," he barked.

It was Marco, telling him to go to Maggiore City Hospital. That's where he'd find Dani.

# CHAPTER TWENTY-THREE

—·✦✧✦·—

Marco met Gabe at the entrance to the hospital's Emergency Room. Gabe couldn't tell by his friend's expression whether the news was good or bad.

"Someone called one-one-eight and said a woman was in the Piazza Bra wandering and looking bewildered. Apparently she was trying to walk but kept stumbling. They thought maybe she was on drugs." Marco was kind enough to keep pity out of his voice. "She was fully dressed and had her purse. Doesn't look like anything was taken. It's a good thing her name is Dunn, or this thing would be all over the morning papers."

Gabe didn't care about any of that. He had to see her. Now. He started to walk past Marco, but his friend cautioned him.

"She's being examined at the moment. They won't let you in there until they're finished." he said. "Regardless of what they find, you've got to keep your cool, okay? Don't make this any more sensational by going off half-cocked…not that you've ever been half-cocked."

Marco's attempt at levity fell on deaf ears. "I will kill whoever did this," Gabe said, his eyes gleaming in the darkness.

"I didn't hear that," Marco said. "Come on, let's see what's what."

They hurried to the nurses' station. Thanks to Marco's badge they were able to go straight to the cubicle where Dani was lying down. Her skin was pale against her dark curls, and her eyes were closed. Gabe walked over immediately and took her hand. She opened her eyes briefly, smiled at him, and closed them again. A doctor was just taking a stethoscope out of his ears. He looked at Marco's badge.

"Signorina Dunn is a very fortunate young woman. She was apparently sedated using ether, which is quite uncommon these days. At least whoever did this knew how to administer it. She doesn't appear to have been harmed in any other way, but we'll keep her overnight to make sure the effects of the sedative have completely worn off."

Gabe turned to the doc. "Hey, is it okay that she's fallen asleep again? Shouldn't we be trying to keep her awake or something?"

The doctor glanced at Dani's heart monitor. "No, she's doing fine. All of her vitals are normal. Really, she just needs to sleep off the effects of the drug."

Marco leaned in to speak quietly to the physician. "This is being investigated as a kidnapping and we have reason to believe Signorina Dunn may be in danger. Do you have a problem with my colleague staying here on protective detail?"

Gabe snorted. Marco knew damn well Gabe wasn't going anywhere, no matter what the doc said. He was just trying to keep the situation from turning into a circus.

The physician smiled briefly at Gabe. He could obviously tell Gabe was more than just an assigned bodyguard. "Not a problem," he said. "Unless we get too busy, we'll just keep her here for the rest of the night."

"What time can she go home?" Gabe asked.

"I'll set discharge for eleven a.m., unless there's a change in circumstances." With that, the doc left the room.

"I'm going to interview the first responders," Marco said. "Maybe they saw something or somebody who can shed some light on Dani's abduction."

"You know where I'll be," Gabe said. "And Marco?"

"Yeah?"

"Thanks for being a good cop—and a better friend."

"No worries. We're going to get these bastards."

Alone with Dani, Gabe pulled up the only chair in the room and sat close to the bed, entwining his fingers with hers. He could feel the adrenaline draining out of his body, now that the danger was over.

He exhaled heavily. Over? Maybe for now. But how soon before the next wave? These assholes didn't mess around. They'd killed Dani's father, probably her aunt, and now they threatened Dani herself. Gabe felt an icy thread of fear sneak its way up his spine. Dani could just as easily have disappeared forever, like that woman Mirela Pavlenco and so many others. Who was next? And for what? To make it easier to sell women and girls as sex slaves? It was beyond sick.

Part of Gabe's time in the LAPD had been spent in Vice, where he'd learned up close and personal about human trafficking. One time he and his partner had raided an old warehouse on a tip and found six Mexican nationals—all girls under the age of sixteen—living in disgusting, rat-infested conditions. The girls were prisoners of their *coyotes* and had to earn their daily allotment of rice and beans on their backs. On the streets, it had always seemed ridiculous to hassle the prostitutes, when most of them were just out there trying to make a living—at least those who weren't forced into selling themselves. But do-gooders felt that busting the streetwalkers was the only way to get them help, especially where drugs were involved. It was such a screwed-up situation, and it wasn't limited to the United States, not by a long shot. Human trafficking was a worldwide, multi-billion-dollar industry, right up there with smuggling guns and drugs. And it was growing. If Santo Forcelli truly had his hands in such a dirty business, he was going down, and it didn't matter whether Dani wanted Gabe involved in it or not.

Time passed and Gabe's lids grew heavy. The last thing he thought about before nodding off was going over a mental checklist of all the things he needed to do in order to keep Dani safe.

—◆◆—

Dani woke to the sight of Gabe sleeping in a chair next to her bed. He looked terribly uncomfortable, but apparently not sore enough to keep him awake. His hair was sticking out at odd angles, and the stubble of his beard was already pronounced. His full lips were open slightly and he breathed heavily, the sound of exhaustion too long denied. He held her hand, and when she tried gently to take it away, he reflexively tightened his grasp, still sleeping, as if it were a lifeline. That little movement brought a lump to her throat. This loving man cared for her and she had rejected him time after time, even if it was for his own good. And still, he kept coming back.

How could she protect him? The Croatian had made it clear Dani had to play ball regarding the hotel acquisition or risk harm to those she loved, Gabe among them. But if the situation were reversed, would Gabe do the man's bidding? She didn't think so. Not because he cared any less for her, but because he would move heaven and earth to stop a situation he knew to be morally and legally wrong. Maybe it was time for Dani to do the same. The question was, how? She thought of the incriminating tape of Santo and how they could put something so sordid to good use.

She gently squeezed Gabe's hand until he woke up. He gazed at her with those gorgeous, chocolate-brown eyes. *"Aida?"* he asked. "What were you thinking?"

She burst out laughing and he grinned, leaning over the bed and gathering her in his arms.

"You scared me to death," he whispered into the crook of her neck. He straightened up enough to cup her face in his hands. "I couldn't bear to lose you."

"Nor I you," she replied, her voice trembling.

Then he kissed her with a gentle sweetness that grew more fierce as the emotion behind it surged.

"Now now, enough of that."

Dani and Gabe broke away from each other to see Nonna Stella standing in the doorway, leaning on a cane. Josefa, her assistant, stood next to her.

"Grandmother!" Dani cried. Gabe stood back respectfully while Dani held out her arms for a hug which the older woman walked up and readily shared.

"I received a call from a Detective Clemente last night that was never followed up on," Stella said, glancing at Gabe and pursing her lips. "Of course I had to take it upon myself to see if you were all right."

"I apologize, Signora Forcelli," Gabe said. "There was a lot going on, and—"

"—and you figured an old woman was the least of your worries."

"No, that's not it. We—"

Stella waved her hand impatiently. "No matter. Irrelevancy comes with old age. I am used to it. The important thing is that Daniela is safe and sound, and you, Signor de la Torre, are going to keep her that way from this point forward. Am I understood?"

"Yes, signora." Gabe grinned, properly chastised and apparently happy with the assignment he'd been given.

"Now, my dear girl, tell me what happened."

Dani glanced at Gabe before speaking. "I...I stupidly walked in the wrong direction after the opera and two men grabbed me. But I put up a fight and they must have decided I wasn't worth it, because after a while they dumped me off in the park and I ended up here."

Stella looked from Dani to Gabe and back again, narrowing her eyes. "Somehow I think there's more to it." When Dani didn't respond, the older woman sighed. "I've seen what I needed to see," she said. "I'll leave you to your rest now, but Daniela?" The old woman caught Dani's dark eyes with her own.

"Yes, Nonna?"

"No matter what you have learned, no matter what the stakes are or what the consequences may be, they are not worth *this*. In the past two weeks I have lost my son and my daughter-in-law, and I am damn well not going to lose you." She squeezed Dani's hand and turned to leave. "Remember what I said, Signor de la Torre," she warned as she left the room.

Gabe stood up and bent over Dani again. "You've got one hell of a grandma," he said. He paused before adding, "Can you tell me what really happened?"

"I can and I will, but not here," she said, stroking his stubbly cheek. "We have some planning to do."

—◆❖◆—

Gabe looked at the small group assembled in Dante's living room. He was more than ready to get to work. "Okay, what do we know?"

After being discharged from the hospital that morning, Dani had insisted they go back to La Tana to shower and change clothes. Gabe readily agreed and was only mildly disappointed when she said no, they'd accomplish those tasks separately. She hadn't talked any more about her ordeal; instead, she seemed all business when she asked Gabe set up a strategy session with Dante and Marco. Everyone decided Dante's condo was the most secure location for the meeting.

"So far I've charted monthly housekeeping staffing levels over the past five years for both the Milan and Verona properties," Dante began. "There is a rhythm to it, although you wouldn't notice the pattern unless you were looking for it. I checked names against payroll records and it looks like we've lost at least five dozen employees, an average of one per hotel every other month, over that period. If that holds up for all ten Stella d'Italia properties, you're looking at three hundred employees who abruptly quit during that time."

"Many of those had to be legitimate attrition," Dani said. "Can you track what happened to them?"

"Some of them, yes, but at least half left no paper trail. They simply vanished, like Mirela Pavlenco."

"And I'm getting the gist of how they managed that," Gabe said. "Picture this. You've got an ops team consisting of Flora in the corporate office, her daughter Dobra, and Goran Novak. Maybe Tino was part of it, too. Maybe others in other cities, who knows. Flora's moving the players on the board like chess pieces. She decides who goes where, when."

"Through the staff sharing program," Dante offered.

"Yes, and maybe sometimes through corporate fiat. When the time comes to move the merchandise, so to speak, she sends Dobra to the next hotel on the rotation, who befriends the girl, or works with whoever they're tied into locally, takes her dancing, introduces her to Novak, who takes her out of circulation."

"Then why wouldn't she have done that with Ines?" Dani asked.

"Ines is a native of Verona," Gabe answered. She knows too many people, she'd be missed. In fact, I bet there won't be any Italian girls on the missing list."

"You're probably right," Marco said. "The most vulnerable are immigrants, usually from rural areas, looking for a better life in the west."

"Okay, so why not just abduct the girls right after they signed up?" Dani asked. "Why go through all the trouble of placing them in hotels?"

"Think of it like money laundering," Marco explained. "A bunch of young girls who all show up missing from the same supposed recruiting company would raise a major red flag. But you work the trafficking angle into a legitimate job program and you've got the perfect cover."

"It's like a shell game," Gabe said. "You can't follow who's going where. The girls move around from city to city, hotel to hotel. Some stay on the job, others legitimately leave. And a few slip through the cracks—not enough to sound an alarm, just enough to have some poor family members wondering what the heck happened to the daughters they lost track of. It really boils down to an elaborate case of misdirection."

Marco had been punching in numbers on his cell phone's calculator. "Good looking, light-haired Caucasian women command extremely high prices in the Middle and Far East," he explained.

"Some of these rich perverts have secret harems and they actually prefer women who are there against their will. A beautiful young blond, for instance, might command as much as a quarter of a million dollars." He punched in more numbers. "If even half those missing women were abducted, you're talking almost nineteen million. No wonder they want to expand."

"Well, we're not going to let them do that." Dani's voice was firm yet controlled, without any trace of hesitation or fear. "Even if it means destroying Stella d'Italia in the process."

Gabe, Marco, and Dante all stared at Dani. The other two men were as shocked as he was. "What do you mean, bella?" Gabe asked.

She reached into the pocket of her jeans and pulled out a USB drive. "Would you put this in your laptop, Dante? I think you should all see this."

The next five minutes were excruciating for all of them. Once Gabe saw what was happening and that it was Santo, he quickly looked back at Dani to gauge her reaction. She wasn't watching; instead she was working hard to maintain her composure. As Marco watched, his hardened expression told Gabe his friend was all in to get the criminals who would perpetrate such atrocities.

But Dante's reaction was the most disturbing of all. He jumped up, walked purposefully over to a chest of drawers and pulled out a gun.

"Whoa, whoa, whoa," Gabe said, striding over to him and taking the gun from his friend's shaking grasp. "That's not how we're going to solve this, Dante."

Dante looked at him and his expression was cold as granite. "He will pay for what he did," he said.

Gabe glanced at Dani, who was concentrating on her hands, rubbing them together briskly. *She's reliving something*, he thought with horror.

Marco had walked over to Dante and put his hand on Dante's arm. "You are obviously personally invested in this, my friend. If you can help us put this monster away, by all means do so...but not with a gun." He gestured for Gabe to hand him the weapon. Gabe turned it over and Marco emptied it of bullets. "I'm going to take this for the duration of this case. File a complaint if you like, but I'll just say I'm checking on your carry license. Now please, tell us why you are so upset."

Dante looked at Marco, then at Gabe and Dani. Gabe saw the anguish in Dante's expression dissipate, replaced by calm determination. "It's not my story to tell," he said quietly. "But I will do anything. *Anything* to make sure that man rots in hell."

Dani joined the circle, a slender column surrounded by three solid pillars. She seemed to have conquered her anxiety for the moment. "The group who wants to force Stella d'Italia to buy Alberghi Paradisi is willing to release this to the public if the sale doesn't go through. If I choose to vote *no*, they have also threatened my family and...and you, Gabriele. They expect me to meet with them tomorrow morning to sign the papers. I am willing to do so. I think it's our best opportunity."

"To do what, bella?" Gabe asked. "Give in to them?" He couldn't believe she was even considering such a move.

"No, to get them on tape admitting to their crimes. That's the only way we're going to put an end to all this."

Wait a minute. Dani wear a wire? No way. If she were caught..."Not going to happen," he said. "There's no way you're going to get Santo or anyone else to admit to breaking any law. That only happens in the movies."

"He's right, cousin," Dante said. "As soon as you try to elicit some kind of confession, they'll be on to you. It's much too dangerous."

Marco had been silent through the exchange, but now he spoke up. "What if she could get them to say something not in the least incriminating to them, but incredibly damaging to someone else?"

"What do you mean?" Gabe asked.

"You talked about the ops team. Flora, Dobra, and Goran. They're doing the dirty work. What if we can get them to flip by showing them how expendable they are?"

Gabe thought about it. Of course. He'd done it more than once in Vice. Get a low level punk scared enough to squeal on the next rat up. "It might work," he said. "Under one condition."

"What's that?" Marco asked.

"I accompany Dani to the meeting...and I go in there armed."

# CHAPTER TWENTY-FOUR

—·❖·—

Dani spent the rest of the day and evening on the computer, preparing for her upcoming meeting with Santo and the Croatian. She knew enough about the various aspects of running a hotel that she could talk for hours if necessary; all she had to do was plug in some specifics related to what she'd already learned about Stella d'Italia and the Paradisi hotel chain to make it all sound legitimate. Whatever it took, she was going to pull this off; otherwise the threats to those she loved would never stop.

Gabe stayed close by while she worked. He brought her snacks and drinks, and when she started to droop, he made sure she took a nap—without him. "Otherwise I'd never let you sleep," he'd confessed, smiling and giving her a quick kiss.

Early in the evening he'd gone to pick up some pasta at a trattoria down the hill. During dinner, Dani brought up something that had been bothering her all day: Dante's extreme reaction to the video.

"I want to talk to him privately about it," she said. "I thought maybe I could drive over there a little later." Expecting a barrage of negativity, she was surprised by Gabe's response.

"Fine. How about I drop you off? I've got an errand to run anyway, and I can pick you up whenever you like. Just consider me your personal taxi service." Once again he gave her his impossible-to-resist smile and once again she wondered how she had gotten so lucky.

They arrived back at Dante's condominium on the Riva San Lorenzo around eight p.m. Dani reassured Gabe she'd call him and only him to get a ride back, and he waited for Dante to buzz her into the lobby before driving off.

She took the elevator up to the top floor of the building and knocked on the door of Dante's unit. He opened the door and Dani was floored to see Agnese standing behind him. It was obvious to anyone paying attention that Dani had interrupted something intimate between them.

"Oh, I'm so sorry," she said, feeling herself blushing. "If I'd known—"

"It's all right," Dante said, opening the door wider to let her in. "In fact, Agnese and I are glad you dropped by. We have some news." He closed the door and stepped back to put his arm around Dani's friend. "This incredible woman has agreed to marry me."

Dani took one look at the unabashed joy on both Agnese and Dante's faces, and squealed in delight. She flung her arms around both of them. "I knew it!" she cried. "I am so, so happy for you!" They all laughed and Dante broke away to get some drinks to celebrate.

"It's only Prosecco," he said, coming back with flutes of the sparkling wine. "We'll toast with something more formal at the wedding."

"We haven't had a chance to talk to Mama yet," Agnese cautioned. "So please don't say anything until we're able to butter her up a bit."

"You've got your work cut out for you," Dani quipped.

Agnese looked lovingly at Dante. "I think I've found the strength to handle it."

They talked of lighthearted matters until a break in the conversation led Dante to ask, "Why did you come tonight, Dani?"

Dani bit her lip. How could she bring up Dante's outburst and spoil this happy occasion? "Uh, oh, well...just to say hi?"

Dante shook his head. He looked at Agnese, who seemed to be giving him permission for something. "I don't believe that," he said. "I think maybe you were wondering about my behavior when you showed us the video this morning. I know it was a bit intense."

"You're right. I've been thinking about it all afternoon. And wondering."

Agnese put her hand on Dante's. "He told me what happened and that he told you it wasn't his story to tell. The fact is, it's my story. You see..." Agnese paused, as if gathering strength. "I became your Uncle Santo's mistress when I was sixteen. It was not something I wanted, and it lasted a few years before I was able to break away, but the important thing is, I *was* able to break the tie and, well, here I am." She smiled at Dante, who leaned in and kissed her.

Dani stared at Agnese in shock. Her uncle had had sex with Agnese? "Couldn't you have called the police?" she asked, outraged.

"It wasn't like that," Agnese explained, a tinge of sadness to her voice. "It was…complicated. My mother was involved. It had to do with money for my aunt's care, and…" She seemed to be shaking off the memories. "Besides, I found out later that the age of consent in our country is only fourteen. They raise it to sixteen if someone in a position of authority is involved. So you see, it wouldn't have mattered even if I had had the courage to speak up."

Dani fumed inside. What sorts of perverse acts *wouldn't* her uncle do? She was filled with disgust that someone so close to her had been a victim, and that someone whose blood she shared would be the perpetrator. She reached out to touch her friend. "I don't know what to say," she offered. "I am so ashamed. I wish I could have done something."

"Please, don't feel bad," Agnese said, taking Dani's hand and squeezing it gently. "You weren't even there. You had just moved to the United States."

Without warning, Dani's stomach began to roil with the familiar mixture of pain and terror she'd experienced before. She wondered if Agnese knew why she had left Italy twelve years earlier. She had certainly never mentioned the reason in the few letters they'd exchanged. If Agnese could talk openly about her past nightmare, Dani could too. "Do you know why I left La Tana when I was fifteen?" she asked.

Agnese shook her head. "No one ever told me. I missed you so much, and I thought at one point that you had left because of something I did."

"No!" Dani said. "Never think that. The truth is, at that huge party, do you remember the one at La Tana? You and I got separated, and I drank too much. But my drink might also have been spiked by someone. At least I think it was. Anyway, a man cornered me on the second floor and tried to rape me. They tell me Uncle Santo stepped in to prevent it."

"What do you mean 'they tell you'?" Dante asked.

"It's crazy, and has caused me no end of problems ever since," Dani confessed. "I think something really did happen to me, but everyone, from Santo on down, says I wasn't raped. He chased the guy off, let me rest in his office, and I fell asleep. Then Nonno Ciro had his stroke and Santo had to leave. When I woke up I told them someone raped me, but Santo said he'd intervened in time. Nonna Stella had Ciro's doctor examine me and he found nothing wrong." Dani smiled ruefully. "Let me tell you, it's hard not to think you're crazy when you feel things no one else says is real."

Agnese looked at Dani with a thoughtful expression. "So do you believe now that nothing happened to you?"

Unexpectedly, Dani's eyes welled up. "I *know* something happened to me," she said. "I just don't know what."

"I remember something Santo said to my mother not long after you moved away. I think they were negotiating the terms of...of my time with him. They didn't know I could hear them. I heard him say, "She is an adequate substitute for now." I never knew what that meant. Who was I a substitute for? His wife? Or someone else?" She looked at Dani expectantly.

The idea of Santo as her attacker hit Dani with the force of a train trying but failing to apply its brakes in time to avoid hitting a car stranded across the tracks. Despite all efforts to forestall the impact, the horror simply could not be stopped.

For a moment she was struck speechless as she processed what Agnese had said. Had her friend truly been a proxy for Dani? Had Santo and not the nameless man been the one to rape her?

No, she remembered the man's breath and his voice and his hands. It had not been her uncle. But after...? If Santo had raped her, why had the doctor said she was fine? And why had her loved ones, every last one of them, assured her she'd escaped a sexual predator? Worst of all, why couldn't she *remember*?

Because it was easier that way, a little voice said. Easier to take Santo's word because his word had always been final. Easier to accept the doctor's report—a doctor employed by her uncle. Easier to blame an unknown man and accept the happy ending of a thwarted attack. Easier to push the unimaginable truth to the recesses of her mind.

Just easier.

After a few moments Dani's emotions settled back down where they belonged. The train having pushed the offending idea off the track, continued on its way. She reverted to the strange comfort of knowing something had happened, but not knowing quite what.

But for the first time ever, she felt a twinge of cowardice because the very real possibility of Santo's wickedness hadn't disappeared. It remained a twisted, ugly wreckage that she couldn't merely wonder about any longer.

Dr. Rudolfo Spada and his family lived in a quiet residential neighborhood in the center of Verona, near the university. It was just up the street from a popular trattoria that Gabe had heard about. He found the apartment easily and only hoped his interview with the physician would go as well.

He wondered if Dr. Spada would remember him; Gabe had only been a boy the last time he'd seen the doctor, and even then it was for just a few minutes. Gabe's mother, Eliana, never could stand to have Gabe nearby when discussing her illness. He wanted to thank the man for helping his mother to the extent he could.

But Gabe's mission went beyond a simple expression of gratitude. Dr. Spada had been there the night of Ciro's death and the night of Dani's so-called "near rape." The doctor had examined Dani using a rape kit. Those procedures were thorough and invasive, and were designed to uncover the smallest piece of evidence that might link a perp with a victim.

The kits were also notorious for ending up on a shelf, at least in the States. The number of backlogged analyses was staggering and in Gabe's opinion, grounds for criminal negligence in and of itself. The good news, if there was any to be had, was that they could stay on a shelf for a hell of a long time and still reveal evidence years later. Something in Gabe's gut told him there was a reason Santo had been so adamant that Dani was fine, and why he'd apparently gotten angry at the need for an exam. Yet the results had somehow come out clean.

Or had they?

Gabe rang the bell, determined to find out.

"How do you feel?" Gabe asked Dani later that night. She had called as she'd promised, and Gabe had picked her up at Dante's. After a light dinner at a downtown pizzeria, they'd returned to their suite and were now curled up together on the couch. Dani seemed subdued but relatively happy, considering all they'd been through. She shared the news about Dante and Agnese, which he could tell brought her a quiet joy, and she said she felt good about the next day's meeting.

"I feel like I've studied as hard as I can for my final exam, and I'm as ready as I'm going to be," she said.

Not wanting to spoil her mood, he didn't tell her what he'd learned from the doctor that afternoon. There was time enough for that. Right now he simply wanted her to feel as relaxed as possible before her ordeal the next morning.

"Knowing you feel confident makes me happy," he said. "Now how, I wonder, can I make you feel even better than that?" He wiggled his eyebrows at her.

"I don't know," she said, her voice deepening just a little. She turned so that she was cradled in his arms. "What were you thinking?"

"Just this," he murmured, lowering his lips to hers.

Gabe made love to Dani as if it were their last time together. Not because he felt some sort of premonition about what would happen. He was going to be in the room with her and he was confident he could protect her.

It was more to show her how much he had grown to love her in just the short time they'd been together here in Verona.

He didn't waste time talking. Instead he communicated with her on a more primitive, physical level. Gone was the uptight young lady who had spurned him for so many months, out of fear, he'd found out. In her place was a loving, sensuous woman who seemed, at least for the night, to share her most vulnerable self with him. The trust she willingly placed in him made Gabe feel humble…and invincible. And he knew at last what true love was all about.

# CHAPTER TWENTY-FIVE

—⊹⊹—

The next morning Dani put all thoughts of what her uncle might have done to her aside and concentrated on the task at hand. She entered Santo's office on her own, a petite general heading into battle.

Santo rose to meet her, impeccably dressed, as always. He looked genuinely surprised to see her, and pleased.

"Daniela. My dear niece. I'm so glad you have seen the light," he said.

*Dear niece, my as*s. She said nothing but shifted her gaze to the other man who had stood up. She knew he was the Croatian with icy blue eyes. Now she saw that he had short salt and pepper hair, and was dressed expensively.

"Signorina Dunn," he said in his low, cultured voice. "I am pleased to finally meet you. Ivan Stolar, at your service." He shook her hand a bit longer than necessary and held her gaze.

The third man, whom Dani knew to be Italian, stood on the far side of the room. He looked at her and smirked. Holding a cigar in his hand, he sniffed it as he looked at her. She fought down the bile.

"I'm sure you won't mind, I've asked my...friend...Gabriele de la Torre to sit in on this meeting. I always find it edifying to have another person listening on my behalf, especially when the conversation is in Italian, which I have not spoken as my primary language in some time. He is also quite...protective of me."

"You have no need of him," Santo said angrily. "I am your family. I am here to protect you."

"Ah, but who will protect me from you, Uncle?" Dani noticed that Stolar was gazing at her, a slight smile on his face.

"I have no problem with it," Stolar said. "Invite him in, please." It was obvious that in this situation, Santo had no real power.

Gabe entered the room, dressed in a dark suit with power tie. He shook hands all around. "Thank you for letting me be a fly on the wall," he said.

"I'll tell you where flies belong," Santo muttered.

"I'd like to start the meeting by saying I have thoroughly reviewed the financials for both Stella d'Italia and Alberghi Paradisi, and I must say I have some concerns."

Stolar and Santo looked at each other. They must have thought it was going to be a cake walk. Well, she was going to make them work for it.

"What kind of concerns, Signorina Dunn?" Stolar asked politely.

*Showtime.* "As you know, I run my own small hotel in the United States, and find, after some reflection—" she stopped and glanced at Stolar "—that I am quite interested in my uncle's offer to run the new hotel division. I am very pragmatic, gentlemen, and my number one concern is for the bottom line. I see several areas in which I can implement efficiencies that will help both operations." She turned to the Croatian directly. "Would you agree that approach is in everyone's best interest, Signor Stolar?"

"Yes, I quite agree," he said.

She almost laughed at the perplexed looks she was getting from her two adversaries. They no doubt expected her to tiptoe in like a mouse and sign the papers for the big bad men. Well, fuck them. She glanced at Gabe, who revealed nothing by his expression except through the slight rise in his eyebrows.

"Which areas do you see that need improvement?" Santo asked.

"I'm glad you asked. This is just a preliminary analysis, of course, but primarily I see several human resource issues that I insist must be addressed." She opened a folder she had brought. "First I'll discuss the structure of the catering departments in each hotel chain and how I see the application of efficiencies of scale…"

During the next forty-five minutes Dani bombarded Santo and the Croatian with useless facts, theories, and proposals about all major aspects of the hotel industry as they applied to Stella d'Italia and the lesser-quality hotel company. She kept going until she could see their interest flagging, and then proceeded to the "eyes glazed over" stage. Every now and again she would glance over at Gabe to see how she was doing. His almost imperceptible nods told her she was right on course. She droned on.

"And now I'd like to discuss staffing issues at both hotel companies. For example, you are overstaffed in the catering, marketing, and housekeeping departments at several hotels, including the Stella d'Italia Verona. As part of my research I interviewed several such employees locally, and frankly, I was appalled. I have listed several whom have no business being employed by a five-star hotel company." She read from the list. "For example, I would ask for the immediate dismissal of Angela Sticoni, Maria deMaso, Dobra Moretti, Cosima Agnoli, and Tina LaDuca. Dobra Moretti in particular is useless. She must go. These employees are simply not up to our standards. They are not worthy of Stella d'Italia nor the brand I hope to build with Alberghi Paradisi. They are a drag on our bottom line."

"A drag on our bottom line," Santo said. "How can you know such a thing so quickly?"

Dani ignored him and barreled on. "At the corporate level, I also see gross inefficiencies. And I do not see the function of—" she looked at her list "—Flora Petrovic, for instance. She must go. Immediately." Dani looked at Santo, who looked at Stolar for guidance. The Croatian gazed intently at her, as if sizing her up. He didn't even bother maintaining the illusion that Santo was in charge.

"What if we say no?" he asked simply.

Dani heaved a dramatic sigh. "Then I'm afraid I cannot vote in favor of this purchase, no matter what. If I am going to run a brand new division, I am damn well going to run it the way it ought to be run." While her insides were roiling, Dani forced herself to look directly at Stolar and challenge him. "I see great opportunity for functional synergy between the two hotel systems and I will not be hamstrung by ineffective leadership. I don't care how you make the changes, but the changes must be made." There was a long pause.

Finally the Croatian turned to Santo. "I detest inefficiency as well, so I don't see any issue with that. I'm sure Signor Forcelli would agree. There should be no problem accommodating your requests."

Santo looked at him with something akin to hatred in his eyes. Dani could practically hear Santo's mental monologue: *Who is this scum, telling me that I now have to take orders from my own niece? Like hell I will.* Outwardly, however, he merely nodded.

"I'm very glad you agree the changes need to happen. I prefer terminations, personally. Flora Petrovic, Debra Moretti...I will give you the rest of the names. The sooner they're gone, the better. She paused, staring at Stolar. "How soon will you take charge of this matter? I like the sound of *immediately*."

"Yes," Stolar said, still staring at her. "Immediately."

"How will you do it?" Dani asked. "I'm interested in expediency, you understand."

"We may simply give them a severance package, or we may determine they have uses in other departments, within the new organization. That remains to be seen."

"Do what you must, as long as they cause me no trouble," she said.

"They won't cause you trouble, Signorina Dunn. I guarantee it."

Dani rose and extended her hand. "Excellent. Now unless my friend Signor de la Torre has any questions—and I'm sure he won't—I feel quite confident we can do business, gentlemen."

"Yes, I'd say it's time," Stolar said.

"I couldn't have said it better. Where would you like me to sign?"

—·✦·✦·—

Dobra was the first to turn. She was just unlocking the door to her apartment when Marco and Gabe approached her. Gabe looked at her and smiled. *You really are one brute of a dame,* he thought.

"You again?" she said.

Marco flashed his badge. "Dobra Petrovic Moretti?"

Dobra scowled at him, her face turning to sour dough. "I knew something was off about you," she said to Gabe.

"I'm afraid you'll have to come down to the station with us," Gabe replied. "You have been accused of aiding and abetting a criminal organization."

"What? That's bullshit."

Marco took over. He was good at laying it on. "No, that's a fact. We have the evidence to establish that you have played a significant role in an international human trafficking ring. You are in very serious trouble. But what you face from the justice system is nothing compared to what was in store for you. You will soon thank us for taking you into protective custody. We might have just saved your life."

"I don't know what the hell you are talking about."

"You will soon enough."

Dobra complained all the way down to the station and up until the time she heard the conversation that had been recorded at a high-level meeting of Azure Consortium big wigs. The conversation she heard went like this:

Dani: Dobra Moretti in particular is useless. She must go. And I do not see the function of Flora Petrovic. These employees are simply not up to our standards. They are a drag on our bottom line.

Stolar. Yes, I quite agree. I detest inefficiency as well.

Dani: I don't care how you make the changes, but the changes must be made. I prefer terminations. Would you agree that approach is in everyone's best interest, Signor Stolar?

Stolar: Well, I don't see any issue with that, and I'm sure Signor Forcelli would agree. There should be no problem accommodating your requests. I'd say it's time."

Forcelli: I'm so glad you have seen the light.

Dani: How soon will you take charge of this matter?

Stolar: Immediately.

Dani: Do what you must, as long as they cause me no trouble.

Stolar: They won't cause you trouble, Signorina Dunn. I guarantee it."

"You're telling me that bitch is a mole?" Dobra asked when the recording stopped.

Gabe looked her in the eye. "I'm telling you that *lady* just saved your life…and your mother's."

For the first time, Dobra's tough veneer cracked. "Where is my mother now?"

"We are watching her, but we wanted to talk to you first," Marco said. "We have witnesses that have placed you and your cousin Goran Novak at the scene where several employees of Stella d'Italia have disappeared. Although we know she is the dispatcher, your mother's role is slightly more circumspect, so we hesitate to bring her in right away. Of course that means she'll be…vulnerable…to the plans alluded to in the recording. There was that emphasis on the word *immediately*. With your cooperation, however, we are prepared to bring your mother in to safety, as well as temper charges in light of your cooperation. You might even get away with probation and simple deportation. What is it going to be, Signorina Moretti?"

"I want to talk to my mother," she said.

"You're an adult," Gabe reminded her. "You must make these decisions on your own."

In the end, to Gabe's great relief, Dobra turned, and so did Flora, when she heard her daughter was in deep shit. They both flipped on Santo Forcelli and Ivan Stolar, thinking they would have been out the door—and maybe worse—anyway. Gabe was glad Marco had brought in the resources of the task force. Their tech guy was an amazing sound editor, and neither of the women had suspected it wasn't one hundred percent legit.

Surprisingly, the women blew the whistle on Goran Novak, too. Apparently they were hoping he'd be treated with as much leniency as they'd been promised, as long as he cooperated.

Gabe figured the chances of Novak cooperating hovered somewhere between slim and none.

— ✦⟨⟩✦ —

Thank God it's all coming to a head, Gabe thought later.

By comparing license plates between the Sexy Pig and the Labyrinth, Marco had found the car linked to Goran Novak and the killer had been tailed all afternoon. According to Flora Petrovic, a new "shipment" (Azure's name for the girls they trafficked) was due to be "processed" at the group's warehouse, located down by the main train station, at ten p.m. Verona was a crossroads city, perfectly situated to move all kinds of merchandise, from sweet potatoes to kidnapped women, throughout Europe. The shipment would be put on a reserved car of the express train headed west to Brescia, where it would be transferred by private jet to points east. Far East.

Under the watchful ear of the multilingual head of the task force, Flora had called Novak, complaining about Dobra giving her a flu bug and telling him to just proceed as planned without her. "*Osjećam se užasno*," she'd told him, sniffling. "I feel terrible."

She should feel terrible, Gabe thought. She just ratted out a member of her own family, which doesn't feel great, even if they deserve it. He'd felt lousy enough keeping his true identity from Dani and reporting to Santo for those months. Even though it was nothing compared to what Dobra and Flora had just done to Novak, he still felt the guilt of betrayal. Dani was part of him now—at least that's the way he felt about her. Time would tell if she felt the same.

Gabe brought his attention back to the present and the perp he most wanted to bring in. Flora had pegged Ivan Stolar as the man in charge of the consortium's Italian operation; counterparts at his level covered the rest of the EU countries. Stolar was almost always present during processing, she said; he liked overseeing the transfers, and spent part of the time in an office on site. Tonight they were moving a young Ukrainian woman who had been working in Florence before being "promoted" to a job in Verona the week before. Apparently she was destined for Jakarta. The plan was to pick up Stolar, Novak, and any of his compatriots as quickly and as neatly as possible. With luck, Santo Forcelli would be there, too.

After seeing for himself that Dobra and Flora were temporarily locked up, Gabe had returned to La Tana and found Dani sound asleep in their suite. Crawling under the blanket with her, he fully intended on catching forty winks himself, but his hands and mouth had other ideas. Soon he was stroking her breasts and between her legs, and she responded like a sleek black cat being petted in all the right places. The first time, he'd taken her gently, knowing what incredible pressure she'd been under to pull off the sting. Physically he wanted to show her how much he admired and respected her, and how sensitive he could be to her needs.

The second time, she'd been the aggressor, seeming to revel in the power she felt as a woman, and the joy she felt as *his* woman.

They hadn't mentioned the obvious. No talk about what would happen once Santo was dealt with, or what their future held once they returned to Little Eden. All that would come eventually. Instead, she'd used her hands, mouth, and body to share her happiness and ride them both to near oblivion. He'd never felt so satisfied.

Afterward he'd jumped in the shower and changed clothes to meet up with Marco at the warehouse. When he came out, she was sitting on the bed, holding his borrowed snubbie with two fingers, as if it were a dead rat she wanted to dispose of. Her eyes were luminous with tears. "Please don't go there," she begged him. "You aren't part of law enforcement here. This isn't your fight."

Gabe's heart caught in his throat; he'd seen the results of too many gun-related mishaps not to be nervous. "These men killed your father, Dani, and they probably killed your aunt too." He slowly reached over to take the gun from her shaking fingers. "The bastards need to face justice, and I can't just sit by and let everybody else do the work. It's just not in me to do that."

"That's bull pucky," she said in a small, firm voice. "That gun is so little it probably doesn't even work, and you're going anyway. You just want to be in on the action, no matter how dangerous!"

"I'll have you know this is a very nice gun," Gabe said with a faint grin, putting the weapon in his pocket and running his hands through her soft brown curls. He kissed her on the forehead. "I promise to come back to you so that you can read me more of the riot act, okay?"

Dani nodded and looked up at him. Her vulnerable, tear-streaked faced nearly did him in. "I…I want this to be over," she said.

"So do I, bella. So do I."

Police surveillance work is two percent terror, seven percent satisfaction, and ninety-one percent boredom, Gabe thought two hours later as he waited with Marco within sight of the warehouse. He often played with those percentages to keep his mind active during the ninety-one percent part of his job.

The place had been staked out since early evening and estimates were that a total of six Azure Consortium employees were on deck for the transfer of the Ukrainian girl. About twice that many agents, all wearing police jackets to ensure they wouldn't draw friendly fire, surrounded the place. Marco had even scored a jacket for Gabe, but luckily he had one more perk in mind.

"You still got Gina's little pop gun?" he asked.

"You know I do," Gabe said. "Sometimes big surprises come in little packages."

"Well here's something slightly bigger." Marco pulled out a Beretta Stampede and handed it over.

Gabe nodded in appreciation. "Sweet. Yours?"

Marco nodded. "It's an Old West Marshall."

"I can see that." He examined the roughly eight-inch-long revolver. "Must be embarrassing knowing your stick's not as long as everybody else's," he said with a smirk.

"Longer doesn't always equal better," Marco said. "It gets the job done, believe me."

Gabe grinned, checked the snubbie and put it in the back waistband of his jeans. "I figure the two of them will equal one of your police issues."

"Let's just hope you don't have to use either of them," Marco said. "I'm on thin ice even having you here, and if you're caught with my guns, I'm gonna say you lifted them the night you came over."

"Glad you've got my back," Gabe said sarcastically. They continued bantering softly, partly to dissipate their nervous energy, partly to pass the time while they waited for the signal to move in.

About nine forty, a black Range Rover pulled into the back parking lot, joining a van and two beat up Fiats that had been parked there for some time. Moments later a large shipping bay garage-style door began to roll up like a giant snake unhinging its jaw. Two men, one of them Novak and the other the fat man from the meeting with Santo, got out of the car and went around to the back of it, pulling out what looked like a person wrapped in a dark blanket. The leader of the task force team kept his hand raised, which meant *don't engage*; it was too dangerous as long as the presumed Ukrainian girl was in the line of fire.

Novak and the fat man carried the girl to the opened bay and lifted her onto the raised platform. Two other men took her inside the warehouse. She offered no resistance, which meant she was probably drugged. *That could have been Dani.* Gabe swallowed the need to charge them, guns blazing.

Novak locked the car and visually swept the area before hopping up onto the platform. The fat man used the steps. Once they were all inside, the giant door came rolling down again.

The team leader called for all units to move in closer so there'd be no chance for escape. Then he signaled for one agent to make his way up to the parking lot and put tire spikes behind all the tires of the parked cars. In case the raid went to shit, at least the bad guys wouldn't get too far.

The noose was tightening. What they needed was two guys to go in and shake things up while the rest of the team closed in for the takedown. Marco volunteered himself and Gabe, and turned his headset so Gabe could hear the response.

"Hell no," the leader hissed. "No way is de la Torre getting in the middle of this." He'd already reamed Marco for letting a civilian—even if he was a cop in the States, and Italian to boot—come anywhere near the operation.

"He knows what he's doing, director. He'll be fine," Marco transmitted back. Then he turned to Gabe and murmured, "You get yourself in trouble here and I'm going to kick your ass."

The leader came on the line again, and again Marco turned his headset so Gabe could hear. "Clemente, go on up with Peretti and make some noise. Collini, Alba, Marino, and Rossi, move in right behind them once they raise that door. The rest of you, keep the perimeter tight and look for strays. All right. Let's move."

Marco shrugged. "I tried, man."

"Shit," Gabe muttered. He watched as Marco got out of the car and met up with Peretti. The two men conferred for a minute then mussed their hair, pulled their shirts out of their pants, hopped up to the bay door and started banging on it. "Hey!" they shouted, trying to sound like drunken louts. "Hey! Let us in!"

In a few minutes the huge garage door opened again and someone called out *"Hey you sons of bitches! Shut your mouth!"* Marco and Peretti drew their weapons and the rest of the team swarmed into the warehouse. Then all hell broke loose.

Not wanting to miss the action, but knowing he'd be screwed if he directly disobeyed orders, Gabe sprinted to the opposite side of the building and ran alongside the wall, trying doors along the way. That was part of the perimeter, wasn't it? All the doors were locked except the one at the far end. He raised his arm and pointed to alert the agents in charge of that side of the complex that he was going inside.

The huge warehouse was lit by widely spaced, scrawny bulbs hanging from the ceiling on long cords. Pallets shrink-wrapped with merchandise from Nestle chocolate bars to cheap portable DVD players created high-walled corridors that formed a kind of maze. Gabe worked his way carefully toward the sounds of shouting and gunfire. Then it died down. He could still hear the *rat tat tat tat tat* of a semi-automatic weapon, but it was sporadic, which told him someone was pinned down and holding out. Maybe he could outflank them.

He was so intent on finding the shooter that he almost missed the light coming from underneath an office door about halfway down the side of the building. Curtains were drawn on the window that faced the warehouse floor. It was quiet but he could see rapid movement inside the room.

*Hey fellas, I could use some backup about now*, Gabe thought. Adrenaline was starting to course through his muscles. Why the hell hadn't they given him a headset like Marco and the rest of the boys? Stolar was likely inside that office and leaving him might give him time to escape; yelling for backup would blow his cover.

Fuck. Too late now. He'd have to draw Stolar out on his own and hope he gave up peacefully. Just as he was about to pound on the door and yell "*Polizia!*" he heard a shuffling and the sound of a click come up behind him.

*Goddammit! Never assume the bad guys aren't watching you!*

He ducked, spun around, and fired. Shot squarely in the chest, Goran Novak went down.

Unfortunately, so did Gabe, dropping his Beretta as he fell.

The door to the office swung open and Ivan Stolar stepped out, a briefcase in one hand and a revolver in the other.

"Ah, the annoying little fly on the wall," the Croatian said with a sneer as he stepped over Gabe. He raised his gun to finish Gabe off, but not before Gabe grabbed Stolar's leg to topple him. As Stolar went down, Gabe reached behind for his Colt Cobra and got off two rounds, which caught Stolar in his leg. Stolar screamed and his shot bounced off the wall. Gabe heard someone yell "Drop it!" but he wasn't sure who the guy was talking to. In fact, everything was getting kind of hazy.

The last thing he remembered was thinking *Marco's going to kick my ass and so is Dani.*

Then he blacked out in a pool of blood.

# CHAPTER TWENTY-SIX

—‹✦✦›—

Dani checked her watch again. It was ten thirty, which meant Gabe, Marco, and the rest of the task force team were probably right in the middle of the raid at the warehouse. Flora Petrovic had explained that Santo liked to be on hand, along with Ivan Stolar, when the women were transported. "Sometimes," she'd said, "Signor Forcelli likes to sample the merchandise."

Dani shuddered. At least by now her uncle would be gone and she could check for the artwork in his inner room. If the paintings were there, she would have them returned to The Grove. Once Santo was arrested, the disposition of the artwork would be the least of his problems. If they *weren't* there, then perhaps it was time to let the memory of them go.

She stuck her cell phone in her pocket but switched it to vibrate so Gabe's eventual call wouldn't wake up the household. Wiping her damp palms on her pant legs, she left the sanctuary of their suite.

La Tana was dark and still, but not lifeless. Tonight, like its namesake the panther, it seemed to be waiting—a predator, biding its time before pouncing on unwary victims. Dani tried to ignore the chill slithering into her. *Remember, it's only a house.*

She made her way down the hall to Santo's office. The door was unlocked. She turned the knob and entered the room, gently closing the door behind her in case another night owl should pass by.

The same small table lamp now lent an eerie glow to the room. She could see that her uncle had been working there recently, possibly that very afternoon. A number of files were stacked on top of his desk, and one drawer stood open, as if he had been looking for something in a hurry. She could smell the faint, musty odor of tobacco and she thought of the fat Italian with his hand on her breast. She shivered.

The door to Santo's inner room was closed, but a light shown underneath the door. Dani frowned. Did he leave a nightlight on when he wasn't home? Why would that be necessary?

*Oh my God, maybe he's already home.*

A frisson of panic shot through her. She turned to leave and had her hand on the doorknob of the hallway door when she heard a deep voice behind her.

"I knew you'd come back."

---

Gabe awoke to the cold, white glare of a hospital room. He was lying flat and several people in blue smocks wearing masks surrounded him. He thought he must have taken a wrong turn and called out "Marco?" to his friend.

Someone in the background said, "*Lasciatemi passare, per favore,*" and Gabe thought *Who needs to be let through?* And then someone who looked like Marco was there, only he was wavering and holding Gabe's hand, which seemed odd, and he was saying, "*Sta andando tutto bene, amico.* It's going to be okay." And Gabe wondered what was wrong, and more than anything, he wanted to go to Dani. He knew, somehow, that she was in danger and he had to tell her something. Tell her what? He struggled to sit up, to go to her, but someone held him down and he called out "Dani" and they said "*Sta andando tutto bene,*" and then the lights went out.

Dani sucked in a deep breath, holding her hand to her heart. It was beating so fast she thought it was going to burst. "You...I thought you were out for the evening," she managed. She thought *Ihavegottogetoutofhere,* but Santo's words stopped her.

"And once again you were going to come into my chamber without my permission? After I told you not to? How very brazen you are. You must really want to see what's in there." He paused, looking intently at her. "That's why you came back, isn't it?"

She froze. Considered. Processed. He was right. She had come for that exact reason. To find out. To remember. She turned and faced him. "Yes," she said, knowing that he'd know what she was talking about. "I need to be sure."

Santo stood in the doorway and beckoned her. "Then come in," he said.

As if in a trance, she walked passed him into the room she'd always thought of as his "inner office." It was in fact a bedroom. The light inside was muted, just as the office had been. A lone bedside lamp illuminated the space. The walls were dark, the gold silk draperies pulled shut against the night. A large, intricately carved wooden bed dominated the room, covered in an expensive golden brocade bedspread. The old anxiety inside of her returned, that mixture of pain and terror. This was the true panther's lair.

"Is this where you raped Agnese?" she asked, finding refuge in anger.

He smiled. "Many times, although I would not couch it in such vulgar terms. Agnese was part of an…arrangement, shall we say. And she did live up to her end of the agreement adequately. Although—" here he paused and pierced Dani with his gaze "— she never did quite measure up to you."

The shock of what he'd said must have registered on her face because he stepped forward and pointed to the wall behind her. "You've been wondering where you saw those," he said, his voice growing in intensity. "You were lying on your back. On my bed. With your knees up and spread apart. You gave yourself to me."

Mute with horror, Dani slowly turned around and saw the two paintings by Lia Wolff that she'd remembered vaguely from so long ago. One was of a young woman in the midst of being taken against her will. The other was the same woman heavy with child. Lia had gone through that nightmare, and Dani now had confirmation that in some respects she had, too. And somehow that knowledge strengthened her. She was not crazy or delusional or some whacked-out teenager who wanted to have sex so badly she made up stories about it. She had been victimized, but no longer would she play the victim. She took a deep, fortifying breath and turned back to Santo.

"Now that I know what you did to me, what do you think is going to happen?" she asked.

Santo continued to gaze at her. "You are back at La Tana," he said. "We can continue with what was meant to be."

"What do you mean 'meant to be'?"

"Us, of course. Together. The purity of the Forcelli blood line at last. We will foist this mess on Dante and build Stella d'Italia into an even greater hotel company than it has ever been. It's in your blood. It's in mine. Together we will be invincible."

Dani looked into Santo's eyes and saw the beginnings of madness, as if his grip on reality were slowly leaving its moorings, a boat drifting away from the dock. "What mess are you referring to?"

Santo shook his head, his demeanor that of a parent chastising a wayward child. "I checked those names you gave us at the meeting, *nipote*," he said. "Only Flora Petrovic and her daughter Dobra were real. I knew you were on the brink of uncovering the arrangement I've had going for the past few years. I knew it was time to shift the focus to Dante. But I am prepared. I am always prepared. I have created a set of accounting records that implicate him. You do not need to worry. He will take the fall for us, *carissima*. Then there will be only you and me."

"What about the…the tape of you?"

"You saw that? Those bastards." He shrugged his shoulders. "I will deny everything, of course. They used a look alike to set me up. The tape was staged. The usual excuses. We will weather the storm, you and I, together as one."

Dani was just beginning to realize how far gone her uncle was when she heard a familiar, yet bloodless voice from the doorway.

"That was not our agreement, signore." Fausta Lombardi stood there, holding a pistol aimed straight at Dani's heart. She looked from Santo to Dani and back again. "Sit down on the bed, Santo," she ordered. When he didn't move she turned the gun on him. "Now!" He carefully sat on the edge of the bed, lifting his arms as if to say *You see? I am obeying.* "You," she said to Dani, gesturing with her weapon, "stand on the side where I can see you. And then don't move."

Dani also did as she was told. She couldn't tell what was driving Fausta; she only hoped once the housekeeper calmed down she would see that Dani was on her side. "I'm glad you're here," Dani ventured, letting relief shine through her words.

Fausta glanced at her. "I wouldn't be, if I were you." She turned back to Santo. "I have called Agnese and explained that the situation has reached a turning point. She is on her way over. You will tell her that you and she are going to be together and that Dani is out of the picture. Completely. And then you will ask Agnese to marry you and she will say yes. In front of witnesses. So that she will not go back on her word. She has always been a good girl that way." She pointed the gun again at Dani. "And if you don't," she said to Santo, "I will remove your precious chimera once and for all."

"But Agnese loves Dante," Dani said. "She has no interest in—"

"Shut up!" Fausta screamed. "You know nothing." Venom dripped from the core of the woman. "Santo gave me his word a dozen years ago and just as Agnese will keep hers, I intend for him to keep his."

"I don't know what you're talking about," Santo said. "Don't believe a word she says, Daniela."

Fausta barked in laughter. "That is rich, coming from you. You want your sweet *nipote* to hear only the truth? So be it." She directed her words to Dani. "I wasn't always a chatelaine, you know. I worked my way up…on my back. I started as a housekeeping attendant in one of Stella d'Italia's hotels. Your Nonno Ciro took an interest in me and brought me to work here at La Tana. But my feckless husband was in the way, so your charming and oh so resourceful Uncle Santo had him beaten to death."

At Dani's gasp she focused on Santo. "You think I didn't know you had him killed? Your father wanted me in his bed and I finally said yes. I let him climb on top of me whenever he wanted for *ten long years*. Why wouldn't I? I needed a job and I had a sister whose care I couldn't afford. And when Ciro died I offered myself to you and you declined because you can only really get it up for little girls, isn't that right?"

Santo said nothing, but his expression revealed he was almost relieved to have all the cards on the table. He looked at Dani, his eyes softened with…love? She wanted to gag.

Fausta nodded in Dani's direction. "Poor little Daniela. You had a taste of her when she was fifteen. So sweet. So young. Too bad her mama finally got smart and took her away. But I came to your rescue, didn't I? I let you do the same thing to my daughter. Over and over again. I even let you impregnate her to show she was fertile! God knows you couldn't get the job done with your own wife. By then my sister's fate was sealed, and you were an idiot if you thought that was my only motivation. I didn't give you my daughter because of my sister's medical costs, or to pay for her education. I did it for your name, Santo. Your *name*. I did it to make my daughter a *queen*." Fausta was so wrapped up in her own diatribe that she didn't notice Agnese and Dante had entered the doorway. When she finally saw them her eyes blazed.

"My father liked fucking you, and I liked fucking Agnese... for a while," Santo said. He had seen the two of them come in, so he directed his poison to Agnese. "Do you remember the last time I had you? You had come home from college and must have taken a class in courage because you announced you were through with me. Imagine. You said, 'Do what you want to me, but this is the last time.' So I fucked you every way possible. And you remember what I told you afterward? I explained that ever since your Aunt Eliana died, you hadn't been under any obligation—that I would have paid for her care and your education regardless. As you can see, your mother knew that too, yet she said nothing to you about it. She pressed you to come to my bed because—" he turned to Fausta "—you wanted me to, what, fall in love with her?" He laughed. "But you never really understood. I would *never* have married her. Daniela has been mine since she was a little girl.

Yes, I tasted her at fifteen, and now that she's back, we'll keep the Forcelli line pure. Together. So stop this behavior or I will be forced, despite your years of service, to let you go."

Dani realized her jaw had dropped and closed it. She found herself in thrall to what seemed like theater of the absurd in which the performers were out to show how completely out of touch with reality their counterparts were.

Fausta gestured to Dani with her weapon. "You just don't get it, do you, Santo? Look at Dani. She detests you. And why wouldn't she? You took her virginity and covered it up so nobody would know that anything had happened."

"But I knew," Dani said, her voice stronger than she thought it would be. "At some level I knew. And all those years I felt like I was crazy for reliving something that everybody said never really happened." She squared her shoulders. "But that's over with. Just like you are, Santo."

"What do you mean?" Uncertainty colored Fausta's tone for the first time.

"She means Santo is going to prison," Dante said. "He has committed several crimes. There are witnesses. He is finished."

Fausta looked at her daughter and at Dante. They both nodded to confirm what Dante had said. In a matter of seconds her expression told the story: Fausta had come to collect a debt years in the making, and now Santo would have the last laugh in spite of everything she had sacrificed. Her face turned to stone. "Then yes, he is most definitely finished." She directed the pistol at Santo's heart.

"Mama, no!" Agnese cried. But it was too late. Her words were cut short by the rapid *pop pop pop* of three bullets entering Santo's chest.

"Oh, Mama, what have you done? He wasn't worth it." Agnese started to go over toward Fausta, but Dante held her back.

Fausta looked at Dante holding her daughter and paused. Afterward Dani wondered what the woman was thinking at the last. Did she feel remorse for all she'd done to herself and her daughter in the name of ambition? Or did Fausta see her daughter in the arms of a man she deemed beneath her and decide that in light of all her failed plans, it was just too much to stomach? No one would ever know, because in the next instant, Fausta put the gun to her head and pulled the trigger.

In the shock of the aftermath it took Dani several minutes before she remembered the many vibrations she'd felt from her cell phone. *I need Gabe so much right now,* she thought. *I'm glad he's back.*

Except the calls weren't from Gabe and when she listened to her voicemail she cried out in anguish. Her cousin Dante caught her as she crumpled to the floor.

# CHAPTER TWENTY-SEVEN

Gabe woke up again with a strange sense of déjà vu. He'd been in a similar hospital room, only he'd been sitting in the chair and Dani had been lying in the bed. Now the situation was reversed and it pissed him off no end. He should be the one taking care of *her*.

"You're awake," Dani said softly. She reached over to brush his hair back from his forehead.

"How long have I been here?"

"You got out of surgery about an hour ago. We've all be waiting for you to come around."

Shit. Surgery? That didn't sound good. He hadn't bothered to check to see if he was missing anything. "Um, what's...what's the prognosis?"

"You'll live. Your left shoulder was torn up and you lost a lot of blood, but the bullet didn't hit anything vital, *grazie a Dio!*" Tears started to roll down her cheeks and he reached over with his right arm because his left wouldn't move. "Hey..."

Dani wiped her tears away. "Dang it, where's a handkerchief when I need one?" She smiled through her tears. "It's okay. Really. I'm fine."

"Look, I know I got Novak, but I don't remember much after Stolar drew his gun on me. What'd I miss?"

Dani let out a burst of laughter, but it didn't sound right, especially since she was still crying. She sounded like she wasn't quite in control.

"Tell me," he said fiercely.

"Tell you what, *amico*?" Marco entered the room along with Dante.

"I asked Dani what I missed and she fell apart," Gabe said.

"You missed a lot," Marco said, his normally jovial face looking way too somber. "Santo is dead, as is Fausta. She killed him and then took her own life."

"Wait a minute—what?"

Dante proceed to tell him what had gone down, how Santo had it in his mind to form some kind of unholy bond with Dani, and how Fausta had gone ballistic over it. Turns out she had made a devil's bargain with him back when Agnese was only sixteen and she expected Santo to fulfill his end of the deal. When he refused, she made him pay the ultimate price.

"Santo admitted that he did…rape me," Dani said.

Gabe could tell it cost her to say it out loud, but he also detected an underlying strength to her admission. He took her hand. "I know. It seems like ages ago, but yesterday while you were visiting Dante, I paid a visit to the doctor who examined you that night. He'd kept the results of the kit but his family was threatened and he was too scared to report what he knew. I was going to tell you after all this blew over." He touched her cheek. "The important thing is, you weren't imagining things."

"No, I wasn't." She squeezed Gabe's hand. "I'll bet this is the one and only time the victim of such a crime is relieved that something really did happen."

Marco and Dante filled Gabe in on other details and it made him sick to hear his cousin was present when the killings occurred. "How is Agnese doing?" he asked.

"She is heartbroken," Dante said. "Despite Fausta's twisted ambition, Agnese loved her. She's with my...with the Mother Superior now. Considering everything she's had to deal with, she's doing all right." Dante looked down and then gave them a half smile. "We're getting married as soon as this all simmers down. I told her we could wait, but she insists. She says we've wasted too much of our lives already and she wants you and Dani to be there."

"Congratulations, *amico.* That's great news!" Gabe said.

Marco kidded Dante about joining the Italian equivalent of the "ball and chain" club and Dante grew serious. "I only hope I can support her when all of this *pasticcio* hits the media."

"It's a mess, all right," Marco agreed.

Dani's voice was strong. "But we agreed it was worth it for Stella d'Italia to take a hit if it meant putting Santo away."

"You know, I still don't understand why Santo did it," Gabe said. "How'd he get involved with those scumbags to begin with?"

"I think it was a combination of greed and lust," Dante said. "I checked through his vacation travel records and it turns out about five years ago he started visiting Thailand as a sex tourist."

"A sex tourist?" Dani asked.

"Yeah, it's really perverse," Gabe said. "Certain countries even offer package deals for men to come over and have sex with underage boys and girls."

Dani shuddered. "Oh, that's...that's horrible."

"Well I'd use slightly different language, but you're right." Gabe frowned. "But what's the connection between a sex holiday and hooking up with the Azure Consortium?"

"A Thai businessman by the name of Somchair Mookjai," Marco said. "The task force has known about him for a while, but he's as slippery as the *olio d'oliva* he puts in his hair."

"He's a businessman. So what?" Dante asked.

"Well, he's more a broker of sorts. Sets up interested parties to create the sex slave version of an underground railroad, like the network the United States had during the Civil War. A secret way to move people—in this case young women—from point A to point B with nobody knowing about it. Like I said before, the potential for profit is astronomical. No doubt Mookjai got a fat commission for bringing Santo and the consortium together."

"My uncle was always looking for a way to make Stella d'Italia more consequential," Dante mused. "He was never satisfied with the status quo."

Gabe gazed at Dani as she subtly hid a strand of hair behind her ear. It reminded him of something. He turned to Marco. "You remember I mentioned that tattoo Ines told Dani and me about? The one behind that woman Mirela's ear? Anything surface on that yet or was it just a coincidence?"

"No coincidence," Marco said. "Turns out the fat guy, Moroni, is a real chatterbox, hoping we'll go light on him. He says that was the way they identified the women they were going to ship. They couldn't afford to accidentally kidnap someone like Ines who knows a lot of people. So goons like him and Goran Novak would check for the tattoo. The butterfly you described was actually part of the Azure logo. I'll bet the Ukranian girl they were trying to move has one, too."

"I *knew* I'd seen it someplace. It was on one of the forms I found when I was researching all those sham companies," Dani said. "I wish I'd made the connection sooner."

"Cases are like that," Marco said. "Sometimes it takes a while before you can see how everything links up."

"Speaking of connections, this has been bugging me," Dani said. "How did they know I was at the opera the other night? Had they been following me?"

"Yeah, apparently since your interview with Ines and Dobra," Marco explained. "Dobra copped to dropping a transmitter in your jacket pocket when she hung it up."

"Huh," Dani said. "I remember taking the thumb drive Stolar gave me out of my pocket along with a little disc. I thought it was a battery or something, so I just left it."

Gabe was having trouble processing everything that had happened and blamed it on the drugs that were dripping through his IV. He tried to get a handle on it. "So Santo goes into human trafficking and uses Stella d'Italia hotels to launder the so-called shipments. The consortium puts the pressure on him to expand, and Dani's father balks because it doesn't smell right. But having his own brother killed? I mean, that is downright evil. And then his wife? How did Ornella figure into all this? Was she going to blow the whistle on him?"

"None of the above," Marco explained. "Moroni said Santo never wanted Armando killed—the consortium just went ahead and did it to speed things along, as well as to let Santo know they meant business. But Santo *did* order Ornella's death." Marco glanced at Dani. "We may never know his true motive. Could be he…uh…got it in his head about that time to remove any barriers between him and Dani getting together."

"It doesn't get much sicker than that," Dante said. "How's the company going to survive such a blow to its reputation? I don't see how it can."

Dani spoke up, sounding surprisingly upbeat. "Stella d'Italia will survive because it's a well-run company that provides excellent service to its guests. Yes, we'll take a hit in the short run, but it will only last until the next celebrity scandal."

"You're pretty optimistic," Dante said. Gabe could hear the skepticism in the man's voice.

Dani looked at Marco. "I'm not sure how much we'll be able to shape the story from your end, but I'm thinking, if Agnese can tough it out, we could explain it as a jealous housekeeper who found out her boss, who had promised to marry her, reneged on it once his wife died. When you think about it, that is essentially what happened. We just don't bring in all the other sordid details. And when the story comes out about the trafficking, we keep repeating that Stella d'Italia is fully cooperating with authorities to root out the evil."

"I don't see a problem with that approach," Marco said. "As far as publicity goes, the task force would prefer to keep as much as possible under wraps. The less we show our hand, the better."

"What about the victims in all this?" Dani asked. "Any chance you can track them down?"

"We scored a lot of logistical information on that raid, so yeah, I think we stand a good chance of returning many of those victims to their families."

Gabe laid his head back down as he listened. It felt like his shoulder was on fire.

Dani leaned over and kissed him. "I am glad you came back to me," she whispered. "I promise I will read you more of the riot act later."

He smiled and didn't remember much after that.

# CHAPTER TWENTY-EIGHT

Dante paced the length of the classroom, pausing every few steps to adjust his tie. He stopped at the small sink in the corner and looked into the mirror, adjusting once again. He glanced at the bouquet of flowers sitting in a jar that he would present to Agnese before the ceremony. She knew so much more about plants than he did; would she like them?

"You look fine," Mother Maria Annunciata said, entering the room with his father. They shut the door behind them. "Almost as pretty as the bride."

"Impossible," Dante muttered. "No one can hold a candle to my Agnese." He looked at his parents and it dawned on him that throughout his life, despite their unconventional relationship to each other, they had always been there for him. He felt the need to confide in them now. "I can't believe she's going to be mine," he said, a hitch in his voice. "Will I ever be worthy of her?"

His father smiled, a wry expression on his face. "No, but because of who you are, you will always try, and she will be more than happy with that."

Dante nodded, comforted by his father's words. "How is it looking out there? Did we outsmart the paparazzi?"

It had been a week since the deaths of Santo and Fausta, and they, along with Ornella, had been quietly laid to rest. With the enthusiasm of hungry tigers being thrown fresh meat, the press had had a field day with the "Sordid Love Triangle Behind the Walls of La Tana." Meanwhile the task force, with Dante's full cooperation, had discreetly gone about unraveling the consortium's Italian operation. Unfortunately, certain strands of the organization still remained out of reach, but at least Azure would no longer operate within Stella d'Italia hotels, or Italy, for that matter, for some time to come.

During the same time, Dante and Agnese had planned their special day.

Aldo nodded. "We've done a good job distracting both the press and the public. Who would have thought a family like ours would stage a wedding inside of a convent school?"

Dante noticed his mother gesturing to his father, as if to encourage him. "Tell him," she urged quietly.

Aldo straightened his shoulders "I have some news," he said.

"What is it?" Dante looked from one parent to the other with concern. He wasn't sure he could take any more "news."

"I have a new job," his father said. "I'm joining the Congregation of Christian Brothers."

"Father, that's wonderful!"

"I agree. Because of my many years of service to the church, they have made me a special adjunct to the Congregational Leadership team based in Rome. I'll be working on programs to encourage older parish members like myself to enter the brotherhood. We may no longer be young, but we still have a lot to contribute to the world." Aldo glanced at Mother Maria, his beloved Luisa. "I...I hope this will help me atone for the wrongs I have done." Mother Maria put her hand tenderly on his arm.

Dante, more buoyant, wrapped his arms around his father's compact frame. "You helped me clean the wound," he whispered. "For that I will always be grateful."

Mother Maria gestured again to Aldo. "The gift?" she reminded him.

"Oh yes, I almost forgot." Dante's father pulled an envelope out of his pocket and handed it to his son. "I should have given this to you years ago. You certainly earned it and I have no need of it. But now it's even better."

Dante opened it. Inside was a letter transferring thirty-four percent of Stella d'Italia to him. *What?* "Father, this is twice your share. I don't understand."

Aldo shrugged. "Yet another sign that God has a sense of humor. Your Uncle Santo made me his beneficiary years ago. He no doubt felt I would always do his bidding, even from beyond the grave. He must be turning in that grave this very moment."

Dante grinned. "He wouldn't be too happy, would he?" He hugged his father again. "Thank you for this vote of confidence. I promise I will make you proud."

"I have always been proud," his father said, gesturing to Mother Maria to join in the family bond. "God has blessed me far more than I deserve."

At that moment Dani knocked on the door and entered. "Anybody in here want to get married?" she asked. "I have one very beautiful bride waiting nervously to walk down the aisle with her soon to be father-in-law."

"That would be me," Aldo said with a smile. "I am ready."

"So am I," Dante said. "More than ready." He took the bouquet out of the jar, carefully dried the stems, and followed his family out the door.

Gabe hadn't gone to many weddings in his life, and he never got worked up over those he had attended, because he always thought of how terrible his own parents' marriage had been. But this one was different. Maybe it was the simplicity of it all. No dog and pony show. No bridal party, no giant reception. Just two people unafraid to profess their love for each other in front of their closest family and friends, who were sitting on folding chairs in a convent garden. It was…nice. He felt a twinge and adjusted the sling on his bandaged shoulder.

"Are you feeling all right?" Dani whispered. "Do you need another pain pill?"

Gabe smiled and shook his head. Ever since he'd gotten shot, Dani had hovered over him like an attentive spouse. He liked the feeling. A lot. Did he have the same courage as Dante and Agnese?

Did Dani? They hadn't talked about the future, and they needed to. Soon.

After the brief ceremony, the guests headed over to the gymnasium, where Dani and Gina had put together a delicious country-style meal of roast chicken, pasta, salad, bread, and wedding cake. Not a fish egg to be seen anywhere, thank God. Gabe was admiring Dani's efficient serving technique when Marco came up to him.

"My kind of wedding," Marco said. "Short and sweet. You got the scissors?"

Gabe patted his breast pocket with his unencumbered hand. "Right here, although I hate to cut up Dante's tie—it's pretty nice."

"I'm sure he won't mind," Marco said. "But keep it in mind when it's your turn—not that you have a favorite tie," he added.

Gabe looked at him. "My turn?"

Marco rolled his eyes. "Only a matter of time, buddy." He gestured to Dani. "You let that one go and you're more of an idiot than I thought."

"Thanks for the vote of confidence," Gabe said. "So, how's the investigation proceeding? You going to arrest me for using an unauthorized firearm?"

"All I can say is, you are one lucky SOB. Not only did I get that little wrinkle smoothed out, I even got you nominated for a commendation for exemplary service above and beyond the call of duty. They might even make you an honorary member of the task force."

"I'd like to see that." Gabe chuckled. "Maybe it'll help me get workman's comp for this." He raised his bandaged arm.

Marco turned serious. "I'm glad you're walking away with just a scar," he said gruffly. "And I thank you for helping us get rid of a major piece of ugliness here in Verona."

"I did it for Dani," Gabe said. "I would do anything for her."

Marco looked across the room. Gabe could tell he was watching Gina. "Like I said, it's only a matter of time. Excuse me. I'm going to go claim my own bride."

The time came for the traditional removal of the garter, and Dante seemed almost shy about reaching up Agnese's simple wedding dress to remove it. Gabe and Marco's catcalls probably didn't help the situation. Then it was time for Gabe to take Dante's tie and cut it up to distribute to the males in the party. In exchange they would give the groom a present, usually money, although in this case, Dante had no need of it.

"I really like that tie," Dante said wistfully as Gabe began to snip away.

"I think you can afford to buy another one," Dani replied. She was standing next to Gabe on his injured side, holding Dante's tie out so Gabe could cut it. He knew she was being protective, but he would have rather been able to put his good arm around her.

Afterward she pulled an envelope out of her purse and handed it to her cousin. "Here's my present," she said. "I finally signed the papers related to my inheritance, so this letter gives you permission to vote my shares in Stella d'Italia."

Dante looked shell shocked. "I don't know what to say."

"Say thank you," Dani said playfully. "And by the way, I'd like my portion of the company income to go toward a foundation I'm setting up to protect young girls from predators like our dear Uncle Santo, may he not rest in peace. I'm going to talk to Agnese about working with me on the project."

Gabe took a deep breath. He hadn't discussed this with Dani, but somehow he knew she would approve. "And I'd like to seed that foundation with the money I'd saved to repay Santo for caring for my mother. Given what Fausta and Agnese went through on her behalf, it's the least I can do." He was rewarded with a radiant smile from Dani. *Yes, it was the right thing to do.*

"Thank you both," Dante said. "But you ought to know something. Santo willed his shares to my father, who has now given all his stock to me. That means I now have controlling interest in Stella d'Italia. Are you comfortable with that?"

"Absolutely." Dani pointed to their grandmother chatting with Gina across the room. "But I wouldn't overlook the asset you have in Nonna Stella. She is sharp as ever, and knows the business as well as you or me."

"I'm going to need a new team," he agreed. "I thought I'd track down Carla Rinaldi as well. Now that the danger has passed, I think she'd be a wonderful addition to our company. We have a lot of work to do."

Dani put her hand on her cousin's arm. "Just do me one favor," she said, glancing at Gabe. "Don't take the love you and Agnese have for each other for granted. Nothing is worth giving up love and family over, not even the best hotel company in the world."

At that moment Agnese walked over, a big smile on her face. She put her arm around Dante and leaned her head on his shoulder. "I missed you," she said. Dante leaned down to kiss her and they seemed to forget they weren't alone. Gabe and Dani exchanged looks.

"Speaking of honeymoons," Gabe said, clearing his throat loudly. "Where are you two headed?" The newlyweds reluctantly broke their embrace.

"Just to Venice for a few days," Agnese said. "Dante must stay close to steer the ship through these choppy waters."

"Well, just remember what I said, cousin," Dani admonished.

"At the very least you have to plan a trip to California to see Dani and me." As he said the words, he caught Dani's gaze and held it. *Understand me*, he wanted to tell her. *This is what I want. How about you?*

# CHAPTER TWENTY-NINE

Dani's insides were tied up in knots and it was her own damn fault. Why hadn't she had the courage to discuss what was really going on between them when Gabe wanted to talk? He'd come to her with a serious expression the evening before and said, "We have to talk about us." She'd panicked, turned defensive, and said in a false, lighthearted tone, "Hey, it's okay. I know. What happens in Verona stays in Verona." Which was the opposite of what she felt.

He'd looked at her a long time, said, "That's lame," and walked away. Later that night he'd come to her bed, however. Without saying a word he had staked his claim, making love to her thoroughly, showing her repeatedly just how perfect they were for each other. She choked up just thinking about it.

He'd been reserved all the way back to Milan and now, here they were, waiting for the first flight of their trip back to San Francisco. He sat off by himself in one of the uncomfortable plastic chairs, killing time before the boarding announcement, acting as if he'd already forgotten everything that had happened between them. A week earlier they'd changed their seats to sit together, but given his attitude, it promised to be an excruciating flight home.

He was driving Dani crazy.

She went over and tried to break the ice. "Did I tell you Dante's going to have those two paintings shipped to me in Little Eden?" she began. "I found a slip of paper behind one of them. It was written by Lia, giving them to my great-grandfather because they had served their purpose."

"Yeah, you told me. That's nice." Gabe didn't appear to be in a sociable mood. He had picked up a copy of *Sports Illustrated* and was thumbing through it, not reading at all.

She tried again. "Nonna Stella called this morning to say she was all for selling La Tana. She agrees with Dante, Uncle Aldo, and me that the place has nothing but bad memories for all of us."

"Makes sense," he said.

The man was *infuriating*.

Dani couldn't stand it any longer. "Okay, you want to talk. Let's talk. You want to tell me you had a good time but it's over. Okay. Fine. But I…I want to say thank you." Her voice broke. *No, don't go all wobbly now. Or at least get it all out before you do.* "I mean it. Thank you for being such a…such a…good friend to me, and—"

Gabe's eyes blazed. He stared at her as if he were trying to see into her heart. "Is that all I am to you?" he growled. "*A friend?*" He stood up and looked around in apparent disgust, shaking his head. It seemed like the only thing standing in the way of him throttling her was the sling he still wore on his arm.

And in that instant it hit her. What her Uncle Aldo would call an epiphany. Gabriele loved her, and he wanted to know if she felt the same. Now it all made sense.

"Yes, you're my friend," she said, approaching him and speaking in a low, clear tone. "My best friend. The one person who knows all my faults, who sees all of my baggage and is willing to carry it for me." She gestured to his sling. "The one who is willing to take a bullet to avenge me." She came closer and Gabe backed up a step. She kept her voice low. "You're also my lover. The one who makes my body sing, who fulfills me on every level. The one whose babies I want to carry. And...and the one I would give anything to spend the rest of my life with, because I love you." She was now as close as she could be to him without touching.

Gabe stared at her a moment longer, breathing rapidly, and she watched his expression as his heart opened and a warmth seemed to spread up through his entire being. Then, with his good arm, he swept her into his embrace. "*Ti amo, bella,*" he murmured, and kissed her reverently at first, then more forcefully, as if he were realizing bit by bit what their declaration to each other really meant.

When they reluctantly broke apart several minutes later, Dani noticed some of the passengers were gawking at them. She smiled at the group and said, "It was just a lovers' quarrel. He really is crazy about me."

Gabe laughed and kissed her again, his strong arm holding her safe within his reach.

Reluctantly, Dani took a deep breath and stepped back. "Gabriele, if we're going to make this work, we can't have any more secrets between us, so I have a confession to make."

Gabe caressed her shoulder with his good hand. "You should know by now you can tell me anything."

Biting her lip, she hesitated. She knew how much Gabe loved Italian food. "I...I can't cook."

"What?"

"I said I can't cook. I even forget when I'm boiling water on the stove sometimes. Nina and Paulo just got this idea in their heads..."

"Ah, you mean the idea that the fastest way to bring you and me together was through my stomach? That I'd fall in love with you over your Venetian meatloaf?"

Dani frowned. "You sound like you aren't surprised."

Gabe smiled that slow, luscious smile that got her every time. "Daniela, I've known from the beginning you can't cook. I could tell from the first conversation we had about a dish you supposedly made. You couldn't remember what was in it. No cook worth his or her salt forgets the ingredients of a dish they just made. But you know something else?"

Speechless, Dani could only shake her head.

"I love you anyway. Completely. Without reservation. Until we leave this earth, and even beyond that. We were meant to be together, bella. I finally believe in fate. And I believe in us."

"Oh, Gabriele..." They kissed again but were interrupted by the announcement that boarding would now begin.

"And now I have a confession to make to you," he whispered.

"What is it?"

"Flying scares me to death."

Dani looked into his eyes and smiled. "Then you are with the right person," she said. "Because I was meant to love you and keep you safe. Now let's go home." She put her arm around his waist and they waited their turn to board.

# EPILOGUE

—·✦·—

**M**irela awoke with a start, panic her first, learned response. She blinked, let out a sigh as she remembered where she was and reassured herself yet again that it was not a dream.

The rocking motion of the train had lulled her into a much-needed sleep, but now that she was getting closer, she knew her mounting anticipation would keep her alert. She focused her eyes on the rolling countryside of her native Romania, but her mind wandered.

She still found it difficult to believe all that had happened in such a short period of time. Just three weeks ago she had been a captive in a secret harem owned by a wealthy Asian businessman in Pak Kret, Thailand. The perverse old man kept both young women and young boys. The only silver lining to her particular nightmare had been the fact that her captor was in poor health and spent more time looking than…doing. The young boys broke her heart, but the other women, who had been there longer and had established a pecking order, were mean to her. Over time she understood why: once a member was deemed no longer "useful," he or she was sent out into the streets to earn a living any way they could.

Then the miracle happened. A group of policemen raided the secluded estate and rescued all of the captives. Mirela, because she wasn't a citizen of Thailand, had been sent to what they called a "recovery house" where they checked her health and started the process of getting her back to her own country. The Thai government didn't want the bad publicity, so they treated her with special care. She wondered what would become of the local women and boys who had shared her imprisonment. Would they just be told to go back to where they came from?

Returning to her own village sounded like heaven. A nice woman from the police agency had contacted Mirela's mother and told her what had happened. When they first spoke on the telephone, her mother had cried for several minutes. "*Puiu*, my little *puiu*!" she kept saying. Mirela had smiled through her own tears. Despite all that she'd been through, she was still her mama's dear little chick.

The conductor came by and announced the next stop: Bârsana, her home village. Mirela wondered how she would be received. Her first reaction had been to hide what had happened to her. She felt so ashamed. Out of habit she touched the small bandage behind her ear. She had asked them at the recovery house to remove the little butterfly tattoo. It was pretty, but she much preferred the scar. It would remind her that something pretty on the outside can often hide ugliness within. Or, as she had heard once, "Be careful what you wish for."

Still, she was embarrassed by the whole ordeal. A part of her felt she'd been foolish and gotten herself into trouble. "Can't we just say that I am back from my job in Italy?" she'd asked her mother.

"No." Her mother, a wise woman, had been firm about that. "You need to be honest with everyone so that the secret doesn't fester within you. You did nothing wrong. You were a victim, but no longer."

After much thought, Mirela realized her mother was right. She had survived a terrible ordeal. It was not her fault and she should not feel bad. In fact, maybe she could do something to help make sure others like her didn't fall into the same trap she did. She would see.

The train chugged around the last bend and its whistle blew. She could see the Bârsana station up ahead. It looked like a group of people was standing by the platform. As she drew closer, she could see that several of them were carrying signs. The signs were homemade and they said things like "Welcome Home" and "We Missed You" and "We Love you, Mirela."

Mirela's mother stood in front of the crowd, scanning the windows of the train. Mirela saw her and waved.

Then she saw him. Simu Fidatof, the big, earnest carpenter she had dreamed about while in captivity, the young man who had been sweet on her, but whom she'd stupidly rejected. He was dressed in his Sunday suit and held a bouquet of flowers, alpine pinks and fire lilies. He waved to her and smiled. She felt tears begin to roll down her cheeks.

She was home.

## THE END

# AUTHOR'S NOTE

*T*he *Lair* has at its core a crime of human exploitation. It's based on the very real problem of human trafficking, which is essentially modern slavery for purposes of forced prostitution or labor. This multi-billion dollar "industry" keeps millions of men, women and children in bondage each year, and according to some estimates is the second-largest crime in terms of dollars spent, surpassed only by the illegal drug trade. It's also the fastest-growing international crime. It knows no boundaries, and is present in virtually every country around the globe, including, unfortunately, the United States and every state in our union.

To find out more about this devastating, far-reaching blight, please contact the Polaris Project.

# THANK YOU

—◆◇◆—

Thank you for reading *The Lair*. I hope you enjoyed it and will share your thoughts with others via social media like Twitter, Facebook, Google+, and Pinterest. Reviews on Amazon and Goodreads are amazingly helpful, and of course I'd love to hear from you. Please visit my website at www.abmichaels.com.

 Twitter       Facebook

 Google+       Pinterest

The Lair is part of my far-reaching romance series "Sinner's Grove." The series follows different generations of men and women associated with a world-famous artists' retreat on the northern California coast. Some of the stories, such as *The Art of Love* and *The Depth of Beauty* (available September 2015), focus on the generation of the retreat's founders, Gus and Lia Wolff. Others, beginning with *Sinner's Grove*, and now *The Lair*, take up the story in the present day. Each is a stand-alone novel.

—┄✦✦✦┄—

**THE ART OF LOVE** (*available on Amazon, Barnes & Noble, and other online booksellers*)

With nothing but a strong back and a barrel full of ambition, August Wolff finds wealth beyond measure in the frozen wilderness of the Klondike. Success, however, comes at an unbearably high price. Now Gus walks alone, and all the money in the world can't buy him what he needs.

In the late 1800's, when women are largely seen and not heard, Amelia Starling longs for a life limited only by her imagination. Blessed with abundant artistic talent and an even bigger heart, she dares to defy convention in order to help the ones she loves. Leaving scandal behind, she moves to the boomtown of San Francisco, hoping to make her mark in a man's world, living with the pain of a sacrifice no woman should ever have to make.

Two wounded yet defiant individuals meet at the dawn of a new century. Finding connection through their pasts and a dream for the future, they discover a passion eclipsing all they'd ever known. They long to build a life together, but can they overcome the dictates of a society known for cruelty and spite?

**An excerpt from *The Art of Love*:**

Gus dressed in formal attire and arrived an hour after the party had begun. No sense in milling around too long and having people think he actually *wanted* to be there. He talked to a few people he recognized and lingered at the back of the ballroom, watching the hoopla unfold. Turns out he'd made it to the Firestones' Pacific Heights mansion just in time.

"And now, may we present *The Family*, a painting by Amelia Starling." Edward and Josephine, Will's parents, jointly pulled a silk cord and the curtain rose, so to speak, on a huge canvas.

The guests erupted in a collective "Oh!" The painting was incredible, unlike any family portrait Gus had ever seen. Instead of everyone in the picture looking straight ahead, they were in the middle of playing croquet on the front lawn of their estate. Will's brother, sister, and Will himself were in it, along with his parents, and Gus got the sense from their particular actions that they loved each other but there was tension too. He started to move through the crowd to see it better, but froze at what, or rather who, he saw next.

"And we are happy to introduce the creator of this brilliant work, Miss Amelia Starling."

The woman who stepped forward, smiling at the crowd, was none other than Ruthie…but not the sweet young girl Gus had met several weeks before. No. This woman was beyond beautiful, her eyes with some kind of color on them that made them seem even larger and more exotic than before, her gorgeous dark hair swept up with some kind of shiny netting woven through it, and glittery diamonds hanging from her delicate ears. And her body. Lord have mercy. Her body was encased in a long, deep-colored dress, a kind of red, he thought, that displayed her breasts and every other curve with elegance and grace. She was magnificent.

Gus was furious.

He strode through the crowd but stopped so that she could see him as she talked to one admirer after another. At one point she saw him and her eyes grew wide. He continued to stare at her and she didn't look away. The man she was talking to—a geezer with money, no doubt—finally had to touch her arm to get her attention. Good.

He waited, patiently, until the crowed had thinned and the Firestones had announced the buffet was open. Then he made his move.

"I take it this is what you meant by 'a little of this and a little of that'," he said.

She smiled awkwardly, looking around the room, probably for someone to come and bail her out.

"No one's going to rescue you this time…Ruthie." He stepped closer and noticed she was breathing rapidly; it was doing wonderful things to her cleavage. "Who is Ruthie, by the way? Did you just make her up on the spot?"

"No. It's my middle name," she explained in a quiet voice. "Look, Mr. Wolff…"

"Oh, so you know *my* name."

"I knew who you were the instant I saw you." Her chin rose. "Your…reputation precedes you."

"Ah. Well, I'll tell you what I tell everybody else: don't believe everything you read." He cocked his head. "Why did you lie about who you were?"

She shrugged her beautiful shoulders. "I don't know. I guess I wanted to hear an honest opinion of my work. You would hardly have been straight with me had you known I painted it."

Gus leaned in to whisper in her ear. She smelled like lavender. "I assure you, Miss Starling, I would be nothing but straight with you."

The young woman stepped back and glared at him. "I'm sure you would be, Mr. Wolff, until the next distraction turned your head." She made a point of looking around the room. "Speaking of which, where is the melodious Miss Lindemann? I don't see her anywhere."

This woman was a pip. Gus wanted more of her. He captured her gaze and answered calmly. "Miss Lindemann and I aren't seeing each other anymore. I haven't been with a woman since before you and I met." He mimicked her perusal of the ballroom, even though most of the guests had migrated to the dining area. "Come to think of it, where is your swain—or swains, as the case may be? Let's see, there's Charles, from the other night, and then there's your *live-in*. What's his name? Sander? My my, how do you keep them all straight?" He smiled wickedly. "Oh dear, there's that word 'straight' again."

Miss Starling's delectable face, which had shown wariness before, now exploded into a storm of outrage. Apparently so mad she didn't care who saw her, she pulled her arm back to slap Gus's face. He caught her arm easily and wrapped it around his waist. Once again he pulled her close and nuzzled her. "I don't give a damn who you're with today, as long as you're with me tomorrow."

"That is never going to happen," she hissed.

"Never say never," he said, letting his breath caress her ear. He let go of her and stepped back, his voice rising to a normal level and his tone serious and heartfelt. "I am giving it to you straight, Miss Starling. I don't know a lot about art, but I do know how something makes me feel. Your work is astonishing. You know how to capture the…what shall I call it? The *truth* of a given moment. That is rare and something to be very, very proud of."

The siren opened her mouth but no words came out. As they stared at each other, Will walked up. "Ah, I see you've finally met Lia," he said. "Isn't she spectacular?"

Keeping his eyes on her, Gus concurred with a murmured, "Yes indeed. Spectacular." *That's not the half of it* careened through his head. He had to have this woman. Had to. He smiled and added, "If you would be a good sport and escort Miss Starling to the dining room, I'm afraid I have to leave. Business, you know."

Will rolled his eyes. "Come on, Gus. It's New Year's. You can take a least *one* day off."

"No rest for the weary," Gus said, heading over to the cloakroom. He stopped halfway and turned around. "Miss Starling. Amelia *Ruth*. It was a pleasure to make your acquaintance. I love your work and want to talk to you more about it. I'll be in touch. You can count on it." He smiled at the frown he put on her face, turned around again, and left before she threw something at him.

**SINNER'S GROVE** *(available on Amazon, Barnes and Nobel, and other online booksellers)*
A startling discovery when she was fourteen left San Francisco artist Jenna Bergstrom estranged from her family; unforeseen tragedy only sharpened her loneliness. But now her ailing

grandfather needs her expertise to re-open the family's once-famous artists' retreat on the California coast. The problem? She'll have to face architect Brit Maguire, the ex-love of her life.

Seven years ago, Maguire spent a magical time with the girl of his dreams, only to have her disappear from his life completely. Now she's back, helping with the biggest historic renovation of Brit's career. No matter how deep his feelings still run, Brit can't afford the distraction of Jenna Bergstrom, because something is going terribly wrong with the project at Sinner's Grove.

**An Excerpt from *Sinner's Grove:***

"What the hell?!" Brit turned around when a second explosion followed on the heels of the first. He immediately wrapped his arms protectively around Jenna.

"My God, was that a bomb?" she cried. She couldn't believe what was happening. She quickly dropped her leg and straightened her dress, fear turning her passion into panic.

"I don't know," Brit said grimly. "Let's find out."

They ran out of the building, passing several workers and a few investors rushing in different directions with terror-stricken faces. The street lights had not gone out, and Jenna saw her brother across the lawn.

"Jason! Do you know what happened?"

"It looks like the equipment barn blew up!" he called as he ran in that direction. "I just called 911."

"Anybody hurt?" Brit yelled.

"Don't know yet!"

Brit took Jenna by the shoulders. "Go back to the Great House. I'll check it out."

"Not in your life," she shot back. "I'm staying with you."

Brit nodded curtly and started running toward the maintenance area. Thankful she'd worn flats to the presentation, Jenna easily kept up with him. As they crested the hill, Brit stopped short and stuck out his arm to keep Jenna from running past him. "Too dangerous!" he yelled.

She grabbed onto his arm to stop her momentum. *Oh my God— this is hell on earth.* The front two-thirds of the huge barn was a fireball shooting flames a hundred feet into the sky. And the heat was so intense, she felt as if even her blood was boiling. Smoke was everywhere, sucking the oxygen from the air. Men were shouting and running back and forth, trying to be heard over the roar of the inferno. *Please keep Jason and Da away from this*, Jenna prayed, her breathing harsh and labored.

"How's it looking, Jack?" Brit called out to the man he'd pegged to help manage the crew.

"Not good." Jack, looking disgusted, tossed a hose on the ground where it joined several others coiled haphazardly in the gloom like somnolent snakes. "Whoever did this cut the hoses. We can't get any pressure, so we're down to a bucket brigade until the fire trucks get here."

"Everybody accounted for?"

"I think so, but it's pretty crazy right now. Maybe we oughta do a head count."

Brit looked around in frustration. In the distance sirens could be heard. "Good idea," he said. "Maybe—"

"Mr. Maguire! Mr. Maguire!" Parker Bishop and Kyle Summers ran up to the group.

"What's wrong?" Jenna cried.

"I think...I think—" Parker seemed to be particularly anxious.

"Spit it out, man," Brit barked.

Jenna glared at Brit. "Give him a chance to calm down!"

"We think...we think maybe that guy Lester's still in the building!" Kyle said.

"How do you know?" Brit asked sharply.

"We were on litter patrol down around the lower bungalows. Parker said he saw him go inside."

"How could you see in the dark?" Jenna asked.

"I think it was him, but I don't know for sure." Parker hedged.

"The light wasn't that good, but we saw *somebody* go inside and close the slider. You can tell when that big sucker closes," Kyle explained. "I didn't think much of it and kept working."

"Me too," Parker said.

"No, you were on the phone, dude, remember?"

Parker nodded. "Yeah, that's right. My dad called. And then, *Kablam*! So we started running back here."

Brit didn't waste a second. "Anybody seen Lester?" he yelled to the members of the makeshift fire crew.

A chorus of "no's" came back.

"Jack, you got a master key on you?" he called out.

The man shook his head.

"Get one!" Brit yelled. He then headed toward the back of the barn.

"Where do you think you're going?" Jenna cried, grabbing his arm.

"If he's in there, there's a chance he's in the back and can't get out," Brit said. "He may not be able to get to the side door. We've got to get it open and help him out."

"But you're not going in after him, right?"

Brit paused and looked at Jenna, running his fingertip down the side of her cheek. "Don't worry." With that he took off, glancing back once before he turned the corner of the building.

Speechless, Jenna watched his retreating figure as if in slow motion. She noticed vaguely that Kyle and Parker had walked up on either side of her. Kyle put his arm around her shoulders.

"It's all right," he said soothingly. "We're here."

Jenna turned and looked up at the large, muscular young man. He had the same glittery look he'd had the last day of school. Then she looked at Parker. He was staring at Kyle and his eyes burned fiercely, just as they had that same day. Fear, slippery and cold, slid over her.

"We need to help Brit," she said neutrally, hoping her voice wouldn't betray the anxiety threatening to overtake her.

By the time she worked her way safely around to the side of the burning barn, several burly workmen were in the process of battering the side door with what looked like a large fence post. The door was already starting to buckle from the heat. When it finally gave way, smoke billowed out and Jenna watched in horror as Brit tore off his jacket, tie and shirt, soaking the latter in a nearby bucket and wrapping it around his nose and mouth.

"Don't go in there—please!" Jenna cried.

Brit looked at her briefly, his eyes communicating what words could not. Then he disappeared inside the carnage. Moments later another deafening explosion ripped apart the air.

"Nooooo!" Jenna screamed. Tears streaming down her face, arms wrapped around herself to keep from falling apart, Jenna stared in shock at the burning, crumbling building, her only words a mantra-like "please God, please God, please God."

She felt someone—Parker, perhaps—urge her back from the heat of the fire, but she couldn't seem to move. Her entire focus was on the jagged hole into which Brit had run. She couldn't believe he was gone. Wouldn't believe it. He was going to walk out again. Any second now. Any second. Any second.

—⁘✦⁘—

**THE DEPTH OF BEAUTY** *(available September 2015)*
In turn of the 20th century San Francisco, Will Firestone is right at home among society's shallow elite. But the handsome, wealthy bachelor senses there must be something more. When business draws him into the heart of the city's controversial Chinatown, he discovers an alien, yet thoroughly enticing new world. With the help of an exotic young mother and a gifted teenage orphan, Will can't help but examine his own values, learning through love and loss that true beauty takes many forms, and is anything but superficial.

Mandy Culpepper has seen a lot of tragedy in her young life, but her spirit is undimmed, even after being forced to leave the only home she has ever known. As she matures into a beautiful young woman, she is determined to remain true to herself, regardless of what society has in store for her. Will she find the soul-deep happiness that has so far been elusive?

**An Excerpt from *The Depth of Beauty:***

The malaise that had dogged Will the night before carried over into Christmas morning. He chalked it up to a change in routine; he wanted to spend time with Tam Shee, but he knew it would be inappropriate to leave, especially since Kit had no idea where he might be going.

He was feeling a touch of self-pity as well, he realized. He wanted to share what had always been a jolly time of year with someone who understood that tradition. Tam Shee had no such reference.

He wanted to take her out to see the lights and decorations of the city, which were particularly festive around Christmas, but he knew it would be difficult if not impossible for her.

He wanted to take Sai-fon up to the mountains so that she could build a snowman. Hell, he would settle for taking her to the ocean where she could collect pretty shells instead of the sow bugs she was forever bringing up for her mother.

Instead he filed those thoughts away, slapped on a smile, and headed downstairs where he knew Kit and Mandy were waiting. His sister, apparently eager to start her own family traditions, had laid out the plan before they'd retired.

"First we'll have a big country breakfast," she said.

"Uh, the staff is off, and since neither of us can cook an egg to save our lives, we'll have to settle for continental," Will argued. "In fact, just coffee's fine for me."

"Oh no, brother dear. Mandy's got it covered. You may not realize it, but she's quite the cook. Half of the goodies coming out of the kitchen in the past few months have been hers."

"Really? She never mentioned it."

Kit gave him a look that said *Did you expect she would?*

Now, as he descended the stairs, he could smell bacon frying and coffee percolating. It was intoxicating. He stuck his head in the kitchen and saw both Mandy and Kit wearing aprons and wielding spoons. Mandy was supervising while Kit poured batter onto a large smoking griddle.

"Is that enough? Is that enough?" For someone as self-confident as his sister, that panicked tone just didn't sound right. By contrast, Mandy's voice was low and calm. She was obviously the one in charge. That didn't seem right either, but he had to admit, the flapjacks and bacon were delicious.

Afterward they retired to the small back parlor, where Kit and Mandy had decorated a small Noble fir. Will had placed his packages there the night before, as had the ladies. He'd never admit it, but he didn't really like opening presents, not for himself, at any rate. He found it embarrassing. Unnecessary, since he could purchase anything he damn well pleased. So instead of anticipation or even a light-hearted sense of fun, he felt only irritation, and a niggling sense of guilt that he should feel that way.

"All right. I'll play Santa's helper," Kit announced, donning a red Santa's hat. She handed a large box to Mandy, who opened it to reveal a beautiful red wool coat with fox trim and a matching muff. Mandy was struck speechless and could only hug the coat and her guardian.

"Try it on, try it on," Kit said.

"Can we get on with it?" Will asked, sounding peevish, which of course, he was.

"Fine, you old mossback. Open your present." She handed him a small rectangular box. It contained a pince-nez style pair of eyeglasses. Kit laughed with delight. "Now you'll look like our dear President Roosevelt," she exclaimed.

Will took off his regular spectacles and tried balancing the new pair on his nose. He could tell in an instant he wasn't going to like them. They seemed on the verge of falling off, and he felt ridiculous. "They're wonderful. Thanks, sister mine." He put the glasses back in their box and handed her a present with her name on it.

She opened it quickly. It was a first edition of the original English translation of Sun Tzu's *The Art of War.* "A worthy addition to my collection. Thank you, brother dear."

Mandy walked over and shyly handed Kit her gift. It was also a book, a novel entitled *The Circle,* written by Katherine Thurston. "She's an Irish writer and is supposed to be very good," Mandy explained. "It's about a woman who makes great sacrifices to follow her dream. And the writer has the same first name as you."

While Kit was saying thanks, Will pulled another small box from under the tree and handed it to Mandy. "Use it in good health," he said. She sat looking at the box for a moment before carefully opening it. Inside was a nondescript pen set one of his business associates had given him that he'd never opened. It came with different nibs and ink. "You can write in your journal, or even practice calligraphy if you're so inclined."

"Such a thoughtful, creative gift," Kit said drily. "What's left?"

"Just this," Mandy said, carrying a medium-size box over to Will.

"You didn't have to get me anything."

"I know, but I thought you could use it maybe."

He unwrapped the box and opened it. Inside was a stereoscope, a wooden viewfinder through which one could see two photographs that replicated what the human eye sees, in three dimensions. Along with the contraption were several dual photographs of places like Niagara Falls and the Grand Canyon.

"I thought maybe you could show it to Tam Shee and Sai-fon, since they never go anywhere, and I know you must want to take them places. So now they can at least see what the bigger world is like. I thought—"

Will's eyes bored into hers, telling her to *stop!* But she didn't catch his warning in time. Within seconds of speaking, however, she realized the mistake she'd made. She clapped her hand over her mouth, making it even more obvious.

Kit had heard it all. "What are you talking about? Who is this Tam Shee person? Why can't she go anywhere?"

Mandy kept looking at Will. "I'm so sorry, I didn't know she didn't—"

*"Enough."* Will took a deep breath and let the poisonous thoughts roiling within him spill out. "Listen, I appreciate the thought, but you're really not part of this family, and giving me things isn't going to make that happen. Has Kit told you we're looking for your real family? I should be hearing from them any day now. I think it best if you don't try to insinuate yourself anymore where you don't belong."

His speech was met with silence. Kit, he knew, was in shock. Mandy looked at him with those mesmerizing eyes and he wanted to turn away, knowing she knew what was inside him. Her next words proved him right.

"To not be close to the ones you love at special times like this is hard. I know. And I know the steep mountain you have to climb." She gestured to the stereoscope. "I just thought maybe that would help you along the way."

She looked around as if she'd lost something. "I ... I think I will take my new coat upstairs and try it on, if you don't mind." She picked up the large box and headed out of the parlor. At the doorway she turned around to face them. "Thank you for sharing your family Christmas with me, both of you. I loved it very much. And Mr. Firestone? You needn't worry. I'll be ready to go when the time comes."

# ABOUT THE AUTHOR

Anative of California, A.B. Michaels holds masters' degrees in history (UCLA) and broadcasting (San Francisco State University). After working for many years as a promotional writer and editor, she decided it was time to focus on writing the kind of fiction she likes to read. "I think it's a control thing," she says. "Life is so darn messy, I just want to make sure some stories end up the way they ought to."

That doesn't mean she won't put her characters through the wringer, however. Her series, "Sinner's Grove," pits men and women against forces ranging from merely corrupt to downright evil. But perhaps the greatest challenge for her heroes and heroines lies in overcoming their own flaws as they search for lasting love.

The writer and her husband now live in Boise, Idaho. On any given day you might see them on the golf course, the bocce court, or walking their four-legged "sons" along the Boise River. More than likely, however, you'll find Ms. Michaels hard at work on her next Sinner's Grove adventure.

Made in the USA
Charleston, SC
09 June 2015